CERTIFICATE OF PROTECT

REF NUMBER: 92592901

REGISTERED ON 29th January 2021 At 16:52:16 CET

REGISTERED BY Megan Innocent

COPYRIGHT OWNER NAME Megan Innocent

REGISTRATION TYPE Uploaded Through Website

I.P ADDRESS 79.68.78.61

WORK TITLE I Am Soldier

Registration certificate issued & certified by:

Protectmywork Limited

Kemp House, 152 City Road, London, EC1V 2NX, United Kingdom.
Company Registered in England & Wales No. 04358873

© Copyright 2021 Megan Innocent
All Rights Reserved.
Protected with www.protectmywork.com,
Reference Number: 9259290121S068

I AM SOLDIER

MEGAN INNOCENT

In memory of all the soldiers who sacrificed for the freedom we have today and for every Holocaust victim that suffered and lost their lives.

Lest we Forget

*"You are about to embark upon the Great Crusade, toward which we have
striven these many months. The eyes of the world are upon you…"*

Dwight D. Eisenhower 1944

U.S 34th President

ACKNOWLEDGEMENTS

To Auschwitz-Birkenau and all of the hardworking and dedicated staff, thank you for all that you do, as well as answering my many questions on my visit. Your staff work exceptionally hard to ensure that every individual's visit is full of informative and constructive information and education. Thank you.

To Eden Camp Modern History Theme Museum and all of the hardworking and dedicated staff, thank you for all that you do to keep the site updated, as well as answering my many questions on my visit. Each visit has brought a great experience that I have been able to apply the information to my research.

To my good friend Jack. There is so much to applause for your continuous support with every book, your knowledge and guidance and the coming to fix my printer every time it has decided to not work! It is without doubt that the work holidays and trips away have been incredible to the writing of this book, including Eden Camp, Poland (Inc. Auschwitz-Birkenau, Schindler's Factory, Krakow) and the many car rides to clear my head of a very frustrating block! For everything, thank you.

To my Dad, for the many hour long phone calls in which you have filled me with your extensive knowledge regarding the second world war that I have been able to apply to this book. Without your interest it could be fair to say that this may not have passed down to me, thank you for everything, including your ongoing support.

To my good friend Nick of many years, thank you for your support in the writing of this book, as well as being so kind as to let me borrow your second world war films! I was able to apply extensive research because of this and I am incredibly grateful, so for that I thank you.

To my good friend Beth, thank you for your continuous support in regards to my books, as well as the book clubs, general book talks and your extensive knowledge on writing that will always astound me. For everything you do, thank you.

To Ryan of Royal Artillery, 4th Regiment, thank you for your patience and vast knowledge that you have shared with me during the writing of this book. It is without question that I would have been very lost without your knowledge that I was able to apply to this book. Not only for your support but thank you for the service provided to our country and the British Army.

To Sam Benterman-Snell of Household Cavalry LG, you have been like a pillar of patience throughout writing this book and despite the many questions, you have been at my aid that has delivered understanding and knowledge. Without your guidance there is great probability that I would still be learning order of ranks as well as many other elements of the British and United States Army. Not only for your forbearance and assistance throughout my journey of writing this book but thank you for the service you deliver to the British Army.

Introduction

From 1939 to 1945 the world was masked with a dark shadow that millions of people across Europe were impacted by in some way or another, during a war that plagued Europe with an evil that even I cannot fully elucidate using words. It is without question that considerable lives were taken on both the Allies and the Axis side of the war that should both be remembered, with their lives honored for their duty to their country. This book does not hold desire to scrutinise or tarnish the name of people, countries or events that happened during the war but to retell a story, that is although fiction, is based on verifiable and historical events that is told from the perspective of both a fictional American Soldier and a Jewish Holocaust victim. The Protagonists, Tritagonists and Sidekicks within this storyline are fictional, though the men of Easy Company and all those of the 101st Airborne (and other mentioned regiments) are in fact real people that fought during the course of the war, though the dialogue contained has been adapted to make this story more personal to the Protagonist.

The aim of this book is to keep the memory of those who not only gave their lives but who lost them, in both battle and in the Holocaust. There are many stories both historical and fictional that have already been told since the war ended over 75 years ago, so why should another be told? Why do we not put behind us such dark times and move on? The answer is relatively elementary. Without such evidence of Anne Frank's diary, a Dutch Jew who went into hiding in Holland to escape the grips of the Germans, Schindler, who was a member of the Nazi Party that saved the lives of over 1,200 Jews in Poland, how could we possibly remember how the world once was and how to evade such adversity in the future that we call today? It is incredibly predominant that lessons from such actions are passed down the generations so that we can learn from yesterday, to live for today.

The world as we know it is a long way from being perfect despite learning of the Holocaust, which is why education is vital into understanding and respecting the diversity amongst humans, whether that is colour, race, age, sex, beliefs or religion. The discrimination against Jews of all walks of life, was not a new approach in 1933 but it was widespread and prevalent in many countries. It would be incorrect to let the Holocaust be consigned to the period of the Third Reich as the Nazi regime manipulated and amplified the latent prejudices of its citizens and did not however create them. Beliefs attached to discrimination and diversity are surviving based on the social expectations that are sceptically being challenged. Every person that walks the earth deserves the right to walk the path of their choosing and although actions may not be taken on a genocide level in todays world, the same notions are being applied that creates stigma and uncertainty. That is why it is important to educate now, so that every person has the right to their own path, being that of sex, religion, beliefs, colour and race and many other factors that make a person, a person.

This book I find necessary for a multitude of reasons, diversity, history, education as well as showing understanding of what happened all those years ago through a prism of multiple places during the same period of war, how lives were somewhat different with people living in unknowing and uncertainty with the hope that the lessons can be applied to today's world. The members of the Army, RAF and Navy contribute to ensuring that we keep the freedoms that both men and women fought impenetrably for all those years ago in conditions that we can only in today's world imagine and reflect on. We owe our greatest and utmost respect for the soldiers of the past, to all those that sacrificed for what we may take for granted today and for those in uniform that stand for our country today.

Prologue

The world is such an extraordinary place, full of opportunities and experiences longing to be grasped. The seas, the ground and the air all make up the place we call home, with rivers, mountains and even on the rainiest of days, a rainbow follows. It would be wonderful to think that this was the way the world worked at all times without the burden of disruption. Sometimes, we are faced with events that force us into making decisions we never thought we would ever have to make for survival. Sometimes, the sea, the ground and the air are filled with decisions that produce devastating consequences and for what? The better good? Who makes that call? The ones being forced to cause the devastation, the ones in high chairs who sit above them, or the ones down below who feel the impact of those decisions?

*

The sky was ignited in colours that should have been beautiful, yet it was anything but feelings of beauty. Amongst the mixture of yellows, oranges and thick black were the screams, painful and heart wrenching screams with the capability of shattering your soul like glass. Streets were ablaze in angry fires that spread from home to home, chasing the next like a taunting game. Everything had changed, nothing was as it had been. The world had turned to chaos, trauma and a battleground of blood in multiple forms. People were falling, clinging onto life with desperate hope that they would be given the opportunity to live through another day, even in the horrors that had unleashed itself amongst the planet. Cities fell in ruins, tumbling to their knees, leaving only echoes of what was once a place where people lived in somewhat harmony, peace and daily life. Children ran in fear, searching for the parents that they had lost, only to be found under broken rubble and foundations, once a happy child now an orphan with no place to go.

In a world that has been spinning for over 4.5 billion years, it has encountered many bloody battles and historical events, from the dinosaurs that roamed our planet for 165 million years, creating what we know as the circle of life, to be wiped out by an asteroid 6-9 miles wide, to the Battle of Hastings in 1066 that took the lives of thousands of people and the first world war lasting from 1914 to 1918 with the Battle of the Somme being one of the bloodiest slaughters in history that took the lives of over one million soldiers. Still, the earth withstands, taking every historical event in its stride, watching as we continue to harm the planet we so desperately need. When will the slaughter end? Is this the way it is supposed to be to make room for the next stage of life that is after us, just like it did with the dinosaurs?

I have often wondered of a world with no bloodshed, no evil and no battles, though it is rather difficult to now think of such a place. The world was getting ready for one of the largest historical events of all time, fitting within the timeline of what would mark as memorable for all the wrong reasons, though not in the opinion of all of course. The world as we know it was once again taking a shift for a bloody battle that would last six devastating years, changing the course of everything as we had grown to believe. The cities that fell to the flames, the people that perished beneath the planes and within them, were all coming and not everybody knew it yet.

September 3rd 1939 - Coronado California USA

I was walking home from the library when I saw the evening paper on one of the selling stands in the square that grabbed my attention almost instantly. I'd attempted to get into writing for numerous newspapers for a job when I was to graduate in less than a year, though some high end student grad always landed the job with the most irritating smirk on his face. It never stopped me glancing at the papers on my way home from work at the library, that I enjoyed but I knew it was never going to be a lifelong goal. Brenda with the too big glasses for her face was friendly enough on the desk, yet she never failed to snap a nerve at least once a day by her over-the-top joy for coming into work to deal with arrogant customers and books that were falling apart. Come home time I'd manage to pull myself together and offer a warm goodbye and smile that was far from sincere yet impressively believable.

As I pulled my aching feet across the pavement my eyes caught sight of *The New York Times* with a bold headline, 'GERMAN ARMY ATTACKS POLAND; CITIES BOMBED, PORT BLOCKADED; DANZIG IS ACCEPTED INTO REICH'. There had been talk of war since Hitler came to power in 1933 and reading the article indicated he had finally done it, with Poland being the first victims.

"You going to buy that or read the whole thing here?" Came the voice of the guy just trying to make a living from selling newspapers.

"Yeah, sorry." Handing him two dollar bills I never took my eyes from the paper. Over several lines spoke of the Gleiwitz episode, the German's posing as Polish military officers to stage an attack on the radio station in the Silesian city of Gleiwitz. Germany used the event as justification for the invasion of Poland with a proclamation by Hitler to his German army stating, *"In order to put an end to this frantic activity no other means is left to me now than to meet force with force."* He'd gone with the self-defense card, people surely didn't believe that. We'd heard his speeches countless times and war had been at the forefront of his mind since he was given the title of Chancellor. It had become evident that Germany were deliberately attacking and the Nazi troops were invading Polish territory along the whole front of old Germany.

As rain began to pour from overhead I became lost in thought for the people of Poland. Images flashed through my mind, horrifying scenes I wished would not be there. Adolf Hitler had started a war that had plunged America into confusion. President Franklin Delano Roosevelt was faced with a question that would change the course of history. *Will the United States become involved in this war?* On the 3rd of September 1939, Britain and France declared war on Germany, widening the European phase of the war. America could be next and despite the grueling depression, we were going about our day unknowing of what was to come. Placing the paper in the nearest trash can and sitting on the bench outside the bakery, taking in the fresh smells that reminded me of Ma's specially baked bread, I look around me, people walking through the streets, busy with their daily routines, all to make it back home at the end of the day to have dinner, to sleep and then wake up the next morning to do it again. Talent and ambition were lost inside the people who were struggling to get by on what money they had, yet nothing compared to the devastation that was crashing through Poland and many more potential countries of Europe that Hitler wanted his hands on.

"Not looking good is it Pete?" Came the voice of Will, the eighty six year old regular who visited the library every afternoon after his daily walk for bread, milk and meat that he would cook for his wife who had begun to lose grasp on her memory with everyday that slipped away. Will, with his top hat and passion for books, carried the pain well of his deteriorating wife, always spreading a smile and a witty remark that had us laughing from our sides.
"Afraid not." I sigh, as he sits down on the bench beside me and takes off his black hat and places it on his lap. Reaching into the trash can he pulls the newspaper out and taps the headline with his fingers.
"Seen it before you know, lived through the first war just twenty one years ago, lost a lot of men we did."

"Did you serve?" I asked, turning on the bench to face his aged and tired face.

"Too right I did, did what was required of you to support your country back then. I was a man of the 15th Cavalry Division, we were to relieve prostrated infantry units in the trenches. We saw things you would never imagine possible and the conditions were much to be desired. It was muddy, cold, the toilets overflowed and many of the men ended up with medical problems, trenchfoot being one of them and I can tell you now, it was not a pretty sight." He shook his head and folded the paper as he looked at me. "You know, if America goes to war, they are going to need men."

"You think I should be one of them?" I asked, shocked at the very thought, though the thought had crossed my mind, I never imagined that I would be a man that served in the army, for my country, I was just Pete who worked in the library while trying to get through highschool.

"I think this country is headed into a bloody battle in the near future and it is going to need men that are willing to go the full stretch to reach the other side of it."

"I don't know," I'd stammered, shaking my head and pondering the thought, "I'm not sure I'm the right person." The thought circles my mind as he chuckles lightly.

"If every man thought that way, America would have nobody to defend it and all the other countries that are going to suffer." He stands and places his hat back on his head while offering me a smile, "you have to think, are you going to sit and watch the war pass, or will you contribute to its triumph?" He nods his head knowing he had left me with countless thoughts to process and walks round the corner and out of sight.

With rain pouring over my face I made no rush to go home that day. Something had been set off inside me that I could not shut off. *There must be more to life than struggling.* Roosevelt knew that this war was different to that of 1914, when Archduke Franz Ferdinand of Austria, the heir to the throne of Austria and Hungary and his pregnant wife were assassinated in June of that year. It had been the immediate cause of war, though other events contributed. Their assassination had been planned by a Serbian terrorist group called the black hand and one month after the assassination on July 28th, Austria-Hungary declared war on Serbia with the backing of Germany who declared war on Russia and France. By August 4th 1914, Germany marched on France taking the route through Belgium, which triggered the involvement of Britain who had agreed to remain neutral with Belgium until this point. As Britain and Germany fought battles at the Battle of Mons in Belgium, this was the start of war for Britain. America entered the war in 1917 due to Germany sinking a number of their ships around the British Isles and by the time the long war ended in November 1918, with Germany and the rest of the central powers being defeated, 20 million people had lost their lives, military and civilian. It was not just Roosevelt that worried for the overall outcome of the Poland attacks in 1939. Europe was at war and

America was hanging over a very thin line over a decision of entering.

As I walked home in the rain I knew that the thoughts in my head would not simply vanish by distraction. If we were plunged into war, what would that mean for the American people? For our economy that was struggling as it was, it was without doubt going to be impacted further. Worry was the leading emotion in every American, yet we still got out of bed in the morning, went to work to provide what we could and carried on in hope that the world would restore itself before devastating results were spread on a much larger scale. As Hitler and his army advanced on Poland and finally gained occupancy in the East, it was a turning point for all European leaders to consider their next steps, though America was still hindering neutralism despite Roosevelts desire to support the allies France and soon to be Great Britain. Germany had taken Austria and Sudtenland in 1938, to which the Munich Pact was created with England and France agreeing to allow Hitler to keep Sudtenland with the condition of no further expansion. Now, in 1939, Japan had entered an alliance with Germany and Italy with the occurrence of the Moscow-Berlin Pact that promised non aggression between the two powers. Hitler broke this pact when he invaded Poland, sending the world as we knew it into a machine that would take the lives of millions of people. It was the beginning of a world war and not everybody knew it yet. I thought about what Will had said, *Are you going to sit and watch the war pass, or will you contribute to its triumph?* Did I want to be Pete the librarian for the rest of my life, or did I want more? By the time December arrived, I had a decision to make and it would be the choice between watching as a bystander or becoming part of the machine that was already in motion. The war had begun and unknowing to all of Europe, it would be many years before a victory over either the allies or the central powers. This was the beginning of the second world war.

September 1st 1939 - Opaczewska Street, Warsaw, Poland

It was early, so early that the light had not yet taken the crisp night air that covered our beautiful city of Warsaw. It was 6am to be exact when our lives were turned well and truly upside down, out of our control and torn apart. I'd gone to bed early the night before the devastation came. As I had curled up in my bed that was now in Mama and Papa's bedroom to make room for Grandma and Grandpa so we could look after them, I had heard the worry in Mother's voice.

"He said it on the radio Hubert, if war does happen, then Jews will be exterminated all over Europe! Will that really happen to us? What will they do to us, to our boy?" Mama was frantic with worry. They had begun educating me on the world of politics which I had found difficult to stay focused on. They had told me about how Jews were suffering and being scrutinised all over Europe and that it was a strong possibility it would get worse. Mama insisted on repeating that we should not be ashamed of who we are but to be proud, while still expecting to be treated differently to non Jews.

"We should not dwell over matters that have not come to present, Marika, war has not been confirmed, Hitler knows not of what he speaks, he is just trying to scare us, now let us enjoy our night." Papa held great power over being able to calm the most anxious of people, which had started to be Mama. She had always been a strong woman who could light up a room with the greatest of happiness, yet with each broadcast the radio spilled, it had begun chipping away at her, tiny fractions at a time until she became so full of worry that she slowly stopped singing and dancing around the room, fear took over her and it was evident in her every step. Papa had accomplished yet again of releasing Mama's worries by dancing around the living room with Mama singing along sweetly to the sound of a woman who sang about twenty three gentlemen looking for a ring.

*

I heard the devastation before I saw it, igniting the city centre in orange and yellows with smoke and fire taking the city by a dominating force that snatched me from my sleep and into a whole new world I was not prepared for. I jumped from my bed at the ear piercing siren I could hear screaming above our homes. As I looked out of the window I saw the city we loved and called home being bombed from the planes above us, dropping unwanted destruction one after another. I didn't understand what was happening, everything was so loud, so fast. It was as though the world had begun to spin at a million miles an hour with no opportunity to take a breath.

The sirens wailed louder as they advanced closer, sending my heart beating so hard in my chest I was convinced it had escaped my body completely. The flashing lights illuminating the sky sent shivers through my body. *What was happening?*

"Jakub, get away from the window!" Came the voice of Mama behind me as she pulled me out the bedroom and towards the basement, legs shaking and buckling beneath me, my breathing out of control with adrenaline soaring through every one of my veins causing me to become lightheaded.

"Marika, get them in the basement, take Mother with you." Papa shouts over the sound of wails, bangs and smashing windows from outside, pushing Grandma towards us as he rushes through the house picking up blankets and food. The wailing sirens continue as they circle above our heads, lights flashing through the windows, cries from people of the city echoing through to the basement from cracks in the windows.

The basement was dark with the occasional glow of fire from the streets outside. Grandma was sitting next to me with her arm around my shoulders and Grandpa sat next to her trying to wrap a blanket around her that she made no attempt to assist with.

"You listen to me Jakub, we are going to be just fine." Grandma attempts to comfort me at little success with so much going on around us. Mama rushes around the basement trying to light a candle and block the windows with newspaper Papa had thrown towards her in a hurried frenzy. My head felt dizzy with endless questions and no time to ask them. Papa rushes into the basement and bolts the door shut behind him. Darkness. Screaming. *Where is that coming from? What is happening?*

From every angle bombs were connecting with buildings, the sirens screaming through the air with the sound of houses and shops being brought fiercely to their knees by the German Luftwaffe demanding destruction and dominance.

"Sit next to your Babica now Jakub and wrap up warm." Mama tells me, pointing to the blanket near Grandma. Grandpa is next to Grandma holding her hand and offering comforting words to us all as best he could, though fear rattled each of our bones the same despite those who tried to hide it. *Would we be alive by the time daylight stole away the night?*

I sat with my head down and covered my ears to block the sound of the German aircraft taking everything we had with each dropping bomb. Mama and Papa were rushing around the basement trying to block the windows so they would not see us in our safe place. Grandpa begins telling one of his stories but the words were muffled, everything playing out around me like a twisted horror show. I attempted to focus on his words, listening to the story about a king who formed an army to rescue the women he loved who had been captured by a jealous night. Upon returning from the first world war Grandpa had thrown himself into writing while teaching me the ways of his words and how they can connect together to create feeling and emotion. He had experienced life on a multitude of levels that deserved no less than a standing ovation and his experience spilled out in his stories in wonderful and exciting adventures.

I had spent many hours after school trying to write short stories though they were never as exciting and gripping as his. He taught me to never leave out a single detail that could pull in an audience to see the story as I did. I began telling my stories to the family who would all cheer, *"Wonderful Jakub, truly wonderful."* They would clap and cheer and it would encourage me to make up another that would please my audience more and more each time. None of the stories I told ever amounted to Grandpa's, he entwined words rhythmically in a way that would have you gripped from the first handful of words. For the very first time his story was unable to keep me focused from the explosions on the other side of the basement wall.

Another bomb falls right next to us, shaking the walls we hid within. Screams echo through from outside, some long and full of pain, others short and cut off too soon. The world as we knew it was falling around us, dismantling through sheer force and fear. I bury my head lower in my hands, trying to block out the reality I was hoping was a horrific nightmare.
"Do not worry now my boy, soon they will leave, be brave." Grandma says cutting Grandpa's story off and putting her arms around me tighter, pulling me closer to wrap me in her comforting embrace that makes the sound of dropping bombs fade out just a fraction, though enough to steady my breathing. I did not feel brave, I felt like a coward, locked away in the arms

of my Grandparents and the basement while those out in the night were unable to reach shelter.

The world was loud, unable to slow down even for a moment, unable to catch up with itself to comprehend what was happening. Buildings were crashing to the ground in devastation, some clinging on to minimal foundations in hope to just stay standing. The aircraft above our heads sending the unwanted gifts of hurt and destruction upon our city, screeching through the air of Warsaw in desperate hope to intimidate us. They were taking our city and crushing it effortlessly with one hand and spitting out what was left, leaving us with only a distant memory of what was once a beautiful and majestic city. It was one of the longest nights of my life, though I would have been naive to believe it would be the last night of horror, torment or pain. This was just the beginning of a very long nightmare that was impossible to wake up from.

September 4th 1939 - Coronado California USA

"What do you mean at war, surely not?" Shouted Jen from the bathroom through muffles of a toothbrush in her mouth.
"That's what the papers say, look, *Britain and France are now at war with Germany. The British ultimatum expired at 11am yesterday and France entered the war six hours later at 5pm.*" I read, moving my finger along the print while angling the paper so she could see it as she walked out of the bathroom and into the bedroom.
"What has the world come to?" She shrieked shocked, skimming over the words I had just read out as if the only way to believe it was to read it for herself. "I can't imagine how it must be for them in Poland right now." As she sits next to me on the bed she looks over the paper and lets out a sigh.
"I dread to think." Folding away the paper I place it on the bedside and turn to face Jen. "You know, this could mean a lot for America." She looks at me perplexed, waiting for me to continue. "If America decides to become allies with Britain and France, then we will be at war too." I rub my temple, knowing I will have to explain further if it means her understanding my reason for talking about the matter. "The country will need men and I wonder if more will be called upon than the army already has."
"Well we do not need to talk about such matters because America is not at war." She'd clicked onto what I was getting at and refused to entertain the idea, as well as the conversation

as she slides inside the duvet and pulls out the romance novel she had worked three quarters of the way through.

"Until now Poland has been fighting the German's on their own. From what I have read about Hitler and the broadcasts he has made he has no intention of backing out of his decision, it's going to get real messy." I was sitting up now, looking her in the face as she pretended to read the book in her hands though I knew she was listening, as much as she didn't want to.

From the very first moment I laid eyes on Jen I knew that I had to have her in my life. Something about her attitude pulled me in, that she cared not for what the world chose to think of her and that just because she was a woman she was just as capable of making up her own mind, without the necessity of a male presence. As I looked at her next to me, I still felt the same, yet I could feel agitation building at her refusal to address the matter. I sit staring at her, knowing that she could sense my eyes burning into hers.

"Peter, I have a pretty good idea where this conversation is going and if you are after my blessing then you will be forever waiting. It is not only not America's war but it is also not yours."

"So the world goes up in flames and we sit back and watch it happen?" I'd lost my temper but somehow managed to keep it to a level that did not require shouting.

"Don't be so dramatic! For one it is not the world it is Poland and two, what could you possibly do as one man to stop it?" She abandons her book and rubs the back of her hands over her eyes. I knew she was becoming restless from the conversation but I had not finished.

"Have you been listening to the broadcasts at all?" My voice had increased volume and I realised it was a bad idea as soon as I saw her change of expression. Holding a hand out in front of me I continued, "Listen, Hitler has been making life a misery for people all over Europe for years, even in Germany! He wants rid of the Jews, how do you suppose he will do that? Ask them nicely?" The long sigh from Jen told me she had lost all interest in trying to pretend to listen and moved down the bed and threw her head on the pillow.

"I don't know Peter, how do you think he will do that?" She was agitated, restless and tired and I knew it didn't matter what I said she would stick to her opinions on the matter with no opportunity of being moved.

"I don't know either but surely that is worse. When America joins this war, which I can see happening, it is going to affect us all, it will change everything as we know it and I for one do not want to be a coward watching it happen." Turning over on my side I face away from her as I fall asleep, for the very first time since I met her. Something inside me told me that war was coming and when it did, our lives would be well and truly thrown upside down. I for one wanted to be ready for it, not cowering in the shadows waiting for it to pass.

September 4th 1939 - Opaczewska Street, Warsaw, Poland

Nothing quite felt the same since the men in airplanes started bombing Warsaw. Our city looked much less like it used to, from beautiful buildings stood tall and proud, to rubble littering the cobbled streets, homes and synagogues left in ruin, standing only by half, naked and exposed to the terrified people below them. The atmosphere had completely changed, everybody was on edge from waking up to attempting to go to sleep, wondering and praying for no more attacks from the air. Mother had stopped dancing around the house with beautiful songs to accompany, no longer did she fill our home with joy and happiness, she had lost the light that had been burning so bright within her the night they first came. It was evident that she was afraid, we all were and it showed through constant tension within our home. She would be looking out the window all the time as if something would change from the last handful of minutes of previously peering out and insisting that I do not do the same.

"Stay away from the windows Jakub, at all times." She would say, over and over again, in worry that we would be hit with another surprise attack from the men in the sky.

It had been three days since they first came and we were living in the expectation that they would come again. They had visited us uninvited for the last three nights and we were sure they would come again, we could feel it with every passing minute.

Part of me just wanted them to leave us alone, never come back and that be that, while the other half of me knew it couldn't possibly be the end, therefore to just get it over with so we would not have to keep living in dreadful suspense and unknowing. I woke up on the fourth day of September and made my way to the breakfast table for bread and jam. Mother was already sitting there looking extremely tense over half a mug of tea that looked long since gone cold and an untouched slice of bread and jam. She left them abandoned as she stared blankly at a newspaper titled *'GAZETA POLSKA'*. I caught a glimpse as I sat next to her and saw big bold letters reading, *'GREAT BRITAIN AND FRANCE DECLARE WAR ON GERMANY.'* When Grandma and Grandpa came to join us for breakfast, he took the paper from her hands and squinted through his glasses to read the print.

"Dam Nazi's don't know when to stop! Britain and France are involved now, I am afraid we are at the centre of a very angry war. We need to be prepared!"

"Prepared for what Grandpa?" I questioned, intrigued and worried into what this would mean for us now.

"Not in front of Jakub, please Wilfred." Mother begs, rubbing her temple and sighing heavily. This was not a conversation to be had lightly and Mother was in no mood for it.

"The boy should know just as much as we should, this affects him too Marika!" Shouts Grandpa, waving the paper around so everyone in the room could see it.

Tension and frustration floats about the air of the apartment in stubbornness to be removed, other than Grandma sitting peacefully at the table smothering jam onto bread.

"The German's have gone power mad son, being controlled by that mad man Hitler to believe they can take the world! They don't know when to stop and I'll tell you something for free, this war has only just begun, it is going to get a lot worse before it is over and that is what we should prepare ourselves for."

"That's enough!" Mother shouts, banging her hand on the table, sending ripples in Grandma's tea, while she carries on about her morning unfazed by the events playing out around her. She has always been the calm one of us all, yet even I am surprised by her lack of emotion to what is happening.

"Marika's right Pa, let us leave it at that for now." Papa had been sat in his chair by the bookshelf overlooking the situation before feeling it was time to step in when Mother began sobbing silently at the table.

As we made our way through breakfast in silence, I stared at the newspaper on the table. Everything around me becomes a blur as the words engrave themselves in my mind. The word *'war'* piercing so deep that shivers ran through my body like lightning bolts. I kept reading the words of the headline over and over until I couldn't stand the torment. *'GREAT BRITAIN AND FRANCE DECLARE WAR ON GERMANY.'* I could feel from the very pit of my stomach that Grandpa was right. Things were going to get worse before the war was over, this was just the beginning.

*

That night we were woken by the familiar and haunting sound of the sirens, loud, echoing and ear piercing. I didn't know what they meant, I assumed it maybe meant for us to hide, a warning maybe, or to encourage us to be as terrified as possible, which was always the resulting outcome. There wasn't much time to think about it as Mother pulls me from my sleep and into the dreaded basement where we would yet again wait for them to leave, taking their torment with them and no doubt many more lives. Mother had heard on her daily food run that the family five doors down had been hit severely by one of the bombs on the second night. She had sat me down at the table, took my hands in hers and attempted to tell me in as gentle a way as possible. I had been very good friends with the Nowak's twelve year old son, we spent most days together at school and during the holidays, now he had gone and I felt a rush of anger towards the German's. They were taking everything with no care at all, destroying not only our homes but the people that lived inside them and they were back, angrier than ever.

Papa is hurrying Grandma and Grandpa inside while grabbing what he can along the way. Mother does the same, taking blankets and food she can get her hands on while pushing me inside. We had started leaving most essential items in the basement like food and blankets, though with the September cold biting harder each night blankets were becoming useless in blocking it out. Food was starting to be stretched with most of the bakeries and food markets being bombed and torn to ruins, therefore we had to make most of what we had, in and out of the shelter.

A thunderous roar and the first bomb of the night connected with the city, exploding and illuminating the sky just as we had learned it would. I tried desperately to block out what it might have hit, our friends, families, businesses that took home zlotys to feed their children under the strenuous circumstances. The bombs as well as the men inside those planes did not care what was in their path, their only goal was destruction. Seconds later another, then another, dropping down on the city in high pitch screams and head splitting bangs. They were showering us in attacks that night, letting us know they meant war, demanding dominance and surrender. Grandpa stood up in anger and began shouting and cursing at the German planes above us, throwing and waving his hands around in an angered frenzy.

"Our men are out there fighting, dying, giving everything they have, while we sit in here like cowardice sheep! This is our country! Be gone!" He shouted over the sound of planes, exploding bombs and collapsing buildings falling to their knees.

"Father please, sit down, you're scaring Jakub!" Papa begged, trying to get him to sit down with one hand on his arm. Grandma had her arm around my shoulders as she always did with Grandpa's thick black coat hanging off her own as she wrapped a blanket around me and tried to block out the sounds to my ears.

"I will not just sit here in fear and let them intimidate us in our own dahm home! You will not scare us!" He shouted louder than ever as he pushed his way out of the basement before any of us could register what was going on.

"He's gone crazy!" Shouted Mother.

"Wilfred!" Cried Grandma, falling into a river of tears as she tried to follow him. Mother grabs her arm while Papa hurried after him. Within seconds, more than our city fell, our whole lives did too.

With another mighty roar a bomb falls that connects with our home. It happened so fast that debris was falling from every angle, my ears rang until my head felt like it might explode. The bomb had connected with the left side of the house, the side of the house that Grandpa and Papa had run through just moments before. The foundations to our home began falling in on itself, pouring to the ground in defeated agony, taking everything inside and crushing it to the ground with sheer force. Then black.

*

I opened my eyes to see the house still falling, fire breaking out from the left side of the house and spreading like a fast infectious disease. I didn't hear the planes anymore, I didn't hear anything, just the constant ringing in my ears that made me throw my hands around my head in hope that it would stop. "Jakub!" I didn't hear it, I just saw her lips move as Mother rushed towards me where I had been thrown back into the corner under a pile of bricks. My legs hurt, burning biting pains that rip through my legs as I try to stop the ringing screeching in my head. The world had slowed down, everything happening at such slow speed it made me feel nauseous and light headed. I felt the tug of Mother's grip on my arm as she pulled me out the debris in panic, with Grandma hobbling and spluttering leading the way out of the basement and out of our home that had gone up in a blaze of angry flames and thick black smoke. We made it out the house and across the street where I began to hear the planes again, distant, maybe leaving. The sirens were still wailing their warnings, rain pouring heavy over our heads with the yellow and orange eyes of the sky offering no protection from anything falling from it. The bite of cold had taken us hostage with nowhere to escape from it. Mother's cries intensified and it was enough clarification to make my stomach drop and my chest pull into knots. Time catches up with itself as realisation kicks in. Grandpa and Papa had not made it out of the house.

Shock takes over and I am frozen to the spot, scanning our burning home for where they could be but it was too late. The house falls, the flames burn higher and the smoke blocks our view.

"NO!" I screamed and cried so hard that night my chest felt like it would explode. They had taken my Papa, my Grandpa. They had taken everything and flown into the night in a cruel and twisted celebration.

Just the morning before we had all sat listening to the radio, huddled around our dinner table with Papa's arm around my shoulder. There was a man talking about an announcement by a British man named Chamberlain and repeating the speech he had made.

> *'I have to tell you now that no such undertaking has been received and that consequently this country is at war with Germany."*

I didn't understand why but it gave me taumenting shivers hearing it over the radio.

"Britain will not aid us son, they cannot come rescue us from this new life of torment but they will fight to stop this war Hitler has reigned upon us. We have to at least be thankful for that. Poland will not fight alone." Papa told me, explaining the announcement in a way I could understand. As much as everybody tried, I still found everything so frustratingly confusing, I just did not understand why this was happening to us and every day that we managed to get through opened up a series of more unanswered questions. Except today, Papa had gone, he had been taken with Grandpa, meaning they could no longer explain any of this cruel and angry world anymore. The German's had stolen their life, taken them with smirks on their faces and cares that were transparently absent. I felt angry, pain, heartbroken, confused, all at the same time. I would never see them again and it tore straight through my heart as I curled into a ball and I sobbed, I sobbed and I grieved for the men I should have been giving a standing ovation to, the two brave men that the fourth of September, 1939, stole from our lives forever.

*

It was early hours of the morning when the sun broke through the thick black smoke that had suffocated our city with the smell of hot burning mortar. Warsaw no longer offered welcoming sights to the eyes or beautiful buildings towering above its people. Instead, a barely standing crying city that had been shaken and bruised through nights of constant air attacks. The planes had left only hours before, taking with them lives and most likely cheers of joy at being so successful in taking down our city. I hated them, despised them and cursed them in my head with words I had heard grown ups use when they were angry. Grandma was still sitting beside me on the sidewalk looking empty and broken as I looked out at the devastation, no longer a sheltered city towering in tall buildings but rather a thick black cloud of smoking debris of shattered and broken homes, businesses burnt to ash and synagogues smouldering in blazing heat.

I felt ashamed that I let sleep steal my consciousness when the German's had stolen the lives of so many people, including Grandpa and Papa. I stood and kissed Grandma on the head to which she remained motionless, staring emptily out at the home that once stood, the home we once called ours. As I walked through the rubble of broken bricks and foundations I see Mother on her knees bent over and crying silently. I lose myself in thought, revisiting every memory brought back through every broken item I saw shattered in the open. What mattered was not the house, not the items within it but the people we had called family that had been taken away when the house came down in an angry blaze of explosions.

As I stood behind Mother I heard her stop crying and turn to face me, her face a rich red and shining in the morning sun with hours of tears. She was holding Papa in her arms, half buried within the rubble with his body motionless and drained of life. Judging by the pile of bricks next to him it was quite possible she had spent hours trying to dig him out. Papa laid still, hauntingly unmoving and stiff. Words were something that did not come easy during that moment. Every emotion flew through my veins, switching and taking a U-turn before repeating all over again.

"Papa." I whispered. He was gone, I knew deep in my heart that he was, yet the desperate yearning I felt flow through me longed for a miracle, that he would open his eyes and tell me everything was going to be okay, tell me everything I needed to know about this horrific war so I could be prepared, teach me about cars like he did on so many occasions, the magic tricks I had soon grown out of that I'd have given anything to have back. My Papa, I was not ready for him to leave me in this world, not yet. He was my hero, my best friend, taken so suddenly, so violently with no opportunity of telling him I still needed him. I had to look away, walk away from what I was seeing to hope that it was not real, hope to wake up from this nightmare that insisted on tormenting me night after night. Mother stayed where she was, holding his motionless body as he laid with heavy beams and mountains of bricks over his body.

I walked away slowly, trying to force my mind to accept it yet not wanting it to at the same time. Never again would he kiss my head when he thought I was sleeping, lift me up and throw me over his shoulder as he had done just months before and I'd told him I was too big for such games. Never again would I hear his voice, the voice of my Papa telling me I was the most important person in his life. He was gone and he was not coming back. I head back towards Grandma when I'm left frozen on the spot. Another pile of broken bricks, yet I see Grandpa's watch through a crack in the pile. Frantically I began digging out the bricks, throwing them in any direction they landed, brick after brick, not feeling the ache in my arms that would have been there. Eventually I stopped. There he was. He had made it out of the house, under the sky of the flying planes though it had not missed him. I wondered if he had said what he wanted to say to them before the house had collapsed and fallen, taking him prisoner beneath it. His eyes were still open and it haunted my soul to see his daunting motionless face engraving itself into my memories, refusing to ever be forgotten. I take his hand and I hold it in mine, crying for the men that we had lost, never to return to our lives.

I heard Grandma shuffling closer behind me and stopping just a handful of feet away. As I turned to look at her I realised the woman she once was had been left behind, pulled from inside her and thrown away. She stood behind me, unable to shuffle her way any closer, the scene before her locking her to the spot. She stared at the two men laying before her, she didn't say anything, didn't move, didn't cry, she just stood there looking completely vacant. I hung my head, knowing that we had all lost them, yet for her she had lost her husband and her son on the same night. It was difficult for us all yet for Grandma I am confident it hit her harder than any of those bombs ever could.

Peering around me I saw the house next door, the Glowaki's. They had taken the majority of the hit. There was nothing at all left that could have indicated to unknown eyes that it was ever a home. Nothing at all stood anymore as the pile of broken bricks were still smouldering, intensifying the air with the smell of burning mortar that was difficult to overlook. Malcolm, their twelve year old son, was my best friend of many years. We would knock on each other's doors with the son of the Nowark's five doors down and go out skimming stones across Warsaw park pond until the sun started to set and we would have to run home fast to make it back in time for dinner. Everything from before the war was ripped away from us, stolen with no opportunity for say in the matter, we just had to deal with the consequences quietly, burying anger and frustrations because there was nowhere for it to go.

I knew from looking at the mounted pile of what was once their home that they were probably laid under there somewhere. I wanted to run over and free them, give them the smallest amount of justice I could by taking all that rubble from on top of them, though I knew I could not do it alone and Mother was too distraught to think about helping anybody other than Papa and Grandpa. Shivers scarred my bones and not from the September wind blowing debris across Poland, they burned into my skin leaving hot raging anger.

Later that day we buried Papa and Grandpa in the Warsaw Jewish Cemetery on Okopowa Street. We were lucky to bury them when we did, as the cemetery was soon cut off for the duration of the war some time after, though we felt the furthest away from being lucky there was. We had lost our home, Papa, Grandpa, most had lost their businesses through bombings or handing over Jewish owned businesses to the German's. All Jewish owned property was to be handed over to the German's whether it be a business or property, home or shop. Everything Jewish people had spent years building for themselves and their families was torn away and stripped with nothing in return but humiliation, starvation and brutality. That was all to come. We thought it was the worst it could possibly be when we buried Papa and Grandpa, when we said our final goodbyes with Mama's soul splitting cries that could shatter any heart into a thousand pieces.

Grandma never spoke another word after losing them, just held everything in, lived the remainder of her days locked inside herself in silence. I still don't know how it didn't eat away at her keeping all that anger and emotion locked inside like that. We said our final goodbyes and made our way out of the cemetery. Our neighbours four doors down in the opposite direction to the hit that took down our home helped to carry Papa and Grandpa to the cemetery. The Jaskolski's were a married couple of twenty three years with three grown sons. They were polite, well spoken and hearts as kind as I'd ever known. They were

Jewish too and would come round often enough for Jewish holidays, each bringing their own contributions. They ran a family run business bakery in the heart of Warsaw that was confiscated from them when the German's took over Warsaw. They were honorable friends of the family and when they had seen the devastation to our home they had offered their condolences and help with carrying Papa and Grandpa to the cemetery while they said goodbye themselves. Walking out of the gates they bowed their heads in respect and made their way home. They had offered for us to stay with them out of courtesy though Mother knew they just did not have room.

They left respectfully as I turned to Mother who was wiping tears from her face to make room for fresh ones spilling from her eyes.
"What will we do now Mama?" It was evident we couldn't go home, there was nothing to go back to other than belongings scattered amongst the street. She had packed a small amount in what she could find that she held closely to her side. It was Papa's suitcase she had managed to forage from the rubble, packing it with photographs that had barely survived the blaze, clothes dirty though just intact and a very small amount of canned food that could be found amongst the bricks and rubble.
"We will have to go to Aunt Lena's Jakub and hope they can make room for us. Hopefully they haven't been touched by those dahm German's like we have."

Aunt Lena lived a fifteen minute walk from us on Przemyska Street. I stayed fairly quiet for the duration of the walk. It didn't feel like Mother was in the mood for conversation and what could I have said anyway? Instead I let questions rattle around my mind like rice grains being shaken in a tin jar until I just couldn't stand the silence anymore.

"Why do they hate us so much Mama? Why do they hate Jews?"

"I cannot be sure Jakub," She says, straightening her composure which surprisingly stops her crying for a short time. "Your Grandpa once told me of when the first world war was not won for Germany. Hitler and many of the German people did not take well to this, especially considering they were made to pay over six billion in charges for damages. Some say he blamed the Jewish people for this." She takes out a tissue from her pocket and gently wipes her nose while walking down the street to Aunt Lena's in the brisk cold wind that made breathing difficult when it blew into our faces.

"But Mama, I thought Polish people fought in that war too?" I asked confused, though starting to understand that little bit more.

"Well done for remembering Jakub though you must remember that Hitler needed someone to blame for them losing and it wasn't going to be his perfect German Aryan Race was it? He used us as his blame card and has hated us since." We turn the corner onto Białobrzeska street and slightly pick up the pace as we near our destination. "You see Hitler believes that the perfect race is those that have pure German blood. Jewish people have been living in Germany for more than a thousand years and he is making Jews in his own country suffer too! He see's Jewish people at the very bottom of his hierarchy of his Aryan Race, we are barely even human at all to him." I saw her mood had changed to one of frustration and anger though I was intrigued, fascinated to know more.

"What does Aryan mean Mama?"

"Aryan Jakub is what Hitler deams as his *master race,*" she says, making bunny ears with her fingers which I don't really understand but let her continue. "Aryan Race to him is blonde hair, blue eyes, tall and pure German blood. Anything else below that he deems as inferior."

"Like us?" I asked, feeling rather saddened that we were thought of in such a way.

"Yes, like us but we should never be ashamed of being Jewish Jakub, it makes us who we are and it has been in this family for generations and generations, we are proud of who we are and no man in political power or not will make us think otherwise, do you understand?" She stopped and waited for my answer, I dared do nothing else but nod.

When we turned the last corner to Aunt Lena's house, with Grandma hanging off Mother's arm and me carrying Papa's suitcase to give her arms a rest, we saw that although the street had also taken the hit from falling and screaming bombs, the apartment still appeared to be standing. Mother knocked at the door while me and Grandma stood behind her like two children being handed into lost and found. The door opened slowly by cousin Kacper who looked at us with wide worried eyes. Kacper being seventeen always held maturity beyond his years, though vulnerability washed over him and stripped him of everything I had ever known about him.

"What is it Kacper?" Mother asked, pushing her way into the apartment to find her sister. I always thought it was a twin instinct that Mother knew her sister was not right. Kacper said nothing, silence overpowering him in a sea of disorientated emotion. Aunt Lena sat curled in a chair silently sobbing that turned to a frantic outburst at the sight of her twin sister. I stood in the entranceway unsure of what to do, words unable to find themselves.

"Jakub, please go with Kacper into the bedroom, I need to speak with your Aunt.

Minutes dragged in what felt like hours, Kacper just sat on his bed silently staring into the distance as though walls were not a barrier of eyesight into the broken city.

"Why is Aunt Lena crying?" I asked on the off chance I would get some kind of response from him, though by his vacant stare that was almost chilling I did not hold out much hope. He turned his head slowly to look at me and I waited, seeing nothing in his eyes but sheer horror. Maybe they were scared of the bombs like we were, though their street had been hardly touched, not in comparison to our own.

"Mama says the German's will come looking for us and kill us, or take us somewhere to work." He hardly blinks as he looks back towards the window. I knew in those short minutes why terror had seeped into their veins like a poisonous fluid. They knew more than me and I didn't know what was more frightening, knowing, or being left in the dark of what was happening outside those walls with every chance of it jumping up and taking us by surprise.

"Papa is out there fighting them back but Mama doesn't think it is working. They are making their way into Poland and taking the lives of any Jew they find. Cousin Tymon informed Mama from Piotrków that the German's were making their way in and were hunting for Jews. They have killed so many, just shot them dead as they ran. Tymon and Uncle Jozef are hiding from them now but we haven't heard from them since. Mama thinks they may have already got into Piotrków but we haven't heard from them. They are coming for us Jakub, it is only a matter of time." A silent tear fell down his face, exposing his vulnerability I had never seen before. I sat in silence and waited for Mother to appear instructing it okay to leave the bedroom. I thought about Uncle Marcel. Kacper and his Papa were extremely close despite him being away fighting on the frontline to defend Poland. He was a brave and courageous man, full of inspirational quotes that could see anybody through a bad day, though it had not been his choice to fight, he had been ordered to like most in Poland because the country needed them and I think that was what hit them both harder. We had visited the day of him leaving and emotions were higher than I had ever experienced, until today.

Poland was losing and there was no doubt about it. The german's were making their way in, closer and closer everyday and we knew the day was exceedingly near that they were going to reach us and that was enough to strike fear into the heart of any courageous civilian. We were like prey, being hunted out and slaughtered at the hands of those with hate coursing through their veins that bubbled and exploded when they saw us. We were Jews, proud of who we were, yet terrified of what it meant for us.

Later that day when we had emerged from the bedroom we saw Aunt Lena and Mama settling the table with Grandma snoozing in a chair in the corner. We sat around the table and enjoyed the best we could the potato pie they had cooked together. Mama always cooked when she was nervous, it took her mind from what was going on around her and I did not doubt it was another *twin thing* that they shared. They were almost identical, other than the way they carried themselves. Mama was more headstrong and could keep things together better than Aunt Lena who would let panic take over her until she was crying and flapping around in an anxious frenzy. Mama always knew how to calm her down, which was more than many could do when she landed herself in one of her episodes. I looked around me, feeling as though the day was almost *normal*, though we knew it was anything but. I locked away the moment, keeping it safe in my memory. From that point I knew it would probably be very little time before such gatherings around the table would be stopped forever. I feared whether we would all still be together by the time the war was won. Won by who? Us? Or the German's? That is what terrified me the most.

January 11th 1940 - Coronado Public Library, California USA

The newspapers and radio were constantly spilling with news regarding the warfront and how Europe as a whole was being affected. In August 1939 the Nazi-Soviet non-aggression pact was signed, only to be broken by Hitler and his army on September 1st when he ordered air attacks on Poland, claiming it was self-defense. Nobody believed it, not after he had been so war crazy for years, yet it didn't stop the world being turned upside down from that very moment. Two days later, Britain declared war on Germany, followed by France just six hours later and on the very same day, the Battle of the Atlantic had begun, which was not given the name until March 6th, 1941 by Winston Churchill, echoing the Battle of Britain to signify its importance. Britain relied on essential supplies from North America, which needed to be transported via merchant ships across the Atlantic Ocean, holding great threat of being attacked by German submarines known as U-boats and warships. To combat the threat, merchant boats were grouped into convoys that were escorted by warships and if it was possible, accompanied by aircraft. On September 2nd, 1939, the first convoy sailed across the Atlantic. Ships were being sunk from both sides as attacks from the German Navy, The Kriegsmarine, took down ships being sent to Britain.

As I sat at the desk in Coronado Public Library I threw the paper in the bin with a sigh of defeat at reading anymore. The morning had been stressful with waking up late, running to Orange Ave to receive an earful from the boss, Marie, about punctuality as she stood arms crossed in her black skirt and blouse, looking at me through her *I'd love to fire you,* eyes. We hadn't seen eye-to-eye since my second day when I had referred to her as uptight for not letting employees talk amongst themselves. Probably should have kept that one to myself, though keeping my mouth shut was not always one of my fortes.

"Looks like you've had a morning from hell." Laughed Will, dismantling his umbrella from the tall entranceway, his thick black coat spilling rain on the floor I was sure Marie would have me clean up just to have a smirk at my inferior presence to hers.

"You could say that." I'd said, half laughing and half sighing.

"Women troubles by any chance?" He pulled a chair from a nearby table and positioned it at the opposite end of the desk as he did every afternoon, placing his food groceries neatly to the side to avoid a trip hazard. "A little advice for you kid, you will never understand the female mind, no matter how hard you try, so don't bother venturing down that path."

"Not so much trouble Will, just a little tense at the moment with everything that's going on." It wasn't so much of a lie but just not revealing all the required information to be one hundred percent truthful. Since the somewhat conversation of me joining the army Jen had been slightly off. With every broadcast and every newspaper article she would give me a stern look as if to say, *I haven't changed my mind*. We hadn't spoken of it since yet it didn't stop it looming in the air like a stubborn bad smell. "Coffee?" A change of subject matter was evident as he lifted his hands in submission and nodded his head.

Over the past year Will had become more of a friend than a customer that came in the library. He was a gentle natured man with wisdom that could take the breath away from any historian, yet get on the wrong side of him and it was as though a caged lion had been let loose. I held a lot of respect for him for that which could not be wavered easily.

"How is Janice holding up?" I asked, placing the hot mug of coffee on the desk before him and taking my seat back at the desk, much to the scowl across the room from Marie who didn't bother coming to lecture me while Will was there, one of the library's most regular customers.

"Hit me with a shoe this morning, which wasn't a plate so I suppose the darkness hasn't taken her memory too much today." He jokes, though I knew he was suppressing feelings he would much rather not admit to. "Coming here gives us both the time we need to ourselves, sometimes I think my smothering is what makes her hit me over the head, not her forgetting who I am." He takes a sip from his coffee and takes his black hat and coat off, hanging them over the back of the chair. "The world right now is a mess Peter and I don't just

mean life at home." He sets the coffee on the desk as he crossed his arms and leaned back in his chair, looking me in the eye as he continued, "Five German armies with 1.5 million men, two thousand tanks and just under two thousand aircraft took on Poland, who in comparison do not have half of what they needed to be successful against them. The Germany army holds occupancy over the East in Poland, the Soviets have the West. I can only imagine that life for the Polish right now is excruciatingly dreadful and it is going to get worse, a lot worse."
"What do you think it means for us?" I asked, leaning back in my chair in thought.
"America is balancing on a very thin line of whether to become involved but I know this, they must. You would have to have a very naive mind to believe that Hitler's army is not strong, it is going to take a lot to bring him down and end the war. I've said it from the start, America will join the war and it will need as many men as possible." He purses his lips as he looks on at me, waiting for my answer as though it were a question.
"Jen won't hear anything of it." I sounded defeated as I shrugged my shoulders, yet I knew deep down it was like an itch that needs urgent attention. "Besides, America is still neutral, I don't really need to be thinking about it yet."

I picked up the pile of sorted books that needed placing back on the shelves as Will let out a long and exaggerated laugh. "You really think that is the case? India, Canada, Australia and New Zealand, they have all issued their own declarations of war. Germany has taken occupancy in the East of Poland, casting out and treating Jews of their own country like dirt on a worn out shoe, the Atlantic sees constant threat from the Kriegsmarine with supplies being transported to Britain, wake up boy, the world is at war, we will not get out of this thing by gritting our teeth and hoping for the best. It is coming and I assure you it will be closer than you expect." He places his top hat firmly back on his head as he picks up his coat and umbrella and makes his way to the literature section before turning on his heel, "It is much more beneficial to be prepared and ready, than to be surprised by orders out of your control." He nods his head and disappears behind a bookshelf for the rest of the afternoon. His words danced around my mind for the rest of the day, trying to work out the riddle he had left me with so irritatingly unsolved. As I stacked books onto shelves I questioned over and over, *do I really want to be doing this for the rest of my life?*

On September 5th, America had officially declared its neutrality but everyone including Roosevelt knew that more needed to be done. By September 8th, Roosevelt had called for a strengthening of the U.S military and began to use his power to call up the reserves as the European war had created a state of limited national emergency. He knew that Europe was in crisis and under the skin of every American we were like sitting ducks waiting for the moment we would be told that our lives would too be changed. I thought about the horrifying news I had heard and seen, worrying about Ma and Jen if the war was brought to America. I'd read the words this morning in the paper, The Soviet Union had invaded Poland on 17th September, sixteen days after the invasion from the German army. The Soviet Union had invaded with forty divisions, many of them waving white flags at a baffled and confused Polish population. The Polish had been unable to put up much of a fight, as the next day Russia claimed the territory that the Nazi's had promised when the two nations had signed the Molotov-Ribbentrop Pact. On the same day a British Navy ship, the *Courageous*, was sunk by a U-boat off Ireland, taking with it five hundred crew members. I'd heard the podcasts of how the British Navy were losing ships to Germany's U-boats, how the Luftwaffe and Britain's Royal Air Force had clashed for the first time on 20th September in the sky over the border between Germany and France, when a German Me109 attacked a Fairey Battle Bomber with the RAF losing two aircraft and the German's losing one. Death was already spilling across Europe and an end to what was a bloody war was nowhere near over. What was to come would change the course of history forever and nobody even knew it.

January 11th 1940 - Warsaw Poland

Everything had changed. Fear screamed through people's veins like an angry lion, caged with no possibility of ever being free. Polish troops had fought brave and hard. Warsaw had endured eighteen days of continuous bombings leaving merely destruction and heartache in its path. Eighteen days Poland had been falling, fighting to keep her feet grounded for her people, until she finally fell, unable to withstand the constant air and land attacks. The 27th September was the day Warsaw surrendered, unable to push back the German Military, machine gun fire, air and land attacks with artillery shells wiping out most of those who stood in their way.

Warsaw had surrendered, meaning we were under the occupation of the Nazis from the west and the Soviets from the East after the Russian invasion sixteen days later on the 17th. We were like trapped sardines with nowhere to go or escape. I had always believed since learning of the war from Papa that the Russians would come to save us. I had never been so wrong. The Russians had already captured 250,000 Polish prisoners during their invasion of Poland and as the Russians had not signed up to the international convention on rules of war, the prisoners were denied any type of legal status, resulting in almost all of the officers being murdered with the remaining soldiers being sent to forced labor camps known as the Gulag. Deep down we felt that Uncle Marcel would have been one of them as we had not heard from him since. Stalin, a Soviet Politician who ruled the Soviet Union from the mid 1920's ordered the murder of 22,000 Poles by the Soviet Police during what was named the *Katyn Massacre,* additionally to this, the Soviet Police rounded up anyone deemed as a threat from intellects, politiciaans to religious leaders and they were executed. The Russians had joined Britian as part of the allies, though with the murder of so many Polish people their precense in Poland felt like it was more as revenge against the Germans than to save us. The crimes being committed by the Soviets from the East were that of mass executions, rape against females and mass deportations, with almost the same crimes from the Nazis in the West, meaning we saw very little hope for our fate being a positive one.

Polish troops had been marched through the city as though their surrender should be ridiculed and mocked. We watched through the windows, longing to see Uncle Marcel amongst the lines of surrendering soldiers, though he was not seen and Aunt Lena had been sure that he had been taken to a Prisoner of War Camp. Watching out the apartment windows, we knew that our fate was now in the hands of the people that had taken down our city then forcing Jews to clean up the devastation caused. It was rubbing salt in the wounds like never before, being made to tidy up the mess the German's had caused with no time for grieving those we had lost.

On October the 1st the Wehrmacht entered Warsaw, pushing out any doubt of Germany's occupation of the west of Poland. Their black leather boots that marched in rhythm with hundreds of others rumbled the streets like a mighty thunderstorm, each mighty stomp to the ground igniting the horror into each of us who watched in fright from our windows, or the streets below. The German's had found quarters in all the bigger, richer houses in the city, forcing out any residence that had been living there. They had made their way in and settled themselves far too comfortably. All Jews were made to go out into the streets under the guard of the armed Germany military to sweep the streets, clean the public latrines, fill the street trenches and remove the dead, taking them to graves and pits dug by Jews themselves in the cemetery.

We did as we were ordered, afraid to do anything else in fear of being shot or beaten. The heavy sticks and whips carried by the German's were not just for show which was demonstrated on numerous occasions when people tried to fight back or if they refused to undertake the strenuous tasks or if they were just not strong enough to keep up with the labor. Nobody was except, men, women, children and even the old were forced to work at the benefit of Hitler himself and his army of men..
"We must do as they say Jakub, don't argue back, do not even look them in the eye, just do as they say and return to me at the end of the day." I'd nod and agree though verbal

clarification was the only form of understanding she would accept.

"Promise me!" She'd shout before breaking down in tears and hugging me so tight my ribs could have quite easily snapped in half. I would promise every time, never breaking my promise.

Each day was a striving challenge to just make it to the next. Notices had been placed throughout the city informing us of our future and that it was a criminal offense to disobey orders given by those in charge. They were asserting dominance in any brutalizing way they could, even when they were not using physical violence. Most were starting to feel the strain of hunger as the communication bridges that brought in food had been bombed and destroyed, meaning food was becoming more of a luxury than a right. All rights we once had were stripped and thrown away like a dirty cloth. We were puppets of a show played out for the German's with not a single opportunity to change how it was. It was out of our hands, we were so low down in the order of priority that people began to starve, sell what they had in exchange for the smallest amount of food to feed their families. When the Blitzkrieg began on September 1st, we didn't think it would get much worse than that, we couldn't imagine how it could and now we were living each day in a tormented journey just to make it to the next day alive. Mother would spend her days out on the streets trying to find food when the rations had run out and I would sit in the apartment as instructed, hiding under the table if the German's were to come.

They didn't enter the apartment until eight days after Warsaw had held up their hands in defeat. The knock at the door rippled horror through each of us as we sat silently pondering the possibilities of what to do. *Was this our time? Were they coming to shoot us like they had so many before us?* Aunt Lena slowly made her way to the door, conjuring the courage that was difficult to come by. Another mighty knock and she flings the door open, closing her eyes expecting gunfire to pour through the apartment in a bloody massacre.

'Kacper Berkowicz?" Came a heavy voice from a tall German standing at attention at the door. We all remained silent, unsure of what to say or what would happen. *Why did they ask for Kacper? What were they going to do with him?*

"Here," Kacper gulps in fright, standing up and looking them in the eye, "I am Kacper."

"Come with us." They instruct, it was a demand, not a request.

"No! You will not take my boy!" Aunt Lena had ran in front of Kacper guarding him with her life, which happened to be literally as the other, smaller German sighed heavily and stormed through the apartment with little patience and no care for what was in his path.

"No! I will not let you take him!" She had broken down into tears and was waving the German's away in hope that by some miracle it would make them turn around and leave. The

German shoved Aunt Lena away so hard she fell backwards onto the floor. We were frozen to the spot, horrified and afraid. I wanted to stand up and hit and smack them, tell them to stop doing this to us and leave us alone, though I knew better than to think it would make any difference other than for them to shoot us faster.

"It's fine Mama," Kacper's voice had broken, shaking before the two men that were about to take him away from us to an unknown destination, "I'm coming, please don't hurt them." He begged as he walked out of the door. The taller German stops him with his hand abruptly and looks him over for a number of seconds.

"Papers." He grunts. Kacper rummages through a draw as quick as his hands would move until his hands fall on his documentation and identification. He hands them to the German who snatches them out of his hands and scans them with his small beady eyes until he looks at the other and nods.

Kacper left us that day and it tore heartbreak through us all, especially Aunt Lena who cried for many weeks after. She never was quite the same, she very rarely said anything or tried to carry on life, I suppose she felt she had no purpose anymore. The German's had taken the two people in her life that meant the most, the two people she lived and breathed for everyday, leaving her with little more than myself, Mama and Grandma who found little success in comforting her. The apartment did not feel the same after he left.

"Where have they taken him Mama?" I asked one day when Aunt Lena was out of earshot.

"I cannot be sure," She sighs while chopping the very few potatoes we had. "I think they are making him work like they have with your cousins in Piotrków. If they have, it is better than other alternatives and that is what we must hope for." I didn't ask anymore after that.

The tanks and armed men just kept coming day after day once Warsaw had surrendered, with two heavy machine-guns that were mounted on each turret, with Nazi soldiers inside the steel armored sheets, shaking the ground with the heavy moving tracks that rotated as they moved. It was as though we were living in an unknown land of terrifying beasts, home so far away it was barely a distant memory, yet we walked amongst its ghost-like shadow in a pitiful memory. We went out of the apartment only when we needed to and never for luxury. We felt trapped most days, confined within the walls of the apartment like they would protect us. They wouldn't of course and we were not naive enough to believe that this was as bad as it was going to get before the war was over. We lived day by day trying to avoid the clutches of the German's while more restrictions were being put in place. All Jews were made to return all arms they may have had and record any contagious diseases to the German authorities. We were given a curfew of 10pm to 5:30am and anybody found violating the curfew would be at risk of being beaten by the SS guards, or worse, shot and killed. We had seen many people lined up on the street, crying, trembling and begging until the machine guns were all we could hear, then silence. They were killing people in mass numbers, sometimes hundreds a day for as little as being in the wrong place at the wrong time was enough for them to point their guns and open fire.

Jewish shops and businesses were failing as most had to be handed over to the German authorities, although those that were still able to operate had tight restrictions with some days being able to open and others not. It was uncertain times, nobody knew if they would see the week out through lack of food or fighting the cold on the streets when they were forced from their homes. We said our prayers before every meal, being grateful for what we had while attempting to lose focus on what we didn't. Mother was always telling us that we still had more than most and we should be thankful for that at least. I knew she was right, we still had a roof over our head to keep us warm and although food was scarce and far between, others were dying from not being quite so lucky.

Matters took another turn for the worse when Grandma fell ill. She was still absent from the world around her which made communication difficult. She had given up a long time ago, we could all see it. Despite Mother and Aunt Lena being practical in making what food we had stretch, the lack of nutrition had caused Grandma to fall into a battling fever. Aunt Lena had moved things around since we arrived. Me and Kacper shared his bedroom while Grandma had been given Aunt Lena's bed, with Mother and Aunt Lena sleeping on a pull out bed on the floor. It had been somewhat cramped though when Kacper had been taken I felt burning guilt that I was still occupying his bedroom. I thought about him most nights as I lay in bed in silence. His bed stood deserted and absent with only his memory occupying the sheets. Aunt Lena refused to use his bed in hope that he would return, though deep down we knew that he was lost to a war that had only just begun. We had stayed up many nights talking about planes and his skills in engineering. Aunt Lena feared that through his skills in the field that he would be used to work on the German war machine. Aunt Lena was constantly worrying and it seemed a long time until it would ease when Grandma had fallen sick during the night.

Mother and Aunt Lena still stayed in the room with her and catered to her day and night, though she was rapidly declining when we couldn't get enough food to bring her back to health. Many occasions I would give her my ration however with the fever overpowering her she was beyond the point of feeling hungry anymore, nor did she have the strength to consume it. One day when I walked into her bedroom I saw both women rushing around the room in panic trying to encourage Grandma to breathe as the fever swelled through her body, leaving her with no energy to fight it. She needed medication though that had become impossible to come by when the hospitals were maxed out with starving and wounded patients. I had suggested she go there though Mother heard nothing of it.

"I will not send her into the pit of those evil men. She would be an easy target to just wipe off the earth. No, we will look after her here and that is that." She had said, though I sensed that even she knew it was a losing battle. They had propped Grandma up on pillows and were trying to control her breathing when I walked in.

"Jakub I need to ask you for something very important now, so I need you to listen to me." Grandma had fallen into a coughing fit though Mother continued as she rubbed her back. "I need you to go to the hospital and ask them for medication for fever. Do not stop running until you reach the hospital Jakub and if you see German's hide! I hate that I have to ask you to go out there but your Babica is sick and she needs me here. Without medication she might not make it." The thought of going outside made my stomach do somersaults, yet it was quite exciting too. I had not been outside in so long, not for anything other than work for the Germans.

I let the confusion of excitement and fright conflict with each other for a number of minutes as I stood watching Mother and Aunt Lena try to give Grandma some water. Going outside I'd have freedom from those same walls I was confined within, yet freedom was a long time gone, as I would have to pass many of those in German authority to get there. It was a risk and

Mother knew that but she would not have asked me if she was not desperate. The Jewish Hospital in Czyste was just over a thirty minute walk from Aunt Lena's. It wasn't far, though I knew I could run into many German's on the way there, I'd have to either run all the way there and risk being caught, or I would need to take my time, hiding between markers like I was on a mission. I decided to go with the latter, better safe than dead in the clutches of those with guns. It was already 8:15pm, curfew hit down at 10pm, I'd need to hurry to get there in time and convince the nurses to hand over medical supplies to a thirteen year old boy, then make it back again without being seen. It was a near impossible mission with the quantity of Germans that swamped the streets of Warsaw, though it was a mission I had been assigned and I was ready.

Leaving the apartment felt chilling and eerie, as though I was breaking every law put in place in the last few weeks. It was not against the law to go outside before curfew however Jews were to walk on the road and not on the sidewalk, meaning it would be a case of blending in with others to not draw attention that I was alone. Aunt Lena's apartment overlooked blocks of apartments that existed through a courtyard. For now the journey was simple, plenty of places to hide, though once I got out into the open I would have to be more cautious to not look suspicious. If they knew I was going to the hospital it would be within high possibility that they would beat me with their sticks, making the journey more difficult, if they let me go at all. I had limited time before the curfew and Grandma needed medical supplies before having to endure another night with only the aid of Mother and Aunt Lena. It was a task I could not fail.

The Jewish Hospital in Czyste consisted of four roads to get there. I kept repeating the fact in my head, telling myself it was not that far, though the daunting realisation of how long each road was tormented my ability to be unable to stop shaking. I'd already told myself there would be times with limited hiding places should I run into the men in uniforms. I had to be vigilant, careful and cautious. The first street off from Aunt Lena's was simple with plenty of places to hide when I saw the German army patrolling the street. The real task started when I reached West Park. Jews had been banned from using parks, along with many other public utilities with signs placed on their outside reading, *'Entrance is forbidden to Jews.'* It was open to the eye and I knew there would be more than a handful of opportunities for them to see me as they patrolled in high numbers across the green and around its perimeter. Stopping at the gate I evaluated my options as well as my surroundings. Two German soldiers patrolled the gates at this side of the park, their sticks in their hands like they had been glued for if a Jew should walk in their line of sight. I could either sneak through the gate as they reached their furthest markers from one another and hope not to be seen and wish for a miracle that inside the park I would make the same successful result, or I could detour by taking Szczęśliwicka Street instead that would add twelve minutes onto my journey there and back. I pondered the possibilities, weighed them up in my head as I hid behind a tree, never taking my eyes from the soldiers walking in perfect sync across the gate.

After barely a minute I had decided. I was going to make a run for it when they crossed each other at the gate and had their backs to me as they walked to the far end of the park. It was a risk, it possibly couldn't get any riskier, though I knew I would need all the extra time possible in convincing the nurses to hand over the supplies and make it back in time for curfew. I stood with my feet itching to make a break for it, nerves like jelly trying to be controlled in a fast moving car, until one...two...three… I had never felt so much adrenaline fire through my body in all my life. As I ran I told myself, if it was like this on the way there, would it be worse on the way home? Or would the dark act as a sheltering aid from watchful eyes? I could feel my legs trying to give in, crumble under the strenuous strain I was forcing them to endure to make it past the soldiers unseen. I felt their eyes burning into me, paranoia maybe, or maybe not, keep running, don't stop, just like Mother had said. As I entered the park there was hardly a handful of people taking their Wednesday evening stroll. It was not a crime for me to be outside however it was a punishable crime for me to be in a park. It had become the law by 1936 that no Jew should step foot in a park, restaurant or swimming pool. I was risking my life to save on a few extra minutes and I wondered whether I was making the right decision as German guards patrolled the perimeter.

Reaching the end of the park I came to a halt. More soldiers patrolling the gates. There was no other way out, I knew there was no time to stop and evaluate again, I just had to run. As my legs carried me out of the park at speed I had never experienced before I did not stop, I kept running, out of the park until I reached the end of the long street, turned the corner onto Tunnel Street and carried on, disregarding my lungs fighting for oxygen and my legs becoming numb and weak. I ran across the junction and stopped. Another park, though this time it was longer, I would have to run for longer to not be seen. I questioned in my mind if I would be lucky a second time, maybe not. *Think Jakub.* Brylowska Street would add two minutes onto my journey. Better to be safe this time. Catching my breath I turn and make the run all the way down until I reach Marcina Kasprzaka Street at the junction. *Left or right? Left or right Jakub?* Frustration overpowered me as I hid from sight behind a bush that looked out onto the road. If I made the wrong turn it could be the fate of Grandma getting the supplies she needed that night. *Think, think.* Rubbing my head I know I had to make a decision. *Right. Or is it left? Why can I not remember?!* I went with my gut and prayed that I had made the right turn. I ran until I met another junction. *It does not look familiar, maybe I have come the wrong way.* Just as I began to turn around I see another junction, I took the chance and as I did I saw the hospital at the end of the road.

Relief washed through my body leaving me light headed, though this could have been through lack of oxygen from so much running. If adrenaline did not take over that day I would sure as day be still making my way to that hospital as the sun disappeared, leaving me vulnerable to the German's. I couldn't get ahead of myself, I still had to make my way home in hope that I would be as lucky as I had on the way there.

The hospital was just as I had remembered it from previous years of visiting with Mother. It stood tall with multiple floors, though it had not been spared of the continuous bombings our country had endured. The air raids had not even spared a hospital that cared for sick patients and it turned my stomach. How could anybody be so cruel to other human beings? Sections of the building had been completely blown out with others barely holding it together. People were queuing to get inside so it was apparent it was still operational even in such dark circumstances. I had to be grateful for that, though if people were lining up outside, did that mean they were struggling under the demand? Walking to the main doors it was clear that many needed medical assistance and maybe it was the reason Mother hadn't brought Grandma here herself. I stood and waited in line as I took in the horrific scenes around me. Men and women barely standing up with little to no energy, their eyes heavy like weighted bricks. Children crying and clinging onto their parents while holding wounds or their stomachs. Hunger appeared to be taking over and there was little to be done with such insufficient rations. The communication bridges that brought in supplies had been destroyed during the air raids and I felt sick at the thought it was probably done purposely, to starve us inside the country with no way out. Not only this but what food was brought in, a substantial amount was shipped to the Reich as part of their mission to eliminate us for being what they referred to us as *'subhuman.'* Mama had told me that the majority of the food was more than likely sent to the German soldiers fighting in the war, leaving us with barely enough to survive. Polish people who were not Jews were given the option of moving to the countryside or to secretly obtain food from farmers, which was surprising as Poles were seen as only one inferior level up from Jews in the Nazi racial ranking. Some that were able did move to seek a much better life with lesser food ration struggles, though not everyone had the option.

It felt like hours of standing in line when I eventually reached the front door with only a woman and her daughter before me. It was nearly dark, meaning the journey home was becoming more and more of a risk to make it back in time before curfew. The scenes flashed through my mind of me still being out when the curfew had landed. Soldiers grabbing me and beating me with their sticks and whips, hitting me until pain was all I could feel, making me stand before them as they pointed their machine guns at me, counting down the seconds until my life would be over. I had seen it with Jews before, they spared no generosity or kindness towards people like us and the thoughts haunted me from the inside out. As I shook the scenes from my mind, I heard a man coughing behind me. I turned to ask if he was okay, though no words could escape me as I saw his wounded face. He had taken a hit severely and the wounds looked as though they were infected as they gaped open with merely a small cloth to cover them.

Realisation hit me harder than the German's ever could. People were struggling, really struggling and resources were limited and running dry while people of the country were being forced to live through the consequences we never asked for.
"Are you okay?" I asked, knowing he wouldn't be given the fact he looked in pain and was waiting outside a hospital, though I didn't know what else I could have said.
"Do I look okay kid?" He snapped while falling into another coughing fit. I looked to the ground and remained silent, I shouldn't have asked, I should have minded my own business and kept to myself. There were a few moments of silence before he nudged my arm gently and offered me a smile.
"What you here for, you don't look sick?" He asked, lighting up a cigarette and inhaling it slowly. I hadn't seen anybody with those for quite some time, nobody could afford them, though it

was quite probable he had exchanged them in hope they would take away some of his pain.

"My Babica is sick, I've been sent to get her some medication to relieve her fever." I watch as he blows the smoke into the misty cold air until it disappears. Noticing my indiscreet staring he pushes the cigarette in my direction.

"No thank you. Mama says smoking takes away your breathing, she says it's bad to smoke. My friend at school did it sometimes. Mama saw he offered me one once and I got told off even though I didn't have any."

"Smart woman. If your Babica is sick why haven't you brought her here?" He threw the cigarette to the ground and pulled the blanket tight around his shaking shoulders.

"She's too sick to move and Mama is too worried that the German's will shoot us if they see us." I stood fidgeting between two feet, time was escaping the day faster with every passing minute. The woman and the small girl entered the building and the rest of the line moved up to make room for more people that had joined the queue.

"She's probably right, they don't seem to hold back do they?" He sighed heavily and nudged my arm again. "Go on kid, make your Grandmama better again." I was being waved into the door by a friendly looking nurse looking so tired her eyes could have fell shut at any moment. I turned back and smiled. "My name is Jakub by the way." He nodded and smiled in return. "Henryk."

Inside the hospital was the most chaos I had seen since the air raids in September. Patients lay in corridors, on the floors, multiple to a bed in wards with frantic nurses rushing around after the constant cries of pain coming from every direction.

"We are very crowded here as you can see so unfortunately if you are well enough to recover from home we would please ask that you do. We have a very high demand of patients, many of whom are soldiers and bed space is extremely limited." She looked me up and down in a polite manner though I could read instantly that she noticed I was not sick.

"It is not me Miss, it is my Babica, she is really very sick at home with a fever." She scans me over again as if in thought as nurses rush around us in and out of wards being unable to keep up with the demand for medical attention.

"I am very sorry to hear that about your Grandmama my boy, though as you can see the hospital is struggling. We have barely enough food or medical supplies to treat the patients we have here, I simply cannot just give them away when I cannot be certain where they are going." I knew instantly she suspected I could have been asking for them to trade in exchange for food or clothes. "We have been caring for a lot of wounded soldiers and civilians, the supplies we have we cannot afford to just give away."

"Please?" I begged, unsure of what else I could say.

"If your Grandmother is sick I can only ask that you bring her in. We treat all people here, not just Jews, we make space where we can, though I cannot guarantee it. Half of the hospital is completely isolated due to the outbreak of Typhus. We have such little room though that is all I can offer you, I'm sorry." She headed back towards the door insinuating my leave. I couldn't go back without them, I had not risked my life to go back empty handed.

"She is too sick to move. Mama and Aunt Lena are trying their best at home but we have such little food we cannot bring her back to health, she needs medical help. I risked my life coming all the way here, I ran through two parks that could have had me shot. We have already lost Papa and Grandpa, Kacper too when they took him, we can't lose Grandmama too. Please, I'm begging you, anything that will get rid of her fever." I'd begged until there was nothing else left within me, watching her stare at me in silence for a number of minutes as she thought about her decision, wondering whether I was here for exchangeable goods or whether my Grandma was actually sick like I had said.

"Wait here." She said, rushing off into one of the nearby rooms that had missed a hit from the German's bombs. It was a number of minutes before she returned again with a bottle of pills and as gently as she could nudged me out the door.

As I walked out of the hospital darkness plummeted the earth like a frightful shadow.

"Excuse me but do you know the time?" I shouted after the nurse as she helped Henryk inside.

"It is twenty minutes to the curfew, you better hurry now." Even by running as fast as my legs would carry me I knew it would be impossible to make it back in time. There was no time to stop and think about it, no time to stop at all, I'd have to run the whole way if I was to be in with a chance of making it home before the curfew fell upon Warsaw. Street after street I ran, through the park, down the street leading up to Przemyska until I ran face first into the belly of a German soldier standing fixed to the spot in his tight fit uniform and black leather boots. I ran so hard into him it knocked me to the floor sending my head dizzy and faint.

"Well, well, well." He laughed in his German accent, though something in my gut told me the situation was all but funny. Fear electrified through my body faster than I could blink.

"I'm s..s..sorry." I stammered, too afraid to talk though quickly hiding the bottle of pills in the back of my trousers. He looked down on me with dark black eyes that sent shivers crawling along my body. *This is it, this is the end.*

"Papers." He demanded, never taking his eyes from me. As quickly as I could I rummaged in my pockets and handed him the documents that clearly stated I was a Jew. His eyes grew narrow as he looked from the papers to me and back again. My heart was beating so fast it felt as if it would jump from my chest and run away in fright.

"You do understand that curfew is at 10pm?" He shoved the papers back to me and stood with his hands in his pockets, a rifle gun at his side. I never took my eyes from it, waiting for the moment he would use it to end my life right there on the street. I eyed the gun then back to his face, I had seen others perish at those guns for not looking a German in the eye when spoken to. I noticed a long thin scar running from the left side of his face down towards his mouth, so thin it almost looked as though a blade could have made an unwelcoming appearance there. He was a young soldier, looking no more than twenty years old yet he brought fear in his appearance all the same.

"Run home boy and stay there. The streets are not safe for your kind this late at night." Confused, I started to run, not taking any risk of him changing his mind. Just as I reached the corner onto Aunt Lena's Street he shouted after me.

"..And don't drop those pills falling out of your pocket, my guess is somebody needs those."

August 12th 1940 - Coronado California USA

I stood at the bottom of the stairs as I had been for the last twenty minutes in a shirt and tie and the smartest slacks I could find that made me feel like a fraud. I was always more of a comfortable attire kind of guy rather than the whole dressing to impress because I simply did not care who I impressed if it was anyone other than Jen, who was still after two hours getting ready to go to her fokes for a dinner that would make us feel like we had been living on the poorest of meals. It was all a farce, everytime we went, everybody putting up acts of something they weren't to impress those that sat at the other end of the table. If the decision had been mine I would have turned up in my most comfortable clothes and let her Mother cast her judgement that went straight over my head and out the nearest window. It was not however down to me, therefore I would take the very precise guidelines from Jen on looking my best.

It didn't matter where we went or how much time we had, she always kept me waiting while she got ready, changing her clothes a dozen times and on many occasions becoming agitated and saying she wasn't going. It was a routine that had set itself in stone and I had concluded from past experience, it was in my best interest to never try and rush her. I was pulled from my thoughts as I saw Jen make her way down the stairs in a blue dress that touched her knees and a pair of small white heels.

"You look beautiful." I said, kissing her forehead and taking her hand. She smiled, as I knew she would. She always said that every person should receive at least one compliment a day to reassure them that they were valued. Another amazing quality I admire most about her.

"You scrub up pretty well yourself handsome." She laughed as she returned my kiss and made her way to the car.

The drive usually took around forty five minutes, though for some reason we had made it in an hour with a traffic jam moving at a slower pace than Jen getting ready. Jen was driving as she knew I needed to have a few whiskeys before facing her parents. I'm not really sure I'd have been able to without sinking a few for dutch courage, meaning I was grateful for the holdup, I'd never been able to stand her folks anyway and it worked in my favor that we had a valid excuse to not be there as long. Her old lady liked to clock off from the day and *unwind* at eight and made it more than obvious we had overstayed our welcome when we were still present at that time, usually by long exaggerated yawns that gave us the hint she was ready for us to leave. Moody sod.

Walking through the door, the same overwhelming scent of meat and potato patties hit me hard in the face. For as long as I'd known her folks they had never failed to keep the impression that they were above everybody else in the world because they had more money than they knew what to do with. The money came from inheritance really but that's not something Jen liked me to bring up during discussions after leaving, which was always in a heated rant about how the evening had panned out. Inheritance and his war pension that he was quickly dipping into for cigarettes and whiskey were what made Jen's Mother feel that they were above the rest of the world with everyone else looking up from an inferior and pathetic height, so she thought. I smiled as I kissed her mother's cheek while pushing down resentment that was all too bitter for the woman. The feeling was mutual and we all knew it, despite having to hide it for appearances. Walking through to the dining room that had been elegantly decorated for the evening ahead, I took a deep breath and told myself it was one night in fourteen I had to do it, then I could go home and look forward to the next thirteen of not having to go round again.

Her dad was sitting in his chair in the corner reading the paper with a cigarette hanging from his mouth that made his wife frown, to which he always went on to tell us the exact same story, "You know, in the war they gave us cigarettes to stop us going crazy with boredom! Said if we smoked um' it would improve our morale, though I know a few men who's discipline could have been tamed a little better, crazy some of the men who were on the frontline, those trenches did things to you, i'll tell ya!" He stubbed it out at this point as he stood up to shake my hand and continued with the exact same story I had heard so many times before.

"Given to us as part of our rations, they knew they were needed to calm the men after the blood baths we'd seen day in and day out. She wants me to quit but I've seen things in my time boy that makes smokin' nothin' in comparison to that. Dam bloody women." He threw an agitated look towards his wife who was busy patting her daughters dress down to ease the creases that were barely visible, while shaking my hand with dominating force for a guy in his late sixties. If I had to be honest, I'd much rather have spent the next few hours with him than his wife. Unfortunately I was never really given the option of choice.

Sitting at the dinner table with my posture on full form, my shirt tucked in and my mouth shut until absolutely necessary I gritted my teeth to make it through a night that I'd much rather have spent at home.

"So Jenny, how has life been at the hospital? I hope they are giving you more time off because they will run you to an early grave all these long hours." Her mum asked, picking up her wine glass and taking an over-the-top elegant sip while keeping her eyes locked on her daughter. Lily Stones, always believing she was more above everyone else than she really was.

"I'm still working the same hours Ma, I need the money but I love what I do and not many can say that about their work." My beautiful Jen, always finding the best in every situation. She had always been the light to enter a dark room and it was just one of the many things about her that I fell in love with as soon as I met her.

"You really should take more care of yourself hunny, how can you possibly make time to give us grandchildren if you're both working all the time?" Lily placed her wine glass down and kept her eyes locked on her daughter, it was obviously not a rhetorical question and the feeling of three pairs of eyes rolling filled the air.

Bill is sitting at the end of the table giving his wife looks of agitation every so often that always gave me the impression he just couldn't stand her, maybe it was too late in life to find anything else worth settling for. Lily didn't notice as she was still insistent on a response to the awkward question that was asked every single time we walked through the door of their home.

"Ma, you know that me and Peter are happy as we are. We have no desire to add further stress on top of our busy work lives by trying for a baby. What is meant to be will be, we should not force it. We graduate this year and we are hoping to stay in our jobs and pick up further hours, it is what we want." Lily was the one to look agitated now as she received the response she hadn't been hoping for. I grabbed Jen's hand under the table and gave it a comforting squeeze.

"I don't want grandchildren when I am too old and useless to play with them Jenny." What she really meant was she doesn't want to look like the old Grandma to all her 'friends' that see newborns as a competition on who can do and buy the best just to brag about it to each other in a depression that was affecting even the richest of people.

I sensed another invisible eye roll so I had tried to swerve the conversation to something else.
"So Bill, Jen tells me you have been working on some cool things in your basement." Jen squeezed my hand back in return for her appreciation of the change of subject. At least it was put off for a while, most likely next time we went for dinner in thirteen days time that I hoped would be cancelled for any reason at all.
"I have boy, a mighty fine collection I have coming along too." He wiped the remnants of his food from his neatly trimmed beard with a napkin so expensive it looked as though it should have been in a glass display unit rather than used to wipe the spilling food from the old guy's mouth.

I took the opportunity for a possible escape away from the old woman who snapped nerves inside me with every passing second in her company. "Planes aren't they? I'd love to have a look sometime." What i was really hoping for was to be out of Mrs Stones glares for as long as possible, even if that meant putting up with the old man's war stories that always made me feel uneasy yet oddly interested.
"Indeed they are, all running like clockwork too. I've just finished painting the replica MB-1 and I'm pretty damn

impressed if I do say so myself." He pushes the chair out to make room for his bloated belly and downs the rest of his whiskey. "How about we leave the girls to it and I show you eh?" He picks his cigarette packet up from the arm of his chair and walks towards the garage. I kiss Jen on the cheek with a sneaky wink as she knows the game I have played. Her smile is accompanied by a slight laugh as she returns my kiss.

Bill Stones' garage was somewhat unexpected to the eye. I had assumed he would be a man of extreme cleanliness with everything needing to have its place. The small cluttered garage was anything other than organised, with empty whiskey bottles scattered around in small drunken piles, oil and paint littered amongst worktops and several overflowing ashtrays hidden amongst rusty tools, begging to be emptied.

"Here we go." Says Bill, proudly holding up the mini plane he had made with two fingers so as to not damage the delicate model with heavy hands. "Took me three weeks to make this bird and she's going to take the prize place on my shelf." Scanning the plane held between his fingers, I take in the immaculate attention to detail. He may be an old guy but he definitely knows his stuff.

"This is amazing," I reply, running my eyes down the wings, "Where did you learn to do this?"

"Good friend of mine fought side by side with me from 1914, told me all about making these things. When we won the war there wasn't much to do to take your mind off the shit you've seen, you have to learn to live with it." As much as his war stories dragged on, I knew he became his true self when not surrounded by his pompous wife. Never would he use language like this infront of her and it gave me a small ounce of satisfaction that he probably saw straight through her too. "So I decided to carry on his little hobby and turns out I'm a firecracker at it." He had a look of sadness that washed over his eyes but he managed a small smile at the memory of his friend as he placed the plane back on the disorganised workbench. "Only nine of these bombers were completed before the end of the war, so quite something to look at now." He gently taps one of the wings with a slight smile before letting out a deep sigh.

"Are you glad you fought in the war Bill? Or do you regret it?" I shift between two feet, wondering if I had asked a question that should not have been asked.

"You don't regret serving your country boy, you regret all of the things you didn't do, sometimes that eats away at you but you have to keep moving forward, despite how persistent the memories are in showing themselves. Why do you ask?" He lights up a cigarette and pours another glass of whiskey that he drinks in seconds. I hesitated for several moments, pondering over the possibility of telling him I wanted to join the army.

"So not doing something you should, would leave regret?" I asked, deciding to answer his question with another to divert the attention away in a cowardice act of being unable to tell him. Looking at me sternly he exhales a cloud of smoke and moves closer. "I have an idea of why you ask, yet I do not wish to hear it clarified, my daughter would never forgive me. The world however is in crisis and there will come a time, in the not too distant future that men and women will be called with no choice. My advice is to do what you want to do, before you are left with no other option. Do it because you want to and leave no room in life for regret, that shit never leaves you. Right now people all over the world are suffering, for some reason or another and their cries echo through our country, not unheard but unaided. At some point the suffering must come to end, regardless of what it means to get there." He points his finger in my direction and stubs his cigarette out on the worktop.

His words pierced themselves into my skin, gaining tenancy into every ounce of thought that circled my mind.
"Are you two coming back inside? Ma is yawning and I'm pretty sure that it is an indication for us to leave." Said Jen, with her head poked round the door with her coat already hanging from her shoulders. Bill snorts a laugh and pats me on the back as he makes his way out the garage. I looked at Jen as guilt washed over me. She looked so happy and I feared that it would be a small duration of time before I would send that happiness crashing down around her and it was something I already knew I would regret. It suddenly felt that the world had placed its weight on my shoulders and was pressing down harder than was possible. Life almost felt impossible to work out, I would be graduating from high school this year and the

library was not an ambitious goal I hoped would see me through until the end of my days. I wanted meaning, something to say that I had really done my part, yet every possibility had consequences. *You regret the things you do not do.* His words play over and over like it had been left on repeat in my mind. War was circling around us and despite the extent that people tried to believe we could escape it, we knew that it was a matter of time before we were plunged into a darkness that the world was already fighting desperately hard to survive. I take one last look at the model planes on the worktop and throw my heavy black coat around my shoulders. Regret was maybe something I would have to deal with, I was just uncertain of which side of life it would come from. Until then, life would carry on as if it were normal, while around us the world was burning in flames that longed to be put to rest, screamed to be freed and liberated from the planes that showered them in further destruction. I'd heard their cries and although at that exact moment I was unaiding, I'd heard them.

August 20th 1940 - Warsaw Poland

I stood staring at the newly raised flags that littered our city with the sign of dominance, power and hunger for more occupancy. The Swastika was placed upon it boldly and proudly. They had ripped down our own flags and replaced them with their own, fiercely reminding us we were not a country of freedom but caged human beings with less human rights with every day that passed.

"To them the symbol is of pride." Papa had told me, days before his life had been lost under the bones of our home. He had spent many hours educating me on what felt so uninteresting at the time, my mind had been so preoccupied I had hardly paid attention. How I wish I had now. Politics, war and antisemitism was never something I had taken great interest in, though Papa persisted to educate me on matters I am sure now he knew I would need to know. Maybe he knew a war was looming over us, people spoke about it often, when Czechoslovakia had been taken over my parents and grandparents would discuss amongst them what Hitler's next move would be. They never liked Hitler, especially Grandpa, I overheard him one evening telling the group of adults of how Hitler wouldn't know where to start in conquering Europe.

"To us as Jews and anybody that is an enemy of Germany, The Swastika is a symbol of antisemitism and terror." Papa told me, drawing the outline of the Swastika.

"What is antisemitism?" I'd asked, though still not fully engaged within the conversation.

"It is the hate towards Jews my boy, the way we are treated because we are Jewish. Do you remember I told you about Hitler, the man that stands in power?" He was leaning across the table at that point, trying to keep his thirteen year old son interested in a conversation of politics. A strenuous task.

"Yes." I'd replied, nodding my head slightly.

"Well, he has the idea that there is such a thing as a *perfect race*." He says, mimicking bunny ears with his fingers that Mother sometimes does. "We are not included in that perfect race. We are so far down the list of being *Aryan..*" Again the bunny ears, "That we are seen as inferior and because he is seen as such a powerful man, he encourages other non-Jews to believe in the same thing as him. He is powerful Jakub but also dangerous and people are buying into his speeches because he makes them sound so good to the people."

"What does he tell them?" I'd asked, becoming slightly more engaged as it appeared that it impacted us specifically.

"He tells them that he will make Europe great again, cast out all those who will stand in the way, all those that will not contribute positively to his *perfect race*," I'd taken a moment to consume all the information, wrap my head around it and understand it.

"This symbol Jakub," He'd said, pointing to the drawing he had made for demonstration, "..is called the Swastika. If you see this symbol at any time from now, you can bet we are in trouble. If you are ever faced with looking at this symbol and I am not with you, it means it is time for you to take extra good care of your Mama and Babica, do you understand?" I nodded in understanding though he continued, harshening his tone and becoming so serious that I had almost been scared just at the talk of it. "Jakub, look at me. If you see this symbol, it means you must stick together, no matter what it costs."

The memory burned in my brain just as much as the Swastika did as I stood below it, burning my hateful gaze into it at what they had done to Warsaw and the people who lived within the city. I carried on walking with barely a handful of rations. I'd managed to make it into line just in time to take home the last portion of bread,potatoes and one egg. This would need to last us for a long time, Warsaw was running out of food at a rate that people were dying. I'd taken the last pieces of bread with the guilty sensation that someone else would be going hungry tonight. As I walk away from the Swastika I glance back and made myself a promise. *We shall stick together, no matter what it costs.*

When I reentered the apartment that day Mother and Aunt Lena were huddled around the radio with Grandma sleeping peacefully in the chair by the window. I joined them as I placed the small amount of food in the kitchen and fell to my knees before the radio on the floor just in front of a big white cupboard that it would be hid behind in the wall, should the German's enter the apartment. People's homes were becoming invaded by German's, The Gestapo, who were part of the Nazi secret police that were given the go ahead to operate outside of the law to repress the public with activity Nazi's deemed as unacceptable. There was the Jewish Police, who would work with the German's telling them where rich Jews lived so they could enter their homes and steal what they could, jewellery, furniture, anything they wanted. They had entered our apartment several days previous and taken Mother and Aunt Lena's wedding rings and Aunt Lena's gold locket, they left the place an overturned mess, though we were grateful that the radio had not been discovered, we would all have seen the death penalty.

We were waiting for an announcement with tension building in every passing second. Music played softly with the sound of a woman singing about a rainbow. I became lost in the words as she sang them so beautifully. As the words danced around us I couldn't help but wonder whether there was still hope, whether the bad times we were living in would soon be over, or was it an empty song I had been delving too much into? I wanted it to be true, as she sang the words and I envisioned rainbows that cast away all the bad that was happening. The world had seen a very dark shadow cast over it, not just Poland but other countries in Europe too which we heard about on the radio. Sometimes we would listen to German announcements from Hitler, sometimes in German and sometimes in Polish and most involved the elimination of Jews. Hitler wanted rid of us and with every announcement it left us fearing for our lives.

Mother kept the radio on low volume, just enough for us to hear the words if we listened with great intent. She was always reminding us of the consequences if we were found in the possession of a radio, therefore nobody ever spoke when it was brought out of the hiding place. When Aunt Lena pulled away the cupboard and reached inside the wall to retrieve the radio we knew it was time for silence. Aunt Lena was able to speak fluently in many different languages through her days of teaching foreign languages at the University of Warsaw before Hitler put a stop to Jews being able to teach or practice. We were waiting to hear an announcement from London that Aunt Lena would be translating into Polish for us. Myself and Mother only spoke part English, meaning we would not understand all that was said without the aid of Aunt Lena. We were risking our lives to do it, meaning the soft sound of that woman singing about somewhere over a rainbow helped us to not be overwhelmed with panic at the slightest noise we would be sure to place on the German's entering the apartment. I always had a feeling that the people inside the radios giving the announcements and the people putting the music on just before knew that some people, like ourselves, risked everything to hear what was happening in the dark and dangerous world we were living in, therefore tried to calm them us the gift of music. Maybe it wasn't the case at all, though it was a thought that always came when eagerly waiting for the next announcement that would settle our fate.

We had heard announcements that Britain and France had declared war on Germany on September 3rd, just two days after the German's started bombing our city. They had declared the war due to Germany bombing us, regardless of the unwelcoming news that they were not coming to rescue us from German occupation. The news that day was bittersweet, we did not know how to react, happy we were not fighting the German's alone, though disheartened to great extent that nobody was coming to help us from the constant bombs that had fallen like rain upon our homes. We had listened to the proclamations by Hitler himself on the isolation of Jews and worried what it meant for us, what would they do with us to *isolate* us that they had not already done? Was bombing our city not enough that they felt more drastic measures needed to be put in place? Every announcement and broadcast just encouraged us to take another risk to listen to the next, leaving us in uncertainty of our fate.

We were huddled around the radio when hearing that Polish Jews between the age of fourteen and sixty would be submitted to the forced labour decree. Kacper had already been taken and every single day was like a waiting game of who would go next. We did our best to stay together, though we knew it would not last forever, one day, whether it be sooner or later we would all be collected and taken to destinations we were uncertain of to work for the Germans. It was as though when we didn't think things could get any worse, it always did.

The music suddenly stopped and we heard a crackling noise that led onto a man talking to the world through the radio. It was always tense with a thick atmosphere that could not be cut even with the sharpest of knives. Mother bites hard into her nails, Aunt Lena has her hand on my shoulders, squeezing harder with worry that is only increasing. The man on the radio begins talking in a lot of jargon I do not understand as we huddle closer to hear the words as Aunt Lena translates. He talks about politics, the war effort and the progress on the battlefront. The Soviets had broken into the Eastern part of Poland and had gained occupation there, while the German's had occupied the West. The man talked about Russia being expelled from The League of Nations, which I try to understand, though I did not dare interrupt the broadcast or Aunt Lena by asking Mother what it meant. I never knew what most of the information meant over the huddled radio sessions, though Mother always tried to explain it to me after, telling me that Papa would want me to know everything that was happening, regardless of her own views on the matter. After several minutes my attention lands back to earth as the man begins talking about Jews. He spoke for a while, telling us information we already knew as well as new information that made us sigh heavily as we continued to listen. It wasn't until I heard the words ...*Jews to wear an armband being four inches wide on their right arm. This is an order by Hans Frank himself and is effective immediately. Those who disobey or fail to comply will face severe punishment.*

When Mother turned the radio off and Aunt Lena returned it to its normal hiding place I stood in silence, waiting for Mother to explain in a way I could understand what had been said. I waited, though when Aunt Lena kneeled on the floor and began to cry into her hands, Mother put her hand on her shoulders.
"We are being reduced to nothing." She cried, "It won't stop here you know, they are labelling us and it is pretty obvious why! They want us marked so they know who the Jews are to send us all away to work and I can bet we don't ever come back." With that she broke into hysterical tears in which Mother pulled her into the bedroom to calm her down.
"Jakub I think it is best that you don't hear this, why don't you start making the soup? Remember, as little as possible." Says Mother as she shuts the door, leaving me in complete silence with my thoughts, other than the occasional sound of Grandma moving around in her sleep.

I prepared the soup for that day with the little food we had and pondered over the thoughts that stabbed at my mind. We were to wear armbands that labelled us as Jews, segregating us, isolating us and worse of all, humiliating us in any way they possibly could by stripping us naked of basic human rights such as food until we little more than bone on the streets. The most frustrating part about it all was feeling so small in a world so big, there was nothing we could do but obey commands and hope that our lives would be spared in the process, though this was not guaranteed or promised. Jews were being taken every day, by mass amounts to destinations we had only heard through rumour.

I made my way to the dinner table one day not long after the broadcast regarding the wearing of armbands, when I stopped in the doorway unseen as I overheard a conversation between Mother and Aunt Lena. My back to the wall and out of sight I listened with curiosity.

"There isn't much for Jakub to do here, yet there isn't much to offer out there besides brutality. Most of his friends including his Papa and Grandfather have perished with the bombs, it's just so much for a young boy to wrap his head around." Mother says as I heard her rustling with fabric. I assumed she was making our armbands with the fabric available and the very specific guidelines regarding them. "They have forbidden schooling for Jews, I will have to school him from home, what will be next Lena? I am worried how far this will go."

"Marika you have always been the stronger one of us both, you can't lose that now or what chance do we have?" I slowly peered my head around the corner to see Aunt Lena placing a hand on Mother's shoulder in comfort. "At least Jakub is still here with you, with us, I have lost my Kacper and there is no way of me knowing what they have done with him, if he is alive. I cannot tell you what that does to you Marika. Every morning I pray that he is alive and that they are not hurting him, the only way I get through the day is believing that he is okay and hoping that he will return to me one day."

"I'm sorry Lena, I don't know how you do it. I just wouldn't be able to get out of bed everyday if they took Jakub from me, I couldn't comprehend it but I know the day is probably nearing faster than we think." Mother stops sewing and looks to the ground with tears falling down her face. I wanted so much to run and hug her but I knew I needed to hear the truth, with nothing held back for my own *protection*.

"We are struggling, yes, especially with food becoming scarce and ration cards not supplied for clothes anymore but we have to stick together now more than ever before. I heard from one of the neighbours that they are sending Jews to forced labour camps, maybe that is where my Kacper is. I beg that they send me to the same one Marika so I can find him and protect him, though we all still need to stick together, do not let them defeat us. Maybe by selling the armbands we can make some more money for food, it should keep us going for a while"

"I worry Lena what will come of us. So many have been taken already and those that haven't risk standing before their guns and truncheons. They have taken our homes, schools, clothes and medical supplies, forbidden us to step foot in cinemas or restaurants, soon there will be nothing left to strip us of but the skin on our bones. People are dying Lena and I don't know how to protect him." Mother breaks down crying at this and I slowly slip away. I had made Papa a promise to look after Mother and Grandma and that included Aunt Lena too. I needed to do more, release some of the pressure placed upon Mother's shoulders. I needed to leave behind the boy that entered the war and walk out of it with my family as a man that had protected them. Everyone had received notices for males of the house to report to the German's for work from the age of fourteen, some went in hope that they would receive food and be spared from the hands of the German's, though very little ever came back. Mother had forbidden me to go, told me that we must stick together. I had thought about going, so I could provide food for the family from work they would have me do, though Mother would not hear of it. My fourteenth birthday was nearing closer and we all knew that I would not have a choice but to work when it came. They would come to collect me like they had with Kacper.

I thought about Shabbat before the German's arrived, how we would all come together every Saturday in the presence of God. Mother would light candles and everyone would dress up for the occasion. It was forbidden to work or partake in any labor on Shabbat, meaning we would prepare everything needed before sundown on Friday and for the next twenty five hours we would drink wine and Grandpa would tell us stories and we would enjoy three meals a day including Challah, which was a soft eggy bread, rich in flavour in the shape of a braid.

Challah was eaten on all Jewish holidays except for Passover when bread is not permitted. Mother made the most tasteful Challah, taking extra care on Friday's to make sure it was perfect. As we sat at the table before eating we would say the following prayer,

"Blessed are you, Lord our God,
King of the universe,
who brings forth bread from the earth."

Mrs Hauldry from our street who lost her husband in the first world war and had no other family, therefore she would come over for Shabbat and even joined in the prayers for blessing children which would be said before and after eating.

"The blessing for daughters asks that they become like the four matriarchs, Sarah, Rebecca, Rachel and Leah, while sons are blessed to grow up like Ephraim and Menasheh, two brothers who lived in harmony."

After this we would make our way to the synagogue that we had washed and become clean for every Friday. Some people in Poland were not fortunate enough to have baths or hot water, so we would make our way to the synagogue, tip the Shamus, which was the wash attendant and he would scrub you down and wash you over the head to make sure you were clean before going down into the Ritual Baths we called

Mikvah. The baths had to be kept clean at all times, hence having a wash beforehand, though it also meant that all Jews were clean for at least once a week for Shabbat. I would enter the Mikvah with Grandpa and they would submerge us in water three times to which we would then exit and sing songs of joy.

The synagogue housed the Torah scrolls which were stored in the Ark that faced the direction of Jerusalem so that Jews had their minds turned in that direction when praying and had an eternal light hanging at the side. A long heavy curtain would cover The Ark that I always saw as protecting the scrolls. The Torah would be read from the reading platform, the Bimah, that was made from the most beautiful carved wood I had ever seen. During reading of the Torah I would daydream and follow my eyes along the lines of the wood, wondering who had made something so beautiful that we were blessed to use within our synagogue. I thought about the Torah and what was read on those Saturday's as they reminded us of the ten commandments, one being that *you must honor your mother and father*. Most of the synagogues were either burned down or bombed and destroyed when the German's arrived, with religious ceremonies forbidden, meaning that when we prayed it would be in secret. This did not stop us being who we are however and Mother always reminded me of the Torah and the commandments within it. As afraid as I was, I wanted to go to work and be able to bring back food, provide for our family that was struggling, even if it could just supply us with the food we needed to celebrate Shabbat in secret, though Mother did not allow it and as I thought of the commandments and how I should honor my parents, I soon realised I had to scrap that idea and come up with something else.

After that day I abandoned the small boy I was and stepped up to be the man my Papa would have wanted me to be. I left the house everyday to search for food, bartering with local townspeople with the possessions I had. We had been lucky that the medication had saved Grandma's life, though there was a risk it would return if food persisted the way it did. I exchanged clothes I had for potatoes and eggs. I rifled through my shoes and kept only the most solid pair I felt would last the longest and exchanged them for cabbages and small amounts of meat that was the hardest to come by. It was not long before the best kind of meat Brisket was a distant memory. Sometimes for Shabbat this would be put in the Cholent and taken to the baker on Friday's. The big sealed pot would be wrapped in rags, containing potatoes, barley, beans and sometimes Brisket, that would be ready for Shabbat. My mouth watered at the memory as I handed over clothes in exchange for some fractions of food. I never told Mother or Aunt Lena where I got them, they soon stopped asking when they failed to get it out of me and was grateful for the food I brought home.

As the weeks went on and I had very little left to exchange it became harder to find food that would keep the family going.

Every morning when the sun broke through on a new and miserable day I would write abstracts that I would read to the family over a small and rationed breakfast of half a slice of bread and a quarter spoon of jam. Then I would brace myself for the day outdoors, kissing Mother on the cheek and telling her I would be home before the sun started to set, signalling curfew. I was never late. After hearing the conversation of how worried she was for my safety I always made sure I was home before she would start to worry. As I stepped foot outside it was always the same horrifying sight that became the new normal. Bodies sprawled across the street of those that did not make it through the night, the shops that were allowed to stay open had to have a sign in the window stating that they were Jews and those that had been looted down to the very last scrap of food looked abandoned and lost, blood on the streets from those that had not been so lucky at the hands of the soldiers became a normal sight. Every single day Warsaw was crumbling beneath the German's and basic human life started failing to thrive under the pressure of just staying alive. As I made my way through the bodies I would start my day in search for food. I stood looking out at the street and stopped to take it in as I saw people beg with what little energy they had left for just the smallest amount of food. It was early in the day and yet many would not know that it was their last.

*

3 years earlier...

"Mama can I have some more potatoes?" I asked after finishing my plate and looking at the bowl of potatoes looking mourish on the table.

"Manners boy!" Came the shout from Grandpa across the table. He was always the first to correct me when I had forgotten to use the word 'please'.

"Could I have some more potatoes please?" I asked again, though this time applying the correct manners.

"Are you still hungry son?" Came the voice of Grandpa again as he wiped away the food from his mouth. Papa looked over and smiled, he knew what was coming and continued to delve into his Seder, the traditional meal of passover we celebrated on the 15th day of the Hebrew month.

"Yes." I replied, piling more potatoes onto my plate and readying myself to dive in and enjoy the rich glorious taste of Mother's cooking.

"Let me tell you a story," He began, placing his fork down and wiping his mouth. Grandma let out an exaggerated sigh. "Brace yourselves." She joked as she carried on eating with her fragile fingers wrapped around the fork as though it would break her fingers if she held it too hard.

"During the war we fought hard against the German's and the Bulgarians and many others and it was not just fighting on the battlefield that made it tough. Do you know what else was tough?" He asked, fixing his gaze on me as he awaited my answer. The table had fallen silent though I could see Papa smiling, which made it apparent he had heard this story many times when he was just a boy.

"I don't know." I replied. I was ten years old and although I had heard many stories of the war Grandpa had fought in, I did not understand.

"Hunger Jakub, hunger. Sometimes food supplies could not be dropped if the supply bridges were bombed, meaning we had to make what we had last. If we ate everything we had, expecting that more would come, a lot more men would have perished at the hands of hunger. We struggled as it was, though we had to know when to put down the fork and save for tomorrow. There were times we would need to sacrifice the little we had, as our bellies screamed for food, to save our comrades. We had to not only fight the war but fight the temptation to not give in to greed when food was at our disposal, as our men may have needed it more and I can tell you that was a challenge. Now, we may have enough food right now but look around you, Grandma has still not had any potatoes, she is a lot older than you and has had a lot less, she may be in need of those a lot more."

Suddenly I felt guilty that I had taken more potatoes when Grandma had not yet had any. I began spooning them back into the bowl when he placed his aged hand gently on mine.

"I do not tell you this story to put it back boy, just to observe around you. Eat only what you must and abandon the need to eat for pleasure. One day this information may come of use to *you, maybe it won't, though tomorrow's fortune may not be as great as today's and that is what we should always be prepared for. Now, let us read from the Haggadah and I'm sure your Mama and Aunt Lena have a song they would like to sing."*

I missed the real message of what he was telling me that day, until now.

*

"Halt!" The sudden noise had brought me back from my memories into the horrifying world of the present. Cold and stiff bodies were being picked up from the night's round of dead and thrown into a cart to be taken away. Every person that moved the bodies were Jews as their armband sat boldly on their right arm. The street stood still in anticipation of what was going to happen next. I stood frozen to the spot as a German soldier towered above a small boy in dirty ragged clothes and no shoes on his bloody and torn feet, his star of David fixed tightly around his arm. He looked no older than ten, maybe eleven as he cowered at the soldiers feet, too afraid to move. He began to cry at the long suspenseful silence.
"Stand you filthy Jew!" He bellowed, as the boy scrambled up from his feet and stood at attention before the man in the uniform, attempting to be silent in his frightful cries. I could feel my body shaking, sweat beading on my forehead, my breathing becoming rapid and difficult to control. Whatever the boy had

done, I stood watching hoping that his life would be spared. He looked so young, so vulnerable.

"Where did you get this?" He asked the boy, snatching the bread from his hands. The boy looked up to the soldier and struggled to find words that would escape from his mouth.

"WELL?!" Shouted the soldier, as he threw the bread on the floor and stamped on it with his big heavy boots until the bread was little more than crumbs. The boy began crying harder in fright and covering his face, expecting to be beaten.

"Did you steal this you dirty Jew?" He asked, taking the boys arm and dragging him down the street. I could feel my blood pulsing harder than it ever had before, anger, fright, I wasn't sure what it was that made me run after them.

"Wait!" They stopped suddenly as the soldier turned to look at me, keeping his grip firmly on the small boy's arm. "He didn't steal it. I gave it to him." I'd said the words before any thought or rational thinking had been applied though now I worried what the consequences would be. It took several moments of silence before the man looked with his beady eyes from me to the small boy before throwing him to the floor and kicking him in the ribs with his heavy boot. Just as he was about to walk away he spat at the boy and laughed to himself as he walked up the street shouting, "What are you all looking at? Back to work!" With that the street resumed as though the situation had never happened.

I ran to help the little boy to his feet as he wiped his snotty face on the arm of his shirt that was torn in multiple places, looking as though it was barely keeping any cold out from his thin bony body.

"Thank you. Why did you do that?" He asked, wrapping his hands around his body in a bid to keep warm while taking particular care of his newly bruised ribs.

"We must all help each other against these monsters. Why did he think you had stolen it?" I asked as I took off my coat and placed it around his shoulders. His face lights up as soon as the fabric touches him in overwhelming gratification.

"Because I did." After several moments of silence we both laugh. I couldn't remember the last time I had laughed like that, or why I even was, maybe it was the graceful feeling of fooling a German and getting away with it with both our lives, despite the Torah stating that one should not steal. Times were getting too difficult not to and no judgement came from me. The laughter didn't last long as he hobbled towards the scattered bread crumbs in the middle of the road. His face fell as he tried to scoop up the larger chunks.

"Are you hungry?" I ask, watching him.

"This was supposed to be for me and Mama. I doubt I will be able to get anymore with *him* recognising my face." He says, shooting an evil look in the direction the soldier had gone. I thought for several minutes as he picked at the pile, pocketing pieces of bread a mouse would have been left hungry with. I thought about what Grandpa had told me about being hungry and sacrificing for the good of others. I wiped my head in stressful thought, Mother may not be happy about this, we barely had enough to go round as it was, yet something inside me told me it was the right thing to do.

"Would you like to come for dinner? We don't have much, I'm going out now to try to get some food for the day, you could come with me and then have dinner with us?" I knew Mother would panic frantically and maybe give me a telling off when he had left, yet it was a gamble I was willing to take. He looked as though food had been a long distant memory until that bread had reached his hands.

"Do you mean it?" He asked, jumping up and down while holding his ribs in pain but a smile spread across his face that was almost infectious.

"What's your name anyway?" I asked, beginning the walk through the city and keeping to his pace as he walked with a limp and held his sides in pain.

"I'm Izaak, what's your name?" He says pulling the coat around his body.

"Jakub," I hold out my hand to shake his, "nice to meet you."

That night after a day around the city foraging what food we could, we sat at the table for Mother's potato stew that had begun to be more watery as rations were more scarce and a quarter slice of bread each. She was not too impressed at first, though after explaining what had happened with the German soldier she soon relaxed to the idea despite her obvious worry about food rations.

"We hardly have enough as it is Jakub." She had told me in the kitchen while Izaak sat awkwardly next to Grandma at the table who eyed the new addition to dinner with cautiousness at his ripped and dirty clothes.

"A German crushed his bread Mama, I don't think he has eaten in a long time, how can we turn him away?" I looked in her eyes and knew there was no way we could have shown him out without food now. "I will give him my share Mama, please."

She takes a deep sigh and bends down to my level. "You are such a caring boy Jakub, he can have dinner with us tonight, we will make it work but please remember that this war is only going to get worse, we cannot feed everybody." She ruffles my hair as though I'm still a young child and hands me bread to cut into quarters.

As we sat around the dinner table Izaak waited patiently as his plate was put before him, eyes burning bright at the sight of it, bulging at the thought of diving into its taste.

"So Izaak," Mother says sitting at the table to join us, "Where is your Mama?" She asks sympathetically. "Does she know you are here?"

Izaak forks food into his mouth gently at as quick a speed as possible that could be deemed polite. "Mama hides in the rubble on Kopinska Street, she doesn't like to come out, she is very weak and worries that the German's will send her away because she cannot work." He says it so casually, as though living within rubble had become the new normal for him. "She says it is better that we are together."

Mother stops eating in shock, unable to take her eyes from Izaak. "Izaak, how have you been living like that? Where is your home?"

"Mama hides in the rubble of what was our home. Papa was taken on the eleventh night of the big bangs and my little sister Rivka ran away and we haven't been able to find her since. I look for her everyday when I search for food but Mama thinks that she has gone too." Everyone besides Izaak and Grandma stop in shock, looking at the small vulnerable boy eating stew as though it was the first meal he had consumed in a substantial amount of time. Mother stands from the table and walks into the kitchen where she disappears for several minutes before returning with bread wrapped in cloth and a pot with several spoonfuls of jam.

"Marika! That is the last of the bread!" Aunt Lena shrieks in panic, "What will we eat tomorrow?"

"Tomorrow is a new day Lena, we will survive, I know it, this little boy and his Mama may not. Here Izaak, take it to your Mama and make sure you both ration it to last you." Izaak's eyes grow large at the parcel of food. At first he doesn't say anything and then he jumps up and throws his arms around Mother in mounts of gratification.

"Thank you, thank you" He shouts, "We have not seen this amount of food in a long time, I just know that Mama will make it with this, she may even be able to look for Rivka with me! Thank you!" He squeezes Mother tight before letting go and turning to me.

"Would you mind if I borrowed your coat for a while to keep Mama warm tonight? I will bring it back I promise." He begs clutching the bread under one arm and holding my coat in the other.

"You can have it, you need it more than I do." With that he bounds out of the apartment in joyful thank you's and back to the pile of rubble that was now his home.

"Do you think he will be okay Mama?" I ask, worried about the new friend I had made. It had been a long time since I had made any friends and I feared that it would be a very short lived pleasure. Even at the time when I was still at school Jew's were segregated and mocked in front of the class, though I enjoyed school all the same, I missed it just as much as I missed my friends.

"We can hope so Jakub, I think you did a very good thing today. We may not have saved them forever though we have at least made tonight that little more comfortable for them. Yahweh will be blessing you tonight." Yahweh was our God who we prayed to many times of the day. Ever since the synagogues were destroyed we prayed from home, prayed that this evil war would soon be over and we would be alive at the end of it.

"Thank you for letting him stay Mama."

"I think you have both been very foolish." Comes the voice of Aunt Lena, spooning the last of her stew into her mouth and throwing down her spoon. "We cannot save ourselves, nevermind people living on the streets! How will we eat tomorrow now?" She looks from me to Mother in a bid to get an answer from one of us.

"We will manage Lena, we always do.." Just as Mother was about to continue the door began to bang from the other side, heavy repetitive bangs that trembled the walls and shook the pictures on the wall. We sat silently, too afraid to answer the door, knowing what would be on the other side. Aunt Lena throws her hands over her mouth trying to calm the rapid sound of her breathing while Mother pulls me close to her. Grandma stares at the door but doesn't react in any way.

"Aufmachen!"Comes the voice of a very angry German standing just outside the door demanding we open up.

"What's happening?" Whispers Lena, though we all had an idea and it stood the hairs on our arms on end, the end was coming and it was just on the other side of the door.

November 1st 1940 - Coronado California USA

The war had been raging through Europe for over a year and in that time lives had changed and turned in every direction possible with very little opportunity for seeing better days on the horizon. During May, the German army had gained occupation of Amsterdam, with their Commander-in-Chief of the Dutch Armed forces Gen Winkelman surrendering, German tanks reaching Atrecht France with Nazi troops conquring Boulogne and capturing Calais, their air force launching attacks on the harbor at Dunkirk in which a British destroyer and six of the biggest merchant ships in the harbor were sunk. After the Phoney War, given its name due to the little fighting and bombs dropped during the first eight months of the war, the Battle of France began in May 1940. As the Allies were losing the battle on the Western Front, Dunkirk was the evacuation process for Allied forces to Britain from 26th May to 4th June. During the battle of France, German tanks travelled in formation through narrow roads of the Ardennes in which they were protected from above by the Luftwaffe. The seven German armored divisions were near Sedan at the River Meuse by the evening of May 12th. French forces rushed heavy artillery to the area along with firing multiple rounds at the German invaders however they were overwhelmed when Rundstedt called for air support to which came the *Stuka* dive bombers and low-level bombers to clear the French lines. By 4pm on May 13th, every piece of French artillery had been destroyed, resulting in the

German forces crossing the Meuse untouched and further resulting in the German's taking the city of Sedan from the French 55th Infantry Division.

By the time June had come around German forces had entered Paris. Norway had surrendered to the Nazis, Italy had declared war on France and Britain and Canada declared war on Italy. The Italian Air Force had bombed the British fortress at Malta in the Mediterranean, the Soviets had invaded Lithuania and gained occupancy two days later, along with Latvia and Estonia and the British Prime Minister, Winston Churchill urging his countrymen with a speech I'd heard on the radio.

"So bear ourselves that if the British empire and its commonwealth last for a thousand years men will say 'This was their finest hour'."

On the very same day, future French president Charles de Gaulle broadcasted to his nation from London, urging them to rally to him and fight Hitler's invading army. By the time the Battle of France had come to an end, Germany held victory as they took over direct control over the Northern half of France, with over two million deaths and casualties. With Adolf Hitler's victory over France, they were made to sign an armistice eight days after German forces overran Paris. Just ten days after the armistice had been signed by France with Nazi Germany, the Royal British Navy sank a French fleet in the North of Africa and the following day destroyed another at Oran, Algeria, resulting in 1267 deaths.

By the time July 10th came around a 114-day Battle began in Britain as German forces began air attacks on Southern England, just months after Churchill had become Britain's Prime Minister. He paid tribute to his country's air force in a speech that was heard by many, including myself and Jen as we sat around the dinner table hearing of the progress on the battlefront, how Britain would not burn to the German's and how America would *still* remain neutral. We sat listening with tension as we heard the words that gave myself and I was sure thousands of others goosebumps that made the hairs on my arm stand on end.

> *"Never in the field of human conflict was so much owed by so many to so few."*

The entirety of the battle was fought by air, resulting in the German Luftwaffe being fought off by the RAF in October. July 23rd was the beginning of the Blitz, the all-night air raids on London that sent shivers to my bones. The British had started evacuating children to the countryside some time before, meaning children were being ripped from their parents to live with strangers just to keep them safe. The world was in chaos, fighting and destruction taking over with lives lost that would never be returned. I stood to click the radio off and sat back at the table in silence, leaving my food untouched.

"Are you not hungry?" Asked Jen, who had begun moving the food around her bowl with a spoon yet hesitating over whether to eat it.

"I seem to have lost my appetite if I'm honest." I sigh heavily and look at Jen, who is looking straight back at me with sympathetic eyes. "The world is burning and crumbling around us, people living in poverty, forced from their homes, rationed food with little hope it will see them through, yet here we are, barely touched by this war and refusing to aid those that are innocent in all of this." I rub my hand across my temple in hope it would relieve the stress building inside me with every announcement we hear.

"Peter, *we* are innocent in all of this, if America joins the war then we are all at risk too, we should be thankful that we are safe, at least for now, shouldn't we?" She moves closer towards me and takes my hand in hers as she offers me a gentle smile.

"It just doesn't seem right." I lean back in my chair that indicates I have given up on attempting to go through with dinner. Guilt and worry washed over me like a river with an increasing current.

"It isn't like we are living a life of gold Peter, as much as employment rates have risen this year, we are still struggling. We are living better than most, yes, we have food, as much as we need to make it stretch, we have a home but we are not living a life of luxury. Maybe we should stop listening to the radio and get on with our lives as best we can. Why don't we go to the theatre tonight? Take your mind from all of this." She waits patiently for an answer as she begins spooning food into her mouth with all table manners in place. It just irritates me more. Her *making the best of a situation* has always been a positive, though at that exact moment, I saw it as arrogance.

"You can't just shut the world out Jen because you don't want to deal with it." I'd lost all possibility of remaining calm and all my tensions had come to the surface like an erupting volcano needing barely a nudge to go off. It was apparent straight away, as I had always known about her, that starting a fight with her would end in a loss on my part.

She never let another person speak to her in a way that disrespected her and I was on the verge of feeling the resulting outcome of that. She stands from the table and looks me sternly in the eye. "I am not burying my head in the sand here Peter, I am trying to keep our world turning while the rest of it goes into complete madness. Don't ever presume that I am turning my back on the world." She looks close to exploding as she pulls herself back and walks towards the door. "I'm going to take a bath," She says, turning her head as she walks, "..and you're going to join me."

*

That night I woke in a pool of sweat with Jen sleeping peacefully next me, just as she had fallen asleep after our passionate moments of making up. We never argued much, though when we did it was much more exciting to take out our frustrations in the best way we knew how. She would call me all the names that came to her in an ocean of seeing red, while I pinned her to the wall and urged her to say it again. We'd collapsed on the bed just an hour later and as I woke from the sleep that I had drifted into, my mind played on repeat the dream that had shaken me to consciousness. Children running from homes crying as their parents perished, buildings ablaze and outnumbered soldiers fighting to keep back an army of men that were pushing their way through to reach cities that were already screaming with pain and violence. It plays over in my mind like a broken record that was impossible to fix. War was surrounding us and we were waiting, caged in, like circus animals waiting for the crack of the whip to make us react.

November 2nd 1940 - Warsaw Poland

"Mama where are they taking us?" I whispered as I followed the herd of people walking silently in line, carrying what little belongings we had been able to gather together in the two week notice they had given us, with very little allowance for taking much with us. Mother had worked herself into a stress many times, worrying about taking essential items we needed to live such as clothes and cooking equipment and sentimental belongings like photographs. I clung onto her arm as she tried her best to hurry Grandma along in worry that she would agitate the men in uniforms with black leather boots who did not take their eyes from us.
"We are going to a new home for a while Jakub but don't worry, we will stay together and hopefully it will not be for long." She whispered back while carrying on in the followed direction with nothing but fear radiating from her. We were being moved to another area of Warsaw like cattle, having to follow the orders given to us by the scary men with guns that looked at us as though we were the most disgusting thing to ever have caught their eyesight.

I watched them as I walked while being cautious of catching their eye. I had come to realise that eye contact with the German's gave them the ammunition they did not really need to beat you with their truncheons or pull you out of line to humiliate and taunt us, yet if we did not look them in the eye when they spoke to us, they would beat us for that too. Keeping our head down and following suit was the safest possible way of arriving at our destination, wherever that was, yet I could not help but peer from the ground at the people around us. Along the street were people lined up, watching us make our way to our new home. None of them Jews, mostly Christians, therefore they could stay, though some of them had smirks filling their faces glad to see the back of us, like they were watching a parade that should be celebrated, while most stood with looks of worry and distress. People watched from windows above us, some threw down food that people scrambled for quickly before falling silently back in line. Grandma began falling behind with her old age and stubbornness to be pushed around which caused attention to be drawn to us and the men with black boots began to shout at us to go faster.

"Schneller!" They shouted while pushing someone in line in the back with their gun. They could have just been standing there, no hands on their guns and they still terrified each and every one of us, even the Poles that were not Jewish were cautious. The Jewish police that accompanied the soldiers were just as frightening. We did not like their treachery and betrayal, they were told if they worked with the German's, themselves and their families would be spared, though we still hated them as they beat us in a bid to impress the Nazi's. They had banged down our door several months before leaving us fearing for our lives as a German soldier and a Jewish officer had marched into the apartment and began taking Aunt Lena's furniture that they deemed would be of good use, though not to us. Aunt Lena had put up a fight though quickly backed down when the Jewish officer had swiped her across the face with his stick, leaving a hot burning scar across her nose under the watchful gaze of the Nazi soldier. I watched them and wanted to pounce on them, cause them as much hurt and suffering as they had done to us. I was not naive enough to believe it would make a difference, I had to follow in line like everyone else and do as we were told.

Most people began crying harder than ever while trying to push those in front along that little faster to escape the clutches of the Germans. We were being marched out of our hometown like a disease that should be exterminated immediately. Grandma was being irritatingly slow and I could tell it was a purposeful act of defiance for them taking Grandpa and Papa. Aunt Lena was next to Mother, clutching at her arm to not be lost in the crowd of cattled Jews all making their way to the same destination.
"Mama, why can't we stay at home?" Came the voice of a small girl looking up at her Mother as her legs struggled to keep up with the pace.
"We are being taken to a new home in Warsaw and we must stay there," She shot a sudden angry look at the men at the side of us and spat in their direction. It took only seconds for one of the German soldiers closest to her firing line to quickly make his way over and drag her by the neck of her dress

abruptly out of the line, with some people gasping in shock and falling into tears of fright.

"Filthy Jew!" He shouted in his German accent, eyes narrowed and showing no sign of being gentle.

The little girl screamed and rusheed after her Mother though a young woman in the crowd of huddled Jews pulled her back quickly and picked the crying infant up into her arms.

"Mama! Mama!" The heartwrenching cries of the small girl sent my chest tight. She began kicking and fighting her way out of the women's arms with no luck as her Mother was being dragged away by her hair out of sight. I stood with no courage to move, the anger and the fear building inside me resulting in tears pouring down my face and my hands shaking. In my head I was begging that the soldier let her go with loss of patience for the situation, that we could carry on in our march with nobody being hurt but the fright inside my body told me something bad was going to happen. Silence filled the street other than the occasional baby cry, hanging off the very tension coursing through the veins of every onlooker. The infant managed to escape the clutches of the woman and ran in the direction of her Mother with the woman following close behind, trying to stop her from seeing what she would not want to see, or from being hurt by those in control.

"Wieder in der Schlange!" He shouted for them to get back in line. The woman snatched the girl up and hurried to get back in line with everybody else. I don't know what happened to the girl's Mother, though I hoped that she was reunited with the little girl that didn't stop crying all the way to the ghetto.

After a while of walking we reached the Warsaw Residential District. Narrow and dark streets held houses with three floors and iron balconies. Residents were already living here, though not all had homes to shelter them, some were on the streets, begging, sleeping, crying and dying of what I could only assume was from the hunger and cold. I had seen the walls being built on my trips for food and when discussing it with Mother when I returned home she instructed that I stay away from the area. I didn't know what they were being built for until now. Everything looked different to where we had come from, there was no colour to the world here, everywhere the eyes met within the walls of the ghetto was dark and grey, soul wrenchingly depressing with very little hope for happiness.

"Is this where we are going to live Mama?" I asked, pulling the suitcase for the final remainder of the journey with an arm that felt as though it would fall off at any given time. It had been a day that had been long and draining, leaving our homes behind and what we had grown up to be around, for this new place that we were told we had to stay.

"Yes Jakub, this is our home for now. The Germans do not think that we should be mixed with other people who are not Jews, so we are to stay here for a while." She looked to the ground and attempted to wipe her eyes that were red and heavy.

We were seen as vermin, a disease that must be squashed from society before it was too late. *Too late for what?* I didn't understand, all I knew was that we were hated, frowned upon and laughed at for the very fact that we were Jews and it was not going to change anytime soon. Those holding the red flag with the Swastika boldly placed upon it controlled us now, while us, with the stars on our arms obeyed in the hope that we were given the luxury of staying alive. There had been a number of people in the march to the ghetto who had tried fighting back or running away and the act of disobedience cost them their life as the mighty bang of the gun stole their lives. It did not take much for people to learn from that. We were to do as we were told, speak only when spoken to and never, ever, disobey the German's. We hung our heads as we were marched into the ghetto, not from shame but from humiliation. We were proud of who we were, yet we were humiliated and degraded to the point we sometimes questioned it.

Everywhere we went we were guarded like criminals, contained and controlled like puppets on a string played with for entertainment with all human rights stripped away with no remorse. We were removed from society like a terrible smell that had already lingered for too long. The Warsaw Ghetto, our new *home,* our new way of life and this was just the beginning. Four hundred and sixty thousand Jewish people were crammed inside at the height of the ghetto, all of us forced to make life work as best we could in an area designed for much less living life. We soon realised it was not just Polish Jews forced into residency here, there were Jews from Germany too. It didn't take long for what felt like the ghetto to push back, showing revenge for too many people trying to find new homes in what was not enough space. Even with families squeezing into buildings with other families, handfuls of people sharing beds and living space it was just not enough room to keep every person out of the cold.

We were not the first to arrive here and we were not the last either. Many had come before us with great amounts of people fighting the cold winter on the cobbled streets with no food or belongings left to trade for a small piece of food that wouldn't come close to keeping them alive for more than just a few days. We walked through the streets, trying to understand our new surroundings, trying to find a building that would house us, which proved extremely difficult, nobody had room, every building, every room was already maxed out with people sleeping on floors or in corridors and stairwells, nine sometimes ten people to a room, just to escape the bite of cold outside. The sight when we arrived was truly heart wrenching, people with wailing cries walked amongst the street asking for pity and food, their feet swollen and bruised, Mother's cradled babies in rags in an attempt to shelter them from the cold. To my surprise some people were even singing, playing music, doing anything they could for money or food.

"Mama, what will we do if there is nowhere left?" I asked in anxious doubt and worry as I was unable to take my eyes from a small frail woman laying on the pavement, with no shoes and a thin flowered dress that offered no protection from the cold, her arms exposed and left vulnerable as they lay over her head. She made no movement and it sent shivers down my spine. I wondered if she was alive though I did not find the courage to find out, the overwhelming shock and realisation for what we had walked into was far more overpowering. People had been living on the streets for quite some time yet this was the worst I'd seen it. Every street, every corner had people begging or laying on the sidewalk, doing their best to keep warm with no energy as hunger took over their bodies.
"I don't know Jakub but we must all stick together, no matter what." She didn't hide the worry in her voice or face anymore. I think she was beyond trying to care about hiding it. What she cared about was protecting her family and keeping them safe. I felt a stab of guilt at the thought, I should be protecting her, doing just as Papa would have done if he was still here. I had tried for as long as I could to be brave and scavenge for food everyday, yet all my vulnerabilities came out that day as I clung to my Mother in desperate hope to feel her comfort.

Walking through the ghetto it became more evident the further we strayed inside that human life was struggling. More and more people spread across the street, some barely alive with others not at all. Children in rags and no shoes trying to forage or steal what little food there seemed to be with little to no luck, people of all ages motionless on the ground. The horrific images burned into my brain with minimal opportunity of ever leaving again. *How could they do this to us?* I watched as a small boy, no older than six hid behind a man and his son laying on the floor before grabbing the small piece of bread in the boy's hand and running away. Neither the man or his son had the energy to run after him or even shout. Warsaw was dying and so were thousands of people who lived within it. We walked through streets where I saw outdoor markets selling various items, basic food and clothing though the feeling in my gut told me there would be a hefty price to pay for them as everybody was struggling to survive.

Posters and notices scattered around the streets reminded us of the constant control, that we were caged and monitored, controlled and degraded. In bold letters I read the words,

"Jews who leave the quarter reserved for them without permission are liable to the death penalty. The same penalty awaits any person who knowingly gives shelter to such Jews."

It was likely the same notices were placed outside of the ghetto, to inform those who would have been willing to hide Jewish people away from the grips of the Germans. As we carried on walking a German soldier instructed that this was our quarter and to 'Go!' Aunt Lena broke from Mother's arm and rushed to a man hobbling into the apartment across the road. We stopped in awe, watching her as she spoke to him and suddenly grabbed his hand in what looked like a plea. They were too far away to hear what was said though Aunt Lena looked as though she was desperate. The man continued to shake his head and point to the top floor of the building while trying to escape her clutches before tilting his head back and chucking his hands in the air as though he had been defeated.

"Come on!" She shouted, waving us over while flinging her arms around the old man. We made our way over in as much of a hurry as Grandma would allow while stepping over motionless people laid at the steps of the building. We followed the man into the building and up the stairs to the top floor. Himself and Grandma had to stop a handful of times in order to catch their breath though just ten minutes later we were walking into an apartment crowded by unknown people.

"He says we can stay here." Says Aunt Lena as she pulled us inside the small cramped living area. Everywhere my eyes met were people, living their life in this new way under new rules and just trying to make it work.

I wondered whether everyone knew each other, or how long they had been here but i dared not speak, it was all so overwhelming. All eyes were on the huddled group of people that had just entered the apartment, silent and probably looking extremely pathetic and vulnerable.

"There's no more room!" Came the voice of a woman with light brown hair and very pale skin hovering over the kitchen sink with a plate in her hand. "We are already sharing three to a bed, three of the kids are basically sleeping with each other's feet in their mouth, there just isn't anymore room Antoni!" She added sharply. Antoni, the old man took a long desperate sigh and closed his eyes.

"Listen, we are all shoved in this god dahm place and I will not see an old neighbour of mine on the streets! Now we will make this work, do you hear me? I will not listen to another word about it."

The woman slammed down the plate she was holding and hurried into the next room to cater to the crying of a young child that had most likely been awoken from a nap by the commotion.

The atmosphere was tense as eyes from every direction stared at the new unknown people standing huddled together in the entranceway. We didn't know what to say, what to do, we had just turned up to their home and disrupted their lives even more, yet we were too desperate to not live outside in the cold to turn around and walk out of the door. Scanning the room I took note of all the people staring back at us. A man and a woman sat at a table with a mug of extremely weak tea, they didn't look angry or upset, more shocked and possibly worried that they would need to find room for four more people in an already overcrowding space. Stood in the doorway to the bedroom was a young girl who looked around my age, her brown curly hair touching just below her chest and the biggest blue eyes I had ever seen. The longer I stared at her the more I was convinced they would suck me in and hold me captive, just like the ghetto. Antoni moves towards the stove to make some tea and chuckles to himself.

"Don't get pulled in by my granddaughter, she's trouble that one." The girl sighed and walked out of the room. Something about her made me feel uncomfortable and nervous, though I couldn't place exactly what it was.

That night I was given a bed to share with Grandma while Mother and Aunt Lena shared a mattress given up resentfully by the man and woman who had been sitting at the table earlier that day. They had somehow squeezed into a double bed with their three children while Antoni and his wife shared a single bed in another room with their daughter who had been resentful earlier that day and their granddaughter sleeping on a single mattress on the floor of their room. It was cramped and overcrowded though we made what we had work. I overheard one of the three children speaking to their Mother and Father after two nights of the new arrangement.

"Mama it is too cramped, I don't like it." She was a small girl with light brown hair that always seemed to be in her eyes with the softest and most innocent voice I had ever heard. The woman picked up the small child as I looked on from the window I had been staring out of at the gloomy streets below.

"Listen, none of us like things this way but you have to remember, we all need somewhere to stay so that we are not outside in the cold. We just wouldn't survive Zofia and neither would any of these other people. We must all stick together until we are free again, do you understand?" She plants a kiss on the little girl's cheek and puts her down where she runs into the other room to play with the small selection of toys that had been brought into the ghetto. The resentful woman walked in the room just as she had finished talking.

"That goes for you too Inga." Said the woman who walked over to her husband and planted a kiss on his cheek before walking out of the room. The woman looked at me to see I was still staring back and smiled before beginning to cut bread into rations that was left by the other woman. I didn't feel uncomfortable around her after that, I felt as though she had come to terms with the fact we were all just doing what we needed to do to survive. After all, there were people dying on the streets below us every single day, if anything, we should have felt lucky we had somewhere with a roof, though it was hard to see the way we were living as lucky.

"Mia is right you know Inga." Says Antoni as he slumps in the chair by the window. "She has three children she is trying to keep safe, you have your Amelia, who we are all trying desperately hard to protect against this awful world we are living in right now. This family who has joined us, they are just trying to survive too."

"I know Papa, I know." She looked at me vaguely and smiled before handing me a small portion of bread as a peace offering. I politely accept her silent apology, as well as the bread that I let sit in my mouth for as long as possible.

Food was starting to become a distant memory back at Aunt Lena's and now we were here in the ghetto we knew it would only get worse. For many months before leaving for the ghetto I had been unable to gather much food. I begged and stole what I could to survive though it did not stop the twisting pains of hunger when I got into bed at night. We had been surviving on one watered down meal a day and although it had seen us this far, I worried it was yet to take another steep decline. Mother would come to tell me a story like she used to when I was small and I would let her as it took my mind from being so hungry. I would feel guilty when the rise of bitterness grew inside me towards the German's for starving us like they were, when there were people on the street failing at being able to stay alive. I knew we had been lucky, been more fortunate than thousands of other people though it did not stop the wrenching pain in my stomach when it cried for food that was just not available.

Mother very rarely let me out of the apartment in worry that the German's would find reason to beat me with their sticks or make me work. I had been lucky so far and I think that was maybe because of my age. When I turned fourteen Mother told me that we should expect a notice for me to go to work. I think what she feared most was that I did not return and after losing Grandpa and Papa, she just could not lose me too like Aunt Lena had lost Kacper. I was able to go for a walk twice a day for no more than half an hour at a time and I was to stay away from the German's.

"If you see them, you hide and come back here to me, do you hear me?" She would repeat to me everytime I walked out of the apartment. I'd nod and agree. It took her several days for her to finally give in and let me outside through constant pleading and begging to just get out of the apartment for a while. I was still only thirteen and being around people a lot older and the children a lot younger made me extremely agitated a lot of the time. Antoni's granddaughter Amelia was thirteen too, though we didn't speak very much. She was always helping others in the apartment with chores that needed doing or brushing the hair of her two dolls she had brought with her to the ghetto. So, I needed to make entertainment for myself, find freedom in a city with walls built ten foot high topped with barbed wire. We may have been like prisoners in this part of the city, yet I did not want to feel trapped inside the apartment too.

We had been in the ghetto a week before frustrations started to show. Food rations were barely going round enough to feed us all and the uncomfortable sleeping arrangements meant someone's back hurt, or others were always tired. The adults were stressed about how the children would be fed and the children were always agitated at having nothing to do. I played with them sometimes, in an attempt to relieve the stress of those in the apartment but it didn't always last very long. I'd make up games that could entertain three children under six years old that would give the adults time to do what they called *'important errands'*. Usually it was to go out to work, look for food, keep the apartment clean or to just take a nap.

My vast imagination and longing for adventure meant most of the time I would sit them in a circle and make up thrilling stories of dragons and castles with princesses to rescue. They would bounce on their knees and make noises to the story in excitement, all trying to have their input into what would happen next. I enjoyed telling the children stories and seeing their faces light up when they were excited. Happiness was hard to come by in the ghetto as living conditions became more and more difficult, so I felt that at least I could make a small difference with the adventures in my stories. Sometimes however they would get bored easily, fight over who wanted what ending and lose interest and this just brought realisation that I could not make them happy all of the time.

Leaving the apartment for the short amount of time I did meant I could leave the frustrations and responsibility behind and just be myself to find fun in such a dark and depressing place. I'd wander the streets and find new and exciting places I could add into my stories for the children. I'd meet new friends sometimes, others who were out looking for food or had no home to go to, though the friendships never lasted long, they would disappear and I would never see them again and I knew in my gut that the hunger or cold had taken them too. It made me sad that I couldn't save them, or bring back more food for everyone living at the apartment though it soon grew to be the way life was. I'd ventured out one day exploring the streets behind our apartment and I must have strayed far as I came across a sight that stopped me in my tracks. The wall. I looked up to see the towering wall looming over me, trapping me within it as the barbed wire and broken glass scattered above it, reminding us that we were animals in this cage. As I stood looking up wondering what was happening on the world outside I felt so small, so insignificant. Surely basic human rights should stand for something, who were they to tell us we must be confined here? As I dwelled on the thought of being on the other side I heard a familiar voice.

"Jakub? Is that you?" Came the voice of a man emerging from the archway of a building that looked long since abandoned. At first I couldn't make out who it was, a skinny and frail man whose cheekbones were on full display, a thin and battered blanket around his shoulders and no shoes on his feet. He must have traded his shoes for food that did not appear to have done much benefit. "Henryk, you remember me don't you?" He asked, shuffling his way over to the wall. I had not seen Henryk for almost a year, he had slipped from my memories until that very moment when he unexpectedly emerged into eyesight. So many people had been dying that I never expected to see him again, it was the common way when meeting people in this war, not many survived and if they did it was luck and nothing else.

I didn't move from the spot between the two tramlines that had been cut off by the ten foot wall that had been built over them, disconnecting life from inside to the outside. I was so surprised I couldn't find words, which appeared apparent as he moved closer and stood next to me, looking out at the wall as I had been. "I wonder what is going on out there sometimes too," He says as he aggressively coughs into his blanket, "yet sometimes I think why bother, the world is a mess right now, wall or no wall, it is all the same."

"How long do you think we will be here for before we are rescued?" I examine the wall and wonder how human beings could be so monstrous as to contain us like they did.

"I've heard word that the allies are attempting to push the German's back though I do not know how successful they are. The Soviets, that's the Russians, are occupying the Easten sector of Poland, while Germany occupy the West, that is where we are." He sighs deeply as he kicks a stone that tumbles along the road and hits the wall.

"Are they coming to save us?" I asked, turning to look at him again and realising from so close just how skinny he had become. His cheekbones stuck out of his face that looked as though they would pierce his skin, his tall and bony frame gave the impression he would fall over at a gust of wind.

"I don't think they aim to save us, I think they aim to stop Hitler and that's my honest opinion but who knows? France has fallen, yet there is still England and the USSR. All I hear is rumours but if I am being completely honest with you I stopped caring a long time ago. I will not be here when this war is over, my body is just not strong enough, I feel it in my bones. Every time the sun rises I know my time here is limited. There is not much I am leaving behind, my daughter and my Esther were shot the day I first met you. This nasty scar here, it is all I have left of that day. I begged them to shoot me too and not leave me in this world without them. They laughed at the very fact my heart had broken into a thousand tiny pieces right before their eyes and they wanted me to deal with that every single day."

"I'm so sorry Henryk." I did not know what else I could say. As he told me his story I felt my heart break into tiny pieces too just listening to him.

As he started coughing he bent to his knees and sat on the road, looking out at the wall as if it was not there at all. He was a man broken by the war and he had no escape from the empty emotion he carried around with him every single day since that horrific moment his family was shot before his eyes.

"I'm sorry too young boy, we have all had our lives taken from us in this war." He says, coughing again though this time it was stubborn to subside.

"How have you survived all this time on your own?" I asked, looking again at his dirty and bruised feet that were turning blue with the cold.

"I do the same as everybody else, dignity is no longer an option when you are a Jew living in today's world. The Torah states that we must not steal or tell lies, though what choice do we have to survive? Sometimes I go to the soup kitchens but there is not always food left" He catches my eyes running over his tiny frame. "I have a mission here, when the mission is complete, that is when I close the curtains on this dreadful world and I open them again to see my girls."

"Mission?" He had spiked my curiosity. Not many Jews had missions anymore other than to survive. He laughed at my sudden interest and fell into spluttering coughs that sounded painful to the ear. After several moments he continued. "You see, I have been getting food, not much, not by a very long stretch but enough to see me through each day that I open my eyes on the next." He was whispering now and eyeing up the empty street for listening ears. The street was deserted other than people motionless on the ground that had not yet been taken by the carts. A policeman patrolled the street to our left who had eyed us up numerous times from a distance but he was probably not in the mood to cause a scene as he saw us sitting there. We had to be cautious but for that moment in time we were fairly safe. The wall was patrolled by Rural Police, Polish police and Jewish Police that all worked for the German's in hope they could save their families.

"How?" I asked, expecting him to recall accounts of him stealing or begging for food.

"We're friends, you and me, yes?" He says, raising his eyebrows in seriousness. I nod and hold out my hand to shake his. He smiled as he returned the gesture. There were not many people that could be trusted in the ghetto, most people would lie and manipulate to get the food they desperately needed for themselves or their children. Others would turn you in to the hands of the guarded police that walked around the inside of the ghetto wall or to the German's themselves in hope they would receive food as a reward. Some people shared, helped others where they could, collected on behalf of communities in need, though not all could be trusted when it came down to it. The challenge was working out who could be confided in to work together in order to survive, many learnt the hard way.

Henryk moved in closer so he could whisper in my ear without looking suspicious.

"Do you see that patch in the wall there." He whispered pointing with a boney finger while shielding it from potential eyes. My eyes moved to the wall to try to distinguish a patch however I couldn't see one no matter how hard I looked at the wall. "You don't see it do you?" He chuckled as he put his hands back to the somewhat warmth of inside his holey blanket. "Neither do the German's, or the police." He whispered even more quietly followed by another laugh and an outburst of painful coughs as a consequence.

"I'm not really sure what you mean." I say confused, wondering if the lack of food was causing him to hallucinate.

"Without drawing attention, look at the bottom of the wall to the right of where we are sitting. There is a hole that has been dug for use in the night and is covered for the day. There are a number of bricks that are loose, they are only placed there during the day and the German's have no idea!" The thought alarms me unexpectedly. Anybody caught trying to escape would be shot instantly, it had been seen so many times, *how could he be so daring at the risk of life?*

"That hole was made by a small boy, younger than yourself. I watched him for weeks come out here in the night and dig away small fractions at a time, loosening bricks until a hole just big enough for him to sneak out and back in again was made to smuggle in food." My mouth fell open at the thought, the risk was so great if caught, yet people were willing to do anything to squash the taunting pain of hunger. I imagined a small boy crawling through the wall and being caught on the other side by the Nazi and Polish officers that patrolled the wall from the outside. The thought made my skin crawl and shake at the fear of it.

"If he could escape, why did he come back inside here?" I asked, confused.

"It was impossible for his family to get through and he didn't want to leave them, so he would go to the other side and bring back what he could. I became part of a mission after he was shot and killed for talking back to an officer. He was a great kid but never knew when to keep his mouth shut around the wrong people."

"What was your mission?" I asked, turning to face him and no longer having my gaze fixed upon the wall that trapped us inside. The thought of such a small boy taking that risk meant he was desperate and I could not comprehend the thought of just how much to make him do it.

"My mission is to wait at that section of the wall at exactly one clock every Sunday morning. Everyone is asleep at that time except the officers who wish they were. At exactly twelve forty five they begin to patrol in the opposite directions. That is when I wait at the hole and I am handed food by somebody on the other side." Shock flowed through my body like a wave of fire. I could not come to grips with the thought. While I had been sleeping through the night Henryk had been here, at this exact spot risking his life.

We caught sight of an officer making his way over and we stood to make our exit.

"Listen kid, meet me back here at twelve fiftyfive. I have a proposition for you that will ensure you and your family do not go hungry again through this war." Before I had an opportunity to refuse or ponder over the idea he had gone, slipped into the night like a clever shadow made of only bones.

*

The air of Warsaw felt different during the night. All was not silent as I had expected it to be, there were still shots of gunfire in the distance from what I had assumed were people trying to flee and escape in the night. I had over-thought the idea so much in my head that in the end I told myself I'd never know unless I went. Henryk had said to meet him at the wall at twelve fifty five, just before he was to receive food from the other side. I had paced all night questioning whether I should go, until I saw Grandma's fragile body trying to get out of the chair and being unable to lift herself without the aid of Mother and Aunt Lena. The thoughts raced around my head like a cat that had caught sight of a mouse and would not stop until it was between its teeth. In the end the thought of my family having some form of food that could help them survive an extra day saw me with my shoes on and the only jumper I had left I had not traded for food.

At twelve thirty I slipped out of the apartment when everyone had fallen asleep. I'd spent the hours leading up to leaving in generous amounts of adrenaline and anxiety. The questions kept pushing themselves to the forefront of my mind with me being unable to control or stop them. *What if they weren't asleep by the time I needed to go? What if the police officers catch me? What would happen then? Would I make it to tomorrow alive? Was I crazy for even entertaining this crazy idea?* They didn't stop me sliding out into the brisk night air that bit and clawed at my skin, sinking its teeth in with a stubbornness for releasing.

Police officers patrolled as they did in the day except some looked as though they just wanted to go to sleep, not on full attention, this could work in my advantage. I slipped between buildings in a bid to stay out of sight. People lay across the ghetto motionless, sleeping? Or had they been taken with the night? I arrived at the wall with a minute to spare though Henryk was nowhere in sight. *Had he thrown me to the wolves?* I hid behind a lamp post with my eyes squinting in the dark, trying to make out any kind of moving life through the thick heavy blackness that fell on the ghetto during the night.
"Psst, hey kid!" Came a voice from behind me, whispering so as not to be heard by any other ears but my own. I turned sharply to see Henryk's thin and fragile body squatting in the archway of a building. I crouch down and make my way over as silently as possible.
"Quickly, get down." He says pulling me into further darkness with him. I scan my surroundings and realise why he had been whispering. A policeman was walking in our direction, if we did not move he would surely see us and we would be shot right there at the ghetto wall. I had heard rumours that smugglers between Jews and the Aryian side had been caught on many occasions, those rumours also told me that they were lined up

at the central lock-up on Gesiowka Street and shot. I nudged away the thought quickly.

I sunk into the dark as far as I possibly could and squeezed my eyes closed. My heart was pumping so ferociously it was near on impossible that the policeman did not hear it. As he walked up and down the wall he stopped just three yards from where we were huddled together, covering our mouths so he could not hear us breathing. *I should have stayed at home.* If the blanket of darkness was not covering the street we would have been seen already, made to stand facing the wall with our hands up and shot with their heavy machine guns. The officer stood so close I could almost make out his face, thin and tight with short dark hair. They were willing to send any of us to the German's in hope for a reward of something that would line their stomachs.

We crouched holding our breath for what felt like hours before he turned on his foot and disappeared out of sight in the direction of the opposite end of the wall.
"Now, come on, we do not have much time." Henryk scurries out of the archway and straight towards the wall. He used his hands to pull out the pre dug hole and as quietly as he could and peered through the hole.
"We wait for the candles." He said, peering through the hole. I bent down and caught a glimpse of the outside world, not much could be seen with the heavy darkness though I did see a faint

flicker of a light that lasted only seconds, not too far away from the wall on the other side.

I stood behind Henryk watching him, trying to get my breathing under control and keeping my eyes fixed on the darkness, we could be spotted so easily out in the open, punished for trying to reach the other side in ways I had heard about, terrifying and brutal punishments that only made people wish they had been shot instead. The air bit at my skin like razors being dragged across every exposed ounce of flesh, I questioned how people survived as long as they did living out in the naked air with no opportunity of warmth.

"Okay Jakub, I need you to reach under the wall for the parcel." He said, pushing me close to the wall with little choice in the matter. My breathing intensifies, falling into frantic and unbalanced rhythm.

"Why don't you do it?" I asked, pushing my hands through the gap while keeping my eyes locked on the street, the policeman could come back at any second and then we would be done for. I scurried my hands inside the gap of the wall hoping to retrieve it and get home as quickly as possible.

"I am too weak to pull the package through Jakub, I just do not have the strength, people are relying on this food, we must get it for them." He sounded sincere, genuine, yet it did not stop the rush of terror at the thought of being caught. This was a serious crime, one that would not go unpunished yet what was the alternative? People would go hungry, more so than they already were and that guilt fell upon me like a sack of stones.

I reached around inside the gap until I felt a hand on mine that stopped me in my tracks. It was the boy on the other side, placing the parcel between my hands and pushing me back inside the ghetto. Henryk was right, the parcel would have been too heavy for him to pull through, his body had become that of glass, ready to shatter and break from cold and poor nutrition. He needed this food, everybody did.
"Pull Jakub, pull it through, that's it." Henryk hurries me as I struggle to pull it through the hole. Suddenly I hear a gasp through the wall, one of terror, fright and sudden panic.
"Jakub, they are coming, pull, now!" Henryk panics as he frantically looks about him, waiting for the moment we will be seen by the wrong eyes. One big pull and the package is through. Before I can see what is happening Henryk pushes a parcel through the gap onto the other side and places the bricks back into place as quickly as his hands would let him while I run into the archway, pushed back against the wall clutching the parcel of food in my hands. Henryk rushes after me, just in time to sink against the wall, his hands over our mouths to stop the sound of heavy breathing. The same police officer was back, patrolling the wall with his eyes moving around the darkness. He peers into the dark in our very direction, my heart stopped as I was sure he had clocked eyes

on us. I questioned whether the boy on the other side of the wall had made it to safety in time.

We waited in that archway for fifteen minutes before the officer headed away again. I breathed out hard, caught my breath and wasted no time.

"Here," Said Henryk, taking the parcel from my hands and opening it, revealing four loaves of bread, a jar of jam and what had made the parcel so heavy, eight potatoes of different sizes. My stomach screamed in excitement at the sight of so much food. "Take this. The rest will go to the orphanage, after I have eaten myself of course." He rummaged quickly through the food and handed me half a loaf of bread and two potatoes. "Same time next week if you want more kid. Believe me, it's scary but it keeps people alive. Those at the orphanage rely on this now, I can't let them down. Now go, go feed your family." He slipped into the darkness and was gone quicker than my eyes could adjust to the dark. I ran home faster than my legs were willing to carry me, through the darkness, through the spotlights and past the guards and their dogs. I did not stop until I reached the apartment, ran up the stairs and slid into bed as quietly as possible so as not to wake the sleeping people crowded in the apartment.

*

"Jakub where did you get this?" Mother asked me the next day, running her fingers over the food in shock. Everyone in the apartment sat around us, eager to sink their teeth into solid food that would ease the sting of hunger that had constantly reminded us for over a week now that we needed to eat. Food had become something of a miracle since entering the ghetto, we rationed enough so that each person could eat once a day, to which they could each decide when they would eat their share. Ration cards entitled us to 180g of bread a day, 220g of sugar a month, 1kg of jam and 1/2 kg of honey. It was not enough to sustain human life and we all knew that the German's were doing this as a purposeful act to eliminate us from the earth, we had heard too many announcements from Hitler to think anything else.

The package now placed on the table with me and Mother sitting around it came as a welcoming surprise that buzzed excitement through every person that morning looking over our shoulders at the extraordinary gift I had presented to them.
"It doesn't matter Mama, all that matters is that we can eat." I told her, finally starting to feel that I was doing my part in helping to keep our new extended family alive. I watched her, as did the many other eyes in the room as she delicately divided the food into portions for everyone, a quarter slice of bread with a small amount of jam on each. I took a bite from my own and felt the taste exhilarate my taste buds like a party had begun in my mouth at the very touch of solid food. I looked

around the room, everyone was smiling, silent, content as they let the food hold in their mouths so as not to let the moment pass too quickly.

*

7 years earlier May 1933

The sound of Mother's radio fills our home with the tasteful aroma of fresh bread baking in the oven, the smell so overpowering we could almost taste it. I was six years old, running between the rooms of the house with my toy airplane with no care in the world while the sound of people singing and pianos playing flooded the room. Papa walks through the front door after his shift at the factory and catches sight of me as he lifts me above his head and places me on his shoulders, my airplane left abandoned on the floor.
"How is my boy?" He asks, circling around the room in the motion of a plane while making the noises that felt almost real. Mother comes into the room and smiles, places a kiss on Papa's cheek as Papa pulls her in so we are all sharing the embrace of a family hug. He looks at Mother and smiles.
"How was work today?" She asks, keeping her arms wrapped around Papa's waist with me dangling from his shoulders making airplane noises.
"The usual but do you know what, it doesn't even matter once I walk through that door. Seeing you both smile is the greatest

gift to my day. Memories of work can soon be forgotten but the smile on your face is beyond priceless and forgettable." He plants a kiss on Mother's head as he zooms around the table with me laughing uncontrollably from his shoulders.

*

October 6th 1940

I look around the room of people as the memory wraps a comforting arm around me, locking me in its embrace, just as Papa had once done. I look at the people struggling at basic life due to conditions out of our control, yet able to deliver a smile at something that should have been within our human rights yet deprived from us to make us suffer. I watch their eyes close as the food enters their mouth, watch the smiles and tears in their eyes as they become so happy even if for a short amount of time. *'Memories of work can soon be forgotten but the smile on your face is beyond priceless and forgettable."* I let Papa's words fill my mind as I watch them. He was right, a smile is beyond forgettable, though unfortunately the world had caused it to be anything but priceless and that is why I knew I had to keep going back to the wall. If the people in this apartment were so overwhelmed by food I wondered about the children at the orphanage, all with something to live for. I had found my mission and I would go back to the wall as many times as I possibly could to keep warsaw alive. I may not have been able to save everybody, I was not naive enough to think I could, though I would do my part in raising Warsaw above its knees once more. We were not animals to be caged, we were not vermin, we were human life and I would do everything I could to even bring a smile to those that felt they had nothing left to smile for and the best way to do that was to fill their stomachs and give them words of hope, even if that meant risking my life to do it.

The apartment held an improved atmosphere that day. We laughed and we sang, we told stories of our lives before the war and we felt happy, despite the world that was crumbling around us. I told myself that day that I would do exactly what was necessary to keep their spirits up. I was standing in my Papa's shoes, living on through his memory and doing what needed to be done to keep us together. I may have only been the small Jew from Warsaw but I was a brand new version, ready to make a change. The German's may have taken our homes, our families, our food but I would ensure they never took the smiles that were so unforgettable.

I returned to the wall every Sunday on time. Henryk was always waiting for me, guiding me with instruction and being the eyes of the street. He would take the parcel after handing me a share and make his way to the orphanage with the remaining.
"Can I come with you, to the orphanage?" I whispered one night while waiting for the candle on the other side.

"It's not a good idea Jakub, these children are in desperate need of this food, I have to make sure it reaches them. One day you will take over from me and it will be your job then to see that it reaches them. It is an awful sight there Jakub, children crying in pain from being hungry, their cries will scar you."

"Why do you take food there?" I asked, intrigued.

"To feed the children." He says as if I should have already known the answer.

"No, I mean why do you take it there rather than eat it all yourself? Most others would do that, why not you?"

"I take my piece, pride will not see anybody through the war. My days left on this earth are numbered, those at the orphanage are struggling, those children's days don't have to be numbered too. My girls are waiting for me when I go, I do not have anything left here but I won't throw in the towel and surrender until I have helped those who need it as much as my body will let me." He looked to the sky as he said it, knowing that his wife and daughter were there, waiting for him to embrace them, just like Mother and Papa had done with me so many times. I held the utmost amount of respect for him after that. He was the unseen hero of Warsaw that sought no credit or gratitude, he was just a broken man, waiting for the day he could reunite with his family.

The candle light made its signal and I reached my hand inside. The parcel felt smaller than the previous and I worried for the disappointment from so many people, from my family, those at the orphanage and Henryk. I pulled the parcel through and Henryk pushed one onto the other side, just as he had done before.

"What do you give to the other side?" I whispered, intrigued, "Is it a trade?"

Henryk pushes the bricks back into place and we rush to our hideout in the archway. He rummages around the bag as he always did and handed me a smaller portion of food to the previous times. Food was becoming difficult on the other side too and we had to make do with what we received, sometimes we had good weeks and others we barely left with more than two slices of bread each, the rest would go to the children.

"Meet me tomorrow evening at four on Chlodna Street. I will show you." With that, he disappeared yet again into the night.

*

The next day I was sure to meet Henryk on Chlodna Street at exactly four o' clock. It didn't take long for Henryk to hobble around the corner and point to the building I had unknowingly been standing in front of.

"You wanted to come with me to the orphanage, here it is." He says walking up the path towards the building. "Janusz Korczak runs this orphanage, he is a wonderful man that looks after his children here after they were forced to relocate from Krochmalna Street. His aim is to offer his children the most comfortable existence as possible with being orphans with no parents, yet the circumstances of the ghetto is pushing down hard on those that live here. This is why I help." He nods in the direction of the building for me to follow him. We walk towards the front door in which he opens it and lets himself in. The door opened up to a great hall with rooms upon rooms trailing off from it. Within the great hall were rows and rows of seats and tables that I assumed were for meal times and education if they happened to do that in secret like me and Mother did at the apartment. Anybody discovered to be teaching, learning or housing such activities would be up against the death penalty, so we would move around and do it in different places, though I wondered whether they were able to do that at the orphanage.

"Janusz!" Shouted Henryk which sent echoes bouncing from the walls and through the rooms upstairs. No longer than a minute passed when a man with no hair and thin rimmed glasses emerged from one of the rooms and greeted us with a friendly smile. He made his way down the stairs and shook Henryk's hand.

"This is Jakub, my friend who has been helping me with supplies the last few weeks. He is a very trusted friend and he has asked me about the packages I send to the other side. Would you mind if he met the children, so he can see who the food has been going to?"

"Of course, though I must warn you Henryk that one of the boys has fallen very ill and I don't think he will make it through the night. Maybe your presence will lift his spirits." He leads us to one of the bedrooms and stands in the doorway as Henryk walks through. I keep my distance and hang back to not intimidate the boy with a new face when fallen so ill.

Henryk walks up to the little boy curled up in bed with a blanket half on and half off his body. Some of the other children were playing around his bed and stopped at the sight of all the company.
"How are you my good friend?" Asked Henryk, holding out a piece of bread and sitting on the edge of the bed at the boys feet. The boy doesn't respond though he makes a moaning noise I assume is of pain or discomfort. He doesn't take the bread so Henryk breaks it into three and gives it to the children sat stationary amongst their toys on the floor, who scramble to take it and gulf it down in one with very little chance for air. I peer around and look at the boy laying in the bed, feeling my heart pull at every emotion until I realise that I have seen him before.
"Izaak?" I shout, moving around and standing next to his bed. "What happened? Where is your Mama?" The boy moves his head slightly and catches sight of me as he tries to string a sentence together.
"The c..c..cold, it took her," He stammers, as Henryk brings the blanket over his shoulders to stop him shivering, "but I found my s..s..sister, Rivka". A small girl with a blanket around her shoulders looked up to me from the floor with a smile. He had finally found her.

"It is so cold in here," Janusz says rubbing at his arms, "I try to keep them warm but it is getting colder every single day, the food you bring keeps them alive but I fear for how long." He runs his hand over his head and sighs deeply in exasperation. I had not realised how many children were housed at the orphanage that Henryk had been taking food to, though seeing the size of the building and how many children were there during my visit worried me. *How would all these children be kept alive in such conditions?*

Seeing Izaak curled up in the bed looking even more vulnerable than he had been when I saw him on the streets sent tears prickling in my eyes.

"How can I help?" I asked, wiping away a tear and attempting to look strong willed and ready for anything they threw at me in regards to saving the children.

"We're grateful for your help young boy though I expect you have your own family that are struggling too." Says Janusz with a soft smile.

"I want to help more, what can I do?" Both men look at each other and Henryk nods in silent agreement.

"Come with me." Says Henryk walking out of the room and leading us down the stairs and into the basement. Confused, I wait for further answers, silently questioning why he had brought me to the basement of the orphanage. He walks over to a wardrobe-like cupboard pressed against the wall and with strenuous effort pushes it away in very little time, revealing a passageway into a room lined with wooden shelves. I stare in amazement. Lining every shelf were items of different uses, brushes, gloves and footwear, sweaters and socks.

"What is all this for?" I ask, "Surely this can be used to keep people warm." I run my fingers over a pair of gloves and feel the leather between my fingers.

"I work in the Embroidery Department on Nowolipie 44 Street, ten sometimes twelve hours a day, that is why you very rarely see me during the day and only at night. We make all kinds of products for the German's to support the war effort, it is the only way we stay alive. When I arrived here at the ghetto all Jewish men were required to report to the German occupation authorities for work. I had no clue how to be an embroider or make such things, I worried I would be chosen in the selection as no use for work, so my friend Adam Halteritz who joined the Jewish police force told me to sign up for the embroidery factory and that one of the other men would guide me."

"So why are all of these things here?" I asked, scratching my head and wondering how it all pieced together.

"We work hard in the factory, not for the German's but for ourselves," He picks up one of the leather brushes sitting in a pile and runs his fingers over the material, "You see the things we make, we can trade." He looks at me now, waiting for the moment I understand.

"You pass them through the wall?"

"Indeed my boy, with nothing to trade, there would be no food, no food means the children perish with hunger, though this is just the small scale of things, it is temporary."

"There is more?"

"This is just the beginning of a much more dangerous but rewarding mission," He says, placing the brush back on the shelf and moving towards a wooden crate on the floor. "These crates are filled in the factory with products, the products are loaded onto the back of a truck and out of the ghetto which is managed by my friend Mr Halteritz. I have received blessings from Janusz to send more than just products in these crates." Suddenly the realisation hits me and shock takes over.

"You want to try to smuggle out children?" I ask, mortified and scared for the consequences if caught.

"You said you wanted to help, I need you to start doing the wall alone, so that I can be at the factory."

"Putting children into boxes?" I sensed the tension in my voice as soon as I said it, this was crazy, there was no way it could ever be pulled off.

"I can't be in two places at once, the children need food but we can not get enough, more and more children are losing their parents on the streets and finding their way into the orphanage, without food we cannot save them, if we do not get them out, they will perish here regardless. We have to save them, Jakub."

Smuggling food and items through a wall was one thing but smuggling a real life person out of the ghetto was another. It would be right under the Police and German's noses and if caught we would be punished in ways I dared not think about. Then I remembered my friend curled up in bed on the floor above, desperately fighting to stay alive.

"When do we start?"

Henryk looks at me with worrisome concern, "Tonight."

*

That night I made my way to the wall and undertook the usual procedure that Henryk had shown me. Mother had stopped asking me where I was going when she caught me sneaking out the apartment at midnight and me refusing to disclose any information regarding my whereabouts or how I brought the food back. I think she must have known we didn't really have a choice, yet she would wait up for me all the same in worry. I waited in the archway for the policeman to patrol in the opposite direction and made my move.

The bricks were harder to remove than I had expected; Henryk had made it look so easy, though I suppose that came with experience in the matter of smuggling at this particular part of the wall. Removing the bricks I waited for the candle to give my signal. It didn't come straight away so I knelt close to the wall and attempted to stay out of sight of dangerous eyes. I thought about Henryk and the children. *Had they been successful? What if they had been caught? Was a child being placed into a crate right now?* I forced the thought out of my mind, I needed to concentrate. The flash of the candle indicates my move, I pull the parcel out of my heavy coat that Henryk had supplied me with to pass through the wall when I hear footsteps.

"Someone's coming." I whisper through the wall.

"It's okay, it is Adam, he is making sure the other officers are out of sight." I had never heard him talk before and he sounded so young. "Henryk spoke to him today and informed him of the plan, he will be moving the crate from your side to this side on a delivery truck. I will be meeting him and taking the child to the convent where they will change their identity and papers." So much thought had gone into the process I wondered how long they had been planning to smuggle out children.

"Why do you help?" I whispered, most other Poles would have given us up to the German's at the first sight of disobedience. There were some Polish residents on the Aryan side that were sad to see us being locked away in this part of the city yet I found it hard to imagine that many would risk their lives to help us.

"I am also a Jew, Papa had my papers falsified so that I would not be sent in there too. We have many friends and family there and we want to help." He whispered so gently and softly I found it hard to make out his words without listening with great intent. He pushes the food parcel through the gap and I pull it through, pushing my own parcel through to the other side.

"I must go now but please, be careful." With that the little boy runs away and out of sight leaving me knelt at the wall alone and vulnerable to the stab of cold air and police that would soon be back to catch me if I did not hurry.

Pushing the bricks back into place I turn to run back for the apartment when I run face first into the police officer standing above me. I clutch the parcel with both hands and question whether to run, my heart pounding through my chest and my hairs stood on end wanting to flee themselves. Adrenaline courses through my veins like a river of larva, burning away at my senses and leaving me light headed. The police officer pulled the parcel from my hand with no force and I did not resist, there was nowhere for me to go, nowhere I could run or hide. I felt responsible for the children at the orphanage not eating for the next few days and it took over my body, left me numb and broken. I wanted to cry right there in front of the officer yet fear stood in the way. Slowly he lifted his finger to his lips and pointed to his arm, showing the star of David on his police uniform. *Adam!* He hands me my share of the food and smiles as he slips into the night in the direction of the orphanage. Everything had been changed in such a short amount of time I had been left almost clueless to what was happening.

Life continued for the next eight months in this way with one child a week was able to make it out of the ghetto, I was able to retrieve the package from the other side of the wall and I had grown to be good friends with the boy who delivered him, the boy I had never seen. Sometimes when we had time we would talk a lot about life in and out of the ghetto, share short stories and on some occasions we would laugh while trying to be as quiet as possible. It had become the new way of life and the feeling of having one over on the German's appeared to feel good too. There was always the fear of being caught. We could not afford to risk being anything but cautious because we were successful so far, we knew we couldn't do it forever though the more lives saved meant more children had a chance to grow into adults, experience life after the war and not be taken by hunger or cold.

Henryk worked overtime in the factory to ensure that more products could be made to move onto phase two of the plan. We had been saving children, that was not questionable, yet there were still those taken in the night by fever and hunger when the parcels were not as heavy. The next phase was to get more crates out of Warsaw ghetto on a more regular basis. I was coming up to my fourteenth birthday and after speaking with Henryk on the rare occasion I saw him, we had agreed that I should put myself forward to work in the embroidery department so I could still contribute to 'the mission'. Mother had been required to work as well as Aunt Lena and the other women in the apartment so it had been fairly quiet during the days. I would look after the children with Antoni and his wife while everybody worked in different factories or rebuilding roads. Mother had been sent to work in the bakery during the day and Aunt Lena doing clothing repairs for the German's. All work was for German benefit with little to no food, strenuous hours under conditions that were taking the lives of thousands in the ghetto. I worried for my family and those in the apartment, meaning it was without a doubt the food parcels were needed to survive.

On rare occasions Mother would be able to pocket bread or on even rarer occasions a piece of cake that she saved for just me, her and Grandma on a nighttime. It was not always possible for her to bring food back, most of the time it was impossible as she would be searched on her way home by SS guards or the Gestapo. Life at home was becoming ever more worrisome when we were searched and raided at the apartment as part of random checks for contraband. We would have no notice other than the bang from downstairs with a sweeping brush on the ceiling which would only give us a few short minutes to pack away learning material or hide food we should not have. We were lucky enough to not get discovered with any contraband though less could be said for others in the building. We would watch in horror as those caught would be dragged violently out of the building and into the square. Some were shot, some were hung and others were beaten until they laid unconscious on the ground in pools of their own blood.

The ghetto was becoming a home that was ever more unlivable as time went on. It had been eight months of smuggling when it was decided to start sending two children at a time in the crates. As conditions became more difficult we had to work harder to save as many as possible. It was a task that did not come easy. More people were dying than we were saving and at times I had to be reminded that one life was still worth saving even if five others were lost. A life was a life and it made each trip to the wall worth the risk. Izaak had come round from the fever which had surprised us all however like most people in the ghetto, he was merely skin clutching tight at bone. The very last time I went to the wall was when I had arrived at exactly twelve fifty five, removed the bricks and waited for the candle. I waited until Adam arrived as he usually did though this time with news that made me want to scream and cry and run up to any German I could find and throw whatever punches I could at them.

"Jakub, Toma has been found with false Aryan papers, we do not know what they have done with him, we cannot trace him." A stab of guilt punctured through me like a bullet in slow motion. We had become friends and I had grown to rely on his company to keep me sane. Now it was too late, another child fallen victim to the hands of the Nazi's, no more food parcels for the orphanage, no more food to take back to the apartment.

I cried hard that night as I laid in bed without one of the thin blankets wrapped around me. Most rooms within the apartment were riddled in damp and cold, so blankets and bedsheets had to be dried during the day and collected before crawling into bed with no energy. I never bothered that night, I had lost care for trying anymore, there was nothing more I could do until I went to work in the factory and even then, it would not bring Toma back. The feeling of guilt never left me, that I was responsible for him being taken away. There was no way of knowing what had happened to him but we knew that at the hands of the German's there were very few who lived to tell the tale.

When my fourteenth birthday came around we received the notice as expected for me to begin work for the war effort. I was surprisingly lucky that I was accepted into the Embroidery Department where I worked alongside Henryk who showed me how to make shoes, brushes, gloves, sweaters and most things made of leather. I picked it up fairly quickly and assisted in the mission to smuggle out more children at a rate we had never done before. We had begun sending three children per crate, some as little as two years old when they had been sent to the orphanage with parents that had died on the streets of the ghetto. Due to the infants being so small and probable to cry, Henryk dosed each with the barbiturate, Luminal to ensure they stayed asleep until on the other side of the wall. This was retrieved from the hospital when Henryk had put his trust in one of the nurses telling them of our plans to rescue as many children as possible. With this being said, the nurse at the hospital would beg for some of the children from the wards to be taken in the next crate, meaning there had begun a demand for smuggling. We wanted to save as many as possible yet it was becoming more and more risky with how population rates were suddenly decreasing rapidly due to terrible conditions, even with three thousand deportees of Jews coming to ghetto from Pruszków, most did not last longer than a few days because of the cold. Between January and March 1941 seventy thousand more Jews were crammed into the ghetto, thirteen thousand died of starvation.

It wasn't long before we realised our mission was only a small scale of help compared to what needed to be done. We had rescued so many children, so many lives that we hoped were safe in the convent until the war could pass, when Poland could be liberated from the clutches of the Wehrmacht, though thousands perished inside the ghetto that we could not save. Since arriving in the ghetto everything that was possible and even impossible had changed. The forced labor had deteriorated people at a speed that the death carts could not keep up with, every single person, even those that had been deported into the ghetto were merely bone and no strength to keep them standing. There were fewer people singing or playing music in the streets than there had been and the black market was selling goods illegally at prices nobody could afford due to the risk of their lives for running them. Children lay silently in Mother's arms on the streets wrapped in rags, offering no protection from the winter cold, children begged and stole, others sold their books on the markets to make money for food at a slow sale pace.

When we thought that situations couldn't get much worse we realised that what we had been living since September 1st 1939 was just the beginning of something so much bigger. People were disappearing from the ghetto in thousands at an alarming rate. I began to have nightmares through the night that the German's were breaking down the door of our apartment and taking us all. Before I ever reached a point in the nightmare where I knew where they were taking us I would wake up in pools of sweat and a rapid heart rate that woke Mother up. I would reassure her I was okay, the last thing I wanted was to worry her but she was no fool, she saw right through me and everybody else was worried too. Towards the end of August 1941 my nightmares became a reality. The dreaded bang on the door told us instantly that they were here. When Aunt Lena opened the door they chucked her across the room as though she was an infectious bug and looked around the room for Antoni, his wife and Grandma. They had struggled through ghetto life, I was surprised they had made it as far as they did however it did not take away the pain that came from that day when the soldiers marched them out of the apartment with no care for how weak and frail they had become. We didn't see them again after that. We were convinced that they had taken the elders to Treblinka and were exterminated at the hands of the Wehrmacht. Mother cried for many days afterwards as did all the other adults in the apartment. Everyone had become so vulnerable, so careless for life anymore, the only thing that kept us going and not giving up completely was each other.

From the summer of 1942 people began disappearing on a wider scale. It was alarming, throat shockingly frightening and worrying. Rumours flew through the ghetto from Jews entering later on, that people were being taken away to extermination camps and being put into gas chambers. Further rumours circulated of other camps that had been built all over Europe and Jews as well as many others that Hitler did not deem acceptable to his *'perfect race',* were being worked to their deaths in worse conditions than the ghetto. We were dubious whether to believe them, though we questioned over and over *what could they gain from making it up? But what could possibly be worse than life here?*

Warsaw was struggling like never before and when August 1942 came around the biggest shock of all came to light. The orphanage had been forced to move to Sienna Street which did not add anything beneficial to their struggling way of life. Janusz and the staff members moved into the orphanage with them however in August 1942 German soldiers arrived at the orphanage to round up the children to take them to Treblinka. For some reason Janusz had been offered sanctuary on the Aryan side and he refused with no hesitation. Where his orphans went, he went. Over one hundred and ninety children, the staff members and Janusz were all loaded into cattle cars and taken to Treblinka in which we never heard from them again. It hit me like a sack of bricks to the face when Henryk told me just days later in the factory. I fell to my knees and cried the driest, hardest cry I had ever heard come from within me. All those children, Izaak and his newly found sister, Mr Korczak, all the lovely staff there, all gone. I never recovered from that. It took a piece of me away that day I never really did get back. I went to work everyday as did the others in the apartment, I'd work but only because I had to in order to stay alive, then we would return to what we knew as home, sometimes to a tiny portion of bread and jam most times we had to do without. While at work at the factory we worked until our energy had run out, then made to work more with as little as a quarter bread for the day and sometimes if demand for the products were high, not at all.

Posters and notices began to spring up around Warsaw to report to the Umschlagplatz at 11 o' clock where the trains left the station to head East for work. It stated that life would be better, we would receive more food and living conditions would be much better than living in the ghetto. It also stated that those who complied would receive two loaves of bread and either margarine or sugar, those that did not, would be shot. It stirred up panic throughout the entire ghetto, many went into hiding, fearing that it was a trap while others were led to the Umschlagplatz by the roaring of their stomachs.

The apartment had been much quieter since the three elders were taken, even the children did not have the energy to fight amongst themselves anymore. Home schooling had long since become a memory of the past and as much as I envied to be back in school as I had been over two years ago, it was a concern that was not very high on the list of priorities. Situations were rapidly becoming ever worse and I'm unsure whether it was through the exhaustion and malnutrition or because everything seemed to be happening so fast with nothing made sense, we did not understand how anything could be worse than the torture we had been living in already.

We battled amongst ourselves within the apartment, with Mother, Aunt Lena, Inga and Mia becoming lost in a flood of disputes and arguments over what was best for everybody. If we stayed, we would be shot eventually, even if we went with Mia's suggestion of going into hiding. It could buy us time but we had no more sources left on the outside. Henryk was taken as soon as the notices went up, against his will so I had heard. He was walking back from work one day and they had snatched him up and sent him to the Umschlagplatz for deportation.

After hours of constant arguing amongst themselves Mia's husband Jerry calmed the situation and ordered that everybody go to bed and matters would be discussed in the morning.

"Nothing is being solved here, we all have different opinions, we must all stick together. We have all become family while living here and we are stronger together than apart. Now, we will be safe by morning, everybody try to get some sleep and do not worry for tonight."

Everyone laid down the argument for the night and took on board what Jerry had said and he was right, we were stronger together, yet come morning, we would be in more fear than we had ever been in before.

January 6th 1942 - Coronado California

The war had been raging through Europe for two years, four months and five days when I signed up for duty at one of the recruiting centers in Coronado California. America knew it was on the horizon, though it wasn't until December 7th 1941 when the Japanese bombed the US naval base, that Roosevelt declared war. Germany had dropped the first bomb on Poland on September 1st 1939, marking the beginning of a very long war that would take the lives of millions of people. We'd read about it in the papers, heard the broadcasts on the radio and yet it didn't really feel real for us until America was attacked. I was nineteen years old when I walked out of the recruitment office with exhilaration, excitement and panic coursing through my veins at one million miles an hour. I hadn't told Ma yet, nor had I told Jen, the love of my life. She had known my intentions and been firm in telling me that I shouldn't do it. *'It was not your war to fight.'* She'd said to me, though I signed up anyway knowing my country needed me and I was unsure of just how bad she would take it.

Now, at nineteen years old, graduated from high school over a year ago and working in the public library I had decided to volunteer my services for a country that needed me. I was driven by books and literature, using words to create emotion and completely change the course of a person's state of mind by the use and positioning of certain words. The library had been a savior to me since graduating, I was able to provide a small and steady income that I was able to use to help Ma out during the depression but I knew I needed to do more. I felt the productivity of my life racing away with every day that was wasted in a job that was coming to a dead end. I needed to do more and my country needed me too. Ma and Jen on the other hand would not be quite so pleased when I broke the news to them.

"How could you do this?" Screamed Jen in tears that had formed faster than I was able to finish my sentence. That's when I knew that I had broken her heart with just six small words, *I've signed up for the army.*
"You've heard the radio, America is at war!" I'd tried to stay calm, reassure her that it wasn't as bad as she thought, though seeing her tears brought frustration in not knowing how to backtrack and avoid them.
"So why is it *your* war to fight? You're not a soldier Peter, you're a librarian! You know I have always told you to chase your dreams, use every day that God has given you to make it worth it but this isn't it!" Her cries had become hysterical and I stood motionless before her unknowing of how to make the situation better.
"It is all of our fight Jen, I need to do this!" I'd attempted to wrap my arms around her which resulted in a drastic fail as she began throwing her hands towards me and venting her anger into my chest. I stood fixed to the spot, letting her spill her

emotions in any way she thought could make things better. After several minutes I grabbed her hand and pulled her towards me, kissing her face as tears streamed down her red face. As she collapsed into my arms I picked her up, carried her upstairs and let her vent her emotions in another way.

She was the love of my life and she knew it and what hurt her the most was that her advice was what had driven me to signing up to the army, despite her several attempts at shutting down the idea. She lived by the motto, *life should be experienced, for what other purpose is there than life itself,* yet on this occasion she refused to accept her own advice was what had pushed me into joining. I wanted to be something, make those around me proud, make my life worth it when I got to the end. My country was in crisis, calling for help from those that were able and I was one of them. Over the course of the next six months I attended boot camps across the States, preparing myself for the intense training that was to come.
"You do your Ma proud, do you hear me? You do me proud and you make sure you come back to me." Ma told me the day I stood on the porch with my rucksack ready to leave. It broke her heart that I was going, yet I could see how proud she was beaming from her at every angle. She was wearing her emotions on the outside, fear, worry and admiration all fighting for the forefront as she stood waving with her handkerchief she used to dab at her eyes. Jen had refused to come out of the house, or entertain the idea of me leaving. She was hurting and

I understood why, yet I knew I needed to go and I hoped she would come around sooner rather than later. I'd kissed her head as I left and promised that I would return to her as she cried into the pillow.

"I'll come back, I promise." I'd said, taking one last look at her curled up body and walking out of the room.

Other than work, we were always together, at home, going to dinner parties, meeting friends and our dreaded fortnightly visits to her parents. We came as a two and that is how it had always been since the moment we met. Now, we were to be apart and I knew deep down in her heart she didn't expect me to return. She'd heard the broadcasts with me, sat at the dinner table with the radio filling the silence with sounds of jazz, that would then finish to the sound of a broadcast. On September 1st 1941 President Roosevelt addressed the nation. *"We shall do everything in our power to crush Hitler and his Nazi forces..."* We had known that war was coming, it lived under the skin of every American, it was just a matter of *when.* Then, just three months later, The Japanese Naval Air Service ordered a surprise military strike on Pearl Harbor. That is when it really started to hit home for the American's. War had been brought to us and we were to fight back, stop Hitler and his German army and the Japanese from causing more devastation to Europe than had already been done.

"Do you wonder what is going on out there?" Asked Jen who had turned the radio off after Roosevelt's announcement that war had been declared.

"I'd be lying if I said I didn't." I'd replied, rubbing my temple in thought, wondering what this would mean for us as a country, what would happen and how our lives would change from that very moment. "Judging by the announcements, a lot of people are suffering already and I fear this war is long but over."

"Suffering how?" She'd asked, placing her knife and fork down, no longer holding an appetite for food.

"I suppose I don't really know anymore than you do, I can only imagine that Hitler is making it very difficult for anybody living in Europe right now. The Russian's are allies with Poland and Britain and now America but when Hitler first attacked Poland, Russia cooperated with Germany in the invasion yet stayed neutral to both the allies and the axis. It was not until Germany attacked Russia in June, with the code name Operation Barbarossa, that Russia joined the allies."

"What happened?" Jen had asked. She would listen to the broadcasts but politics and understanding what was happening on the warfront was not her forte, therefore she would bombard me with questions after each speech and I would educate her as much as I possibly could. I'd always said it was important for her to understand what was happening for if we were ever affected and now we were.

"Well Germany, with their axis allies Japan and Italy, began the invasion of the Soviet Union. Four and a half million troops were deployed from Poland, Romania and Finland. In just a week, German forces had advanced two hundred miles into Soviet territory, taking out almost four thousand aircraft with over six hundred thousand Red Army troops being killed, captured or wounded."

"What happened to them when they were captured? Are they still alive?" Jen had completely abandoned her dinner now and was leaning over the table with a look of horror spreading wide across her face.

"I do not know, I can't imagine they would want to be if they were still alive though. Right now, the Germany army are in sight of Moscow," I continued, finishing the wine in my glass and setting it down on the table to refill, "..but with the notorious Russian Winter the German's are struggling." Taking the bottle of wine with one hand while standing to take Jen's hand, I led her upstairs in a bid to end the talk of war. It was enough for her to process for one night.

During the month of December 1941, German advances in Russia had come to a halt due to the winter that was nicknamed, General Winter. By December 5th, Germany suffered 775,000 casualties, 800,000 Soviet's were killed, with an additional 6 million being wounded or captured. Hitler's plan to conquer the Soviet Union before winter came to a fail, despite their advancing efforts. Many BT-7 and Sd.Kfz-250 half-track Soviet tanks were taken out and destroyed along with many soldiers, though Germany suffered a loss that would cost as a turning point in the war.

As I climbed into a cab, leaving Ma waving frantically, I heard Jen shouting from inside the house. Within seconds she came running out onto the porch, down the grass and threw herself into my arms harder than she ever had before.
"You better come home to me." She cried, wrapping her arms around me tightly with no intention of releasing any time soon. "You be the soldier you need to be but you come back and be my Peter." The emotions were running higher than they ever had before as I lifted her and wrapped her around my waist. I was leaving for training, though it was evident within us both that we knew it would be a long time until we would be together again. "Promise me!" She cried, her head in my chest with tears falling uncontrollably from her eyes.
"I'll come back to you, I promise." It was a promise that I would carry with me over the course of the war, ensuring that I survived whatever was to be thrown at me to make it back to them. I wouldn't break my promise, I couldn't.

For America the war was just beginning but for much of Europe they were in the pit of the lions den that they had been dragged into two years ago. As the cab pulled away I thought of Ma and Jen but I thought about German occupied countries too, I wondered how they had been affected by a war I hadn't even walked into yet. I became lost in thought of what I would see, how it would change me and what the outcome would be when all weapons were laid to the ground at the end.

September 1942 - Heading East

We were being shoved into cattle cars like sardines, a suitcase with names scribbled on clutched in each person's hand with children hanging onto parents with every ounce of strength they had left. We had been rounded up in the night by the Gestapo and SS guards and taken to the Umschlagplatz to head East, or so they told us. We never received the bread and margarine as they had stated though we were not shot either which we counted our blessings for. They marched into the apartment and gave us little time to collect our belongings, to then be dragged out of the building with hundreds of other residents of the ghetto. They did not hold back in using brutal force while shouting at us. "Hurry, out, move!" Over and over they shouted until eventually they grew tired of waiting for the women of the house to collect what belongings they could. We had been somewhat prepared, had our cases packed for several weeks when we realised people were going missing. When Mia and Inga came back from the work day one evening after having to run from the grips of the guards, they told us of children being snatched from the streets and taken away. They kept the children inside the apartment after that and Mother was worried constantly that I would be taken too.

People were being taken everyday on their way home from work in the ghetto, so many had been taken already that Mother and Aunt Lena felt everyday would be their time.

Without fail Mother would tell me every night when we climbed into bed how much she loved me and that no matter what it took, staying together was the best chance we had of surviving the war that was raging angier every single day through Europe. It wasn't just Poland suffering, other countries too were going through the same, we had heard on the British radio Aunt Lena had smuggled in with her and kept under the floorboards of the kitchen, that Jews all over Europe were being gassed and killed. France had fallen already though we clung onto the hope that America, Britain and the USSR would defeat the Nazi's so that life as we had grown to know it would be over and we could live once again without fear in every breath, in every loud noise. When we heard that Japan had attacked America and that they had declared war on the axis, we guiltily felt that maybe there was a possibility that America would aid Britain and Russia into stopping the war and saving us.

Not only had we left our home in Warsaw, we were now forced to leave our city to a destination nobody knew for definite and that was the scariest part of all. After hearing the British announcements on the radio we could not help but fear that we too were being sent to our deaths. They told us they were resettling us in the East for a better life, yet we had not become naive enough to believe them after causing us so much suffering. In every cattle car one hundred people were crammed inside, no room to sit down or turn around and no facilities other than a dirty bucket in one corner. Women and children cried while men tried to calm everybody down, a lot of the men cried too, with others sitting motionless in a corner, no expression, no emotion flowing through them at all. I think a lot of people had begun to give up on life, we had so much taken from us already that many simply could not see reason to fight anymore, with the German's or simply just to stay alive. Some were calm and collected, believing we were travelling to a much improved way of life.

I stared at those around me looking vacant, In all the chaos, shouting and crying I knew I had felt like that many times within the ghetto, with Amelia and the three little ones trying for days to just make me *feel* again. The pain of losing so many I had considered friends had hit me hard, the pain of Papa and Grandpa, Kacper being taken, Izaak and the orphans and Henryk being deported appeared to weigh on my shoulders leaving me with the perception that the world was crumbling around us. I felt every stab of loss, while feeling completely numb. It wasn't until Mother sat beside me one evening, looking the most frail I had ever seen her and she spoke words that I will never forget.
"Jakub, when I met your Papa he made me feel as though I was alive. Of course I had been alive since the moment I left the womb of my Mama but meeting your Papa was the moment I truly *felt* alive spiritually and not just physically. I feel as though before him I had just been existing, waiting for the moment he would come into my life. He was my purpose for

living back then. When he was taken, a chunk of my heart was ripped right out of my skin. Do you know the only thing that fills it, makes me carry on in this dark and painful world right now?" She looked at me a handful of seconds as I sat staring blankly out of the window and took hold of my hand, squeezing it within her own. "You Jakub. There is nothing in this world I wouldn't do to make sure you are safe. It pains me to know that there are so many things out of our control right now but I will tell you this, no matter what happens, no matter where we end up, if we are not always together, we must hold on to make it back to each other because my world would cease to turn without you, you are my purpose Jakub." Her words changed me that day, made me realise that I could not give up, that I did deep down, still *feel*. I questioned through the chaos and panic whether there was still that hope buried deep in these people too, or whether the light had completely burnt out. Hope for better days and an end to the war in the not so distant future is what would carry people through, push them to survive because they had reason.

The door slammed shut on the cattle car leaving us with minimal light amongst the crowded bodies huddled together. There were no windows, leaving us in beams of light only through the wooden cracks. So many people were packed inside such a small car that sitting down on the damp straw was impossible without disturbing and aggravating other people. I clung to Mother's arm the whole journey, holding her up when she became too weak to stand on her own. For the majority of the journey she stood with her body weight lent against mine, her head on my shoulder. She was weak, dehydrated and hungry and there was nothing I could do to help her but keep her upright. Mia and her husband held their crying children and attempted to calm them with soothing songs with very little success. Everyone was hungry, needed water and air and we were deprived of it all as we stood bounding towards our destination.

"Mama I'm hungry." Came the gentle voice of Zofia who lay half conscious across her Papa's chest, the two twins of three years old clutching at an arm of their mother.

"Mia did you pack any of the food that was left?" Asked Jerry as he began rocking the six year old for comfort, her short blonde curls bouncing to the rhythm. Mia placed the twins on the floor and looked through her suitcase at the aggravation of the other passengers with most looking on eagerly at the thought of food. Mia pulled out a handful of bread wrapped in rags and before she could give it to Zofia the cattle car broke out in frantic chaos.

"She has food!" Comes the voice of a man squashed against the door fighting his way through the people for the bread held in Mia's hand.

"That's for the child!" Came the voice of a woman trying to shield Zofia and her parents.

"Why don't you share it, we are all hungry!" Comes the voice of another woman with an angry look on her face. Before I could do anything, everyone had broken out in arguments, shouting and pushing one another to get their hands on the bread.

"Listen! If we fight like this now what hope do we have!" Came the voice of a young man squashed in the corner with his hands in the air. "If we fight amongst ourselves they have won this war already! We must remember the Torah! Live by it and help one another." Most passengers fell calm while others, including a group of Hungarian women muttered under their breath in a language I was unfamiliar with.

"Please, feed your child, the children must be fed first." Says the woman shielding the family.

"If anybody has any food they would like to share maybe now is the time people, we must pull together." Says the man in the corner, now with his hands in his case looking for whatever food he could find in the limited light.

The little food that was found within suitcases did not stretch the whole of the cattle car though it had been agreed that women and children were to eat what there was before anybody else. I had been offered some bread though I had turned to look next to me at Amelia who was savoring the taste in her mouth like it would be the last food she would ever receive. Turning to the left I noticed an elderly man with thin rimmed glasses and cheekbones that gave the impression they would pop out of his skin at any moment. He looked sad, broken, that he had given up any hope of life being happy again.

"You can have my piece." I said, holding out my hand. He looked up at me slowly and offered me a gentle smile. Looking into his eyes I became lost in a world of darkness and emptiness, yet I could see the gentleness of his nature, that he was a good man that had undoubtedly lost everything.

"You are a very special young man, not many have the same qualities towards others as you. You should eat it, you will need it more than I will." He smiles again and looks towards the ground. Nobody around him appeared to acknowledge he was there, I assumed he had lost all the family he had. He looked as though he had experienced a long life with wisdom filling the most part, wondering if knowledge for where we were going was more of a curse than a blessing.

"I want you to have it." I said, placing the bread on his arm, not taking no for an answer. He ruffles my hair with his fragile hands and runs his fingers over the dry, crumbling texture of almost stale bread just a few centimeters in size, yet possibly a sight he had not seen in quite some time.

"Thank you." He says smiling, breaking the small piece of bread in half and giving it to a man looking painfully thin on the floor. It was enough for merely a taste and nothing more, though I hoped it would make some kind of small difference.

"We all deserve life," I reply, "all of us."

Throughout the rest of the journey most people shared what they had, helped others who fell from weakness while others who were strong enough sang songs to calm the nerves of the children and their parents. The smell within the cattle car was so pungent that it turned my stomach, a thick, fusty smell of bad sanitation and hygiene as we had been deprived of hot and cold water in the ghetto. By the time the train came to a halt I noticed an elderly man and woman sitting against the wooden sides of the traincar who were not moving. At first I thought they may have been asleep though when prodded by a young boy to tell them we had arrived neither of the couple moved. Everyone looked on in silence at first, even the more agitated people felt their hearts drop when seeing the old couple locked hand in hand, together at their final moments in such awful conditions.

The men wearing hats took them off their heads and held them to their chest in respect, women sobbed silently while children shrieked in panic and hunger. At the far right of the train car was a woman crouched in the corner cradling her baby in a blanket full of holes, she too lay motionless. No sound came from the small infant. *What were they doing to us?* I thought to myself horrified. *How could they be so inhumane?*

It was not a long way to where we were going but with railway lines being bombed we were rocked back and forth, shuddered along the lines not knowing where they were taking us. Even with the journey not being for a substantial amount of time, there were those that were just not strong enough to make it until we arrived. There was very little time to show respect for those who did not make it as the train doors thundered open with a mighty crash to a completely new world of terror and fear. The evening sun streamed through the doors revealing a vast platform with reflectors lighting up everything it touched, revealing bodies everywhere, SS guards in their uniforms with tight belts around their waists, shiny black boots and guns on their backs. Dogs stood fiercely at their side amongst the platform, barking at the herd of people panicking and rushing around them, ready to sink their teeth into anyone who disobeyed, men in striped uniforms helping people down from the cattle cars, some whispering quickly into peoples ears as they held their hands and took their luggage from them. Chimneys stood tall in the distance with smoke rising into the sky, I don't think anybody knew what they were. I assumed it was a factory and that we had been sent here to work as ash blew through the platform like snow on a winter's day. A wooden watchtower stood tall above us housing guards that skimmed through the crowd below, pointing their guns at us, electrifying fear into each and every one of us.

The world we knew had been left so far behind it was merely a distant and long lost memory on a completely new planet. Terror flooded the platform as thousands of people, men, women and children exited the train carrying their luggage that we were made to deposit at the side of the train, with shouting coming from every angle. "Leave all belongings, they will be returned to you later." "Form two columns, women and children this side," They said, pointing to the left, "men this side." They shouted pointing to the right. Those who were too frail to walk were escorted onto trucks, most being those of old age. Someone within the herd of people translated the German in a panic as children fought to stay with their parents, others falling into frightful tears as loved ones were separated, some cried out in anger, fright and worry to which the SS guards assured them, "Together again afterwards." The SS guards and doctors flooded the platform portraying a calm and gentle approach, that we should not worry.

"When asked, say you have a trade." Whispered a painfully thin man in what looked like striped pajamas and hat as he helped us off the train then moved quickly onto the next person. His words confused me, left me with numerous questions though there was no time to ask them, he was quickly and timidly helping others off the train by taking their luggage then helping them down, to pass them their cases and move onto the next, whispering in some of their ears as he had done mine. I'd seen it in the ghetto, how having a trade could be the difference between survival and death, yet here it felt much more than that.

It became impossible to concentrate on any one thing happening around us, the cold air stabbed at my skin as I pulled my long black coat around my body. I had started to feel the cold more in recent months and I was unsure of whether this was because we were so weak our bodies could just not fight the cold or whether it was the winter making a harsh appearance. It hurt my bones as I stood hanging off Mother's arm, refusing to let her go to be lost in the sea of distressed bodies. People were crying, not wanting to be separated, clinging onto the arms of their husbands and parents while guards pulled them apart reassuring them they would be reunited soon.

"Jakub, keep hold of my arm, do not let go." Mother shouts pushing her way through to the group of women and children and Aunt Lena following close behind. I gripped Mother's arm so tight I feared I was cutting right into her skin, unable to control my breathing in fear of what was happening.

Within just minutes of us huddled together in lines, SS guards marched through us, interrogating women with older children such as ourselves. "How old?" "Healthy or ill?" We'd heard the rumours of those who were not deemed fit for work, many women were being held up by others in a bid to fool the guards into believing they were healthy, anything to stay alive. An SS guard and a small man who looked like a doctor eyed up Mia and Jerry before his eyes fell on their two twins.

"Twins?" He asked bluntly. Mia and Jerry both nod in fear, unknowing of what would happen with their answer. "Take them." He said, before moving down the line and repeating the process. The children were snatched from their parents arms with Zofia screaming in fear and clutching at her mothers leg.

"You can't take my babies!" Screamed Mia in tears and cries that held the capability of splitting a person's soul in half. Jerry looked worried, tried talking to the guard in a way he hoped would give them back their children, though the guard grew restless and struck him across the face with his whip. We stood amongst the crowd, shaking in fear and waiting for further instruction when a tall, thin SS guard appeared in my face shouting, "How old?"

"Thirteen." I trembled, not taking my eyes from his. He looked me up and down several times as if he was trying to make a decision.

"Ill or healthy?" He asked, trying to come across as though there was nothing for us to be fearful of.

"I'm healthy sir." My legs began to buckle and shake with fear as his stale cigarette breath stroked my face.

"Do you have a trade?" He asked, narrowing his eyes.

"Embroidery." I nodded, remembering the whispering man's advice.

"Experience?" He asked, never taking his eyes from me. I had to think on the spot while not taking too long that would come across as suspicious. "Warsaw embroidery department sir, my uncle trained me and I worked for him for three years, mostly training but I am skilled. I can make almost anything from leather, gloves, boots, brushes." I held my breath, waiting for a conclusion, a verdict that would most likely be on the fate of my life.

"That way!" He shouted, pulling my arm and directing me in the direction of thousands of men huddled like penguins in silence. As he pulled my arm I tried in a desperate bid to keep hold of Mother, yet the sheer force of his strength pushed me in the direction of the other men, ripping us apart and separating us. I had never felt fear like I did at that moment. Up until then I knew I had Mother, we protected each other yet I knew deep down that I needed her. Suddenly the world opened up and swallowed me whole, surrounded by thousands of people yet I felt completely alone. I tried to look for Mother as I shouted for her but she had already been lost, my only vision being of endless strangers' heads. Fear pierced my skin, sunk into my bones and buried deep beneath. *What will happen to Mama? Will I see her again? What is going to happen to me?*

"This way!" Ordered an SS guard pointing with his truncheon, the men in striped pajamas leading us from the sides. We were led through tall gates and towards a wood until reaching a wooden barrack, everyone in line shuffling along like sheep being herded to an unknown destination.
"First you must shower. We take hygiene very seriously at Auschwitz." Came the voice of the leading SS guard. *Auschwitz!* I had heard rumors of this place, none being pleasant, that people were working to the point of exhaustion. Surrounding us from every direction was a barbed wire fence that suffocated us inside with signs of electricity that passed through it and I knew it meant a warning for those that had

ideas of escaping. They had tried to keep us calm yet the fear striked through every person enclosed within the three meter high fence. Once inside we were told to undress quickly so that we could shower. At first the thought of a shower after so long with limited water and poor sanitising facilities sounded overwhelming, until we were ordered back outside with no clothes to shelter our body from the brisk biting cold to wait for the showers.

We pushed along the stoney path, every part of our bodies on display in a humiliating performance of men and young boys fearing under the commands of the guards. I could feel my heart pounding in my chest, biting cold that stabbed at every inch of my skin with stones cutting sharp into my feet. We were ordered to wait outside a building lined with windows that had a striking resemblance of a prison. We were exposed and humiliated for an hour before entering. I stood shaking, thoughts screaming in my mind at whether they were putting Mother through the same humiliating procedures, it made me fill with boiling anger at the thought. The world suddenly felt so big, so vast with me being such a tiny fraction of a person within it. I stood amongst hundreds of men and young boys who I did not know, everyone around me strangers. I had never felt so alone. In the distance screams could be heard of hundreds of people, blocked from view yet the screams travelled through the air across the camp, into the souls of those whose ears they met. It was impossible to shrug them off, to not hear the desperate cries of help and screams of pain. Wrapping my hands around my body for warmth, I let myself cry, let myself pine for my Mother.

Shouting from the guards came from the front of the line of men which indicated them to enter the building. I didn't understand his German, though everyone around me started taking off jewelry and wedding rings and throwing them inside a box as they entered.
"Disinfection!" Shouted one of the guards with those in pajamas pushing us along to get us all into the showers. The concrete building offered no protection from the cold, if anything my bones shook more after being hit with warm water to then be stood naked in the cold air. We had been pushed into an open concrete room lined with shower heads above us, made to wash in the presence of hundreds of other men with dignity and pride so far gone I wondered what it felt like. My body shook painfully as I wrapped my hands around my body desperately hoping it would offer some warmth.

Upon leaving the showers we were prompted abruptly to stand on stools to be shaved. I held myself in agonising horror watching skinny, frail looking men shaving the new arrivals from head to toe, leaving almost no hair visible. The men shaving us were skinnier than all of the new arrivals, skinnier than I had ever seen a person, even in the ghetto. When the men stepped off the stools and walked into another room it was as if they had left behind the person they once were. I'd never before imagined that hair could change someone so remarkably by having it stripped away, some looked like they were in a trance of sadness that could not be broken. I stepped up on the stool, embarrassed as another man silently shaved my body at speed that suggested he had been doing the same task for a substantial amount of time, or he was afraid of not doing his job quickly enough.

"What is going to happen to us?" I whispered, trying to hold back frightful tears. I felt like a small boy again, desperate for the embrace of my Mother with her nowhere in sight.

"Just do as they say kid, there's no escape from here. Your only chance of ever getting out of here is if they lose this dahm war. If they think you're not capable of working for them anymore.." He moved the sharp blade across his neck, inches away from his skin with a look of horror on his face as he glided his hands horizontally. *Death.* He quickly continued shaving my head as an SS guard patrolled down the line. When finishing he pushed me in the direction of the next room. It was unquestionable that he too was afraid of the guards. There was no time to turn back or retrieve any answers to questions as I pushed along into the next room with hundreds of other naked men waiting in another line. We were herded through the line, swallowed up and spat back out in new versions of ourselves, happiness drained and squashed out of us.

We were each tattooed a number on our forearm with a needle approximately 1cm long that engraved our number with ink then being rubbed into the bleeding wound. We were referred to by that number from then on and never our name. We had our role as humans stripped away, dignity and rights laughed at while being used as part of the German war effort to exterminate ourselves and make their army stronger through the labor they forced upon us The rumours from the ghetto began to feel real, that concentration and extermination camps had been built and I was now a number added to Auschwitz-Birkenau, the largest of them all. After receiving a striped uniform with our numbers stitched into the chest, it hit me hard that I probably wasn't going to make it out alive. I placed the given hat on my head, buttoned up my striped shirt and that was it, I was no longer Jakub of Warsaw Poland, I was number 198216 and nothing more. I was no longer a human but a set of numbers, a statistic to work for the people we hated more than anyone in the world.

That night I lay in the barracks thinking of my Mother. The barrack consisted of rows upon rows of bunks on three different levels. I had been lucky with being one of the smallest in the barrack to squeeze between six other men on the top bunk. Those that had the strength welcomed me graciously, though it did not make life seem any more pleasant.

"You don't want the bottom bunk kid, rats will eat you alive down there. Better with the middle, don't get the draft from the windows up top. Rule is, the younger you are the higher up you go, old'uns can't pull themselves up there see. Luckily for you, old man died last night in his sleep, they carted him off this morning, so you might as well have his place, looks like you got a lot of life left in you, no point wasting a strong one to the cold up there, get enough of that outside in Appell." Said a Polish man with thin rimmed glasses by the name of Binem. I felt anything but lucky and to hear that an old man had died in his sleep made me worry ever more. My stomach turned in knots and screamed to be fed. I clutched it tight, hoping to forget the pain.

"You are Polish?" I asked, trying to get comfortable between six other men, some already sleeping and moaning at the conversation keeping them from falling asleep. We were to sleep on wooden beds, one mattress and blanket to share with around eight other men, some bunks even more.

"I am, came from Warsaw with the first transports, dahm Nazi's made me build half of this place. Pfft.. building our own prison, couldn't make it up could you?"

The first week in Auschwitz was a wrecking ball of emotions. I longed for my Mother, to know that she was alive, that she was not hurt however the women's barracks were separate to ours meaning finding her could have been almost impossible. I began work in what the other men called *kanada*, unstitching clothes and sorting possessions brought in by prisoners that would either be used within the camp or be transported to

Germany. When told that we would be relocated East, we were also told that we could bring essential items, unknowing that they would find themselves in the abundant warehouses of the camp, never to be returned to their owners. Despite the harsh conditions of the camp and the daily routine I knew I had fallen lucky working in the Kanada. It was like a gold mine for being able to smuggle items, if you knew how without getting caught.

Daily routine began at 04:30am in the spring and summer, while Autumn and Winter it began at 05:30am. Nights were strenuous and challenging to sleep with the sound of cries and moaning from the other men who were in pain from hunger, exhaustion and medical problems that stemmed from it and the cold that forced us to use one another for body heat like penguins in the ice. At the sound of the call bell ringing loudly through the camp, we woke up, tidied our sleeping area, attempted to wash and relieve ourselves, which meant getting to the front of the line as close to first as possible or there would not be time, to then have *'tea'* or *'coffee'* before heading out to the parade ground to be counted in roll call, known as Appell. Every morning was as daunting as the last, mountains of people who had passed away during the night were piled outside the barracks like they were objects holding little to no value.

The first morning shocked me the most, seeing piles of corpses like I had never seen it before, some still with their eyes open, haunting my soul as they lay with no life remaining in their frail and stiff skin. All the men that lay there had their uniforms hanging loosely from their exhausted bodies, though their wooden shoes had been taken during the night. When I questioned Binem why, he told me that in order to survive you needed to be able to push away guilt of taking from the dead, they did not need the items that could save those that were still living. It daunted on me that we were living in the worst version of hell possible. I was ushered along by men in the barrack to avoid a brutal beating by the guards to line up for roll call. We were to line up in rows of ten by block sections while counted by the guards. If the numbers did not add up to what they should be then we would have to wait outside in whatever weather and wait longer, which was exceptionally difficult for those suffering from exhaustion. Many prisoners would be held up with the aid of others to avoid being sentenced as *unfit for work*. When this happened they were sent away and we never saw them again, though I knew it couldn't have been to a good place. Nothing about this place offered light or comfort.

The end of roll call forwarded on to the order to form up into labor sections, where we would walk out to work accompanied by the sound of the orchestra who were not required to line up for roll call. The sound of the music would circle around my mind, sending me to a parallel universe in which I was still living at home with Mother, Papa, Grandma and Grandpa. I'd walk to the Kanada every morning and look over the fence at the women walking to their labor duties, desperately hoping that it would be the day I would see her. I'd let the musical notes send me into my memories, before the war hit our city and destroyed our lives, ripping us apart from each other, before radios were banned and we would stand in the kitchen watching Mother dance and twirl across the floor with happiness radiating from her. I thought about it every morning, reminiscing about the memories I would have done anything to bring back as I was left with a hole of emptiness and disappointment at another day of not finding her.

I'd been in Auschwitz-Birkenau for three months before I was able to establish contact with the woman's camp. The SS guards who were on duty for marching us to our labor duties had fallen behind at a scene of distress with a man too exhausted to walk. They beat him with their truncheons over and over, sending the cries of pain through the camp. I carried on walking, if there was anything I had learned it was that there was never anything anyone could do in those situations with the guards, so I chose not to let myself see it. It was the only way not to let the situations in Birkenau completely pull you into the dark. As I pulled my feet across the ground, begging them not to give in to the knot of hunger and exhaustiveness that spread through my body I caught a glimpse over the fence at a group of women aiding another. I watched in dreaded anticipation, if she was caught she would be sent away. It appeared that the guards in the women camp were also preoccupied with other matters and had not yet noticed the woman in aid of support from other prisoners. Something inside me told me that I could not look away. We saw this everyday, from waking up to going to sleep at lights out, though I had the extraordinary notion that I should keep my gaze on the other side.

After several moments of the woman composing herself and finally managing to stand unaided she turned to look over the fence and that was when everything changed. Every ounce of giving up I had accumulated since arriving at Birkenau was gone as I looked into the eyes of the woman who looked back at me, pale and blue from the cold, hair shaved, exposing the bones that were making an appearance from her cheeks, legs like that of matchsticks and just as brittle.
"Jakub?" Came the voice of a fragile and suffering woman, looking into my eyes as though a ghost had been placed before her.
"Mama!"

July - December 1942 - Camp Toccoa, Georgia

I think it would be fair to say we were all different. No two men in Easy Company were the same. We had all come from different places across the state with our own stories to tell. Those stories would carry us through a war that had already begun when all 140 men and seven officers who formed the original company found their place at Camp Toccoa. Me? My old man left for the army as I was fresh to the world so I can't say I remember him, I never met him. When he was taken in combat Ma was devastated, yet she brought me and my two younger sisters up with honor and pride in every hard decision, even more so when times were hard, as she used to say, *"It is through the hardest times we find our strength from those around us."* Despite her greatest efforts it would be a lie to say I grew up with money weighing my pockets down and when the depression wreaked havoc amongst the states things only progressed further down a spireling slope of struggle.

On June 4th 1942, The Battle of Midway turned a corner for America in the war. The major naval battle in the Pacific Theater between the U.S and Japan, just six months after Japan's attack on Pearl Harbor, wiped Japan's hopes of neutralizing the U.S as a naval power and effectively changed the course of the war, though America still needed men in the sea, air and on the ground.

I'd heard the benefits, heard the briefings and to be honest, I enlisted to be part of Easy Company, 506th Regiment of the 101st Airborne Division to serve for my country when it needed me most. Well, that and we had heard we would be jumping out of planes. *Who wouldn't want to fight for their country while doing that?* It was about making America proud, serving our country with pride and honor. The ordinary infantry was an option, though we wanted to go into combat with men we trusted would have our backs, fight with us and for us, not to be carried through by the comrades surrounding us. Choosing the infantry was too much of a risk, I wanted to fight for my country but I wanted to do everything possible to make sure I made the journey home too. Joining the paratroopers was much less of a risk, something that was taken into careful consideration when enlisting for a role. It was going to be dangerous, it would be very naive indeed to think otherwise, yet we loved our country like we love our Ma's, not really much love stronger than that and although it meant leaving behind a life that had barely begun, we did what needed to be done for the war that we did not start but would fight through anyway for the greater good.

They'd told us about the training, said it would be the hardest experience of our lives and I can tell you that they were absolutely right. I didn't know too much about the airborne when enlisting, just the basics of it, that it was going into combat by jumping out of planes and that it was a voluntary position. It hadn't been formed long so it was still brand spanking new, meaning the training was nothing like we had ever done before, even for those that were in the reserves. We knew that a fight was on the horizon for a war that had been raging for years before the United States stepped in. When the Japanese bombed the US naval base in Pearl Harbor Hawaii, president Roosevelt declared war on Japan that had already joined with Germany and Italy in the axis powers. From the Japanese attack on December 7th 1941, America had been declared at war with Japan and we had left our homes and life as we knew it behind.

I'll never forget the death hill at Toccoa, a hill that raised one thousand foot above the parade ground. Three miles it took to get to the top. As expected a number of the men were lost on the very first day, taken down by the mighty mountain itself. It wasn't surprising, running up that hill for the first time felt like your lungs would explode right out of your chest and your legs would fall and surrender to the incline. You had to tell yourself this was the way to your future, this was how you made it into the airborne. It was a year before the units were attached to the Airborne, after training that broke some men, others it made stronger, which was the aim of Colonel Robert Sink, to harden our shells, prepare us for jump school with the basic training that would result in a regiment that could be led into combat. Within the space of seven days we were able to run up the hill and back again. The training was intense but it was evident that it was working. By the time the end of the second week came, more men were sent home due to failing to make it to the top of the hill without taking the ambulance back down after eating an immense portion of spaghetti in the mess hall during lunchtime, unknowing that we would be running that day. Sick covered the shirts of almost all men, me included, yet every man gave it their all and that is without doubt.

That day made me realise the bigger picture, what I wanted from life and what needed to be done. The hill was a metaphor for all of that. It showed me that no matter how steep the climb, you're only going to get from life what you put in. If I didn't want to reach the top of that hill, regardless of the spaghetti wanting to make a sudden reappearance, then I would have given up and taken the ambulance ride back with some of the other men. I wanted to succeed, I didn't care how big the hill was, I was going to reach the top because there was no way I would see myself fail. I watched the earth move around me, pulling at every step taken, longing to see me fall and I told myself I had two options, succeed, or fail. The latter was not an outcome I was prepared to let happen.

We ran the hill three or four times a week, pushing to limits we never even knew possible. By my side was Bradley Hiker, a skinny little thing but could outrun any of the men when he put his mind to it. He was humble, heart of the purest gold that would carry any man of the United States Army through combat if they needed it and not because of his role but because it was the way his heart worked. He had one purpose and that was to fight for his country and return to his girl and kid when the war was done. Sounds simple when it is said so bluntly, yet the training, exercise sessions, jump school and combat lessons were all stepping stones for him to returning back to them. Despite the many jokes that flew around camp, each man knew that we all had a family we wanted to return to, whether that was by blood or romance and it was respected beyond any jokes made. Jones stood out amongst them all to me, held his heart in his sleeve for his family and was never stirred by mockery, he would laugh along, be a friend and brother to any man yet he never let any of it dim his passion for talking about them and I think the other men respected him the most for that too.

It had been a long day of training on the obstacle course, knee-ups, push-ups and pull-ups and running up the hill known as Currahee. It was said that Currahee was an Indian word for *We Stand Alone*, which was fitting to say that was how we were expected to fight. It became our battle cry for the 506th paratroopers.
"You got a lady back home?" Hiker had said to me later that night as we settled into our bunks.
"I do, often worry about her while I'm here y'know, never really spent much time apart, this will be the longest since I met her." I sighed, though he looked at me and smiled as he handed me a photograph.

"Worrying over situations you can't control will eat you alive. I've looked at this picture everyday since I've been here and I don't worry, I just tell myself I have to make it back for them when the job is done." Looking back at me from the picture in my hand was a woman with short brown curls standing in a field with a baby in her arms. Hiker stood smiling with his arm around her looking into the camera. Her white dress flowed into the flowers around their feet and she held a smile that spoke a thousand words. They were happy. I understood from that moment that having something to make it back for could push you through limits that would make you crack in any other circumstance.

We were trained by Captain Herbert Sobel, born to a Jewish family in Chicago, Illinois. He attended Culver Military Academy in Indiana and by 1934 he had graduated from the University of Illinois. At the outbreak of war in 1941 he joined the US army and gained an officers commission as a 2nd Lieutenant and after a promotion to 1st Lieutenant he was sent to camp Toccoa in Georgia in 1942 as part of the 506th parachute Infantry Regiment. He was given the command of Easy Company, to train us and push us to limits that would harden us ready for combat as soldiers. We knew that as a drill instructor he would need to be harsh, test our boundaries and limits that would prove vital in the war, yet we held our opinions on him from the very beginning. Weekend passes were almost always revoked due to slightly rusty bayonets, which was abundantly demonstrated when Joe Liebgott got all our passes canceled because of it.

"I wouldn't take this rusty piece of shit to war!" Shouted Sobel angrily into the face of Liegbott who stood at attention without so much as a flinch. "I will not take you to war in your condition!" We all lost our passes that weekend because of such minor infractions that we had begun to hold a silent grudge over it. Arguing with Sobel was a mistake you would only make once. I think it would be fair to say that all men of Easy Company had their own war with Sobel that could not be pursued due to us desperately wanting those wings. We looked at him as arrogant, in lesser physical shape than we were ourselves and he knew nothing of training and working in the outdoors that we did not already know. Back in the barracks on an evening most men would curse quietly to one another about how Sobel would use punishment simply for not liking a man of the company, which he would put down to us being disobedient.

"F'ing Jew, if those dahm Nazi's don't get him in the field i'll make sure my rifle is pointing his way." Cursed Terrence Harris, one of the first privates of Easy Company. He had served in the Navy before volunteering to be a paratrooper so we nicknamed him Salty and his liking for Sobel was much to be desired. Some of the men didn't *hate* Sobel, like myself and Hiker, though we did consider his actions and punishments beyond fair on more than several occasions.

We had started with a close order drill that progressed onto night marches with our entire field equipment that was eleven miles when we started and every march after an extra mile was added on, sometimes two. It was out of the question to do the marches with a break or a cigarette and the worst one of all was to not drink out of our water canteen. After every march Sobel would stand us at attention and inspect each one of us, including our canteens. Those who had taken a drink were ordered to complete the whole march again. It was grueling and exhausting the first time around, which is why fighting the temptation to have even a sip of water was vital in not having to start all over again. Some of the lesser punishments included twenty pushups on the spot, which meant we had got off lightly in comparison to weekend passes being revoked or remarches.

Himself and Lieutenant Winters were silent rivals, neither spoke it aloud though it was thick in the air and everyone knew it. We held respect for Lieutenant Winters and he had it for us, treating us as men without the need to shout constantly unlike Sobel who came across as having a point to prove that was never really proved. He was unable to map-read or train us in the way that Winter's did and it was beyond any reasonable doubt that Sobel knew this. Sobel held even more hate towards Winter's when Colonel Sink had walked by a training session in calisthenics run by Winters, the training sessions undertaken for strength, flexibility, coordination and endurance and had promoted him to 1st lieutenant just a few days later. Sobel gave him the worst possible jobs after that in a bid to take out his loathing for the man though Winter did his duties and never complained. As much as nearly every man hated Sobel, we knew he was turning us into fine and sharp soldiers that the US Army needed for war, yet we obeyed due to fear, not because we were training to be the man that he was and it stood out by miles in his presence, in comparison to being in that of Winters.

Camp Toccoa wasn't just about the physical exercise, we underwent training in the basics of becoming a soldier ready for combat, lectures, demolitions, infantry tactics, radio equipment, map and compass reading, codes, weapons and switchboard and wire stringing. Even under the least amount of physical training, we were constantly learning and training, preparing us for what was to come. We had become so familiar with stripping down an M1 Garand, a .30 calibre semi-automatic rifle, that we could do it with our eyes closed and half asleep. The 9.5 pound rifle could be field stripped without tools, meaning an easy enough disassembler when out in combat. We were to treat our rifles delicately once we were issued them, to have on our person in the field and to care for them like we would a loved one we had left at home. Once we made it through jump school successfully, we would receive our silver wings that would be placed on the left pocket of our jackets, with a patch for our left shoulder and one for our hats. After jump school brought another gratifying reward of being able to wear the trousers we tucked into our boots, the uniform of a paratrooper.

Before our wings were gained and our patches worn with pride, we had to make it through jump school first, meaning we could not train any less than hard. We were prepared for jump school by a mock tower at Toccoa that stood at 35feet tall, to which we were strapped into a parachute harness that was attached to risers at 15foot. With the risers attached to a pulley running from a cable, we jumped from the 35 foot tower in our harness and slid down the cable, that when landing, made it feel like we were paratuting and landing for real. I had never experienced it before and although it was training, my twenty year old self found the training exciting and exhilarating. I wanted to be on the planes and jumping out after that first training session at the towers. I became familiar with the training of jumping extraordinarily quickly. Some men took longer than others however once we were able to jump successfully, we were moved onto the next section of training.

All 140 of us had grown to be a family of brothers, we drank, we fought, we reinforced each other and we chanted in unison, bringing us together as one in a way that no other family or lover ever could. Men would slander the name of others women, Mothers and lovers, where they had come from and a fight would break out that only ever brought the men closer together. I'd picked up on the way of a soldier's life early on, how it worked, the exhaustion, how each man treated another, how much they liked to swear because it made them feel like tougher soldiers. The only man I never heard use foul language or discredit others was Hiker. I have to admit, I fell into the category of men who lost my temper when the men brought up Jen and would end up in a brawl resulting in a black eye that would cost me later. Hiker however would laugh it off when mocked, never raised his fists to another man in the unit and spoke with only the utmost respect for his comrades that we became.

"How do you keep so cool all the time, don't you ever get the urge to just fly off the handle?" I asked him one night as we'd returned to the barracks after a heavy evening of drinking, smoking, playing cards and chanting.

"Why would I fight my own? We're here to fight together, not against each other, what good would that do in the field, the enemy would have already won." He laughed, pulling off his boots and shirt and sinking into his bunk.

"Yeah but don't you ever feel like just letting it all out? I don't know how you keep it all in sometimes." I pulled the picture from under my pillow and starred at Jen, laughing uncontrollably as I threw her over my shoulder. We had been drunk ourselves that day, spent countless hours on the porch visiting a vast variety of emotions, laughter, tears, exhilaration and excitement. Ma came out of the house and did her usual stand and smile at the memories being made while capturing it in ink that I could keep in my pocket. She was a big believer in capturing a memory so that it could never be lost. I'd told them I was leaving for the army that day. Ma cried endlessly while Jen let all her anger and hurt fly out at me, I never stopped her, though we made up for it later as we climbed into bed and made love like it would be the very last time.

*

"Close your eyes," She ordered, her body weighing almost nothing above my own, "..and do not open them until I say so." She was smiling, taking pleasure in being completely in charge. "What if I open them?" I smirk, running my hand up her thighs, towards her back. She slapped me away playfully and I knew exactly where things were going, she was taking out her frustrations at me leaving, while devoting her love for me at the same time. It was an incredible mix of emotions that made my hands want to explore every part of her body. She'd been so insistent on me not signing up, though when Pearl Harbor had been attacked, she must have known that my departure was nearing closure. I'd had countless nights of terrifying dreams leading up to the attack and although she never said the words out loud, she knew America and all of its people had to do their part.

"For every time your eyes open Mr Mcclough, a piece of my clothing goes back on. She was taking the sexy domineering approach and by god was it working. Pulling her hair from her headscarf and throwing it to the floor, her hair bounced *effortlessly down my unbuttoned shirt she wore so well. "I believe your eyes are still open."* She says with a smile, every attempt at being domineering in full motion as she kisses my neck, moving her lips across my body as I close my eyes, every sense kicked into full power, not knowing where she will touch my body next with her soft playful lips or what she will do. She purposefully moves her body against mine, using my hands to run across her chest, pushing herself into my hands as she breathes in my ear and whispers, "If you are leaving for the army sir, I better make sure to give you a night that you won't forget."

*

Running my fingers over the black and white ink of the woman I had left behind I smiled and remembered I was doing it for her, not just myself. Hiker was oblivious to my wandering mind as he looked at me with a grin.
"The more I keep in, the better soldier I will be when it is needed." He winked, turned on his pillow and was snoring before I could even process the meaning. His way of thinking was unquestionably catching, he rubbed off on many men in the company and his life quotes he seemed to have stored in a filing cabinet in his mind ready for a time it could be well used, were ones that would be remembered by every person he had dealt them to.

Basic training came to a close at the fall of November 1942, where approximately eighteen thousand men had volunteered for the paratroopers, with roughly six thousand completing the course to move on to the next stage of training. Every private found their strengths, with myself and Hiker falling into the strength of using rifles. Every officer and private were able to complete any task within the platoon to at least a basic level. We understood the roles and responsibilities of a sergeant and a corporal and if it was needed for any of us to take their place we were fully in the position to do so. We were to head to Fort Benning Georgia where we would complete advanced airborne training from packing our own paratutes to jumping out of real C-47 planes rather than towers and mockup planes on the ground. In the mess hall the evening before I sat at a table with Hiker, Ranney, Salty and Taylor and celebrated the end of an era.

"We did it boys!" Shouted Ranney, throwing beer across the table in his celebration.

"Yeah, even with Sobel training us, who'd have thought it?" Laughed Salty as everyone lifted their mugs and banged them together with a cheer.

"We finally did it!" Cheered Hiker as he pats his hand on my back with a smile stretching from one side of his face to the other.

"It's good to see you so happy buddy." I shook his hand and embraced him as a brother, afterall, that is what we had become and not just the two of us, the company as a whole were a family of brothers that would see each other through combat.

"One step closer to home!" He laughed and began singing in chats with the rest of the men, though when I looked at him, I did not just see the incredible soldier that he was to become but a man who loved his family unconditionally that would do whatever it took to get back to them. He was to be a soldier that I so desperately wanted to be.

September 1942 - Birkenau

The fence stood at three metres high, running the full length of the camp at 17km, with concrete posts, ceramic insulators and metal lamps mounted on every third post for the aid of guards monitoring the grounds at night. Not only that but the fence had a total of 760 volts running through it, making it next to impossible for any prisoner to escape. The fence was what stood between me and Mother, so close, yet separated by equipment that would kill us within seconds. We were divided by two worlds of evil with no possibility of escape. The overwhelming difference of emotions tore through me leaving my head light and dizzy and speechless on the spot.
"Jakub! You're alive, you're alive Jakub!" She cried and fell to her knees, reaching her hands in my direction though being so far apart.
"I've been looking for you everyday Mama!" I wanted to cry with happiness that she was alive, yet I wanted to rage in anger at the German's for causing her suffering and making her so weak she was unable to stand unaided for more than a few brief minutes.
"Here, take this, you need to eat." She hands a piece of bread to a woman next to her who she held a lot of faith in to not steal it with how much hunger spread through the camp, who threw the piece of bread over the fence. I rushed to pick it up within seconds, if caught she would be punished severely for not only storing food in her shirt but also throwing it over the fence and

sharing it. I stuffed it in my shoe as I bent down and when I looked up again she was being dragged away by shouting SS men who began beating her in the back with their sticks. Mother's splitting cries rang through me as I stood unable to help her. With every strike to her body I felt on my own, thunderous blows that punctured the skin right through to the depths of the mind. Tears fell and my heart ached for the woman across the fence I was so powerless to save.

"Mama no!" I shouted, to which a man behind me put his hand over my mouth and moved me along in hope to not arouse suspicion of the guards making their way up the line. No matter how much I cried there was no possible way of me getting over the fence to pull her to safety. I was the most powerless I had ever been and it tore at my soul and left me with questions hurtling through my mind for the rest of the day at the Kanada. I needed to know she was okay, that they had not punished her by taking her life, not for giving her son a piece of bread, not for anything.

The work day lasted eleven long hours, with a break in between for the noon meal that usually lasted from twelve until one. I arrived at the Kanada that morning with my mother in my mind more than ever. Guilt washed over me leaving me unable to eat or perform tasks of sorting through prisoners clothing and possessions. On some days I would sort through the cases and pile up the belongings, photographs in one section, clothes in another, utensils and other miscellaneous in another and on some days, such as this day in particular, I would be instructed at roll call that I was on duty of unstitching clothing to be made into something more practical for German use, as well as finding anything of value that may have been stitched into the clothing as a hiding place such as money and jewelry. On some days when I had seen the SS use brutal force on prisoners unable to carry out their duties due to exhaustion, I would think of ways of using the needles and other tools at our fingertips to hurt the guards, I never had the courage to follow through with the scenarios that played out in my mind, I had seen what had happened to prisoners who had tried such acts and more often than not, it left them without their life. On the day I saw my mother for the first time since being separated at the platform of Birkenau, I thought of only her.

Nine hours into the work day I had barely sorted through any possessions, my mind wondered, walking amongst daydreams of different scenarios that could have happened to her.
"You know, not working will get us all into trouble." Comes a familiar voice from behind me. I snap back to reality as I turn and look into the face of a long departed friend.
"Henryk!" Before I knew what I was doing I had flung my arms around him and was squeezing him harder than his body would find pleasant given the petite and frail physique of his body.
"I'm sorry, I..I thought you were dead!"
"Well that's no way to think of an old buddy is it." He chuckles though cautiously, if the guards caught anybody laughing they

would become suspicious at what could possibly cause happiness in such bleak and dismal surroundings.

"What happened to you?" I asked, pulling a grey shirt from the pile and beginning to unstitch the seams to appear as though I was working.

"On my way back from work in the ghetto the guards grabbed my arm, pushed me towards the Umschlagplatz with hundreds of others." He says, following suit and sorting through a pile of men's trousers. "It was all so sudden, chaos leaking from every molecule of the air. Women and children were crying, people dragged from hiding, we were made to wait there until there were enough of us to fill the train cars to bring here. We waited days for the guards to round enough people up, by that point people were dying of hunger, dehydration, babies' cries faded, mens anger slithered away, until we were shoved on that dahm train and brought here." He shakes his head as he says the words, the memory of the night bleeding back to the forefront of his mind like an unwelcoming memory. "I started work in a camp next to this one when I arrived, repairing and making shoes, though until today I was moved here."

Working alongside Henryk made the long labor days more tolerable. I confided of the cruel and heartbreaking position I was living in everyday in regards to trying to get back to my mother and although there was nothing he could do to help me, he pushed me through the days reassuring me that when the allies reached us, my mother would be waiting for me, just as I was for her. It was many weeks before I saw her again at the fence, more frail than I ever thought possible, bruises visible on every inch of her skin. We were on the walk to work when I caught sight of her, waiting at the gate for what I knew was me. My heart raced and bounced between the walls of my chest, she was alive and regardless of her weak state I knew I had to be grateful for that.

"Jakub!" Came her soft, struggling voice from meters away.

"Mama!" I felt the emotion rip through me like a lion tormenting its prey. The anger and frustration boiled within me, I had the most desperate longing to be with her and knowing there wasn't a single thing I could do to make it happen sent mixed emotions colliding and crashing with one another inside me.

I stood at the fence and looked into her eyes, seeing the pain she was so desperately trying to hide.

"You have to keep going Jakub, you have to keep fighting and being strong. Promise me? Promise me now that you will keep going no matter what and never give up? Promise me!" She cried, tears rolling down her pale cheeks. Before I could answer I had been grabbed by the arm and pulled away. Mother's cries travelled through the fence and rang in my ears.

"No! Please!" She fell to the ground as I was pulled out of sight, confusion and fear taking over as I was pulled out the line of walking laborers.

"What exactly do you think you are doing?" Came the voice of the SS guard with his grip tightening on my arms. Something about him seemed familiar yet I could not place it. I had seen so many SS guards that it had become impossible to remember them all yet something about the man standing towering over me sent my mind into overdrive, studying his face and delving deep into my memories to try and place him within one.

"My Mama, I'm sorry." I say, sheltering my head for the potential blows coming my way. After several seconds of silence I look up to see him staring at me, no fists or hands heading in my direction to send me into extreme levels of pain.

"I've seen you before." He says, narrowing his eyes and as if a light bulb had suddenly been switched on above his head, his eyes widen. "You're the Jew from Warsaw, you had the medicine." The memory flooded back instantly. He had been the guard that stopped me on my way back from the hospital and spared my life when I was sure I would have been punished for breaking curfew.

"Why did you let me go?" As soon as the question had left my mouth I knew I had entered dangerous territory.

"Not all of us like what's happening here, we just don't have much choice, like you." His voice softens into almost a whisper, like his vulnerabilities were exposed on the outside. An overwhelming sense of confusion crashed around me like waves desperately trying to reach the shore. This could have been a trick and I was falling straight into his nicotine stained hands.

"My Mama is just on the other side of the fence, I just want to talk to her." I cried, my own vulnerabilities making an appearance before the SS guard standing before me. He eyes me up quizzingly, pinching the skin between his eyes and taking several moments before speaking again.

"You are assigned to the warehouse, yes?" He says, eyes darting between the shuffling prisoners making their way through the tired and trampled mud. I nod in agreement, excitement unexpectedly building with every possibility of it being crushed in seconds. "You bring me what gold you find tomorrow after Appell and I arrange for you to see your Ma. Do not get caught, I cannot take responsibility for you." He turns on his foot and begins to walk back down the line.

"Wait," I shout after him as he reaches a small handful of yards away. He turns back and motions his head to say *go on*.

"I don't understand why you are helping me. Is this a trick?" I don't know why I felt the need to ask, even if it was he would not have told me, yet the question still burned away at me, begging to be answered.

"I was assigned to Auschwitz, it was not a decision made willingly." He whispers, cautious as ever. "I work for my family, without them I would have no purpose, no real reason for being alive, just as I knew you made that trip to the hospital regardless of the risks, you did it for your family didn't you?" He pulls out a cigarette from his pocket and lights it, inhaling sharply. I nod again, something told me he was genuine however falling victim to the guards tricks could cost your life.

"We don't get a choice in being here, just as you don't. It is best to make the most of bad situations, there is really nothing more than can be done." With that he walks away and I walk to the Kanada feeling confused yet exhilarated. If there was even a small chance I could see Mother again I was going to take it, despite the consequences if I was wrong.

Work at the Kanada felt worthwhile that day, that despite the freezing cold that krept within the creases of my dirty striped uniform, I was not just working for survival, I was working to finally see my Mother again. I confided in Henryk, told him that day of the trade I would make with the guard. He was sceptical at first, told me I was falling head first into a trap, though upon further explanation he seemed to warm to the idea.
"I just don't understand why he would help you." Says Henryk, emptying the contents of a men's jacket to find cigarettes and some loose photographs. He pockets the cigarettes in little more than seconds and carries on as though it never happened.
"I don't really know either but I have to at least try, I'm not sure Mama can prove she is well enough to work much longer, I'm worried about her. Maybe seeing me will encourage her to keep going, this war can't go on much longer." I'd tried to convince myself that the war would be over soon but the truth was, nobody really knew. Even when the war was over, what then? Most had lost everyone they had, their wives, husbands, parents, their children and it was evident to see in those that

had fallen into themselves and given up. Happiness was leaked out of every person upon arrival at the camp and only the strong would survive it. You had to find the balance between becoming emotionless and forgetting the life we once had on the outside world and having something that kept you going.

Henryk kept watch for me that day and distracted the guards at risk of being beaten, so I could hide what gold I found in my clothes and clogs that were three sizes too big and had started to cut into my feet. Clogs were hard to come by in Auschwitz and were often a goldmine for trading, food being at the top of that list. If you could stop yourself from eating the three inch black bread on an evening during free time then it could be used to trade for other survival tools. In the first week of me arriving at Auschwitz-Birkenau, Binem and the other men in my bunk had told me of the black market and what was of value. I had managed to save my evening bread for three nights which I traded for a metal mug that would store the watery soup. The grainy coffee substitute had no taste and offered nothing against the hunger but nonetheless I reminded myself it would be beneficial in the long run. Those in possession of utensils were often given later portions with bigger pieces of vegetables, rather than failed attempts at trying to consume soup from cupped hands, to which it would leak out through fingers and be lost to the floor.

Clogs were not always available when coming from the *'showers',* so many were made to do without, meaning their feet would be exposed to the icy cold air during the night or the long hours stood in snow during the winter Appell. I never removed my clogs and slept with my mug to avoid the risk of theft that was always running high within the camp. As Henryk walked up to a guard he began showing the stitching inside a woman's jacket, asking questions he knew the answers to while trying to avoid the guards agitation and his truncheon making an appearance. As he held the conversation as long as he could I stuffed a gold necklace tightly into the inside pocket of my jacket that Henryk had shown me how to make. It was a great way of storing and hiding items that the German's had not yet caught onto, though when they did the consequences would be beyond imaginable.

"You are going to get us killed!" Cried the voice of a German Jewish prisoner, eyes wide and fearful at witnessing me pocket valuable items. His weak brittle frame shuffled away in an attempt to show no involvement.

"Only if they see you." I whispered, storing three gold coins in the inside of my pocket that gave a small *clang* as it hit the necklace. Looking over to Henryk I nod slightly to suggest the items had been pocketed. The system appeared to work for the rest of the day until the German Jew added complications.

"You steal items and for what? If you are caught, who is to say that we will not all be sent to the chimneys!" He cries in panic, keeping his hands busy in fear of SS guards and the Kapo, who were the first prisoners to arrive at the camp who were placed in positions of power over regular prisoners and they almost always showed it. "There is nothing stopping me from walking over there and telling them what you are up to!" I knew where it was going before the words could leave his mouth. It was the way of survival in Auschwitz, the only way some were able to eat or keep warm.

"Okay, tomorrow I will bring you my bread, just keep your head down, you haven't seen anything." I sigh at the thought, another night without food would certainly be painful but I knew it would prove worthwhile for the chance to see my mother again, if I was not being lured into a trap.

That night I stared at the wooden bunk above me with sounds of heavy snoring from exhaustion rattling through the barrack. Binem laid beside me humming a soft tune to himself at the frustration of other prisoners trying to sleep. He acknowledged their sighs though he was not a person to give into such signals.

"What are the chimneys?" I whispered over the constant screams of hunger coming from my stomach.

"That is where the weak go to die lad. The chimneys are what we work to avoid." He says, rubbing his temple, knowing the question would have been coming sooner rather than later.

"I know that but *what are they?*" I sat up on the bunk that caused frustration amongst the other men. When one person moved or turned over it meant the whole bunk had to follow suit due to the little quantity of room.

"I'm afraid I don't know anybody that has been sent there and returned to tell the tale. I've heard talk that they are the showers we are to fear, showers that *gas you*!" He emphasises the words like he is telling a thrilling and exciting story. "I came here with my wife and three children, I have not seen them since arriving here and something inside tells me that they were sent to the showers. Those chimneys," He points a finger in the direction, "Those are the remains of those we love, finally leaving the camp." The words haunt me, penetrate fear and shock through my skin.

"Why are they sent there?" I stare into his deep shadowed eyes waiting for answers I probably already knew.

"If they can't use you for work, why would they keep us alive? It is all part of Hitlers Final Solution, to cleanse Europe of our kind by using the worst killing machine imaginable." He appeared so calm given the words that were spilling from him.

"Are you not scared?" I asked, looking around at the sleeping men who were hungry and tired, stripped of their dignity and everything they once were.

"I have been here since the beginning, built this place up from the bricks and wood torn down from nearby villages. I avoided becoming part of the Kapo because my morals tell me I will not contribute to what is being done here if there is even the slither of choice. What happens to us is not our choice, we work to survive but I have grown to accept that what will happen will happen, being afraid of the inevitable will not change the course of what is our fate. There is only one way out of Auschwitz and that is out of those chimneys." He slumps his head back and shuts his eyes. He would not go down until his last breath, yet deep inside, he was one of the many that had given up hope. Maybe he was too old to try talk himself into a positive mindframe, or maybe that was his way of being positive, by not worrying over matters he could not change.

The next morning I woke up anxious with adrenaline pumping hard in my veins. At first bell I'd jumped out of bed, tidied the sleeping area, rushed to the front of the line to relieve and wash myself and was straight outside into the frosty snow that had fallen during the night. I kept my shoulders back, showing no sign of weakness or being too unfit for work with the bread hidden up my jacket sleeve that I had tied to my arm with a piece of string pulled from my striped trousers in the night. The gold jewellery and coins sat hidden in my inside pockets. I tried hard not to make a sound as I walked quickly into the courtyard. Appell lasted for hours, from early hours of the morning until every last prisoner had been counted and recounted. We were to stand as still as possible, show no sign of fever or exhaustion until we were given our labor details for the day. The SS mens boots crunched in the snow as they walked back and forth. Dr Mengele from the hospital camp was making his rounds and pulling sick prisoners from their lines. I'd heard the men talk about experiments that were carried out in the hospital camps that left prisoners severely ill or caused them death. I feared him more than I feared most of the guards and Kapo. Benim had told me of his friend Jaosz that had been chosen from roll call to be sent to the hospital camp with Mengele. He was one of the extreme few that had returned for his work efforts to be monitored afterwards. They were taken from Appell in a van to the hospital where painful experiments were conducted on them.

"Jaosz was chosen because of his exhaustion and weight. His liver was experimented on by Dr Kremer in the main camp. He never said what had happened to him, what they did, though he was in the Musselman state before he even went."

"What is the Musselman state?" I asked, intrigued.

"The poor physical condition of a prisoner, one that has no will to live. Some people call them the walking dead, or the wandering corpses. It pained me to see him so broken, so empty of willing to carry on anymore. Unfortunately when he came back he only lasted two days before whatever they had pumped into him killed him."

"Did he try to fight it?" I could feel the sadness pouring from within him at the mention of his good friend that was no longer by his side.

"Life simply does not wait for us to be prepared for challenges, it would not be a challenge if it did, merely a stepping stone. Life launches us into the depths of survival and sometimes with no warning. Jaosz had no warning, he was gone a long time before he went to those hospital wards." During Appell I thought of Mother and Aunt Lena and whether they had been experimented on like Binem's friend, or the twins that were taken at the platform. My heart sank in shock, knowing that it was more than possible that that was where the twins had gone.

I stood in the snow with items of value that would reunite me with Mother even if it was for a short time. My heart thumped violently in my chest, my nerves running at one hundred miles an hour at the risk of being caught. Appell lasted longer than usual that morning as prisoner after prisoner was chosen for experiments by the Dr's that patrolled the lines, making judgements on those that appeared too weak. I kept my shoulders back in a bid to look healthier than I felt. My legs shook under the strain of my body weight after days of not eating enough to simply stand for four hours in the snow that had started to blanket around us.

It felt like an eternity before we were given our work details and sent out to the day. I had been sent to the Kandada for another day of grueling hours with little to no food. When reaching the fence I looked for my mother, through crowds of shaved heads, through streams of floating prisoners to realise that she was not amongst them. A lump bore tenancy in my throat as I feared the worst. For those who even looked across the fence the SS guards hands would twitch towards their guns, yet I had somehow been able to manage it for as long as I had. I carried on walking, peering my eyes without turning my head, pleading with the air that she would appear.

"This way." Came the voice of the SS guard I had been waiting for while slowly walking to the Kanada. I followed behind him and turned behind the barrack in his path. When I was sure no prying eyes were in sight I quickly took out the gold from my jacket pocket and shoved them into his hands, waiting for the moment I would realise it had been a trick, my hiding place exposed and given up, my longing to see my mother crushed in just a few short seconds.
"Come." He whispered, heading in the direction of the latrines as he pockets the jewellery and coins quickly.

Upon entering the latrines I questioned if it would be the time I was going to be beaten within inches of my life, taught a lesson for believing that stealing from the Kanada would gain me privileges. He walks slowly up to the door inside and opens it, motioning his head for me to go inside. I stood fixed to the spot, unsure of what was going to happen.
"You have five minutes. I cannot risk any longer than that. Make it worthwhile." He stood at attention at the door and closed it behind me as I walked in revealing a sight that will forever haunt my dreams, wake me from my sleep in pools of sweat that would torment my memories for an unwelcoming duration of time. What I saw when I walked into that room ripped apart my soul and smashed it like glass..

November 1942 - Fort Benning, Georgia

We were moved to Fort Benning, adjacent to the city of Columbus in Southwest Georgia, the home of the U.S Army Infantry with the mission to produce the world's finest combat infantryman. Upon arriving we were thrown straight into parachute training through stages A to D. We completely skipped the first stage due to the 1st Battalion arriving first and being able to complete the physical exercises much more effortlessly than the Sergeants. With them being laughed at and mocked for being in much less physical shape than those they were teaching, the Sergeants spoke to the C.O and every company within the 506th Parachute Infantry Regiment were moved to stage B.

During our first week at Benning we would fast march to the packing sheds every morning where we had learned how to fold and pack our parachutes, to then head for the Frying Pan area for our midday meal. From there we would endure an afternoon of different exercises or learning activities such as jumping into piles of sawdust from mock airplane doors attached to a mock body of an airplane that stood four foot off the ground and on some days, jumping with a parachute from towers at thirty foot with a steel cable. We'd been training soldiers at Benning for six days when Hiker turned to face me after a long day of physical training and jumping from the thirty foot towers, with a smile on his face stretching from ear to ear.

"What are you so happy about?" I laughed, throwing a towel in his face and collapsing into my bunk with a heavy and exhausted sigh.

"Buck really showed them how to do it today didn't he?" He shook his head in disbelief and leaned back onto his pillow, closing his eyes in a sign of defeat for the day's hard training.

"You're not wrong, just picks it up straight away and does it like he's been doing it years." I say just as he walks into the sleeping hut placed on thin soil that made the place feel much worse than Toccoa. It probably would have been if it was not for the great company of the men and training that felt like we were edging closer to becoming a part of the airborne.

"Buck," I say, nodding my head as he slumps awkwardly on the end of my bunk and lights a cigarette. "Really gave it some today, think it showed Sobel a thing or two." We laughed at the thought as he nodded his head with an exhausted smile.

Hiker takes out the picture from under his pillow as he usually did on an evening and stares at it for numerous minutes with a soft smile.

"Do you ever stop looking at that thing?" He says, stubbing out his cigarette and lighting up another.

"This picture reminds me of why I must train harder, so I can make it back to them both." He smiles at the photograph as Buck lets out a sigh while rolling his eyes harmlessly. Amos Taylor, otherwise known to the men of Easy Company as *Buck,* was one of the 140 men that came from Toccoa as part of Easy

Company, 2nd Battalion, leaving behind his woman and Mother while himself and his three younger brothers were sent out to the army for training. He was a good, honorable man, that along with Darrell Powers, received the title of expert marksman for their skills in shooting. We had become friends that would become brothers right from the first meeting at Toccoa.

"You don't agree?" Smiles Hiker friendly to Buck.

Guess so, Ma made all four of us join different branches in the army so she wouldn't lose all of us at the same time, kinda made it feel real, that it's a war we're training for, it's realistic to believe that we might be the unlucky ones that don't." He shrugged his shoulders and rolled off the bed to head for his bunk, where he fell into his bed and looked as if he could have been asleep within seconds.

During the second week we entered stage C, that consisted of us making jumps from towers that stood at 250foot where we made numerous day jumps and one during the night. In order to learn how to dismantle our parachutes once we had landed. It wasn't until we reached D stage that we undertook our very first real parachute jump from C-47 Douglas planes. We were nervous, excited and exhilarated, some men were so ready to take that first jump that they were bounding in energy as we were waiting to be loaded onto the planes.

"Here we go fellas! This is it!" I shouted, patting the men next to me heavily on the back and laughing with excitement. We chanted, we sang, we joked and we laughed, all emotions possible dancing around us like a figure on ice. We had spent many hours the previous day packing and checking our parachutes and equipment until almost midnight, to be up and ready at five thirty for the day of jumps and yet there was so much excitement soaring through our veins we felt anything but tired. We took our experience from the towers 1,500 feet in the air, waiting in formation of twentyfour men for our turn to jump. One we had reached the designated height, the plane circled, the red light came on and everyone's hearts were in their mouths, excitement and fear fighting for the opportunity to be a leading emotion.

The Sergeant instructor's voice filled the cargo, "stand up and hook up!" So we did, attached the line to our backpack cover of our main parachute to the anchor line that ran the length of the cargo. The jump master's voice now, "Sound off for equipment check!" We knew it was still training but it also felt so *real*. Jumping out of the plane was happening, though it wasn't into a war and we still felt the realisation of what we were doing pulse through our veins as if we were as we shouted 'O.K' to our number being called for the check. We stood in formation, watching as man after man held onto the outside of the plane and made the jump, disappearing into the air to be followed by the next, then the next, the adrenaline took over. I had never jumped from a plane before in my life. This time last year I was a librarian and now, I was a training airborne infantryman about to take my very first leap out of an army plane. There was no time for thinking of home, as Hiker stood at the door, hands on the outside of the plane and disappeared within seconds. A tap on the leg told me it was my turn. I stood in the door, hands on the outside, looking out at the horizon and not at the ground as our training had instructed and leaped into the air, taking my breath and sending my legs like jelly that could not be controlled.

In what felt like seconds, the static line that was attached to the hook on the anchor line pulled back the cover of my chute and the break cord that was attached to the apex of the chute pulling the parachute out of the pack, resulting in my parachute parting and the prop blast distending the chute. I could feel the opening revelation as I floated through the air, down towards the ground, all thoughts absent other than the incredible feeling of what I was doing at that exact moment. I looked around me, saw the sky littered with parachutes holding cheerful men '*woooo*'ing and '*yeahhhhhh*'ing through the sky. A war was raging around us, bringing the world to its knees that it so desperately tried to withstand, yet that day, at that very moment, we let it all fade away to feel the rush of excitement, happiness and exhilaration. Just for those moments we felt like the young men we were, all of nineteen and twenty that were joined up to the army that would stomp out any sign of boys to transform us as men. Later that day we completed the jump again yet this time, I had no nerves as I waited in line or stood in the doorway, I felt a longing to do it again, like an addiction for more that I could not suppress.

When December 25th came around everything felt completely new.

"First Christmas for us all away from family, yet most of us chose to be here. Least we get a good meal though." Said Buck, biting down on a strip of turkey that took just seconds to disappear. We had completed another jump the day before on Christmas Eve and been given the day off on Christmas from all training and we made the most of it the best way we knew how, smoking, drinking, eating, joking and laughing. There were no animosities between men on Christmas day, as much as it felt like just a day off from work it was a day that we spent as the newly formed family that we had become.

"Jen will be lonely today but I'm sure Ma will keep her entertained." I'd said to Hiker who was working his way through his dinner like it would be taken away from him. He saw me watching him as I started to laugh and patted him on the back.

"What? It's good food!" He laughed and picked up his beer to toast with mine. "Merry Christmas Mcclough." I toast him as I down the rest of my beer and join in with the loud and boisterous chants coming from the rest of the men in the mess hall.

The following day, on December 26th we were filled with the utmost pride and gratitude when we were represented with our wings. What we had trained so hard for over the last six months meant we were now a qualified and fully trained parachutist and as they pinned the silver wings on our uniforms, we drank and we sang like we never had before. We had done it, faced the training and braved the jumps, hurdled our fears to get to this exact moment. This was not however the end of the line, this was merely a stepping stone to the bigger picture, yet we delved into the reward as much as possible and celebrated as parachutists of the 101st Airborne, chanting our battle cry, *Currahee, We Stand Alone Together!"*

December 1942 - Birkenau

"Mama! What happened to you?" I cried, flinging my arms around her neck and causing her to flinch against the freshly littered bruises staining her skin. Tears pricked in my eyes, of shock, hurt and anger. Her face had been completely disfigured through what I assumed was countless beatings and hits to the face with more than what could be done with a person's hands. Her skin looked battered though not just from beatings, it looked as though chemicals swam within her veins, poisoning her from the inside out.

"I was working in the kitchens and the Kapo caught me trying to hide food. Sent me straight to the guards. I'll be fine, I want to know how you are. My poor boy." She fell into tears as she forced her head up to meet her eyes with mine. "You must be hungry." She says, wiping away a tear from a face I no longer recognised. Her beautiful hair no longer bouncing with curls at the end but shaven and holding deep scars that still looked fresh. She takes out a piece of sausage from the dress of her pocket and hands it to me shakily. "They didn't find it all." She motions again for me to take it to which I silently refuse. I look into her tired and heavy eyes as though I had forgotten how to speak.

"You need it more than I do Mama, please, I want you to eat it. Did you get these cuts from trying to get food for me?" I asked, unsure of whether I was overwhelmed with love for her or angry that she could put herself at so much risk.

"Please, take it Jakub. I do not have the strength to get through another work day, my body simply will not allow it. What is more important is what I did to get here. The guards, they can promise anything if they have a body to use in return."

"Why are you telling me this Mama?" Tears were falling down my face faster than I could wipe them away.

"I tell you because they have no limit, they have power and they will use it to get exactly what they want. If you refuse, you put your life in their hands." I watch her as she leans against the cold wall in defeat, my heart screaming for me to make things right, to save her. "I want you to promise me that no matter what, you will do everything you can to survive, you will never give up. Promise me Jakub!" It would have almost been a shout if her lungs would have allowed her.

"I promise Mama but you need to do the same, I cannot survive here knowing that you aren't." I turn away and pace the floor, pondering over possibilities of how to save her, how to make the war go away, only to be left answerless.

"I love you with every single ounce of my being, your Papa would be proud of you. My biggest fear that eats away at me every day that I am in here is that we live on this earth without each other. I worry that you need me and I am gone but you have to remember, me and your Papa will always be around you, do you understand?" She says, resting her eyes, sleep must have been deprived from the women's camp too.

"I understand Mama but we will get through this together and when the war is over we can go home, we can listen to your radio again and eat your Challeh and everything will be fine again." I stop pacing and look at her tired face, "I love you Mama." I plant a kiss on her forehead to realise that she does not respond.

Shaking her gently I attempt to wake her up, beg for her to wake up and tell me again that she loves me. The guard walks into the room and sighs heavily, though not surprised by what he sees.

"Come on kid." He pulls at my arm as I cling on to Mother, unable to let her go knowing that it would be the last time I ever saw her. I couldn't comprehend it, I couldn't begin to imagine a world without her in it.

"Mama!" I screamed her name and begged that she open her eyes, that she was alive. The guards hand covered my mouth as he carried me out the latrines and calmed me down with one of his cigarettes. My soul felt like it had split into two, broken at every possible seam with no opportunity of ever being fixed again.

"She can't die! She can't die in there! Not in here! Not in this place!" My cries had turned soul splitting, heart wrenching and painful.

"I'm sorry." It was all he was able to say, there was no way he could have saved her though I took my anger out on him, he was the closest person I could blame and I needed somewhere for it to go.

"This is your fault!" I screamed through pouring tears. "Why do you all do this to us?" I began hitting into his chest, hard fists one after another. I could feel my heart shatter within my chest, pouring with pain and begging to be released. He just stood there, letting me release the pain in the only way I could until I dropped to my knees and let the world swallow everything around me.

I worked that day because I had no other choice. I had not entered the musselman state because I could still feel hot burning, raging anger that would suddenly change to pitiful cries that echoed through the Kanada. The SS guards had twitched over their guns at the disturbance and annoyance to them, though the guard who had helped me see my mother for the last time, who never told me his name, would walk over and whisper in their ear that made them lower their hands and walk off with a hunch. Through breaks of cries and anger I would question over and over why he had helped me, on more than one occasion. Maybe he was different to the others, yet I found it incredibly difficult given our circumstances to believe that there were good men who were part of the SS. It did not take long for the small German Jew to ask for his slice of bread in return for keeping my secret. Pulling it from my sleeve I placed it in his hand without saying a single word to him and walked away.

That night I was given my three inches of black bread and a spoonful of margarine. It was mine to have, no saving for trades or exchanges, yet I could not face eating.

"You need to eat Jakub, we don't get enough food as it is." Says Binem who is accompanied soon after by Franck, a French Jew in his mid forties that played for the camp orchestra during morning and evening roll calls. They sat at my feet on the end of the bunk eating their bread and accompaniment while trying to get me to eat my own that lay abandoned on the bed.

"Keep walking." Says Franck who had spotted one of the other men eyeing up my bread. I had no desire to engage in conversation, or eat, or even sleep. I was sinking into a black hole of emptiness and I just wanted Mother to be there with me, to play her music and dance around the barrack telling me that we would soon be going home. It was so far from ever being possible that the thought almost tore at my mind. Binem placed the bread inside my sleeve to which I made no effort to respond.

"Poor kid," Franck whispers as they jump off the bunk and head to the latrines in hope they would make the line in time before the second gong, which meant lights out, anyone out of bed at this time would fall into the hands of the Kapo's or the block elders that would be sure to turn you into the guards for a reward of extra food.

Before the sun had barely risen the next morning the gong sounded at five thirty, indicating another long and painful day. I had slept not nearly enough to not feel the heaviness in my eyes, like they were attached to bricks that were pulling against gravity. As soon as my eyes opened I remembered where I was, remembered Mother lying in the latrines, motionless, beaten and weak. I remembered she had gone and I was truly on my own. I had no desire to eat the bread stored in my sleeve. On an evening, the three hundred gram bread was suggested to be halved for breakfast. Very few were able to wait, meaning the watery coffee was the crueling substitution until the soup at noon. I could not face the bread, or the coffee, or the soup. I kept the bread inside my sleeve though the soup I gave to Binem and Franck who guiltily let the dull tasting substance pour into their stomachs.

"No point in it going completely to waste when we are hungry." exclaimed Franck, who patted me on the back reassuringly and smiled in a way to say *I'm here when you're ready to talk.*

I entered the Kanada that day with mixed emotions. I was sad, angry, hurting, wanting to scream from the top of my lungs to release the pain that was sitting so heavily on my chest. As I sorted shoes and suitcases into piles I was hit hard in the back by a male Gestapo guard, chunkier than the rest of us from the food he reveled in on an evening, carrying no guilt for punishing his own people to receive it. I flinched though I did not say a word.

"Faster!" He shouted, hitting me in the back again, to which I remained silent, refusing to show any kind of emotion towards the people I saw as traitors. Not all the Gestapo were as bad as the others, some took a lighter approach, whereas others would beat you to an inch of your life to impress the SS guards and receive privileges in return.

"You're no better than them!" Cried an old man just a few feet away, pointing in the direction of a group of guards huddled near the gates, smoking cigarettes and laughing at prisoners falling in the mud from exhaustion. "Can't you see he has lost someone! You should be ashamed of yourself!" Shouted the old man pointing a finger in the Gestapo's face in anger, blood running to his shaven and scarred head. Fear flowed through me like a burning river, desperate to be put out.

"Stop, please, I will work faster, you will get yourself killed!" I shrieked at the man, who had obviously lost all sense of patience and control of his emotions. The Gestapo walked over to him in an alarmingly calm tone and stood before him in tense silence. The old man hesitated on the spot yet refused to remove eye contact, refusing to show fear. With a sudden swing of his arm he hits the old man in the chest with his stick that causes him to fall to the ground in cries of pain. Within seconds everyone including the guards had stopped working and was watching the scene play out before us. My legs trembled and anger boiled so deep within my skin I lunged forward, "Stop! We will work faster, just stop!"

"Unless you want to be next little boy, move aside!" His voice vibrated through the air as he pushed me away. The man stood up shakily holding his chest and gasping for the air that had escaped from his chest. With another swing of the stick the Gestapo hit the old man again and again, until he could no longer stand and had to be carted away by other prisoners.

Unfortunately it was not the only violence within the camp, if anything it was one of the more lighter punishments. Binem had told me of the more severe punishments that required the cells in the main camp. "Well there are four standing cells in block eleven, which they cram four people inside with only room to stand and two inches of a hole for air. Then there are the regular cells and dark cells where you would be most likely to sleep on the floor and put to death by starvation. Then there are the other punishments, in the courtyard outside block eleven you'd either be lined up against the *Death Wall* and shot or flogged while counting the number of blows in German, if you lose count, right back to the beginning you go and I can tell you those bullwhips feel like the life is being knocked straight out of you. Then there's The Post.."

"What's *The Post*?" I'd asked, shocked at what I was hearing. I had been so naive to believe that everything I saw in Birkenau was all that was happening, I had never been so wrong.

"The post is a punishment that every single prisoner should fear. They tie your hands behind your back and hang you from a post by your tied up hands so your feet don't touch the ground, most people pass out from the pain and when your shoulders rupture, that's it, they send you to the chimneys because you can't work no more."

"Why do they do such horrible things to us?" I'd cried turning in the bunk and annoying three other prisoners.

"We are all part of their master plan, use us for what they can then dump us in the ground. Well I could say a few things about Hitler's *Final Solution*.." He'd said, using a mocking voice, "We are living inside his killing machine and there ain't no way out I'll tell ya. Most of these punishments, the cells, the basement jail, all of them, the majority of the time they are used because people try to escape. Make an example out of um' see, those that are caught are either sent to the cells or sentenced to hanging right before our very eyes to set an example, show there ain't no getting out of here, not unless it's through the chimney." Scoffed Binem in hate towards the Germans.

"How do you know all this?"

"I was sent to Auschwitz main camp not long after I arrived here, guards decided I worked too slow and made an example out of me." He lifted his striped shirt over his head to reveal the many lines of deep scars imprinted in his back. "They flogged you?" I gasped, unable to hide the shock in my voice.

"Yep and I saw the punishments of others when I was there too, hence why I keep my head down, work as I should and come back and curse about them on a night. Only way to do it."

After that day at the Kanada I spoke only when I nèeded to, worked through the pain of hunger and exhaustion and went back to the barracks after the seven clock roll call and cursed the German's for enduring so much pain and suffering on us. There was simply nothing else that could be done. Auschwitz was a killing machine and we were making it run, keeping it moving and in motion yet powerless to stop it. Every night I closed my eyes and thought of Mother, wished by some miracle she could come back and take me away from the cold, damp, typhus ridden camp that I now called my home. Unfortunately, Auschwitz would be my home for too many years before I would leave.

December 1942 - Coronado California USA

It felt like centuries since I had placed a pen on paper and let the words flow from my mind into the ink that spilled before me as I struggled to find the words to express how much I had missed Ma and Jen in those moments I returned. I locked them both in my embrace, never wanting to let go. It had only been six months but during that time it had felt like my life had completely changed. Not only was I no longer Pete the Librarian, I was a qualified parachutist of the 101st Airborne for the United States Army and the confidence that radiated from me and left a shining glow that even mountains couldn't crush easily. I felt honourable, that I was a man serving his country rather than cowering within it.

Colonel Sink had held a regimental parade that gathered all the men around him as he stood raised on a platform, stating that we were members of the finest regiments in the United States Army and as a result, in the world. He stood on the platform and delivered news that changed our Christmas from an ordinary day off, to one that made us want to throw our arms around him and squeeze him in gratification. We were being sent home on a ten-day furlough to carry on with the notion of military life, care for our appearances and adding on at the end, *'stay out of jail.'* The ten days I was home felt the shortest duration of time I had ever experienced. Time seemed to slip away in what felt like moments before I would need to head back to Georgia.

It would be fair to say that I had not missed the in-laws visits every fortnight which I felt I had to do while back, yet Bill Stones held out his old and wrinkled hand and shook it fiercely and proudly for a man of his age. "Knew you could do it son. Proud of you, really." I could tell from the look in his eye as he shook my hand that he held a great deal more respect for me than that of before I had left for training. Something inside me told me that he missed serving for his country and it wasn't until that moment I understood why. The feeling of incredible improvement within yourself when completing what you have in the army is one that could never really be described in words and I had been using words my whole life for that very purpose, to create meaning and understanding. The feelings I held at that moment were beyond possible to fit into words and I enjoyed every part of it. I had become the man I had been so desperately aiming to be, all within just six months. Lily Stones was still her uptight and pompous self yet she managed to force a smile and congratulate me on my successes. I knew it wasn't genuine, her hate for me had burnt too deep to ever change but we knew it would be impossible to avoid disputes if she had done anything else. I offered a fake smile back myself in gratitude and offered my thanks as we spent the evening talking of my training, including jumping from the planes that Bill roared in excitement about, throwing his hands into the air with a mighty *'Go on!'* Deep down I knew that he missed his days in combat, moreso to get away from the judging and piercing glares of the wife he was stuck with and Jen knew it too but we played happy families for the sake of politeness and returned home at the end of the evening, Ma sleeping peacefully in her room as we fell into bed and made love like it was our very first time.

*

"Just look at you! I knew you could do it boy!" Will had made his way across town to congratulate me during my time home and it was a welcoming visit I had plenty of time for. Jen and Ma had gone out of their way to make an appetising dinner that would line our stomachs before the alcohol was heavily brought out that evening. Her parents were due round within the hour and I decided I'd stick close to Will's side to avoid unpleasant runningin's with her Mother. The neighbors from all up the street were to join the party who had welcomed me home with banners and cheers, sending my sense of pride in overload.
"I haven't actually done much yet Will, just the training." I replied, shaking his hand and attempting to stay humble, though the beaming pride for what I had accomplished could be seen through the smile that had never left my face.
"Oh don't be submissive with me, I know what the training is like, you should be proud!" He says, taking a glass of whiskey from Jen as we both take seats on the porch.

"I have to say, it was something else." I wrapped my coat around me as the winter air blew around my body, though it was not completely unwelcoming. I felt relaxed and energised for the first time in six months and even though I was to return, I was enjoying every minute of being back.

"Well, I want to hear all about it, from start to finish!" He says, lifting his glass up in a toast. "To your deserving successes!" I couldn't help but smile, as I sat for hours delving into every experience of the last half a year.

"Sobel is hard work, can't tell his left foot from his right half the time, I really don't know how he got the job in the first place." I laugh, as I top up our fourth glass of the night.

"Ah! Get people like him in every battalion since the start of history. Most of the time it's not what you know but *who* you know. Take him with a pinch of salt my boy, he can't use punishment against you if there's nothing to punish!" He says it with a finger in the air, pointing it at me with every word said, like each was filled with experience and wisdom. As the sun disappeared behind the trees we made our way inside to exchange polite words with all the neighbors, family and friends that had been enjoying the flow of drinks that had been a long time coming since the depression.

Throughout the night people had questions they urged me to answer, *what is it like? Is it terrifying jumping out of a plane? When will you be home again?* The night was one that was much needed that released all the tensions of the war that people had been carrying. As the last guests left I closed the door and saw Ma sleeping peacefully in her armchair, her favourite book sliding out of her hand that she had fallen asleep reading. She had taught me everything I knew from being polite and giving, to always practice my studies, never give up on life despite how hard it might get. She did it all while doing it alone and as I watched her sleep peacefully, I kissed her head and carried her to her room. Pulling the blanket over her shoulders I knelt down next to her bed as she softly slept.

"I couldn't have done this without you Ma." Placing a gentle kiss on her forehead I stood and left the room, silently thanking the old and frail woman that slept before me, for all the life lessons that had got me as far as I had.

It was day three of my furlough when Ma fell ill. A rapid fever had taken over her body and left her bedbound, unable to care or aid for herself. I did what I could, bought the medicine she needed, placed cool towels on her head to bring her temperature down, yet nothing appeared to subside the fever that spread like wildfire through her body. Jen did all she could as a nurse, though during the night the fever had turned to an aggressive form of pneumonia that left her struggling to breathe as the air sacs in her lugs began to fill with liquid, resulting in an angry cough that would not subside. Just two days later her lips had turned blue, she was almost completely unable to breathe and suffered from severe chest pains. I sat at her bed the entire time, holding her hand as she had done with me as a young boy when I came down with the cold or flu.

"You gotta keep fighting this Ma, you have to." I cried, holding her hand in mine and stroking the hair out of her red and tired face. She turned her head slowly in a combination of coughs and wheezes and managed a small but loving smile as she looked at me.

"You listen to me Peter." It was evident that speaking had become a strenuous task yet I knew what she was going to say was important to her, quite possibly something I would not want to hear. "You are a man now, I have taught you everything I possibly can about life, how to be kind and gentle, how to stand your ground when you need to, there is nothing left to learn from me now. Do you remember the song I would sing to you, when you were a boy?" She takes a breath and puts her blue lips together to sing me the song she always sang, dancing around the room with the utmost happiness radiating from her very bones, igniting the atmosphere with her energy. *"Please don't be offended, if I preach to you awhile, tears are out of place in eyes that were meant to smile."* A tear runs down my cheek as she falls into a pit of coughs, fighting for the energy she once had.

Wiping my face that left room for more tears of happy memories, I dropped the needle on the record player, playing her favourite song, *Marion Harris, It Had To Be You*, that filled the room with the woman's voice that brought a smile to Ma's face as she closed her eyes to let the words and memories surround her and her hand tightening around mine.

"There's a way to make your very biggest troubles small, here's the happy secret of it all."

*

1928

"What happened to Daddy, Mama?" I'd asked, tucked in bed like a cocoon with Ma sitting next to me on the bed. Her face fell, as though a dreaded question had been asked she knew would come one day. Her eyes met mine as she pursed her lips and took a number of seconds to put together an explanation.

"Well Peter, he was a very good man, always doing what he could for everyone around him. He felt like he wanted to do more, make a difference." Her eyes glaze over as if lost in his memory. "He enlisted for the army, to do good for his country. He sacrificed his life to save many others and I can tell you, nothing really beats that in terms of being honourable." Tears prick her eyes though she doesn't let them fall.

"Do you miss him?" I asked, cocooning my six year old self further into the covers to block out the cold that tried to creep in. Ma smiled as her eyes filled with tears, eager to fall and let her emotions be worn on the outside. She held it together better than anyone I ever knew.

"I miss him terribly Peter, though his memory will forever be alive as long as we remember him. He left for the army just before you were born, he was very excited when I told him I was expecting you." She reaches under the bed and pulls out a box containing several old and crumpled letters. "I wasn't going to give you these until you were a little older, though I suppose you have reached an age of wanting questions answered. This one.." She said, smiling down at the handwriting on the paper and brushing her finger over the words, "..was the letter he wrote back to me when he found out we were to have you." She hands me the letter with a gentle sigh. Running my eyes over the words once written by my father in a battlefield, feeling the cold and brisk air stab at his skin, wounded and crying men surrounding him as they longed to be back home. He was excited and happy to say the least that he was to become a father, adding further purpose to him returning. He never did return and Ma was left to raise me single handedly while suppressing every ounce of hurt and pain to give me the very best life she could.

"Do you think one day I could be in the army, just like Daddy?" I asked as she took hold of my hand and squeezed it in hers.

"I think that you can be anything you want to be in life, as long as you allow your mind to believe that you can." She kisses me on the head and stands to make her way out of the room.

"Mama, will you sing me the song that he used to sing to you, until I fall asleep?" I'd sat up, longing for her to say yes, to fill the air with his memories as though he was here, so I could feel his presence like all the boys at my school who I'd see hugging their Father's. I wanted that too and the only way I could was through her voice.

"Look for the silver lining, whenever a cloud appears in the blue, remember somewhere the sun is shining and so the right thing to do, is make it shine for you." The words dance around the room as her soft and gentle voice fills the air with his memory as though he was back with her, singing the words as I drifted into a peaceful sleep, dreaming of my father and following in his footsteps.

*

1942

The memory was welcoming, reminding me of who I was, what I had achieved and why I had tried so hard to be the man I was. The record spins on the turntable, spinning with no notion of time like I was taken back to a time the world appeared so much more giving. As she sang the words, *"So always look for the silver lining and try to find the sunny side of life…"* It was at that moment her grip loosened on mine. She had walked into the memory with me, surrounded by my father she had been so strong living without. She walked into his arms again, knowing she had contributed to the life I had in only the most fulfilled ways.

September 1943 - Birkenau

We crowded around the smuggled radio hidden beneath the floorboards of Hans' bunk. He was a German Jew sent to Birkenau in early January of 1942, transferred to our barracks in March 1943. His nature was strong, not easily broken at the hands of the Nazi's and we looked up to him for reassurance when Auschwitz got the better of us. His old age meant nothing when it came to working hard to keep his life going, he would tell us on an evening while eating our black bread and discussing progress on the warfront that despite his many years on the earth, he was still not fiished yet and no Nazi would tell him his time was up. Two men would stand by the door, watching for the Kapo doing his rounds, ready to alert us of their presence so the radio could be placed back under the floorboards and out of sight. Crackling the radio to receive a signal we wait in anticipation for an announcement on the warfront. Nobody spoke a word, the barrack was eerily silent as though it had been long since abandoned. Suddenly the voice of General Eisenhower flooded our ears.

'Italy has signed an unconditional armistice with the Allies...' Men suddenly began smiling, hugging one another and celebrating as quietly as possible so not to be heard, yet joyful enough to give us hope that we were closer to reaching the end of the war with a German defeat.

"Shhh.. listen, there's more." Hushed Hans who moved his ear closer to the radio to listen. '*The surrender was signed five days ago in secret by a representative of Marshal Pietro Badoglio, Italy's prime minister since the downfall of Benito Mussolini in July. The Italian Government has agreed to end all hostilities with the United Nations. All Italians who now act to help eject the German aggressor from Italian soil will have the assistance and support of the United Nations.*'

"Kapo!" Shouted Franck from the door. Panicking, we rushed around trying to hide the radio, replace the floorboard and put his belongings back over the top. Even as the Kapo walked through the barrack, tapping his stick along the beds as we lay looking asleep, we were smiling inside that the allies were taking control. In February we had heard of the German's defeat as they had marched into Russia. The Soviets had stopped the German advance into Stalingrad Russia, which was a turning point for the whole of Europe. We had begun to see light, that the allies were winning, slowly but surely and it gave us hope that one day the war would be over.

In April a number of Polish men were housed in our bunks with very little space to occupy them. We shared beds, blankets and mattresses yet it was not always possible to save everyone from the cold during the brisk nights that bit at your skin. A man by the name of Marek had come from Warsaw Poland and told us of an uprising that had been led by the underground resistance to liberate Warsaw from the German Army.

"What happened?" I'd asked, intrigued as to what had happened in the city I had come from. Warsaw had been long out of my mind since arriving at Auschwitz. I thought of home on many nights that I lay amongst hundreds of men, fighting to stay alive in conditions that made it impossible, yet it had also started to feel like a dream. It felt so long ago that I was living at home, untouched by a war or the bombs that rained upon us that some days I simply felt that Auschwitz was my home.

"The Soviets were advancing, we needed to take back control of Warsaw before they reached us. I'd attended all of the underground meetings with the Home Army, offered my hand in anything to stop them and we were promised aid by the Soviets who had encouraged us to do it. Unfortunately many lives were lost, thousands of people died to bring justice that I am afraid didn't really come." He shook his head, hanging it in respect for all the people who had sacrificed to make Warsaw free again. "The Uprising failed because of the lack of promised support from the Soviets, British and American unwillingness to demand that Stalin extend assistance to our ally. The Soviets advancement into Poland stopped on the Vistula River, it just wasn't enough." I thought of my friends that could have still been in Warsaw, if they had survived the deportations, extensive work days or lack of food and shelter. The thought bit down hard at my chest, the not knowing while we were caged away made everything feel so much more worrying. We were locked away, unknown to the world outside, as many thought and all we had to rely on was the radio that we would be put to death for if found as well as the word of new inmates.

We'd huddled around the radio when the allies had taken the island of Sicily from the axis and we had celebrated, so hearing that Italy had surrendered brought further hope that we desperately needed to carry on, to not give up or let the German's take our lives. The joyful celebration never lasted long, we were always reminded of the brutal conditions when a prisoner was beaten to death or stolen in the night by cold or hunger.

"We'll get through it you know kid, the allies are winning." Hans had told me one night as I struggled to get warm. I'd tried to cut out emotion, to not feel anything as it left you vulnerable to defeat in Auschwitz but some nights were more difficult than others. The screaming pain in our stomachs would override anything positive we had tried to put in place to survive.

"I don't think I can take much more." I'd said, pulling my uniform tight around my body to ease the cold that shook my body through the night.

"What other choices do you have, hmm?" He was looking straight at me with a stern look on his face, sympathy far from in sight. We were all in the same situation and he made no effort to hide the fact. "You going to roll over and let them take you? The allies are out there fighting them back and you just want to give up?" He shook his head in dismay, as if disappointed. "Then I am afraid we will not be celebrating the victory together at the end will we?" I knew what he was doing, yet the thought of celebrations after the war was over was a feeling of bittersweet. We would all be overwhelmed and relieved at the end of such suffering but we had lost our families, our friends and everyone we loved, how could we celebrate that?

"It feels like the war is never going to be over." As I moved within the bunk everyone else followed suit, much to their discomfort and aggravation at being disturbed.

"We're not the only ones living like this you know. Britain has suffered too, the air attacks, the bombs, children being evacuated and separated from their parents, food and clothes rationed, lives lost. There is no comparison to who has it worse, we must all push through together, your life is important, just as every single other person is and just because we are not in control of situations right now, does not mean you are not in charge of your own survival. That my friend is down to you." He pats me on the leg gently and stands to make his exit to his own bunk.

"That does not mean we cannot feel though, Hans. It is impossible to stay positive in a place like this."

"No but it is possible to keep going, if you allow your mind to believe it." He smiled and nodded his head, indicating the end of the conversation as he walked away.

Auschwitz resembled the root of all evil compressed and stored within one camp that we could not escape from. Every single day that we opened our eyes to start the routine all over again, we saw death, violence, hunger and pain. I wanted nothing more than to be able to see something positive in each new day, though Auschwitz made that impossible. I watched as the people I had become so fond of deteriorate to nothing, crippled by the pain of hunger, crushed by the emotional strain of the muselmann state, all while turning to bone, the size of walking matchsticks that would resemble the walking dead.

The allies were perhaps winning against the axis, yet to us our lives were slipping away with each new day, wondering if the world knew about us and if they did, why was nobody coming to save us? The most difficult part was trying to believe there would be something I would leave the camp for if we were saved. I had lost everyone, Mama, Aunt Lena, Kasper, Grandpa, Grandma and Papa. What would I do after the war if I was to survive it? It wasn't long before it took over me, left me with no will to want to survive, I just was. I was trudging through each long day trying to get to the next, hoping that one day it would be over, yet not trying desperately hard to ensure that tomorrow came. I was to see another year in Auschwitz-Birkenau before situations changed and whether they were for the best, I was completely in the unknown.

September 1943 - Brooklyn Naval Shipyard, NYC Harbor

The sky was lit up in fluorescent pinks and oranges the night the ship pulled away from the harbor that captured the prayers of every man silently confining in its confidence. We had been lined up in single file to walk the gangplank, carrying our barrack bags and weapons as we stepped onto the Samaria, an old India mail liner and passenger ship converted into a troop transport designed to hold 1,000 passengers and resulting in 5,000 troops being boarded inside. Our names were called with a marker signing us present. Some men knew how to get out of going, with sickness or illnesses that would require them to stay behind, though most, including myself and Hiker stepped aboard the ship that took us closer to Hitler's war.

We were part of the 101st Airborne, considered fit to fight after nine months of training and exercises. We had the finest performance record in the whole 2nd battalion and the title came by crossing boundaries in training most would think impossible. When returning from our ten day furlough some of the privates were unable to adhere to the strict instruction given by Colonel Sink. We were not to return late. Nine men learned the hard way that those instructions were no joke. In a public display of humiliation their wings were stripped, uniforms demoted and were condemned to the regular infantry as punishment. Despite the passing of Ma, I knew I had to carry on my father's legacy and return to Easy Company.

Upon returning we were moved across the Chattahoochee River to the Alabama side of Fort Benning for training that concentrated on house-to-house fighting, learning and demonstrating explosions, firing blanks and other privates and throwing smoke grenades that we would understand how to move and fight amongst. While there we made our sixth jump, the first being with rifles. The rush never seemed to fade, with each one making us feel as alive as we had ever been. It is safe to say that moving across the river was of beneficial improvement, beds were comfortable, the food was better and the movie theater meant that those of us who longed for entertainment could somehow fulfill the desire.

By March, we were moved to Camp Mackall in North Carolina, with heated barracks and beds with mattresses, five movie theaters, six spacious beer gardens that many men would suffer at the hands of whiskey or a provoking Easy Company private, three 5,000 foot runways on an airfield and a hospital containing 1,200 beds. Camp Mackall was the home to the Airborne Command with training strengthening further more, with jumps with rifles and other small arms and light machine guns and a bazooka that had to be jumped in one piece. It took two men to split the 60mm mortar and its base plate, while being attached with ammunition, hand grenades, food, maps and high explosives to make the jumps. Afterwards we were faced with multiple days in the woods undertaking exercises such as quick troop movements and operating behind enemy lines as large forces. We were under the command of Sobel, who didn't know his left ear from his right ear, meaning we had lost count the times he would become lost during exercises because of his inability to read maps. The hate towards him grew in camp from the men of the company and most would think up blissful scenarios of how to take him out on the battlefield.

Regardless of heavy training and the constant feeling of exhaustion, May swung around quicker than expected, which saw us packing our barrack bags to join other companies of the 506th for a stop-and-go train ride to Sturgis, Kentucky. Most men were delighted and not just at the coffee and doughnuts at the depot but the girls of the Red Cross that delivered our last comfort for the foreseeable month ahead. Young girls were everywhere and for men who craved a woman's touch from being surrounded by men for so long, fleurtations were high. We were marched into the countryside from then and although we pitched up pup tents for sleeping barracks as well as dug our own latrines to relieve ourselves, we did eat our favourite troop field meal of creamed chipped beef on toast, or Shit on a Shingle as most of the men called it. It was no meal made by Jen or Ma but out there it was the best we could wish for and at Sturgis Kentucky, we got it.

From June 5th to July 15th 1943, we were combined with the glider troops in a large scale exercise, officially joining us as the 101st Airborne Division. We were not experiencing combat, though we expected it was as close to combat as they could make it to prepare us for the real thing. We completed three jumps, underwent extended night marches, waded through streams, climbed the far banks and stumbled over rocks, stumps and roots causing constant exhaustion and iching that felt like it would never subside. By July, we received a commendation from Maj. Gen. William C. Lee, the Commander of the 101st who had fought in the 1914 war, for *'spending aggressive action, sound tactical doctrine and well trained individuals.'* The confidence and enthusiasm only grew and tightened more from the reward.

From Sturgis we were moved to Camp Breckinridge, Kentucky, where the camp was overflowing and we slept again in pup tents with the ground for our mattress. Most men had gained a ten day furlough, including Hiker, though as I had been found with contraband of canned food, my pass was revoked, much to the aggravation of Jen who was furious when I wrote and told her. I carried on training while the men were away, strengthening my fitness and completing runs and marches. When they arrived back at camp we took trains as an entire division to Fort Bragg, North Carolina, with better food and beds that did not consist of lying on the floor and hot showers that felt like personal hygiene mattered.

"I'm telling ya, we're being shipped somewhere coming here." Came the voice of Hiker as he sipped his beer and placed it firmly on the table before him.

"What makes you say that?" I asked, lighting up a cigarette and inhaling it sharply before blowing it out in an exhausted sigh.

"Come on! You can't seriously think we are here for more training! Look at the staging area, it's for shipping us out overseas! We've been given new clothes, weapons and gear, if we aren't going overseas then I'll bet it's straight to war!" He finishes his beer and orders another, refusing the temptation for the more stronger option of whiskey like the men of Easy, who ended up in a brawl with the glider troops who did not receive the $50 bonus until July 1944 they were not volunteers or the regular soldiers stationed at Bragg and as a result of being unable to handle whiskey that wasn't usually our forte, fights broke out amongst the men.

"I don't know, we've been training here, to use rifles and machine guns, if they were shipping us out wouldn't they have done it already?" I lean back in my chair and watch the village people of Fayetteville discussing their own matters over spilt beer and thick clouds of cigarette smoke.

"I'm telling ya, give it a few days and we'll be out of here. Just hope the showers are still hot, sick of washing in little more than a dahm puddle." Thanking the guy who brings over his beer he leans back, crosses one leg over the other and downs the entire contents of the bottle in one. I couldn't help but laugh, as much as he missed his family he made the best of every situation, getting drunk and having a knees up with the men because, *why not,* we were here, might as well enjoy it.

It wasn't until half way through August that Hiker punched me in the arm and called in his winnings. We were called to regimental formation as the band played, the Red Cross girls cried at our departure as we were boarded onto twenty trains that were to take us into our next step towards war. We were headed North, towards Camp Shanks with promises of passes to go into New York City that were never kept. We were vaccinated to the point our arms felt like they would drop off at any moment and were lined up to make the march onto the docks.

"Would of been nice to go through the city." I'd said with a sarcastic eye roll and half a cigarette hanging out my mouth as we lined up to board the gangplank.

"Apparently we couldn't, in case *enemy spies knew* we were being shipped out." Said Buck with emphasis on his words that he must have thought would make us feel better.

As we stood at the railings aboard a ship that would take us to our next destination, it was evident that every man was lost in thought under the luminous sky above us. I stood beside Jones who waved to the people below, knowing that this was really it, we were going towards a war that we could not turn back on even if we wanted to. I don't think any of us felt like the same man we were before volunteering for the airborne, though we were all leaving behind a world of people we loved when we pulled away from the harbor. Sobel had written letters that were sent to every man's Mother, with mine being sent to Jen after explaining the recent passing of Ma during furlough. We all hated him, though a small fraction of that eased with the smallest amount of sympathy given by him when I had come back and explained what happened. He was still the same arrogant man who had earned the utmost hatred amongst the company, yet he had found it within himself to send a letter to Jen, rather than not at all.

I let the night circle around me, with Mother's memory dancing within it. Without her I would never have made it through the training, her unquestionable confidence that I could achieve anything was what saw me through every grueling hill march, every terrifying jump and every night of sleeping on the cold, hard ground. I stood hanging over the railings, watching New York become little more than a shadow in the distance as I told myself I could do it. I could be the soldier she told me I could be.

*

1929

"I can't do it Mama, it's too hard." I cried, throwing my head into my hands and letting tears overtake my willingness to learn. I had been given homework from school that needed to be completed and returned the next day and I was struggling to work out the numbers that came to an answer that looked right.

"Why do you cry son?" She asked me, sitting down next to me with her head resting on her hand and moving away my own so I could see her as she spoke to me.

"Because I can't do it. I have been trying for hours and I just can't. With a gentle laugh she takes hold of my hands and places them on the table, away from my face and wipes away the tears with her handkerchief.

"Let me tell you something. Life is one big challenge that we must face to understand what our greater goal is. If everything in life was easy how do you think we would learn things, understand what we were good at or how would we be able to improve?" She smiles at me gently then takes on another approach as I was still unable to feel better with her speech.

"Life is like a tree Peter, the stump is our beginning, it is our starting point to grow into something much bigger. Then one day, our first branch will begin to form, leading us onto a completely new path with different lessons and challenges. We live with these challenges for a time and then one day, another branch appears, showing us another path and more hurdles that must be taken."

"Why must we take them Mama?" I asked, looking at the ground with a bottom lip almost touching it.

"When a tree has blossomed and all of its branches have reached in many different directions, what do you think comes next?" She looks at me for a time before realising I was waiting for her to continue. *"It grows Peter. It grows and it grows, becoming stronger with every new branch that appears. The branches are your lessons, your challenges and your hurdles that you have accomplished. The tree will forever grow tall, as high as the clouds if it is let be that way, the only way it isn't is if it is cut down. If you give up now, cut down your tree, how will you ever know what it looks like at the very top?"*

1943

We stood crowded on that ship for what felt like a lifetime of anticipation, waiting to see where our journey would lead next. I thought about Ma the whole time, wishing that her words could still fill me with encouragement and courage when I returned, though I knew they were in the air and in my mind, that could never be taken away. Some of the men were playing cards, holding conversations over a beer and a smoke, others reading magazines I'm sure the women they had left at home wouldn't be happy about, though it helped to distract our minds from reality for just a few brief moments. The sound of metal chains and muffled conversation, the salt water and thick cigarette smoke all filled the air that day that offered no compensation to the fact we were leaving behind our lives in America.

I remember the conversations about children and the women we were leaving at home. We laughed and we smiled, some even broke out in brawls over women they had never met before, though inside we had to either believe that life as we once knew it was gone, or we would make it back for them if nothing else. As we hung over the railings of the ship that took us to England, it was unquestionable that every man wondered what their fate was, whether we would return when the war was over to celebrate with those we loved, or whether we would be remembered if we didn't. Some were full of adrenaline and excitement while others full of anxiety and worry about what we were edging closer towards. As much as most of us tried to hide it, it was certain that nearly every man I stood on the ship with that day was thinking of who they were leaving behind and whether they would return. Some were just better at locking it away and masking it behind jokes and fights than others.

I thought about my precious Jen as I let the air brush across my skin, so gently it could have almost been innocent, though I knew it held secrets and unknowing promises of thousands of men with hearts so big it was a wonder they hid it so well on the outside. She stayed orbiting my mind from the moment I kissed her goodbye and never left my mind since. Her long brown hair that fell onto her chest and curled slightly at the ends, her smile that could brighten the darkest of rooms, her laugh being so infectious it was almost impossible for it not to be catching. I thought about it all as I held her picture to my chest and said goodbye to the States.

We were heading to a county in England where we would continue our training in close combat, street fighting, chemical warfare, the use of German weapons, all while undertaking physical training. I had told myself I was ready for what the war would throw at me, for all of us as a division. We were heading into Hitler's war as the United States Paratroopers of the 101st Airborne. It was exhilarating to think of ourselves as fully trained parachuting Infantry men that had gained our wings through tough training, after entering training as little more than boys in comparison.

I stood beside my good friend Hiker and even though we did not exchange heavy amounts of words before the ship pulled away, we respected each other's reasoning behind it. We were saying our silent goodbyes and preparing ourselves for what was coming. His woman and child he had left at home was all that really mattered to him, the rest was for them and nothing more and the respect I held for him because of that exceeds what words could even begin to describe. They were the reason we stood so strongly in the regiment, knowing we had to make it back for them. Seeing the fire ignite in his soul when he spoke about his girls was truly a blessing. Not many men that would openly admit that the women in their lives were everything, that they gave him so much purpose. Some of the men within the battalion were more concerned about public opinion and leaving behind scenes of what they would call *weakness* back at home. They didn't speak much of what they'd left behind, they would tarnish the name of women in jokes and laughter which I suppose was their way of getting through training and the war ahead. Every man dealt with it differently and still I had to respect that even though I did not agree with the methods of doing so, it was *their* way and we were all entering this war together, as brothers.

The air felt thick with hidden speeches, unspoken words of messages to home and the begging of every man to God to look after their women and send them home alive after the war. I remember thinking how Jen would explode with exhilaration and the overwhelming sense of excitement for the sky being so beautiful. She would tell me a story of a sailor, how he would receive positive weather the following day just from the sky being lit up in pink the night before. I never really concentrated on the story that much, she was the most beautiful thing to meet my eyes and no sky in pretty colours could compete with her. She would insist that we lay on a blanket and watch for shooting stars and as daft as it may seem, I never regretted any time I spent in her company. She could have had me doing cartwheels across the garden for light entertainment and I would have undoubtedly done it to see her smile. It was her smile I knew I would miss the most, to hold her and tell her I loved her and see the smile that would flood her face, right from one side of her face to the other in a giant beam of happiness. When the war broke out in 1939, those smiles became less frequent as the stress of life took over.

It was the smallest of things in life she enjoyed the most, hanging her head out of the car window with the wind blowing her hair. She would tell me on occasions with a smile spread widely across her face, *'It is a chance to start again isn't it? For the wind to blow away all of your worries so you can live your life with only the purest of happiness inside you.'* I don't know where she got that from but her mottos for life and her positivity for everything in it endlessly made me smile. That was before the war lay heavy on our home and started to take small fractions of her energy away, piece by piece. I would think about her every single day until I returned, I knew that, though it was evident that if I was to make it back to her I would need to say goodbye for now. I kissed her picture, took a deep breath, closed my eyes and under my breath I said my final farewell. "*America, until I return, look after my Jenny.*"

The journey to England on a ship that was painfully overcrowding was unpleasant to say the least. Showers consisted of cold salt water, life jackets had to be worn at all times, with cartridge belts attached with canteens that resulted in frequent bumping into each other while passing, the two meals a day were not the worst, with boiled fish and tomatoes from large pots, though the cooks looked like their stained clothes could have been attached to them for several days at the least with no sign of a wash. Fresh water was rationed to the point we could only drink for fifteen minutes intervals for an hour and a half per day. Sleeping was another issue with overcrowding. We shared two men to a bunk, meaning it would be alternated, while sleeping in our clothes. The entire journey was uncomfortable, with a thirst that could not be tamed and a smell on the ship that just grew stronger everyday. I'd tried to keep myself entertained to avoid blowing off the handle like most of the other men who had reached breaking point by walking along the decks with Hiker or participating in a game of poker that almost always left a guy with no money or lots of it.

By the time we reached September 15th we had docked in a new country, further training awaiting our arrival and experiences that would remain imprinted in our minds forever. We were yet another step closer to the raging war and we were not just fearful of it but excited too. Stepping off the ship in Liverpool, England I felt a completely new man. I felt a proud soldier of the 101st Airborne and I was ready for what was to come next, whatever that might have been.

June 1944 - The Bauzug

I was prisoner A-198216 of Auschwitz-Birkenau for almost two years before I was transferred onto the Bauzug, the construction trains that were headed for Germany to repair damage to German cities and to clear rubble caused by the allies bombing. Transportations out of camp were not unusual, prisoners were needed elsewhere to contribute to the German war effort. People were sent to factories to work on machinery and aircraft, others sent to work in German homes, sent to other camps in which prisoners were needed and like myself, transported on the construction trains to fix bombed out areas in Western Germany. I was given no notice for my departure from the camp though it came as a relief to get away from Auschwitz. In my heart I knew I would miss Binem, Franck and Han's, yet being away from Auschwitz still brought a welcoming relief. No information was provided as to where I would be going, how long for, or whether I would be returning to Birkenau. Deep down I felt that where I was going it was unlikely I would return. Despite the relief to finally be leaving the camp, I was undoubtedly anxious as to whether I would be going to a destination worse. If there was anything that the war had taught me, it was that nothing was impossible anymore.

I was comforted by the fact that Henryk had also been chosen for work on the Bauzug, meaning we shared one of the three tier bunks on the freight cars along with another Polish Jew named Jan who did not say very much yet it was evident he was not a man to be broken so easily. He held strength mentally that most in the ghetto and Auschwitz would have been envious of. He reminded me of Han's, which brought comfort in such bleak and depressing times. The food rations were an improvement from camp, so when we laid on our bunk during the blistering cold winter of September 1944, eating the bread and accompaniment we did not need to worry about trading, we spoke about our lives before Hitler crashed it around us and found comfort in sharing what we would do after the war.

"I lived in Krakow all my life, my parents were well off Jewish residents that I'm sure all of Krakow respected. My father was a dentist and my Mother a nurse, they brought me up with the belief that helping others is the meaning to life. The city is truly beautiful, hence the reason it wasn't bombed, Hitler wanted it preserved to use as the capital of the government, yet it didn't stop us being shoved into the ghetto like caged animals." Jan sits up on the bottom bunk as I lay watching him with my head dangling over the edge. "They beat my family before my eyes, tried to get me to crack, I did, I just never let them see it. That is how they win, by seeing your soul break before their eyes and watching as you can do nothing about it." His words spiral around me as I think about the SS guard who had reunited me with Mother before her last breaths. *Had he known she was going to die and wanted me to endure the pain of watching her? Or was he really one of the nice ones? Was there such a thing?*

"Where are they now?" Asked Henryk, sitting up on the middle bunk and rubbing his swollen ankles.

"I do not know. Mother and Father were taken in the opposite direction when arriving at Auschwitz, I have no doubt they were taken to the chimneys, along with my brother and sister and their children. My brother was too weak from the ghetto to be able to work at satisfaction, my sister was led into the woman's camp, I do not know for sure where my family are but in my head I have already prepared for the worst." My heart sank at the thought, not knowing was worse than knowing those we loved had perished but it still meant that hope was on the horizon, giving us something to push through the days for.

"My wife and daughter were taken too. I watched as their lives slipped away, I have to say I have not been as strong as you Jan." Henryk comfortingly smiles as Jan bows his head.

"Unfortunately it has not always been the case. Many nights I wake at night wondering if this is all just some bad dream, hoping beyond anything that it is and my family will walk through from the next room and laugh at my continuous nightmares. I am yet to wake up." The sadness washed over him yet he still held it together, not even craking at the seams in what I assumed was stubbornness for the Nazi's to break him.

The train shuttled along through German cities that the allies had bombed in retaliation. Some days we were repairing railroads, others clearing rubble, putting out fires and rescuing people from burning buildings. The days were backbreaking, still hard work that needed to be done to stay alive and many men were lost to the air raids or collapsing buildings. We were constantly under the watchful eyes of the SS guards, though retrieving food from abandoned buildings meant we were able to eat more than we had been used to. Every night was a struggle to sleep, I'd revisit Auschwitz in my dreams that convinced me it was real, we were still there, being beaten, starved, watching the ones we love fall before the Germans. The roll calls and hours standing in the biting snow or burning heat was imprinted in my memories that came back to haunt me every time I closed my eyes. The construction trains were not a life of paradise and tranquility, they still held most of the indistinguishable risks that had hovered over our lives in camp. We were hit with sticks, threatened with guns if we did not work faster and worked until exhaustion was the only thing we really knew anymore. That being said, food was easier to come by with food stores being hidden in basements, some men were even able to escape due to an increase in successful hiding places.

Initially the train was sent to the station in Karlsruhe Germany, which at the time was a prime target for allied bombers, meaning we were all at risk from the air raids and falling buildings. While in Karlsruhe the air opened up for an attack from the air. Life from before the ghetto flashed before my eyes, reliving the same horrific scenes as I witnessed while living in Warsaw, except this time, my family were all gone, lost to a war we had never asked for. The bombs lit up the sky, demolished buildings with civilians inside. I was hiding behind a collapsed wall of a house when I thought to myself, *does this make us as bad as the German's?* I pondered the thought amidst the falling debris and smoke filling my lungs when I remembered the ghettos, the camps and the starvation. Another bomb screams through the air hitting into the building just two houses away. I question whether I run or whether I hide, the two options spirling around me in an anxious whirlwind begging me to make a decision before another bomb hits closer.

*

"Are you afraid when they come, Jakub?" Comes the voice of my Grandpa sitting opposite in the dimly lit air raid shelter of our basement.
"Yes, aren't you?" I asked, huddled into Grandmama for protection, my vulnerabilities on show with no attempt to hide them.
"They are scary yes, but what is it you really fear?" He was looking straight into my eyes, not flinching from the explosions vibrating around us. I think for a few moments before shaking

my head, was this a trick question? I had always believed that if he was faced with situations similar to what he encountered in the first world war, that he would struggle to get through it.

"You fear the unknown, you fear, what will happen to me, to us? You fear, will I be hurt? You fear the things that you are not certain will happen. Fearing the unknown is your enemy and those in them Stuka planes know that. Why do you think they come without warning?" I let his words fill my mind, digest them like something hard to swallow. "Your strength is to rise above that, face what comes when exactly it comes and not before, or it will eat you alive from the inside out."

"He's right son, your superpower is your own mind." Papa says, ruffling my hair as he sits beside Grandmama.

"Then why do we hide?" I questioned, unsure of the exact meaning of what they were saying. Grandpa leans in towards me and smiles, "If a lion has its mouth open you wouldn't walk straight in would you?" He waits for the moment I finally link the two scenarios and nods when he sees in my eyes that I had. "You see it is all about being smart, waiting for your moment while not letting fear make you reckless. Everything that happens is for a reason and do not ever forget that. It does not matter how bad the situation may seem, it is always a blessing or a lesson."

*

The ground shakes beneath my feet as I struggle to see through the thick smoke and blazing flames. I think about Grandpa's words, wondering how he could have been so reckless against his own advice. *Was that the lesson?* To run but at the right time, to not fear what I do not know will happen or not happen. Amongst the smoke I looked for Henryk who had been in the building next door saving a family of five with another Polish prisoner. With my hands out in front of me I cautiously walk on the rubble and see that the building had been completely brought to the ground. There was no sign of Henryk or any other prisoners, no sign of SS guards or the family inside the home. In a frantic panic I rush inside what remained of a once standing building.

"Jakub?" Came the struggling voice of Henryk beneath a pile of beams and concrete. Rushing over I begin pulling them off to which he stops me. "Jakub, you need to run." Shocked and dismissing his words I carry on pulling bricks and broken furniture off his body. ""Listen," He coughed for a duration of time that sounded painful, long aching coughs that made it difficult for him to breathe. "Most of the SS guards fled when the planes came over, they probably think we are all dead, you need to run, I will never make it and I will slow you down." The planes had passed leaving the city in ruins though it was inevitable that the SS guards would return. "I'm not leaving you, I can get you out." Tears began filling inside my eyes, through anxious desperation and adrenaline at being captured and taken back to the trains, or worse, Auschwitz.

Henryk's body is no longer tense as he places his only available arm on mine. "Everything happens for a reason, I can help one more person before I see my girls again. Now go, you do not have much time." He pushes me away with what strength he had and begins banging on one of the beams with a rock close to hand. "No! I know what you are doing! You're distracting them while I run but I'm not leaving you here, they will kill you!"

"Look at me, I'm not going anywhere am I? Now go!" My heart beating in my chest and the sound of trucks approaching from the distance I let out a defeated sigh. I smile with tears streaming down my face faster than I could blink and turn and run, faster than my legs would allow, knowing it could be seconds before I am in the hands of the guards or shot for running. I run until I reach the corner of the street and hide behind a somewhat still standing building. Two SS guards get out of their trucks and run inside the building where Henryk is still banging on the beam. I question over and over, *should I have stayed? Have I just left him to die?* The questions plummeted around my mind until I heard a roar of a gun and suddenly, the banging stopped and as it did, I closed my eyes and I smiled. I smiled because I knew he was walking into the arms of his wife and daughter, just as he had been waiting for. I saw his arms wrap around them in a beautiful reunion in my mind, his smile so wide and infectious. He had given his life to so many, the orphans, prisoners at Auschwitz, me. Our country had needed people like him but it was finally time for him to cash in his reward and he did when he walked hand in hand with his family, what he had been waiting for since the moment they were taken. As the clouds of smoke began to disappear so did Henryk and I smiled knowing that he was finally with the two people he had been waiting so long to see. As I ran I looked up to the sky. "My greatest ever friend, thank you."

1943 - 1944 - Aldbourne, England

On 15th September 1943 the Samaria docked in Liverpool England, to which we were taken by trucks the next day 80 miles West of London, to Aldbourne, a small English village with narrow cobbled streets lined with cottages and a church with its bell chiming the hours through the day. Our barracks consisted of nissen huts; prefabricated steel structures, made from a half-cylindrical skin of corrugated steel. A twin pot-belly stove heated the huts, as well as a mattress cover we were given to fill with straw. The heavy wool blankets helped with the cold on a night, though come morning we would be itching all over. Throughout the village were five beer houses that were a welcoming escape from training if passes were not revoked to visit them. We were briefed on the customary mannerisms of the British and given strict instruction on how we should fit in with them while holding tenancy in their country. We were to drink quietly, hold off on the brawls and eat the food that they did, which included powdered milk and eggs, horse meat, brussel sprouts, turnips and cabbage and dehydrated apricots and potatoes. Our mission while here was to prepare for the invasion of Europe and nothing else, that was done through extensive training.

Arriving in England from the States ensured that any doubt we had about entering the war was long lost. It became that ever more real when the training started and lasted for over nine long months. The longest we had stayed in one place so far. Training exercises kicked any lack of confidence men may have had right out of them, leaving us strong and ready to face Hitler's war. Hiker was by my side in every step of training and I knew deep down we pushed each other on without even really realising it. We were just what each other needed, used the other as ambition and willing to keep going through training most men would find impossible and although Aldbourne was different to Toccoa and Benning, it held the same training intensity if not more.

During a night of extreme rain and biting cold we were ordered out of our beds to endure strenuous training with the rain hitting hard against our skin from all directions. Sobel had waited for this night I was sure, one that would push us to our limits, one that would not make it easy by a gentle midsummer night breeze. The rain lasted six solid hours, taking away fractions of vision though it was no excuse to fall behind. Every man needed to complete the course of obstacles and track within six minutes, anyone failing to complete it within that time was made to do it again, back through thick mud that was gaining rivers of water, slowing down your pace begging you to give in and accept defeat. Once completed within time, we were to 'dig in' and remain on guard until morning. Myself and Hiker shared a foxhole that night. While he slept with his rifle clutched to his chest I kept guard, hearing him mutter in his sleep about the family he left back in the States and something about a dog that never stopped chewing shoes. When he woke, he did the same while I slept for what felt like small minutes squashed into a tiny pocket of time.

When we were both awake, looking up to the sky that washed the earth with endless rain, we spoke about the women we craved to see again. None of us judged, the feelings were mutual, to just be back at home, yet to defeat Hitler's war at the same time.
"She's great my Rosie you know, I'd love for you to meet her. No question about it, she would have the teapot hot and ready with a saucer of biscuits before your foot stepped through the door. Loves visitors she does, always says it keeps the spirit alive, stops life getting boring. Think she could be right." He told me, a smile itching on his face at the picture in his head. It didn't matter to him that the air was biting exposed skin, or that rain was encouraging cold to seap beneath our clothes or that a hot meal may have been a long time coming, the thought of that woman made his heart swell, made him train hard just to get back to her.
"When we walk out of this dahm war you have my word we will all meet for a beer and we'll celebrate taking every one of those Krauts down." We both laughed at the thought, yet deep down we agonized over whether we would make it to the end of the war to celebrate. It was a worry every man carried. As we slept in our foxholes that the platoon leaders had instructed to dig deep, which proved strenuous in the hard soil, an armoured

team of Sherman tanks began shaking the ground, heading in our direction up the hill. The lesson was learned that day to dig your hole deep enough.

Days were stretched to their absolute maximum in order to cram in as much training as possible. Tiredness had to be forgotten, sleeping just wasn't always an option, despite how much your body wanted to fall to the ground and not wake up for a long duration of time. Sleep became a distant memory though we knew we still had it good here, this was just training for the real fight to come. Six days a week at eight to ten hours a day we were in the field, making fifteen to twenty five mile hikes, undertook street fighting exercises, learned map reading, first aid and about chemical warfare, went on night operations and spent an hour every day in close combat exercises that would prepare us for Hitler's army and his allies. Multiple times a week we would venture out on two-to-three day exercises that would teach us the basic knowledge of infantrymen and how to use the ground, live within it without disablement of physical competence. Our bodies were exhausted, begging us to give in yet we were able to override it with a mental attitude that always kept us going.

It was throughout our training in England that we really started to know the men within the company, it drew us closer as comrades and even through the regular jumps in full gear, in cold that sent our feet numb, that would come as a shock when hitting the ground, we learned to trust one another, how each man moved and carried himself and in combat, it would be the knowledge needed between life and death, how to save the men you served with as well as choosing the right decision over the wrong one in the face of danger or threat.

Situations with Sobel didn't improve in England, which made men of the company tense and eager to get him in the field to use a rifle on him. His pettiness for discipline meant that almost all men of Easy Company had come to their last nerve with him, yet not much could be done.

"I swear that man has got to be my biggest enemy." Complained Salty after a heavy lecture from Sobel about his field techniques. "Like he knows what he is doing! I could lead this whole platoon better with my eyes closed compared to that guy, all he does is flap around with his hands in the air. I'm telling ya', we go into combat with him, we will all be dead within a few hours."

"Don't be so dramatic," Shouted Ranney coming back from the showers, "More like a few minutes." The men laughed at Sobel's expense though deep down we all knew that going into combat with a guy who couldn't even read a map would surely leave us open to the enemy.

"Isn't like we can do anything about it is it?" I'd said, pulling a clean shirt over my head and jumping into the uncomfortable straw mattress with the blanket placed over me. "We go to Sink, what exactly are we going to say? *'We have the finest performance record but the Captain is useless, can we have another one?'* Think he would have us for mutiny before we had even mentioned Sobel."

"Somethin' needs to be done because we might as well write our wills now if that man leads us into combat." Joined Buck, holding a book in his hand that he had been attempting to read since stepping foot on the Samaria, with barely a chapter being read.

"*Aye!*" Agreed all the men in unison within the hut. Sobel and 1st Sergeant Evans remained in command for the foreseeable future but we knew it could not go on for much longer. With the battle of Normandy drawing in closer by the day, our concerns over Sobel's commanding techniques and lack of skills increased with every exercise that Sobel led.

It wasn't just us that Sobel had got on the wrong side of, he had wound up Winters to the point that it had caused a silent rivalry between the two men. We respected Winters, and wanted him to command us, rather than Sobel, who everyone hated, which only grew more when Winters was transferred out of Easy Company and was made battalion mess officer. Not only had this riled Winters but also every man of Easy, including myself. Sergeants Ranny and Harris had called a meeting soon after to get together all N.C.O's of Easy Company for a proposal.

"Either Sobel is replaced, or we turn in our stripes." Said Harris, the tension within him rising to the surface, showing no opportunity of hiding itself. "There isn't much more we can do at this point. They aren't going to take us seriously any other way."

"We say that to Sink I guarantee he will have us for mutiny. If we take this risk we need to all do it together." I added, looking at each man for their agreement. "Every one of us needs to be on board otherwise we're in for big trouble."

"I'm in, Sobel's gone too far, can't go into combat with a man like that, it's just asking for trouble." Hiker agreed, nodding his head enthusiastically like he couldn't wait to get on with it. I wrote my letter of resignation that would give Sink and Strayer an ultimatum.

"I, Peter Mcclough, hereby turn in my stripes. I no longer wish to be a N.C.O in Easy Company under the command of Herbert Sobel."

Once all the letters had been written, C.Q Sergeant Lipton collected everyone's letters and posted them in the 'In basket' belonging to Sobel. Just a few days later we were called before Colonel Sink for a lecture of a lifetime.

"You have disgraced this company, I could put you all in the guardhouse for such mutiny." Sink bellowed, looking in the eye of every N.C.O who stood before him. *'Knew it.'* I thought, standing before him daring not to make a sound or movement. If it wasn't for the fact we were in preparation for combat, we could have been shot for acts of such mutiny. To us, we knew the risks and we went ahead with them anyway, that is how much we did not want to be commanded by Sobel. 1st Lieutenant Patrick Sweeney from Able Company was brought in to be Executive Officer of Easy, who made 1st Lieutenant Thomas Meehan of Baker Company, Captain, meaning the days of being under the command of Sobel were over, as he was sent to run a training camp in Chilton Foliat.

We were commanded like a normal company from that point on, with training intensifying even further that taught us how to catch food that we could eat, to be resourceful with what was around us in order to survive should we need to put it into practise. We continued to make jumps, some during the night and when Christmas and New Year came around we were given the day off, with enough turkey to feed twice the men that were there. We made the most of the time off which was a decision made rightly, as come February we started to train with seven other divisions as part of rehearsals for the upcoming attack on Normandy France.

March 23rd brought a day that I would never forget in all my days of training. We were, along with the 3rd battalion, to jump from C-47's under the watchful eyes of British Prime Minister, Winston Churchill, Supreme Allied Commander Dwight Eisenhower, The U.S First Army Commander Omar Bradley and many other big names that would witness the jump that would be a demonstration of how the attack on Normandy would happen. More than 1,000 men jumped from the planes that soured through the skies that day, including myself and Hiker, who waited in excitement for our spot at the door.

"Don't mess this up man, lot of people watching down there." Shouted Hiker with a laugh over the sound of rattling and wind. He was excited, there was no doubt about it, we all were, the confidence and pride that filled us that day was beyond any day in training could ever compare to. Once we reached the ground we disassembled from our parachutes and in speed that came with the longing to show what capable men we were, we began putting together the M1 Garand we had become so accustomed with.

Later that day we were assembled before a raised platform to be inspected by both Churchill and Eisenhower who went along the ranks asking men questions.

"Soldier, where are you from?" Came the voice of Churchill looking me in the eye.

"Colorado California." I answered, feeling honorable to be stood before him answering his questions.

"What do you think of England?" He asked, not taking his gaze from me though with a slight smile that indicated it wasn't completely a trick question.

"I like it very much indeed, I was a librarian and college student before joining the Airborne and I have read a great deal of books about England and its history." The moment was truly memorable on every level, something I would not forget in all my years of living. I felt proud, honorable, overwhelmed and full of excitement.

Straight after these jumps witnessed by Churchill, Eisenhower and the other big names that attended that day, we completed bigger exercises of joining with the gliderborne units, ground forces and the forces from the air and the navy. The air drops as well as the land and sea force took place throughout the Southwest of England. I completed each exercise as though it was the real thing, putting every ounce of effort into being an honorable soldier that my comrades would feel safe and proud to drop into combat with. Some days were hard, as exhaustion and hunger would make an unwelcoming appearance, yet we strived through regardless knowing that when the time came we would be soldiers that would put an end to Hitler's war. Training was preparing us for the day that would mark our first real drop. The day we attacked Normandy from the air, land and sea. I wore my uniform with pride, held my rifle with boldness knowing I would not be afraid to use it to contribute to the ending of the war that was battling through Europe. Our time was edging closer and as much as realisation kicked in, nothing would stop us in our mission. We would do whatever was expected of us when we jumped from that plane into occupied France.

We had sat through countless briefs instructing us on what would happen during the attack. The 101st, the 82nd Airborne and the 4th infantry were combined together to take the base of the Cotentin, given the code name Utah Beach, from the extreme right flank of the area of invasion that extended from the debouchment of the Orne River to the east with a distance of just over forty miles from Cotentin that we were to take. Our hurdle would be the German army dug in behind Hitler's Atlantic Wall, a series of fortifications that Hitler had ordered to be built to guard Europe's west coast from Allied assault. We were exposed to other risks too, one being that the German Commander, Field Marshal Erwin Rommel had flooded the fields we would need to take off the beach to approach inland, with the intention of pushing us onto the roads, which would be defended by German Infantry troops that could take us out from their camouflaged positions and bunkers. Our mission, given by Eisenhower himself, was to cause a disturbance that would throw them off and appropriate the causeways and before the German's had time to respond, we would eliminate them. This would be done by a night drop, though the danger held great, meaning we were to train and prepare by means of rehearsing the mission beforehand on similar ground to that of Utah Beach.

During our training in England, we were to carry out the rehearsals for D-Day at Slapton Sands, Devonshire as it held great resemblance to that of the Utah Beach in Normandy. Over 3,000 civilians had been evacuated from Slapton, Strete,

Torcross, Blackawton and East Allington in South Devon for the training exercise code named Operation Tiger.

"Just like the real thing ay Mcclough!" Shouted Hiker over the sound of rotating tires on bumpy roads, a cigarette hung loosely from his mouth with his rifle sat comfortably in his left hand.

"Especially after sleeping in that field all night." I joked, taking a cigarette from the packet he held before me. "Going to see some real action today my brother!" It was evident we were excited, nervous, though not quite fearful as we knew in our minds it was a training exercise, nothing more until the actual invasion. We had spent the last two years training and at this very moment we felt we were finally putting it into action. Hiker laughed with one eyebrow raised and an eye squinted with the cigarette hung from the left side of his mouth, "Time to make our women proud!" The men of Easy laughed and joked all the way in those trucks to the drop zone at Slapton Sands, where we assembled and marched to the defensive positions a mile back from the beach. Slapton Sands bore resemblance to Utah on a multitude of levels, one being that two bridges crossed from the coastline upland. Once we had reached our defensive positions we were to guard the bridge until dawn.

During the night we were ambushed by nine German E-boats, alerted by heavy radio traffic in Lyme Bay, that slipped in amongst the eight tank landing ships, using the blanket of darkness as their cover. The exercise had been vital to that of the D-Day landings that commanders had ordered live naval and artillery ammunition to make the rehearsal as real as possible so we would be accustomed to what we would experience on D-Day. The E-Boats intercepted the three mile group of ships, resulting in three ships being aggressively hit by German torpedoes. The absence of the British Navy Destroyer, that had been ordered to Plymouth for repairs, as well as the error in radio frequencies resulted in what was meant to be a training exercise being a real attack from the German forces. Over 900 Americans lost their lives that day due to ships being sunk and improper training on the wearing of lifejackets that led to many men perishing to hypothermia in the freezing temperatures of the sea. We watched from the beach astounded, how a training exercise had converted to a genuine attack in such a small amount of time, how we had been so unaware of the German's making their way through Lyme Bay to take the lives of so many American servicemen and sink military equipment, including an American Sherman Tank that would lay at the seabed, intact, for many years to come that would tell the story of what happened that day. We had been ordered to remain silent about what we had seen that night so as not to affect the moral of men going into battle in the invasion of Normandy. Any man, including officers, to speak of what happened would be threatened with a court martial. Later that afternoon Easy Company marched 25 miles then took temporary shelter in the woods for the night, where we took trucks back to Aldbourne on the morning of April 28th.

Operation Eagle took place between 9th and 12th of May, which was a dress rehearsal for the D-Day landings in France that the entire division took part in. On the 10th and 11th of May we were briefed of our mission and on the 11th we began boarding the C-47's on Upottery airfield, the same airfield we would use to fly to Normandy. We took to the sky with all our equipment and gear that we may have needed for any possible emergency.

"Talk about sweating, I think I could ring this thing out and fill a good few buckets." I snapped, pulling my combat jacket as far away from my skin as possible in an attempt to feel air.

"You're not on your own with that one." Laughed Buck three men in front of me.

"I think I'm itching more now than what I do under that dahm blanket in Aldbourne." Shouted Salty, scratching at his skin that his vest had touched. Every man's uniform had been impregnated to repel a possible chemical attack and as we waited aboard the C-47 we did nothing but itch, sweat and become agitated for the entire two and a half hours over England. Our mission was an artillery battery that was covering the beach and despite the itching and sweating from carrying equipment that made us weigh twice our weight, the exercise was a success for Easy Company.

On May 31st we said goodbye to Aldbourne, its village, the experiences and the women that lined the roads waving and crying as we marched to trucks that were to take us to the marshaling area on a wide open field next to the airstrip at Upottery that we had used for Operation Eagle. After twenty two months of almost continuous training it had come to an end and we were as ready as we could ever be, as strong and knowledgeable soldiers that were willing to fight for and with our comrades.

"You scared?" Asked Hiker, stuffing chicken into his mouth before he had finished the bread he was chewing on like he hadn't eaten in months.

"Fear is there, of course but we have known it has been coming for a long time now, that is probably what makes it worse." I mumble through a mouthful of bread spread far too much in butter. "We've just been sitting on the fact for so long that every possibility has had a chance to manifest." I shake my head in thought as I push the second plate of food away from me in defeat.

"I can't help but feel excited about it y'know, don't you feel that?" He had followed suit and placed his plate away from him as though he couldn't look at food anymore.

"I wouldn't say excited, more apprehensive but eager to get it over with. If Slapton taught me anything it was that we should be prepared for the worst. Doesn't mean I won't enjoy taking out those dahm Krauts." I hold my hands in a rifle position, squinting my eyes as if pointing at a German, then click the trigger that would have been there.

"Going to be a long time for that, might as well make do with my company." He says, patting me on the back with a smile.

"Better make sure we end it sooner rather than later then." I joke, yet we both knew from all the men of Easy Company, we had become the most like brothers. We would die for our comrades, kill for them, fight for them, yet the space I had for Hiker had grown exceptionally large.

"We'll see them again you know," He says smiling, "when it is all over, they will be waiting for us." I nod my head in agreement, seeing Jen in my mind waiting at the porch, only the memory of Ma beside her. "I know, which is why we have to make it back for them."

June 1944 - Pforzheim Germany

It had been a mix of walking and running for six hours before I reached the city of Pforzheim. A beautiful city in Western Germany that had suffered air attacks by the allies. Buildings looked like a doll's house fallen subject to the temper tantrum of a child. Some were completely reduced to rubble, exposing broken beds and furniture, others still standing with blown out windows leaving shattered glass glistening on the ground. It was strange to think that Warsaw was not the only city in the world to suffer damage and destruction, though I remembered what my parents had told me when they were still alive, that Germany had started this war, yet the broken homes still made me question the survival of the people who lived inside them. So many innocent people dragged into countries disputes, lives lost who probably wanted no part of the powerful situations around them.

As I urged my feet to keep carrying me I heard the rumble of my stomach crying out for food. It had been what felt like forever since I had eaten and my body was beginning to remind me of the consequences. Energy and strength were so far away from reach I worried I would collapse in the street and be captured by the SS. I could not risk being sent back to Auschwitz now, or the Bauzug. Although I was still under threat of being captured, I had not been this free in over two years. It was too soon to have that taken away again already. My feet wandered to a destination unknown. I was in an unfamiliar country fleeing the grasps of the German soldiers, no family, no money and no food to aid my survival. I sink myself between two broken walls and rub my head, *what was I supposed to do now?* I wondered whether the SS knew I had gone, or if they assumed I had been killed in the explosions. A distant radio played softly in the distance, the streets were abandoned and vacant. I assumed most were either under the remains of houses or had fled the scene in evacuations when the planes had appeared.

Just as I let the music take me into an exhausted sleep I heard the voice of a young girl.
"You..American?" I looked up to see a girl no older than myself standing before me in a mucky white dress and a red bow in her messy golden hair. I stared perplexed, unsure of whether she would run to the German authorities and inform them of my presence. I shook my head in silence, watching her every move, waiting for the moment she would run away, indicating my own escape. She tilts her head to the side and looks at my striped uniform. I had forgotten about my clothes, if anything would make me stand out to the German's it would be the blue and white stripes of my trousers and jacket.
"You..hungry?" She asked, looking at my thin and pale face in sympathy. I nod again, remaining silent. She turned on her foot and walked towards a building only minorly damaged by raids. I watched in awe, confused and weak as though the last three

years had finally all caught up with me at once. She turned again and motions me to follow. It could have beeen a trap but what other choice did I have? I was so hungry I could have been walking straight into the lion's mouth just because it was open.

We entered her home to see a woman I assumed was her Mother clearing glass from the carpet and an old man hobbling across the floor with a wooden stick. They began speaking in German as we entered and the woman gave me a watchful eye, judging and cautious, it was apparent she had ideas of where I could have come from and was worried that I was standing in their home. The young girl and her mother continue to talk in what looked like a heated discussion, how I wish I had understood the German language when being taught at school. It had been nearly four years since I had received regular education at the school in Warsaw that was now a shattered and bruised building in a pile of debris. I missed my friends, my family, the way life was before this war started, I missed being a boy and not having to worry about adult ideologies for the sake of just trying to stay alive. Everything had changed since Hitler dropped that first bomb on our city, he had taken everything from me, leaving me with only the skin on my bones and a voice that was impossible to use for systematic change.

After several moments her mother looked over to me again and forced a grin before dramatically turning on her heel and heading for the kitchen. The young girl motions me to a wash basin with a rag, indicating I have was to have a wash. It had been so long since I had been able to wash myself properly. Before roll call in the morning it was a fight to get to the latrines and wash areas and even if you did make it in time before hundreds of others, water was near impossible to come by. I had seen some use their mugs to collect snow and let it turn to water for drinking or washing though keeping on top of hygiene was simply impossible due to the restrictions Auschwitz held over every prisoner. Not only had we lost our families, we had lost our identities, our dignities, therefore taking off the striped uniform in the middle of the room to wash myself down brought no embarrassment. The young girl emerged from one of the bedrooms with some clean clothes. The last time I had worn normal clothes was stepping off the freight cars onto the platform at the camp that took so many lives. Pulling the jumper over my head I began to feel like a person again, that I was Jakub, not prisoner A-198216.

"Greta." Says the young girl, pointing to herself, "You?"

"Jakub." She had straightened up her bow and changed her dress to a fresh green one that sat loosely around her knees. The more I looked at her the more I realised she was truly and remarkably beautiful. I offered my hand out to shake hers as Papa had suggested to me, to always be polite. She smiled, sending my stomach into somersaults as she gently took my hand and shakes it.

We suddenly burst out laughing at the thought of acting like mature grown ups, we were still kids and sometimes the war forced us to forget that. The sounds of our laughter were interrupted by the sound of Greta's mother's over-emphasised cough. We turned to see she had a bowl of food in her hands, meaning we had been instructed to sit at the table and stop the childish nonsense. Greta spooned potatoes onto my plate as I silently said my blessings. I spooned the food into my mouth so quickly that I received looks of concern and disgust by Greta's mother. Embarrassed I slowed down, reminded myself I was no longer in camp and that manners were still compulsarary on the outside world. It was not long before the meal was finished and the mother and old man walked into separate rooms to clean the dishes. My stomach had never felt so full, the fear of being dragged away from such mouthwatering food after it had been placed in front of me ensured that I ate the entire bowl that was given to me, even after my shrunken stomach had warned me I had forced enough down.

Greta was incredibly distracting from the nauseousness I felt afterwards, showing me photographs of her family and the poems she had written. I could not understand any of them as they were in German, though I smiled and nodded in approval, her bold blue eyes pulling me in as she laughed. I had never felt such peculiar feelings before other than towards one single person. Back at the apartment in the ghetto I had become very good friends with Amelia, who I suddenly thought of, knowing I would probably never see her again. I had felt such rushes of excitement, like bombs had been going off from inside me but only the most marvelous and extraordinary kind.

*

"Amelia, can you show young Jakub here how we dry out the sheets." Antoni had said, nudging my arm gently and winking at the same time. Amelia came bounding through the apartment, full of life and energy despite the dreary surroundings.
"You know, there really isn't much to it." She'd said, picking up the sheets from Antoni's bed, "We have to dry them out because of the damp that gets in, we can't really wash them so every morning we hang them to dry and come bedtime, they are nearly always dry again."
"Do you miss your home?" I asked, changing the subject. She sighs deeply and hangs the sheet to dry over the balcony.
"I miss my friends and I miss being able to walk through the streets and pick pretty flowers and feathers I find to put in my scrapbook. I miss home yes but a home is where you make it and that is here for now." Her attitude towards life even under the sufferable circumstances we were living always knocked me back in my stride. She was so strong willed and determined, made whatever she had work and I wished that I could be more like her.

"What do you miss?" She asks, sitting on the bed just inches away from me, gazing her eyes into mine, all sense of concentration and focus being lost.

"I..I miss..er.." I stutter embarrassingly as she leans in and plants a gentle kiss on my lips. It takes me by surprise, I had never kissed a girl before though the feelings running through me left me confused but exhilarated. I didn't move away but I did kiss her back. My first kiss and she made it magical, just like I'd seen in the theatres Grandpa would take me to.

"Life is nothing without a little excitement." She says smiling, "you have to give yourself something amazing to wake up for, otherwise we are wasting time."

*

I dropped my head in memory of her, she had been separated at the platform when she had stayed with our Mothers and Aunt Lena, who was another family member I was sure had been taken with the camp. I shrugged away the thought, pushed away the images of the chimneys as my mind told me they had been sent there, never to return. I was pulled from distracting thoughts at the sound of a thunderous bang on the door. I jumped up with my heart in my mouth and my legs shaking in fear. As I had somewhat expected, Greta's Mother had called the authorities who had turned up to the door with guns hanging from their backs and black leather boots shining in the dimly lit corridor. Greta began shouting in German who was pulled back by her Mother while the two SS men pulled me into the corridor and outside. As they pushed me into the back of a truck I took a last look at the girl who had taken pity on me, who had helped me when I had become so sure there was nobody else left in the world to offer such a thing. She was crying, refusing to stand near her Mother as she stood with her hand over her face in frustration. She took one last look at me and through streaming eyes smiled as I was hurtled into the back of the truck labeled with the dreaded Swastika.

I was in the hands of the German's once again, feeling like the war would never be over. I had escaped their grips for a while, felt freedom though not in its truest form but it was enough. *Everything happens for a reason,* Grandpa had said and I believed I had met her for a reason, to bring back hope into my life after it was almost gone. When Mother had lost her fight I subconsciously began to believe that there was nothing else to reach the end of the war for. If I was to survive, I would be walking out of it alone, my family gone. Greta was placed at that very moment of my life to guide me into remembering that I wanted to *feel* again, I had so much left I wanted to do and being happy again was one of them. Being happy was the only thing Mother ever really wanted for me. As I sat in the back of the truck with three other prisoners, all still wearing their striped pajamas, I pictured Mother, though not laying on the floor of the latrines at her weakest moment but dancing around the kitchen to the sound of women's voices and her freshly baking Challah filling the home that was once so free of war.

The truck bumped along the road, knocking us into each other in silence as we awaited our destination. *Back to Auschwitz? Back to the Bauzug? To our deaths?* It was impossible to know exactly where we were going, given that the truck had no windows. We sat in the dark with our thoughts as the truck bumped and shook us to a destination we could not see. After over two hours, that felt like many days, the truck came to a sudden halt. SS guards exchanged words outside before flinging the doors open and ordering us out. "Schnell!" Ordered a guard dressed in green with a mustache that hid his true expression. He could have been smiling at our misfortune and we were none the wiser. I followed in line of the other men, making sure I kept up with the pace to avoid being hit in the back with their guns.

As light shone on our surroundings I realised I had arrived at another camp. The truck had pulled into the camp train station consisting of three platforms with railroad sidings behind them. I was crowded amongst hundreds of other prisoners and led towards an adjacent camp. Once rounded up we were divided like worthless items and sent to numerous other camps in the vicinity. Upon arrival we were yelled at straight away by the Jewish Kapo. "You have arrived at Dachau, Kaufering labor camp, none of you will get out of this place alive." There was almost a laugh in his booming voice, emphasising that he believed he would leave this place while we would all be worked and starved to death.

The whole camp carried the stench of wet dirt, poor hygiene and death, as bodies laid sprawled across the ground that were left for days, stripped of their clothes and lice crawling under their arms. Until I stepped off the truck in Kaufering I believed that nothing could ever be as bad as Auschwitz. Here everything appeared worse on a level that would almost be unbelievable to anybody not witnessing it with their own eyes. I followed the herd of men to the registry where we were assigned labor details, given dirty and damp uniforms if not in possession of them already, such as those that had been transported straight from Auschwitz. I was given a new uniform with my tattooed number of 82521 stitched on the chest with my clothes taken away and we were all ordered to surrender all belongings such as money, documents and items of value.

Once registration had been completed we were ordered to stand in formation for roll call.
"This, you dirty pigs, is going to be your food. This is all you are going to get until you have fallen dead!" Came the voice of SS-Rapportfuhrer Kirsch as he began instructing us of our responsibilities and duties within the camp. I looked around me sharply, at the deceased bodies laying on the floor, the barbed wire closing us in, the guard towers at every one hundred foot

and in every corner each containing a member of the SS holding a submachine gun, waiting for anybody who dared go within eight foot of the fence to start firing. I had been taken to a camp housing rows upon rows of huts that were half built into the ground, earth covering the roofs to hide from Allied aircraft and a trench that ran through the middle that was so dirty it was almost impossible to determine whether water was flowing through it or feces. At both the left and right of the trench were six foot wooden platforms at knee height that was covered with excelsior which were our sleeping barracks. There was only one entrance to the huts with a double window at the far end. Much like Auschwitz they forced more people inside than was physically liveable. Fifty prisoners were crammed in a hut, though in some cases, over one hundred, all with one blanket each with water that came up to sleeping level during the rain.

It was as though the last two years at Auschwitz was beginning all over again, except this time in much more grueling conditions. When I had reached the city of Pforzheim I was hit with a sense of liberation and finally being free, yet the horrifying truth of the war was that it could snatch everything away from you in a blink of an eye with no warning. I had never been so ready to go home, yet I had never been so far from reach. Auschwitz-Birkenau in some small ways, was like a luxury compared to the harsh conditions I would be facing at Dachau and I didn't even know it yet.

June 6th 1944 - Normandy France - D-DAY

We were headed towards the C-47's on June 4th when we were told to stand down. The wind had picked up and with much thought, Eisenhower had decided to delay the invasion, so instead, we made our way to a wall tent to watch a movie, with much commotion and conversation amongst the privates who had mentally prepared themselves as much as they possibly could for the invasion that would now not be taking place until a later date. The feeling was bittersweet. We were relieved from fear, yet disappointed from how much we had hyped ourselves up for the jump. It wasn't until the next day at 8:30pm that the sky cleared and we were marched once again to the airfield, eerie silence in the air as every man began to be hit with realisation that we were headed to what we had been training for. With our blackened and painted faces of green and black we made our way to the Gooney Birds.

We'd heard the speeches as we stood before Colonel Sink. "Tonight is the night of nights, may God be with each of you fine soldiers." Followed by a speech from Eisenhower straight after, "Soldiers, Sailors and Airmen of the Allied Expeditionary Force, you are about to embark upon the Great Crusade, towards which we have striven these many months. The eyes of the world are upon you." I cannot be sure what it was about their speeches that rattled the most terrifying fear through my body. This was it, it was time to face combat like we had never done before. It had all been practice before now, preparing, learning, yet stood before the Colonel and Eisenhower made it ever more real that we might not return and that was the reality of it.

By 10pm we were being told to mount up as the jumpmasters pushed us onto the steps carrying over 100 pounds in weight. We wore our combat jacket and baggy combat trousers, holding cleaning patches, a spoon, razors, a flashlight, our three day K-rations plus an emergency one, two fragmentation grenades, an anti-tank mine, smoke grenade and a Gammon bomb used for blowing up tanks. The cigarettes we continuously smoked out of nervousness sat in the pocket of our trousers as well as our socks and maps. Attached on top of our uniform was a webbing belt with braces as well as a .45 pistol, a first aid kit, bayonette, a shovel and a water canteen. Over the top of this was our parachute harness with the main parachute in our backpacks and the reserve chute hooked onto the front. Our legs held a gas mask on the left and a bayonet on the right, though at the last minute we had been given leg bags, designed by the British Airborne to carry more ammunition and medical equipment. Across our chest, diagonally downwards, we held our musset bags containing spare underwear and additional ammunition that included our broken down rifles. Over the top of everything that we carried was our Mae West life jackets and a helmet. The weight was indescribable, we had trained to carry as much as 100 pounds, though that day we carried the added weight of the unknowing of whether we would return. We were given metal dome store crickets that we could squeeze to release a *click* for identification, one squeeze to call, two to answer.

We waited on board the planes for over an hour in nervous anticipation and hot stifling sweat before they took to the night sky. We were in the sky for over two hours when we heard the pilot shout to Winters, "Twenty minutes out." The door of the plane was removed, sending the rush of wind through the cabin, waking the sleeping soldiers who had been knocked out by the sickness tablets they had given us before setting off. Looking down we saw a sight that we had never seen before. Thousands of ships lined the waters below, naval combat ships, landing ships and landing craft, ancillary craft and merchant vessels. Even while flying to France, it did not feel real until that very moment. As the red light flashed on Winters called, "Stand up and hook up!" We flew through a sea of clouds, causing the formation of V's the thousands of Airborne had flown in, in sets of three, to break up. With formations broken, the side planes of what was once a part of the V had no device that would instruct the pilots to turn on the green light.

As we began to feel fear like never before, we were hit with German fire from all directions, causing the polits to react by increasing speed to 150 miles per hour and pressing the green light without knowing where we were other than Normandy. From every direction we heard planes screaming to the ground, artillery shells hitting metal and the wind that rushed through the cabin from the open doors.

"We need to get out of this goddamn plane!" I shouted, never had I been so eager to jump out of a plane in all my life. The air held smoke, fire and planes that screamed to the ground with its men still inside. The sky had become a flying graveyard. Thousands of parachutes littered the air in an anxious bid to be out of the aircrafts that were vulnerable to being hit.

"Let's go!" Shouted Winters, pushing each man towards the door and out of the plane, wasting no time for preparation or cold feet. I could feel the adrenaline and fear hurtling through my body at a million miles per hour. Hiker was next to jump after I had kicked out my leg bag and had been plunged into the air holding endless antiaircraft and allied planes fighting for dominance and survival. As I had jumped my leg bag had ripped loose, spiraling towards the ground and becoming lost in the war amongst it. I had no time to look for Hiker as I released my chute just moments before falling towards trees at a speed that would have killed me if I hit them. Lifting my legs as far as they would go I hit the ground hard, leaving every bone in my body battered and bruised as I took out my pocket knife and cut myself free of the chute. The trees had beaten at my legs as I descended though I remember thinking, *'that could have been a lot worse.'* All around me was machine gun fire, roaring planes overhead that fought to stay in the sky and protect its men. I thought about the mission, what we had been sent there to do. We had been briefed on our mission on 2nd June from 1st Lieutenant Nixon and Captain Hester on sand tables showing a demonstration of Normandy and where we would land, what we were to accomplish and how we would do it. They had told us that we would be dropped near Ste. Marie-du-Mont just over six miles south of Ste.Mere-Eglise with the objective of destroying the German garrison within the village and capturing the exit at causeway number 2 that was a road leading from the coast just north of Pouppeville. I stood at a tree, taking in the horrifying scenes before me, planes falling, men with the most heart wrenching cries as they lay wounded, crying for a medic to assist their wounds, holding their comrades with no life left within them, artillery shells firing from every direction, the sea a mass graveyard as ships sunk, taking down the crew that was once within it.

Before me, just beyond the trees I could see a PzKpfw V Panther tank approaching in my direction, carrying German's with aims of wiping us out. The heavy tracks imprinted the ground, shaking it in its steps over the sound of gunfire and falling aircraft. I stood at that tree for an amount of time I will never really know, looking into the sky through the battlefield of war from every angle, from the air, sea and ground, igniting the sky, sending the sea into flames and the ground a tormenting nightmare of walking dead. The sound of artillery fire began to fade as I saw a single star forcing its way through the devastation. It was as though for that moment in time I had taken myself away from the hell unveiling before me, away from men with loss of life and away from the screams that littered the sky in endless flows of pain, engraving themselves in my memories that would never be forgotten. Looking up to the sky, seeing the one single star through fog, smoke and flames, the sound of gunfire, explosions and heart wrenching cries faded around me.

*

It was 1938, Begin the Beguine by Artie Shaw spilled through Mother's house and into the street lined with trees freshly renewed of leaves for the awakening summer. The sun was shining in glorious rays of generous heat with not much sign of cooling anything in a hurry. I was painting Mother's porch in what I was hoping to be a job worthy of the meatloaf baking in the oven, letting off the teasing aroma that danced in the air refusing to be forgotten.

My body moved in sequence with the sound of trumpets, saxophones and Artie Shaw on the clarinet. I'd sat for a rest beneath the scorching sun, closing my eyes and letting the heat smother me. Until I saw her, walking down the street in a yellow dress that just covered her knees. My eyes fixed, her walk so elegant and carefree, until her eyes caught mine and she laughed as she walked by carrying the most beautiful smile

I had ever seen. She twirled in time with the music, sending her dress in a rhythm of dance.

"Have you had a good enough look?" She strides by then looks back at me before coming to a halt and making a U-turn.

Embarrassed though slightly impressed by her confidence, I hung my head and tried to hide the smile stretching across my face. I lifted my head as she sat beside me, the smell of her perfume fighting for the limelight with the meatloaf from the kitchen coming in at close second. Her big brown eyes looked into mine, not backing down or moving her gaze as she waited for my answer.

"I'm sorry Ma'am, my intentions were pure." I said the words through a smile, though inside it was as though my nerves had started a party at the sight of such a beautiful woman. She didn't say anything at first, she just leaned back in an attempt to work me out and see behind the strangers eyes looking straight back at her. She made me nervous, it was more than obvious that she knew it and boy did she thrive on it. After a number of seconds she leaned towards me with her chin on her hands, her eyes bigger than ever.

"Oh really? And what were your intentions, may I ask?" She asked me with a grin, knowing if there was anytime to put someone on the spot it was then.

"Well Ma'am, if I might be so bold, to ask if you would care for a drink with me?" Two could play at that game, though by her reaction the nerves inside her were all but still in comparison to my own.

"I don't even know your name, how could I possibly drink lemonade with a stranger?" She was a woman that carried confidence and back then, not many did, not like her.

Benny Goodman takes over on the radio at that moment, filling the air with sounds of fresh trumpets.

"Peter." Within seconds she had taken the lemonade out of my hand and sank the entire contents before wiping her mouth and handing the glass back to me.

"Nice to meet you Peter." She stood to make her exit as my mind raced on what to say to keep her company for a little while longer, worrying that I would respond before I had time to control my nerves.

"I don't even know your name." She pauses for a moment, as if pondering the possibilities. Spinning round in an effortless twirl she looks me in the eye with a smile, "How about you get another drink and you find out?"

We sat for the remainder of the day exchanging laughter and our stories. When the sun began to fall making way for the dark sky above us, she insisted I lay a blanket on the ground so we could lay under the sky. I didn't hesitate, I was not ready to lose her in an ocean of the world's people. I let her fill my night with her stories and life's mottos that quite obviously made her the fun and energetic person she was.

"What is your purpose?" She asked me, moving her head parallel with mine just inches away.

"What do you mean?" I asked bewildered, kneeling on one elbow and looking into her eyes.

"We're all here for a reason aren't we? What is yours?" She turns her head and looks me in the eye, her brown hair sitting comfortably across her chest.

"I suppose it is to make my Ma proud, do something with my life that will make her the most proud of me." I said it back in my head and regretted it straight away, she probably thought I was some nerdy kid.

"I think that is lovely." She smiled, taking her eyes from mine and back to the stars that littered the sky above us.

"What about yours?" I ask, interested to know her response.

"My purpose is to feel the greatest love you could ever imagine. To be ignited with those feelings like everyday is a beautiful display of fascinating colours." She was smiling more than ever, letting her passion for life come out in those few moments. "I want to feel it all, y'know? I don't think there is anything more powerful than love itself, to feel loved and be loved are the most treasured things of all." I nod my head in agreement, unable to stop smiling at the passionate woman laid before me I had been so lucky to spend such wonderful time with.

"Do you know that the stars are those we have lost looking down upon us?" I turn my head to see the stars shining blissfully in the clear sky and look back at her to see she is *deep in thought, her gaze so deep in the night air I wondered whether a response would reach her.*

"What about in the day? Where do they go then?" I challenged, interested to hear her philosophies and how her mind worked, how it made her the person she was to make me feel so many crazy emotions all at the same time.

"Do you think they disappear in the day?" She adds, "They may not be visible, yet they are still there. They make themselves seen in the dark, to offer light when it may seem so far away from reach." I never forgot those words, not once.

I turn to face her and she instantly does the same, her skin so close to mine I could almost touch her, though I would have never dreamt of disrespecting her in such a way. She had not only caught my attention that day, she captured my heart and everything that came with it. I felt the beautiful sting of a thousand flying butterflies as she planted a gentle kiss on my cheek.

"Jennifer, my name is Jennifer."

*

The sound of heavy German fire brings me back to reality. Somehow from so far away she had the capability to give me strength to see beyond falling men, the screaming planes and the explosions that rattled my eardrums. Looking at the star flying lonesome in the sky I remember her words. She had given me strength without the credit of knowing. The mission was still before us, despite that we had become separated by the night's unfortunate events.

"I'll do it for you Jen, I'll come back to you."

Walking through the trees making as little sound as possible, scanning every indication of movement with my .45 automatic at the ready in sweaty hands, I looked for my comrades of the 101st with eyes holding alertness that did not cease to make room for vulnerability. Sudden movement in the trees freezes me to the spot. Using my clicker I identified myself. One click...followed by a two click response that told me it was not an enemy. Coming closer into view I knew straight away who it was just from his small-framed silhouette.

"Dammit Hiker, where have you been?" I shout in as much of a whisper as possible, both angry at sneaking up and happy that he hadn't got himself killed.

"Got bit on the beach, dahm Krauts." He says, shuffling closer with one hand over his arm and another on his .45.

"Oh Christ." Taking out my medical kit I wrap the wound in bandages to stop the bleeding. "We need to find the others, still got an objective even with a lousy arm."

We didn't know where we were, though we had been told to link up with other units, defend positions and fight the Germans. By the time morning broke through we had taken down fifteen German's between us, each as terrifying as the last yet we never let them see that when we put a rifle bullet through them which was as easier than we had imagined after experiencing what we had in the air.

"We need to get to Ste. Marie-du-Mont," I said aloud, taking the map from my trousers and opening it up. "We're here, Le Grand-Chemin, just under two miles from where we need to be." We carried on towards our objective, keeping our eyes open and our wits constantly on edge, ready to take down Germans with rifles or artillery men hiding in the hedgerows.

It was around 6am when we ran into Winters as well as the Captain of Dog company, Captain Jerre Gross and forty of his men. A number of other 2nd battalion staff had also joined the unit, meaning we were becoming stronger as a group. It was a welcoming relief to be joined units and even more so with Winters. It was evident that as we neared closer to Ste. Marie-du-Mont, the commander of the German unit defending the area, was also gaining on the village. He had three battalions, one at Ste.Mere-Eglise, another battalion at Ste. Marie-du-Mont and another in Carentan. An hour later we moved into Le Grand-Chemin, a small village just under two miles from our objective. We were ordered to sit and rest by Winters, which we did with no hesitation.

Hiker rubbed his forehead as he lit up a cigarette and drank from his canteen. "We've only just entered this war and it feels like we've been fighting it half my life." He was a good soldier,

strong and willing, yet the day's events had compiled themselves together and come to the surface now it had opportunity. I copy his idea and take a smoke from my rations, striking a match to light the end. I sit on the road and let the wind brush my face, "We're nearly there brother, keep it together." I put my arm around his shoulders and gently shook him as I let out a sigh. "Hell of a day." He laughs quietly as he draws on his cigarette and throws it to the ground.
"Yeah, hell of a day."

Fifteen minutes later Lieutenant George Lavenson, previously a member of Easy Company came into view from down the path and had started talking to Winters. Within a handful of minutes he came over to where we were resting and instructed us on our next move.
"There is a four-gun battery of German 105mm cannon two hundred or so metres across from some hedgerows and open fields. Opposite, there is a farmhouse with the name Brecourt Manor. There is a fifty man platoon of infantrymen defending the position and has gone into action firing on Utah Beach. You are to drop all of your equipment, keeping only your weapons, ammunition and grenades. This will be a quick direct assault with aid of a base of fire from numerous positions. These need to be as close to the guns as possible." With that, he began setting up the two machine-guns that would give covering fire as we were moved to our positions.

Three machine-gunners were placed along the hedge that led to our objective with strict instructions to lay down covering fire. As Winters began crawling we waited at our positions to see him take his M-1 and fire two shots at a German that had been making his way through the trench with his helmet visible from above ground.

"Nice shot." Whispered Hiker in my ear as we watch from our positions, waiting for the word when we should attack. Compton, Guarnere and Malarkey went to the left, Lipton and Ranney to the right. We were led by Winters down the hedge as he whispered, "Follow me."

It wasn't until that day that I turned my combat training into experience. MK-2 Grenades were thrown into the trench and across the field, M1 Garands firing into the backs of the enemy as they fled towards the farmhouse, constant machine-gun fire from the German's, it all made my heart pump ferociously with adrenaline that no amount of training had prepared me for. After just fifteen seconds since the charge, we had captured the first cannon that was covered by three men, while Toye and Compton began firing towards the next. I felt the man I once was slip away, with a new version of myself pushing through, one that would complete a mission and take down the enemy with no amount of remorse. The M1 gripped between my fingers, firing one after another, straight through the enemy and taking them down. Hiker was three men up from me, shouting as he fired, "Take that you dahm Krauts!" Taking a grenade from his musette bag he launches it towards a group of fleeing German's and takes them out as it hits the ground beneath their feet.

After tremendous fighting, firing and grenade launching we were successfully able to destroy a German battery of 105's looking towards causeway number 2 onto Utah Beach. There is no doubt that the men of Easy Company who had been shot during the assault made an incredible difference to the outcome that day. They had given their lives to the mission without a single shred of doubt and for that we respected them. Four men were lost on that mission, a further two wounded, yet they had contributed to the taking down of fifteen Germans with many more injured and captured twelve German prisoners. As a company, we had destroyed the fifty-man platoon of German paratroopers that had been defending the guns and the celebrations afterwards were to be remembered.

As late afternoon approached from a very long and tiresome day, we reached Ste. Marie-du-Mont, to which the Germans had moved out. Myself, Hiker and the rest of the 2nd battalion were marched just over a mile away to a small village of Culoville where we rested for the night with Winters setting outposts in place during the night.
"What a crazy few days fellas." Sighs Buck while swallowing down his K rations of chocolate. Many men cheered in agreement as they ate and drank the powdered coffee.

"We're here to win and that is what we will do." Shouted Ranney lifting his coffee in the air to which we all followed suit.

"I think we definitely did that today, if the Krauts aren't scared of us yet they soon will be!" Joined Salty from the back who was vigorously rubbing at his legs that had begun to bruise from landing. More cheers from the room and an outburst of individual conversation.

"I never thought I could be the man I was today, always thought I'd be too soft but in a weird way I think I enjoyed it. I'm not really sure if I should feel guilty for that." Says Hiker as he changes his socks and lays down in an exhausted retreat.

"Why would you feel guilty?" I asked, though I knew what was coming, the heart he wore amongst his sleeve would always be there, despite how many Germans he took down.

"I enjoyed taking a life, surely that's not normal." He laughs a little yet I knew it was bothering him from the scrunched up expression on his face that indicated he was thinking deeply about it.

"They started this war, we're finishing it, Hikes. If there is anything that I have learned it is that thinking that way will have you killed. Still got a long way to go brother, so might as well enjoy it rather than it eat you alive." He nods his head as though processing the information and smiles.

We had survived the D-Day landings, pushed out the Germans in Ste. Marie-du-Mont, seen men fall who we had become like brothers, captured a German battery of 105's and still, it was just the beginning of a journey through war that raged on angrily. We had far to go and what was coming was far from predictable, yet far from impossible for us to win. As we somewhat slept that night I dreamt of the horrors I had seen while jumping out of the C-47 Gooney Bird, dreams that would haunt my sleep for an unwelcoming duration of time.

June 1944 - Dachau Concentration Camp, Kaufering

The night I arrived at Kaufering the rain showed no mercy in just how terrible it was to sleep on the wooden platforms with water coming up to our level and leaking from the roof. Some of the men took off their uniforms to sleep, though I took note of the other mens ideas and kept it on through the night so I would not have to endure putting on a wet, cold uniform in freezing weather. I had made the mistake at Auschwitz, though I only made it once. We huddled together during the night, for warmth and through lack of choice with crowding.
"I came from Auschwitz, told I was fit for work and was needed here. They didn't even tell me where *here* was, just chucked me in the train car with hundreds of others for days with just a piece of bread and margarine. I'd been on them dahm train cars before when they deported me from Lodz but this time just felt different, felt worse." Gersw says shivering between Tomasz and Lukasz from the summer rain that had made its way into the hunt causing everything to turn wet and damp. "Maybe it is because I didn't know what to expect at Auschwitz, this time I did but it was much worse." Gersw was an old man who had lost his wife and four children upon arrival at Auschwitz-Birkenau. Two of the children had been twin boys and unfortunately he had heard the stories of Dr Mengele's experiments, meaning he had said his silent, silent goodbyes to ever finding them again. He rubbed his temple in frustration,

letting out a sigh of desperation that said *we have had enough now, we just want to go home.*

"I lost my Mama in Auschwitz." Saying the words out loud was like the memory had burned stronger inside me again, relighting a fire I had desperately tried to put out.

"Chimney?" Asks Gersw, pulling his blanket around his shoulders with his worn out clogs slipping off his feet. I shake my head as I see my Mother laying on the ground, beaten, bruised and weak. They had stripped her of everything, let her die in the most inhumane way with no heart to ever feel guilty for it.

"No, they beat her when she was too weak. I didn't really get to speak to her for very long so anything could have happened during the time before I found her again."

"She'll have ended up in the chimney anyway." Snarls Tomasz, the more abrupt and to the point prisoner in the hut.

"Tomasz!" Cries Gersw, his eyes wide with shock and horror. "Give the boy a break! I don't think that is what he needs to hear!"

"What the truth?" Snaps Tomasz rubbing his swollen ankles in a bid to relieve the pain. "Everyone we have lost went through the chimney, the sooner we face the facts the better." He slams his feet down on the wooden platform and attempts to lay down amongst the other sleeping men.

"It's okay, I knew they would send her to the crematorium, it's the only way anyone ever really gets out of Auschwitz, unless they are sent away to work like us." My heart stops at the thought of her being chucked into the metal equipment like she was merely a broken toy that needed to be destroyed. "She didn't just look beaten though, her veins looked strange, like chemicals were pumping through her. Her and my Aunt are twins, I worry that Dr Mengele got his hands on them and that is maybe what caused her death. I guess I will never know."

"There is a high probability son, especially if they were identical but listen, you'll survive this war, I can see it in your eyes. A lot happened to ya but you got a long way to go before they break you." Lukasz smiles as he gently pats me on the back. He was another of the younger men within the hut, late twenties from what I could work out from his shaven head and thin face. I seemed to like Lukasz the most, he was young, lost his family, the woman he loved without really knowing what happened to them, he was a skeleton attached to bone, frail but never stopped pushing through each day to get through the war and find the ones he loved more than anything else in the world and he always managed in some way, to bring a smile to the depressing and damp hut every night. He spoke about them every single night though not a single person grew bored of it, not even Tomasz who was always grumpy from the day's work and having to wear cement bags on his feet through having no clogs. It gave most a sense of normality away from being a prisoner and reminded us of who we used to be before a number branded our whole lives.

Our hut had been set to labor in the nearby mountains, digging tunnels that would be put to use by the Germans for underground aircraft. Hundreds of satellite camps that were attached to major concentration camps were created in 1944 and 1945 throughout the German Reich. We were to hollow out the sides of the mountains, or sometimes caves for vast systems of factories and tunnels that would be safe from Allied bombers. On some days when not sent out to the mountains in whatever weather poured on us, we were to work on building new weapons that the German's could use against the Allies such as the Jet-fighter or V-2 rockets. Many men thought of building the weaponry purposefully wrong though under the burning eyes of SS guards not many succeeded or dared to take the risk.

Much like Auschwitz our day began at 4:30am. During the summer months this was bad enough however during the winter and cruel weather that beat down hard on our tired and cold skin it was like murder, which for most, it was. During roll call many would collapse, to then be beaten by the SS guards and Kapo with their sticks or piece of rubber-covered cable until they physically could not stand up, to which they would finish them off by kicking them in the ribs or the face and ordering them to be carted off. We were to jog to the roll call area and stand at attention for an hour and a half no matter what weather was given to us that day. We were shouted orders, *"Hat on, hat off, drop to the ground."* I could tell they were fishing out the weak from the healthy and on most mornings many were selected to be sent away, to which they never returned. Myself, Lukasz, Gersw and even Tomasz helped each other on days when exhaustion took over, holding each other up until the SS came round so we would only have to stand unaided for a short period of time, shared the food rations we received which were mediocre at best and helped to create warmth in the clothes and clogs that we had, or didn't have. We had become somewhat of a team, brothers who looked out for one another and on many nights I thought of Henryk, how I missed him yet I did not cry for him. He was exactly where he had been waiting to be. I'd told the men in the hut about Henryk and even Tomasz held back on his remarks as they all bowed their head and said their respects for a man who did so much but gained so little.

As we stood at attention and obeyed the orders shouted at us, we were informed that five prisoners were sentenced to hanging as a result of making foot-rags out of blankets. They were escorted out of the potato cellar by Kirsch and Kramer and we were to watch as each man's life was taken. They were killed for attempting to save their own lives, the sad irony of it caused boiling hot anger to rise within me as I saw the life drain from each man's face. A young boy by the name of Baruch, only eighteen years old, hung in the very same place for taking his blanket with him when he marched off to work, infested with lice that was an ongoing problem in Kaufering, to keep himself warm against the bitter cold and killed in the roll call area for it. I had seen so many deaths, seen so many people die and as much as it chipped away at you, pieces at a time, changing who you are from the inside out, sadly, from the increase in witnessing them, it became more bearable to keep your eyes on them as they hung while SS men and Kapo patrolled round, beating anybody who looked away with their iron bars, rubber-covered cables, sticks and rubber hoses.

After roll call, our black water with no coffee or sugar in it and attempts at washing with hardly any water and no soap, we were sent out on our labor details. We marched to the mountains, feet in clogs that were too big or cement bags that rubbed and caused scarring, ankles swollen and bruised, hunger striking down most on the way to work or on our way back. For those that fell during the work day we were ordered to carry them back so they could be counted at roll call. While tunneling through the mountains we were given Mollsuppe, three cups of water with dried vegetables but for many it was not enough to lessen the hunger that rifled the camps. We returned to camp on an evening at eight, sometimes ten and received the camp soup, being thin and watery with mostly two unpeeled potatoes. On our walk back from the mountains many men would rush to grass they could see and begin wolfing it down like it was chocolate, or search the lice-ridden dead for mouldy bread that could be devoured, only to be beaten by the guards for such attempts. When returning back to camp we would undergo another roll call as well as waiting in line for our evening soup and slice of bread. My feet would pulse beneath the weight I had been carrying for sixteen hours, my ankles would swell and send sharp shooting pains up my legs as we stood in line in front of the kitchen and waited for our soup bowls that were never washed but handed from one person to the next. They were not always used as soup bowls, as time went on in the camp they were used as wash bowls and bed pans, they were somewhat of a luxury in camp and we were to make do with what we had.

"I think I have forgotten what it feels like to not be hungry." I say to Lukasz who was hovering over a small iron stove in the centre of the hut. Sometimes when it was possible we would use the stove for warmth but it didn't do much against the harsh climate that made its way inside.
"Me too kid, me too." He places the green moldy bread we had been given into a tin can and poured *'coffee'* over the bread rations. My stomach had been in knots for months of being in the camp, most days I felt I would not be able to make it through the day, I sometimes questioned how I did.
"Do you think the German's will win this war?" I asked, feeling my bones vibrate against my pale and fragile skin as I breathed. Lukasz uses a piece of wire to hang the tin can over the stove and purses his lips together in thought. "I can't say for sure, I hope not, or we will be cooking mould off bread for a

very long time." He smiles and ruffles my hair as he sinks back into his bunk and lights a cigarette.

"Where did you get that?" I asked, shocked and horrified at the same time. Men had died for being in possession of such luxuries. Tomasz smells the cigarette and sits up quickly, which disturbs every man next to him. Lukasz laughs and hands him the rolled up cigarette.

"Favour for a favour and all that." He says, winking in my direction and taking the cigarette back from Tomasz before he became too greedy with it.

"I don't know what I will do after this war." I say, hanging my head and remembering everyone I had lost. "Everyone I know is dead, I don't have anybody left." As the words left my mouth I realised how pathetic I sounded and swung my hand in the air as if to say *forget I said that.*

"Same here small one, same here. I tell you what, we both make it out of this prison you can come live with me, how's about that? We can eat and drink as much as we like and curse these goddamn animals every night for the rest of our lives for putting us in here. How's that?" Gersw sits up from the wooden platform and raises his hand as he takes the cigarette from Lukasz, 'Here here to that!" He says, inhaling sharply and holding it for several moments before blowing it out again. "Here here to...that!"

June 7th - July 12th - Carentan - Normandy France

On the 6th June, 1944 we landed in Normandy France under the Command of Maj. Gen. Maxwell D. Taylor. More than 6,000 paratroopers landed on French land beginning in the early morning hours after jumping from C-47 Transports. A further 6,000 paratroopers under command of General Matthew Ridgway's 82nd Airborne Division jumped into Normandy slightly after us. Glider missions supporting both divisions of the 101st and the 82nd followed later that morning and evening. The sights I saw that day were not ones that could be explained easily. Death chewed up the beaches that day, spitting out only the remains of what was once great soldiers. We had however achieved our D-Day objectives of securing the causeways and now we were to head South towards Carentan to join with American units coming West from Omaha Beach.

We had managed to clear Vierville from the enemy before moving onto Angoville-au-Plain with Easy Company in reserve and spent the duration of the day fighting off counter attacks from the Germans 6th Parachute Regiment. Over the course of the next three days we were to take position to defend regimental headquarters with the 1st Battalion of the 506th taking St. Come-du-Mont. During this time we were able to regain energy which would be an understatement to say we needed it. Sleep in its truest form was still a distant memory with counter attacks and mortar fire, yet we were not out in the field and we were grateful enough for that. Not only were we battered and bruised from the landings, some men of the company had taken hits while seizing the causeways and the German battery, so three days that were less intense came as a welcoming break on some part to most of us. Hiker had seen a medic at Culoville which left little damage where he had been shot other than a scar that would probably always remind him of it.

We linked up with the 29th Division that came from Omaha Beach on 10th June, yet we were unable to progress the secured beachhead until German forces were drove out of Carentan, which proved a strenuous task given the inadequate supplies and artillery as well as the establishment of the German 6th Parachute Regiment that were defending Carentan with everything they had. The endless 6ft high hedgerows with narrow lanes held possible enemies that could attack during the infantry assault, yet it was a task that could not be avoided. We were therefore sent on a nightmarch Southwest, around the town of Carentan to which synchronized attacks would start at 5am on the morning of June 12th, following Fox Company through marshes, over a bridge and across fields that led us to the railroad.

"Wish they'd hold up a little." Sneered Ranney, fighting his feet through the thick mud that attached itself to his feet with every step. "They've already trampled through this, makes it harder to walk in!" A few of the men laughed though we were all on the receiving end of walking through mad that had already been churned from endless marching feet of the leading company before us.

"Don't think they are bothered, haven't seen one of them turn round yet to see if we're still following." I snap as I look at the men in front gaining distance between us.

"It's like being back training with Sobel again." Laughed Hiker, which lightened the mood of the surrounding men.

"I suppose even this is better than being back under Sobels command." I laugh at the thought, "Though it would be funny seeing him trying to get through this with his 'Hi-Ho-Silver!' No doubt he would have fallen face-first by now and *that* is something I wouldn't want to miss." We were whispering, trying to remain as inconspicuous as possible and surprise the German's with an attack they were not expecting.

"Quiet!" Demanded Winters, not wanting to give our game away, though I was sure a smile was trying its hardest to not show an appearance on his face at the thought of Sobel trying to get through those same marshes. "I'll try to communicate with them again."

The most frustrating part to the whole mission was digging in and setting up machine guns, to be told by headquarters to once again move out. The mission was to reach Carentan through Vieirlle to St. Come-du-Mont then cross the river. Even after crossing over the Douve River we lost contact completely with Fox Company, who had not spared a thought for keeping the two companies together. With a sudden outburst we were ordered to *'Get down!'* as we were hit with a counter attack from the left by a German MG-42 machine gun that was undoubtedly our most terrifying enemy, more than any German that stood behind it, we could take them easy, yet the machine-gun they fired with would rip you apart within seconds if exposed to the eye of the gunner. Hitler's *'Buzz Saw'* we called them due to the high scale capabilities of the weapon itself. It was a weapon that fired so rapidly with a sound like ripping cloth as it tore through the air, that we feared the very name. You didn't have to be in combat for a long time to know that it could spit out 1,550 rounds of high-velocity, 7.92 millimeter ammunition per minute, working out at 25 rounds per second. With bullets firing in from the left we had to think quick and respond even faster. Within seconds Lipton had ordered his machine-gunner to set up facing the Buzz Saw, which proved a difficult task to remain unexposed with how loud the gun was. Luckily incoming fire ceased and we were back on our feet and marching towards the railroad.

As we marched through the night we remained cautious, expecting attacks at any point from positions unknown which required us to be ready for a counter attack at all times, despite how quiet the road seemed.

"I don't like it when it's quiet." Whispered Hiker, clutching at his .45 with both hands.

"Makes you wonder where they are doesn't it?" I whisper back, scanning every possible hiding place, expecting fire from each one. It wasn't that it made us paranoid, which could have been a good thing if we were, having too much confidence could probably have killed you, it was more than we were always alert, which made the difference between life and death.

"Half expect them to jump out at any second, would rather them all steam out at once, least we would know where they were." He jumps, realising it was a man of the company standing on uneven ground and scraping his boot.

"They wouldn't get past you anyway Hikes, you're always ready." I joke, accompanied by harmless laughs from Ranney and Buck.

We'd reached the railroad, set up a defensive position and expected to be firing rounds at hidden German Infantry, though no attack came. It turned out that the Germans had pulled back from Carentan due to low ammunition from firing so many rounds during the beach landings with no incoming supplies. They had left only one fifty-man company with a machine-gun to fire up the road directing towards the Southwest, as well as 80mm mortars that were positioned on the edge of town at the T-junction to hold Carentan for as long as possible while they reloaded and prepared to attack from the Southwest.

"What now?" Asked Lipton, already knowing the answer yet waiting for orders from Winters for clarification.

"We head northeast with the objective of attacking Carentan from the T-junction. The 6th Parachute Regiment is defending it, we take them out, we take Carentan." Replied Winters, making it sound easy though he knew we were capable, even without a full unit of men. "The last stretch of road to the junction is straight with a slope leading downwards. There are ditches on either side, Fox Company will take the left flank, Easy will head straight down the road with Dog Company in reserve. We need to move into Carentan and join with the 327th that are coming in from the north.

"When do we headout?" Asked Lipton, ready to inform the rest of the battalion though we were listening and dreading the walk down the road as soon as Winters had said it. We would be exposed in the open, vulnerable to German artillery like wide open targets with backup from the left.

"Now." Ordered Winters, already preparing the men and walking towards the city.

That night we became restless, longing for just a fraction of time we could close our eyes and sleep with no disturbance, which was impossible through constant setting up positions to be moved out again.

"Sir, when will we attack?" Asked Lipton, scratching his head beneath his helmet as he had grown agitated.

"Orders are to attack at 0600 hours." He replied bluntly, becoming frustrated himself by the constant rearranging of positions. "1st platoon on the left, 2nd on the right and 3rd in reserve."

We laid in the ditches on the right, waiting for the signal to attack, like lions stalking their prey, waiting for the moment to pounce and claim dominance over an enemy we had grown to hate that were remaining silent, not giving away their positions that left us in eerie silence for a duration of time that became tantalizing.

When 6am arrived we heard Winters, "Move out", that started the advance of men towards the junction. Within seconds the enemy had started firing from their Buzz Saw that shook the entire road with its power. Men began splitting up, darting to the left, to the right, bullets firing down the road in directions unseen.

"Keep your head down!" I shouted, pushing Hiker's head down further into the ditch to avoid incoming rounds of continuous fire.

"Move out!" Shouted Winters, with fear and anger filling his voice, trying everything he could to get us to move.

"I can't! We'll die!" Shouted Hiker through terrified screams, keeping his head down and huddling into the men that were doing the same. We were being attacked by the weapon we feared most and bravery was so far out of sight we wondered whether we would ever gain the courage to listen to Winters orders.

"Move out!"He shouted again. Still, we stayed where we were, hoping the attack would die down so we could get out of the ditch while still clutching at our lives. Still, the machine-gun roared through the night, hitting anything that was in its path. I remember the fear paralyzing me as I looked into Winters eyes looming over us, unable to move as my body remained frozen in that ditch, the only thought that circled my mind was *'If I move out of this ditch I will be ripped apart by that gun.'* Winters turned into somebody I had never seen before as he threw down all the gear he was holding, keeping his M1 firmly in his hands and started to kick us in the back, in the legs shouting like we had never heard him do before, "Get going!" Then to the opposite side shouting the same. He was standing in the middle of the road, somehow avoiding the shells that were screaming through the air around him like he was a ghost that could not be touched. It was difficult to distinguish what we feared more at that point, though judging by our exit from the ditches it was most likely Winters, who we had never before heard shout the way he did that day.

Following Winters up the road we heard his orders, "Turn right at the intersection." As we ran we threw grenades from our musset bags and pockets at the machine-gun, throwing with little to no aim in fear of dodging the bullets that spat in every direction. A mighty explosion and suddenly, the machine-gun sat silent, along with the men who had been behind it. We had taken them out, even with fear screaming through us, certain that we would lose our lives to the MG-42 we had achieved what we had set out to do and the confidence it gave us was evident in every man, yet we had not finished. We ran into the intersection with legs that had trained for such combat, yet adrenaline sending us numb. We were sent to the right to clear out any houses of enemy fire. Grenades were thrown, rifles fired, everywhere your eyes met was buildings being blown up, men falling with the aid of a medic with morphine to numb the pain.

Running into a house with my M1 clutched in my hands, I stand behind the door, throw a fragmentation grenade inside as I cover my head, hear the explosion and move inside, two men behind me. I couldn't see Hiker, he had taken another building just left of me. Pointing my rifle I spot a German crouched at a window pointing his rifle outside and firing. One shot to the head and he fell, his K98k rifle falling with him along with a Potato masher stick grenade. I take the grenades and exit the room, my M1 pointing in each room before entering, waiting for a target to stand before it. Motors fired in from an opposite building, sending shrapnel from the street through the broken windows. Suddenly, a sharp and agonising bite to my left hand makes me drop my rifle and fall to the ground. The pain was not one to be described easily, other than that one thousand pieces of glass were cutting into me at the same time. Using my other hand I instantly apply pressure, keeping my head down as bullets fly around me. As I looked down at my hand I had been shot, blood squirting from my hand though it had passed through just below my index finger. Hastily I take a bandage from my first aid kit and wrap it around my hand just in time to move away from the door I had been sat against as a mortar blew in from the entrance of the building, leaving shrapnel cutting into my feet and ankles.

By the time it hit 7am we had captured Carentan successfully, though many had wounds that needed to be bandaged or medically seen at the aid station. I was one of them as a medic put sulfa powder over the wounds followed by bandages around my hand and ankles. The shrapnel had been tweezered out with the aid of morphine for the pain. Scars would remain imprinted from that day, yet I knew I had left with my life and I thanked God many times for giving me that.
"Looks nasty." Came the voice of Hiker as he walked over with a smile.
"Just a scratch. You get hit?" I ask, looking him over and seeing no visible wounds.
"Nope, like you said, they can't get past me." He laughs as he sits next to me and takes a sip out of his canteen. "Bullet hit my helmet though, pretty sure if it had been a few to the right it would have gone straight through my jaw." He was looking at the bandages on my ankles and smiled again. "Can you walk?"

"Yeah, can't take me down that easy.." I joke, "..and what are you laughing at?"

"Just feeling lucky brother, God has been on our side."

*

We were positioned to the right of the railroad track when we witnessed enemy tanks in a hedgerow a handful of yards away, that began firing in our direction. Only when Easy let off a bazooka were they drawn back. We headed southwest down the railroad where we set up a defensive position behind a hedgerow with the enemy right in front of us in another, pondering over their triggers for anyone that dared move. During the night we caught up on sleep, as much as could be expected and I thought of Jen. It felt like a lifetime since I had been laid with her head on my chest, talking into the night about matters of everyday life, neither one of us expected it to be this way now.

"You're thinking of her aren't you?" Asks Hiker laid beside me eating tinned meat with his spoon.

"All the time." I sigh, leaning back to open him to conversation. "I told myself I wouldn't when we left for here, yet she doesn't seem to leave my mind."

"I think it's the same for us all, it is what will see us through to the end of the war you know." He chucks the tin down and licks his lips. "Just got to find that line between seeing you through and causing a distraction, just like you have told me. My Rosie is on my mind all the time and my daughter, I can't wait to get back to them but you have to remind yourself that they are your protection, not your distraction." He spoke sense and I knew everything he was saying was right, to not fall into daydream yet let them sit peacefully within your mind. The world at that moment was about survival and not much more, for everyone living in Europe, to just see the next day and hope that the war would soon be over. That was our real mission, the bigger picture that was important for us to not forget.

We stayed in position, eating our rations, holding quiet conversations, sleeping for small quantities of time, fixing our bayonets and smoking into the night that held a cool and steady breeze. By 5:30am we were ready to attack, though just as we were given the order to move out, the Germans 6th Parachute Regiment released their counterattack that we had expected would come during the night. We gave everything we had, rifle-fire, motors being fired, grenades launched through tiredness that had long since taken over. Sherman tanks rolled in and offered artillery support though they were shooting into their own men, the whole scenario felt a disaster, unplanned by the surprise attack we had expected much earlier. What turned situations worse during extreme fire was that Fox Company had fallen back, meaning Dog Company was completely exposed, so they also fell back, leaving us alone with the enemy. We didn't back down, we fired with every ounce of strength we had, machine-guns set up at the entrance to the hedgerow, mortars just ten meters ahead sending shrapnel flying through the air with no care for where it landed, or who it landed on. The officers were running up and down the line, ensuring everything was done to stop the enemy.

Pulling my M1 into clearer view I spot a German behind a machine-gun, firing aggressively towards Easy Company and its men. I set my aim, amongst the chaos and continuous fire I wait, line up the target, then pull the trigger. The German fell in an instant, though more were still firing and right where Fox Company should have been a German Panzer tank rolled in, heavy tracks imprinting the ground with its dominance. McGrath and Welsh took no time to rush into the open field with a bazooka that they aimed straight for the tank. Aim, fire. It hits the tank though bounces straight off and with just moments passing, the tank realigns its 88mm cannon and aims for the two men, fire, just missing their heads as a result of the tank trying to make an appearance through the hedge. The bazooka was reloaded in an anxious cry to be fired before the cannon. The bazooka aimed, it fired and it hit in exactly the right spot ensuring within just seconds an explosion had ripped through the tank in illuminous orange and black flames and smoke that flew towards the sky.

The celebrations were far from present, despite the German tanks behind falling back at the sight of the explosion. We stood our ground, held our rifles between our hands and fired like our life depended on it, which it did. It was us or them, no mercy. Motors ripped the sky heading for the target, M1 bullets following their path, shot after shot, grenades being thrown in an attempt to take as many of the enemy as possible. My hand was excruciatingly sore for weeks after I had been shot, though in those moments of pure pumped adrenaline, I had forgotten all about that wound. It was amazing what that did to you, pumped you so full of life during a time when it could have also drained you. It was not until 4:30pm when we were relieved by the 2nd Armored and infantrymen from the 29th Division that took our places. It was the most welcoming sight we had ever seen. We were worn out, exhausted, some badly hurt with wounds that needed to be attended to at the medic station, Hiker being one, as he had taken a bullet to the right side of his left foot, ripping straight through his boot and puncturing through his skin, shattering bone and leaving him in immense pain. The tanks stormed across our lines and headed into the German's hedgerows, taking out anything in its path as though it was not there. The infantry walking beside them were a sight for sore eyes, they took over from us and I had never been so happy to just close my eyes for a few brief moments and breathe in the French air.

Back in the heart of Carentan we were placed in undestroyed buildings to remain on division reserve. Hiker had been in the medical station for several hours before finding me in an abandoned house, just opposite a bombed out bar.

"I could do with some of that." Shouted Hiker, hobbling over and looking at the bottle of whiskey placed in my hand.

"How's the foot?" I ask, pouring the whiskey into a tumbler found in the kitchen. "Looks like they can catch you after all."

"They took the bullet out with some tweezers though I'm not sure I'll be on the next objective." He sighs in disappointment before necking the full glass and handing it back for me to fill up again. "Where'd you get this? Not bad."

"One of the stores. Didn't have much to choose from but I suppose I got lucky with this one." I hand him back the glass to which he drinks at a much more reasonable pace. "I was worried when that tank came in, pointed straight for McGrath and Welsh, would have taken them out in one if they weren't trying to climb that hedgerow."

"All part of the game isn't it? One day we're here fighting for our men and the good of Europe, the next we could be gone." He says it so matter-of-factly that I wondered whether he had come to terms with it long before. He shuffles into the bedroom opposite and lays down his gear before reappearing with his helmet in his hands. "Y'know, ever since that bullet hit my helmet I've been a little worried to take it off, then I remember, everything has to happen for a reason doesn't it?" I purse my lips together in thought and left the question unanswered. That would be another day's story.

We were pulled from the frontline June 29th, sweaty, dirty, exhausted and in need of a night's sleep that would not be disturbed by the sound of heavy artillery and enemy fire. The 83rd Infantry Division took our place with faces of shock as they saw us so worn and ridden with dirt. The sight was overwhelming on both parts, they were so clean, so fresh and ready for action, whereas we were ready for anything that did not include lifting a rifle or sleeping in a ditch if even for just a handful of blissful days. Carentan was our last action in Normandy as we were pulled into a field camp just North of Utah Beach. During the time we waited for our departure back to England we kept our rifles and bayonets clean, patrolled the area around the field as well as endured hot showers that were the most welcoming.

As we remained in the field we were visited by Gen Omar Bradley for an awards ceremony. He stood on a raised platform and read out the Citations for Distinguished Service Cross for eleven of Easy Company's soldiers. Afterwards, he told us of the excellent work we were doing so far and to carry it on throughout our next objectives. Excitement filled the field that day and not just from the awards but from being told that we could be in Berlin come Christmas time. We silently all hoped that we would be able to spend Christmas at home with family, yet we understood this was a slim, if not impossible chance. By July 1st Winters had been promoted to Captain that we were all in agreement was well deserved. He showed courage and bravery like no other man that dropped into Normandy and the endless selflessness guaranteed that no other man deserved it more. It was not until July 11th we were marching up the ramp of the landing ship craft and said the most joyful goodbye to France we ever thought we would make. The next night we arrived in Southampton and we were taken by train back to Aldbourne.

I sometimes wonder how the events of Normandy did not eat me alive, though deep down I know that we worked not as friends but as brothers that had become family. Without the trust and bravery of all those other men I would not be walking out of Normandy. The nightmares hold frequent tenancy within my mind and I know that every man, not just of the 101st but all those that dropped onto those beaches will hold the same burden. There is no greater accomplishment than successfully completing what was set out to do for a war that needed ending, yet it did not come without sacrifice. The men we lost would never be forgotten as they spared their lives on those beaches. I think about those that fought, those that did not make it home and those that are forever troubled by the sights that we saw every single day and it is with great pleasure that I do, for without remembering them, how can we be truly grateful for what was accomplished.

September 1944 - Dachau Concentration Camp, Kaufering

The cold was starting to make its way into camp like an unpleasant and unwelcoming visitor that we hoped would hold off. We hadn't needed to huddle together quite so much during recent months to keep warm and with the wind blowing that little icer everyday we knew it was coming. There was an order to survive living in camps, the first being that of eating and drinking. Food and water were so scarce that some would eat the grass that so rarely grew on the muddy fields on the way to labor. Of course if seen by the SS guards they would be brutally beaten, not all left with their lives yet the ones that were, wished they hadn't. That was the unfortunate way our lives had become. To see blades of grass and feel desperate enough to risk falling out of line to just put something in their stomachs. Risking their lives for blades of grass that would do so very little in terms of squashing hunger, yet most were willing to take that risk. It was not just food and water that was deprived, it was warmth that came second on the hierarchy to survival. During summer months it did not pose as much of a threat to life, though when the winter months showed signs of appearance we knew that not all prisoners would survive it. Most were just not strong enough to push their bodies through a winter that hammered hard against their skin.

I had managed to make friends in Dachau and as much as making friends through the war proved to end in heartache, they also saw us through. On days that felt like our last, the companions we met were a needed aid to push to the next. Friends however, could not always determine life or death and that was the cold fact that was witnessed many mornings in Dachau.

*

"Marcin, it is time for roll call." Came the voice of Gersw who was shaking the man next to him to wake up. The man grunted in pain though made no attempt to move. "Marcin! You need to move, come on!" Again the man remained still, holding his stomach with sounds of pain that filled the barrack. Most prisoners were already shuffling their way to the wash basins they would have only twenty five minutes to use between the whole barrack. I watched as Gersw touched the man's head and jumped back quickly in shock.
"What is it?" Asked Lukasz, hobbling over with his eyes puffy and red.
"I think he may have typhus." Worried Gersw as he stood over the man, watching him shake beneath the thin blanket.
"We need to get him outside otherwise they will kill him." With that both men lifted the man with what strength they had and took him outside.

We stood in line, waiting for the guards to do their rounds of counting us before we would be sent out for the day's work.

Marcin leaned against Lukasz and Gersw in an attempt to stay standing, though it was by far evident that he would not make it through a full labor day, he couldn't stand unaided and could barely keep his eyes open or stop his body from shaking. The leather boots came stomping down the line, tension grew with each footstep, every person questioning if they would make it to the end of the day. I kept my stare forward, avoiding eye contact with the tall, thin guard with eyes that could burn right through your skin at only a glance. He stopped before Marcin with an evil smile that spread from one ear to the other.

"Release him." He ordered to Lukasz and Gersw who had been holding him up. The two men looked at each other in anticipation before slowly taking Marcin's hands from around their neck. Marcin wobbled, his determination to survival still inside him yet strength to accomplish it extremely distant. He shuffled between two feet, his eyes in a blur as he struggled to focus on the guard in front of him. The guard did not move as he watched the man before him struggle with every ounce of his being to stay upright, before he fell to the ground at the guards boots. Within just seconds, he took out his pistol and fired a bullet into his head. The sound of the gun echoed through the camp, stabbing fear in every other man that stood in line, not daring to move their eyes to the body that lay on the floor. I could feel anger swell within me like a volcano needing only a nudge to be erupted. Tears pricked my eyes, my fists clenched at my side, *how could they be so cruel?* Lukasz and Gersw stood perplexed, unable to come to a final emotion as their friend lay unmoving on the ground between them. The guard bellowed a loud and exaggerated laugh, spitting at Marcin as he continued down the line.

Roll calls were always the most tense, having to prove you were fit to carry on living, judged by the men in uniforms who held the weapons to end your life in split seconds, before you could even have time to come up with an excuse as to why you should be allowed to live. Later that night the men in the barrack were almost silent. Marcin had been a positive contribution to the barrack, always helping the other men around him when they needed it, offering kind words of wisdom and guidance that ensured another day someone would not reach the muselmann state.

"He had been here a long time," Said Gersw with his head bowed down in respect as he sat on the edge of the bunk in thought. "He was old, yet he did not let the guards tamper with his longing to live. He had just reached his time and I am afraid there was not much more we could do." He lets out a heavy sigh and wipes his forehead in a sadness I had never seen him hold before that very moment.

"His body had given up in the night, he was merely a corpse before light had broken through. Even if we had found him in the night it is with great sadness that I say the same outcome would have still happened." Says Lukasz as he attempts to fix the hole in his clogs.

"I hate this stupid war." I say, kicking a stone and thinking about home. "I miss Warsaw, my life before all of this, yet I do not know what I would even return for anymore. My Mama has gone and I can not be sure what has happened to my Aunt and cousin. Kacper was taken first and none of us knew where. I don't even know if he is still alive." Lukasz and Gersw look at one another then back to me as if in thought. "What?" I asked confused, looking over the two men whose expressions had suddenly changed.

"You said his name is Kacper?" Asked Lukasz as he abandoned the hole in his clogs and put them back on his feet before shuffling closer.

"Yes, he is my cousin." The two men were looking at me with half a smile and half a look of concern that made me worry.

"There is someone by the name of Kacper here, I have spoken to him only a handful of times but maybe he could be your relation?" He asks as though a question yet frustration and excitement both build within me at the same time.

"Where is he?" If there was a chance that someone in my family was still alive I had to find out, yet I worried for the disappointment after if I was left with answers that I knew were a possibility.

"He stays four barracks up from here to the right, I must warn you that if he is your cousin, he has not been doing well for quite some time." Gersw had jumped from the bunk and was stood before me with his hands on my shoulders in sympathy.

I lay restless that night, unable to fall into any kind of sleep with the pondering thought that Kacper could be sleeping just a handful of huts from where I was. I had to find out. As quietly as I could I climbed down from the concrete bunk and made my way to the door.

"If they catch you, they will kill you." Comes the voice of Lukasz who was still in a sleeping position with his eyes closed.

"I have to find out if it is him!" I whispered as I carried on towards the door.

"I will come with you." He stretches restlessly as he pulls himself up with no effort to not disturb the men sleeping next to him.

"If caught they will kill us both! No, I have to do this on my own." I say the words though I knew that with Lukasz accompanying me it would be a task much less terrifying. He laughs as he climbs down from the bunk and pats me on the back, disregarding the idea completely of me going alone.

Outside the night held winds that were so strong we struggled to keep our frail bodies upright. If we were to succeed we needed to be fast and unseen. The slightest glimpse of movement would set gunfire off from the towers in our direction faster than we would be able to dodge them. We waited for the spotlights to move to the far end of camp before making a crouched run behind the next hut. SS guards patrolled with their guns on their backs, their presence dominatingly powerful as they held the decision between our life and death. We kept out of sight, waited for the moment we could make the run to the next hut. It took merely a handful of minutes to reach the hut that could be housing Kacper and as we did I was hit with the realisation that I could be disappointed. We crept inside to see over fifty men sleeping on the concrete bunks, identical to our own.

"You take that side, I'll take this side." Whispered Lukasz as he began looking over the men on the right. It was abundantly clear that all the men within Dachau had only fragments of life left within them that they fought to keep alive, desperate to see the end of the war and reunite with any loved ones that could have made it. I walked down the line, scanning each face hoping to see Kascper huddled amongst them. It wasn't until I reached the end of the line feeling disappointed and disheartened that Lukasz whispered me over, waving his hands in his direction indicating that I followed him. It was at that moment, during the bitter night, that the world around me began to spin again with order and purpose. Before me, sleeping peacefully yet with struggle lining his every bone that pierced his skin, was Kacper.

September - November 1944 - Operation Market Garden

On September 15th 1944 we were briefed by Colonel Sink for one of the largest Airborne landings in history that would consist of three divisions and be of surprise to the German Army that held occupancy in Holland. The operation was code named Market Garden, with the airborne falling under the 'Market' title and the ground forces falling under the 'Garden' designation. The operation was a large airborne and ground offensive in Holland that aimed to allow us to take control of the bridges on the Rhine. The overall plan was required for the final push into Germany that was hoped to end the war throughout Europe by Christmas 1944. Before leaving for Holland I wrote to Jen, hoping it would at least offer some comfort during our time apart.

To my Jenny,
Life in the army is really quite extraordinary, one day we can be fighting on the frontline, bullets just missing our skin and the next celebrating a victory and drinking beer and the finest whiskey I have ever tasted. It is quite expected that you are spending your days in overwhelming worry for my return however know that lives must be given for the better cause. I am living everyday in hope that I will return to you soon but for now understand that this is what needs to be done to end the war we have all grown so tired of and I will do everything to

ensure my return. It has been said that we could be home for Christmas yet I do not hold unquestionable assurance of this. During the nights we spend within the soil I look to the stars and feel you there. I hope you are doing the same.

With much love,

Your Pete

We were placed under the British command of the 2nd Army while also regrouping the 82nd American Airborne Division and the 1st British Airborne Division. Just two days after the briefing on September 17th 20,000 allied paratroopers jumped into the Dutch sky, which was much less of a threat than Normandy however we still encountered air attack from the German air force. Nerves filled the Douglas C-47, though with planes remaining in formation during the attacks those nerves were eased if at least by a small fraction. The landing was successful, just over eighteen miles behind the front line and much less painful than that of France, as we dropped from the sky into a field that left little difficulty in cutting our chutes and heading to the assembly area lined with smoke grenades. A lot less could be said for the gliders as they suffered many losses during landing to both life and material.

The objective was somewhat simple when put into words. We, as the 101st were to land north of Eindhoven with the objective of capturing the town while moving through Son towards Veghel and Grave to open the southern end of the line of advance. Afterwards, we would take control of the bridge over the Wilhelmina Canal at Son while doing everything possible to keep it intact, then group with the 3rd battalion in attacking Eindhoven and hold the city and bridges until the Guards Armored Division passed through. The first mission Son, the second Eindhoven, with the end result being an open road to Berlin.

We were moved out from the assembly area almost instantly with 1st battalion through a field located west of the road. We were following behind D Company with Battalion HQ behind us and F Company behind them. As we entered Son I had never experienced anything quite like that very moment. The civilians lined the roads, cheering, waving and thanking us in both Dutch and English for our arrival and saving them from the Germans who held occupancy over their city. They were so joyful and grateful at their liberation they began giving away food, cigarettes and beer to us as we marched down the road.
"Please, take these, we cannot thank you enough that you are here." Said a man pushing a packet of cigarettes into my hand as he shook it with his, holding a smile from one side of his face to the other.

"Thank you very much." I replied, unsure of what else I could have said. We were still to fight back the Germans though our arrival gave them hope that the war was coming to an end and I did not have it in me to take that away from them with truthful facts. All down the line soldiers were receiving gifts that meant more than they usually would if Holland had not been suffering food shortages.

Making our way out of Son, Hiker showed me the cigars he was gifted by a male civilian that had been adamant that he took them. He lit one with the matches in his musset bag and offered me one with a smile. "I don't think war is *all* bad." He laughs through a cloud of smoke as I light my own, only to be taken aback by German fire shooting straight down the road in the direction of where we were marching. A German 88mm Flak, with a firing range of over six miles and explosives causing the downpour of shrapnel we knew, with the machine gun fire, that the Germans would not let us pass without a fight on their hands. D Company covering the right and E Company covering the left we began firing back, repeated rifle fire towards the enemy until our hands felt bruised and sore, throwing mortar shells that shot out after being loaded into the tube and hitting the fixed firing pin that fired the rounds towards the enemy.
"Take that you dahm Krauts!" Shouted Hiker, taking extra care to avoid being hit after his foot was barely healed. He was told that it would be best to stay in England for this mission, though

his determination to *do his part,* proved that no matter how many hits he took, he would fight this war through to the very end.

"Keep moving!" Shouted Winters from the front, indicating we push forward and not fall back as we fired everything we had at them.

It wasn't until we reached the bridge that we realised their plan. They were stalling us so they could blow up the bridge, which they did as we edged closer. A storm of wood and stone hammered down over our heads in an unmerciful shower of destruction. We covered our heads as the Germans wasted no time in falling back now their plan had succeeded. The platoon engineers were able to fix the bridge as best they could though it was unstable in terms of carrying too much weight, therefore it took many hours for all the men to cross to the other side.

That night we slept in haystacks that we found around the fields with outposts being set by the platoon leaders. The Guards Armoured Division were running behind schedule as they were caught by German Flak they were fighting back that were stationed in Eindhoven. As our days work had come to a standstill waiting for them, we made use of the time to regain energy.

"I think we were lucky nobody was hurt today." I sighed, doubting my cigarette and slumping back onto the haystack. "They came out of nowhere."

"I wouldn't say lucky, I'd say we were ready, despite not knowing they were there. If Normandy taught us anything it was to never not expect an appearance from them dahm Krauts."It had become evidently clear over the last few months that Hiker was holding an increased hatred towards the Nazis. We all hated them, though there was something else buried within Hiker that made his combat fighting ten to none.

"Something tells me it's becoming a little personal." I look at him as I narrow my eyes, if there was anybody that knew him better than himself it was me and I knew there was something eating away at him. He shifted on his heels for a few brief moments before looking at me with giant eyes.

"Rosie wrote to me back in England, my daughter isn't doing too well." He hangs his head as if in defeat, knowing that while out here there was nothing he could do.

"What's wrong with her?" I ask, sitting up on one elbow with a concerned look.

"Rosie says it's a fever but she can't get her temperature to go down, she doesn't know whether to keep her warm or keep her cool. She's having a really awful time at the minute and she's struggling." For the first time since I had met him I saw his most vulnerable side as he angrily wiped away a tear before the other men noticed and mocked him for situations they did not understand.

"Oh man, that is rough but from what you have told me about your girl she is tough, she will be fine and that goes for your daughter too. With your blood in her she will be a fighter and pull through it." He doesn't say anything as he looks to the ground feeling helpless. "She'll be fine Hikes." I assured, though deep down I knew I was the furthest away from being at a right to offer such comfort, I had never met his family but I knew how much they meant to him and a distraction like that would surely make him reckless or vulnerable. For the rest of the night I left him to his silence though I worried about him as he lay on his side, eyes open in deep thought for the majority of the night.

The next morning the march continued, with men still tired from the uncomfortable nights sleep, yet with more energy than we would from sleeping in a foxhole or ditch. We were following behind 1st battalion on the road heading south, both battalions marching in formation with little to no words said. We entered Eindhoven with only a small amount of fire from snipers that held no difficulty in taking out. Once again we were greeted and cheered by the Dutch for our arrival, bringing us hot tea, milk and fruit that they could spare to show their gratitude. Others were singing and dancing as they raised their orange flags once again in joy that Hitler and his army had ordered to have taken down. The Germans goal was to conquer France while bypassing the French defence line at the eastern border by going through the Netherlands and Belgium. Their occupation of the Netherlands aimed to prevent England from setting up a base of operations on the European mainland.

Despite Holland's attempts to remain neutral as the war took hold in Europe, German forces invaded the country on May 10th 1940. Soon after, Holland was under German control. It had been nearly four years under the occupancy of Germany and the Dutch were overwhelmed at the thought that they were now being liberated but we still had a mission to complete and pushing the Germans back proved to be a strenuous task that did not come easily. I was unsure of whether they were oblivious to this, or whether they were overflowing with hope after it had been drained for so many years that they celebrated anyway with cheers so loud we couldn't hear ourselves think. Hiker even managed to forget life at home for a while as he joined in on the celebrations as he marched, taking food that was offered to him and shaking hands with the civilians. Although we knew we were far from a victory it filled us with pride and confidence that day, something that I knew every one of us would remember long after the war was over.

It took most of the day for the officers to push us through the crowds of cheering people so we could get through to capture the bridges over the Dommel River. Later that day the British tanks arrived and we were able to celebrate with the city people properly. Again, they provided food and alcohol as we stopped for pictures and autographs, sending our confidence ever higher in being able to do exactly what it took to claim a victory. If they thought we could, what was stopping us?

We soon found out, when we were led on a march to Nuenen by Winters, which posed no German threat until we had just passed the town and witnessed the 107th Panzer Brigade fifty tanks strong, attacking towards Nuenen. The British tanks came forward, only to be blown up effortlessly by the Panther's 7.5 cm long barrelled high velocity anti-tank gun.

The Germans were not allowed to build or possess any tanks after WWI. Soon however the German military realised that the tank would be a vital weapon in a modern army and they were fully aware that any act to design or produce a tank would be a major breaking of the terms of the Versailles Treaty. The projects that were launched were therefore camouflaged by means of agricultural cover-titles. All development projects received phoney agricultural nick-names and tank chassis were addressed as tractors. The destruction of Army Group Centre in June 1944 and the collapse of the Western Front that followed the Allied invasion of France in the same month caused a major drain of German manpower and material. Within just two months dozens of divisions were wiped from German Order of Battle by the Russian offensives in Byelorussia and Ukraine, or bled white in the war of attrition in Normandy. In the summer of 1944 the German army was beaten both in Russia and in Western Europe and fell back in full retreat. The German army reserves were not able to cope with the dreadful losses and necessary measures were taken in order to stabilise the situation. A new kind of unit saw their arrival that summer.

Infantry divisions were raised as so-called "Volksgrenadier-divisions" and new tank forces were made in the form of 'Panzer-Brigades.'

With only six British tanks available at that very moment, with four being hit, the British tanks fell back, along with Easy Company. We knew we were outnumbered and their superior tank force had left us no option than to head back to town where we found shelter in buildings and set up a return fire. The day, although being able to hold up the Germans and stall them, had been unsuccessful as we had been unable to push them back and men were lost during the attempt. We retreated to Tongelre in which we sought food and a place to sleep for the night. We felt saddened by the day's events, spirits were not high like they had been during the civilian celebrations and we were beginning to feel like we had left them down. That night we witnessed the Luftwaffe soaring overhead and bombing the British supply column. We could only sit and watch, with resources limited we were unable to offer support during the attack that left the city severely damaged.

It was September 22nd when we were mounted onto trucks heading for Uden, to defend the town against a Panther attack coming from Helmond. Once in Uden the Germans had us surrounded, leaving us with a sickening feeling that once again we would be pushed back, however with three British tanks and Easy Company, along with Battalion HQ setting up numerous roadblocks on all roads leading into Uden, we were able to drive the Germans back with them assuming we had more men and tanks than we actually had. Sniper fire meant setting up defensive positions with machine-guns and explosives that would prepare for an enemy attack.

"If the panthers come, we take them out from the second floor windows by dropping composition C charges on the tanks." Winters told us as we held our positions. "Be ready. "With that he made his way to the other end of the town to set up roadblocks that would be supported by a British tank.

Two days later the enemy had lost Uden and Veghel but they were far from a surrender. They began attacking from the south of Veghel and were able to cut the road. They had already taken back control of the Arnhem bridge which was crucial to us to have open, as it allowed Allied supplies to pass through. Being unable to take back control of the road and ensure it stayed open, the mission would go from defeat to an absolute disaster, therefore we were given a new mission of taking out the German salient that was south of Veghel. We set out once again on a march with us in reserve of 1st and 3rd battalions. As we passed through Veghel the two battalions began their attack which started off as a hopeful success, though German artillery soon increased when Tiger tanks dug in along the road with their 88mm guns and machine-guns. After digging in, Colonel Sink set the order for the 2nd battalion to make a flanking move to the left that would be assisted by British

Sherman tanks. British Shermans were equipped with 75mm guns as well as secondary weapons of .50 and .30 machine guns, with an overall speed of 20mph. The Sherman weighed 33 tonnes and had a 75mm gun, compared to the Tiger's 54 tonnes and an 88mm gun. The Tiger also had 3.9 inch thick armour, so shells from a Sherman literally bounced off it, meaning we were not optimistic about the British tank support against the Tigers, though it was better than none at all.

We were called to formation, readying our rifles, the machine-gunners reading their machine-guns and 60mm mortars offering support. We advanced through the field yet halfway across the Germans released their machine-guns sending us all straight to the ground with our hands over our heads. The ground ripped up around us, bullets piercing the air in a fight to find contact with anyone in its path. Clutching my rifle, my body remained frozen to the ground, unable to move or counterattack as the ground ate bullets that flew inches from where we were. The Germans artillery was too strong, we couldn't match them, not with how vulnerable we were in the middle of the field, so Winter's ordered that the machine-gunners opened continuous fire until we reached the woods, where myself, Hiker and a few other riflemen shot our guns into the air, indicating that the machine-gunners fall back too. Winters gave orders to two British tanks that stormed through the trees, taking them down with their heavy tracks, only to be blown up by the Tigers that had been waiting for them.

On the evening of 27th September I opened my first letter from Jen that I had received since leaving England just ten days before.

Peter,

Do you remember our first meeting, how I told you that the stars are those we have lost looking down upon us? I do not look to the stars because that means that I would have lost you and I am not ready for that, I could never be ready for that. I am living each day in hope that they will send you back to me, if even for just a brief time and not just because I miss you but because while you are here you are safe. I cannot pretend to be confident in your place out there, this war is evil and although I do not lack the belief you are an incredible contribution to our country's army, I worry that you may not return.

I am working endlessly at the hospital with hope that I too can make a difference here and it occupies my mind away from the worry. I cannot wait to see you again, hopefully long before this war is over, until then, I will not look to the stars, I will look to your return.

My forever love,

Your Jen

With a heavy sigh I place the letter in my backpack and remain lost in thought for a while, wondering what she was doing at that very moment, if she was thinking of me like I was her. I longed to be back home, yet I did not regret my decision in joining the airborne. The war needed men and if everybody relied on everybody else to fight instead of them, there would be no men to fight at all.

"Tough one?" Asked Hiker as he looked over with a sympathetic smile.

"Could be worse, how is everything for you?" I asked, rubbing my head and trying to block it out to offer comfort to the man who had become my best friend. He lifts the letter in the air with a laugh that almost sounded fake, "Rosie says she's on the mend but I'm not sure if she's just telling me that to stop me worrying, y'know?" He hangs his head and sighs deeply as he places the letter in his backpack carefully as though creasing the paper would cause it to be lost to flames.

"I'm sure she is telling you the truth, besides, you can't think like that out here, let it be of comfort to you that your daughter is doing well again. You'll be back with her soon buddy." I smile again though I know he is unsure by the worried look spread across his face.

"They mean everything to me, I have to get back to them, back to Pasadena. I don't think Rosie will cope on her own, not if I don't make it back."

"Woah! Who said you're not making it back? I haven't seen a performance record like yours from anyone else in Easy, if anyone is making it back its you. Here, have some and calm down, just because we have failed here doesn't mean we have lost the war." I hand him a tin of canned meat with a spoon, indicating I wasn't taking no for an answer.

"We failed to get the bridge at Son, failed to get through Nuenen, failed the drive at Uden and failed the attack on the German salient. That's a lot of failure Mcclough." He takes the food though doesn't rush to open it before falling into panic again. "The Krauts army is strong, too strong for us, count my words."

"We may have failed here but we didn't in France, besides, the Krauts army are not stronger than us, they have sufficient tanks and equipment for sure but put a Kraut and an American together in a field to fight who do you think would win?" He nods slowly and doesn't say anything, knowing that one bad mission did not mean we were losing the whole war.

The truth was in fact that we had failed. We failed to secure the key bridge at Arnhem, which meant that we had been halted at the Rhine. The operation failed because of a failure in planning, intelligence, and a lack of understanding of the terrain's nature. We had not received experience with working alongside the British tankers and it was shown as an obstacle that was unable to be hurtled during Operation Market Garden. The German army had many more men and their artillery and ammunition meant that we were unable to match their artillery or manpower in the field.

From the Market-Garden drop to the last of the division being relieved, Easy Company spent 69 days in combat zones in Holland. Towards the end of the operation the weather was wet and despairing as we spent nights in foxholes, barnes and fields. We had spent many of those days in severe frustration at the artillery fire and the food in most part was not a lot to be excited about in such mere conditions of combat. We had drawn rations from the British, being that of beef and yorkshire puddings that tasted of nothing short of dreadful, there was no coffee and even the British cigarettes did nothing to ease tensions. With the majority of Holland being evacuated there were numerous opportunities for retrieving goods left behind but even then the British troops had got there first and taken everything worthwhile.

While in Holland we were sent out on patrols, fought off attacks, fired ammunition in quantities one could only imagine, many had been lost or wounded to an operation that had failed. We had failed to achieve all our objectives, one being to secure the key bridge at Arnhem and open a gateway to the Ruhr by outflanking the German Siegfried Line, which meant that we were halted at the Rhine. If we had been successful, the plan would have liberaterated the Netherlands, outflanked Germany's dreaded frontier defences, the Siegfried Line, and made possible an armoured drive into the Ruhr, Germany's industrial heartland. The plan failed largely because of 30 Corps' inability to reach the furthest bridge at Arnhem before German forces overwhelmed the British defenders. Allied intelligence had failed to detect the presence of German tanks, including elements of two SS Panzer divisions.

In some places the advance was made difficult by marshes that prevented off-road movement. Throughout the battle the Germans also showed a remarkable ability to put together battle groups that fought to delay the armoured columns. The crossing of the Rhine and the capture of Germany's industrial heartland were now delayed. We would have to fight our way into the Reich on a broad front with no quick victory before Christmas as was planned. It was hoped that the US troops, along with the British 1st Airborne Division, would launch a heavy strike across the Maas, Waal and Rhine rivers in Holland that would pave the way for ground troops to advance swiftly into Germany and end the war by Christmas of 1944.

We did not hold doubt that Market Garden was a failure, though the northern flank of the Allied armies was extended some 65 miles across two canals and the Maas and Waal rivers with a large amount of Dutch land had been liberated from German occupation. We had taken out a large amount of Germans as well as capturing over 3,500 however we had suffered over 2,000 casualties ourselves. We had held out positions on the

Island until later November when we were withdrawn and pulled from the line by Canadian troops and taken to Camp Mourmelon by trucks stationed outside the French village of Mourmelon-le-Grand. The Dutch lined the streets and were cheering us as we rolled by in trucks down Hell's Highway, the road we had fought the Germans to get through to Arnham. We were the furthest away from being in the mood to celebrate as we didn't feel like the heroes they looked at us as. Once in Camp Mourmelon we were able to rest, refit and take a shower, which we had been unable to do for sixty nine days. We had made two jumps into enemy territory and still, the war raged on through Europe like an angry bull and what we had left to witness, not one of us expected.

September 1944 - Dachau Concentration Camp, Kaufering, Germany

"Jakub?" Came the voice of Kacper looking up at me, still half asleep and huddled between the other men in his bunk who were silently sleeping.

"It's really you!" I could have almost shouted with joy if not for the fact that German SS and Polish Kapo were patrolling outside the hut. Looking into his tired and worn eyes it was if the world had begun to spin again, everything lining up as it should, finally making sense in a world so full of hate. For a few brief moments no words were said, we just looked at each other in disbelief as Lukasz hobbled over to the door to keep a lookout for unwelcoming company. Since the passing of Mother I had believed I was the only one left, that everyone had been taken in a cruel and bitter exchange for labor that only benefited the Nazi war effort.

Kacper lifts himself up slowly, his face a mere shadow of what it once was all that time ago at the apartment in Warsaw. His cheeks were pale, like all life had been sucked from his bones with merely a strand of survival clinging on. He was looking at me as though I was a ghost, like he was dreaming and was unsure of whether he wanted to wake up from a dream that came as bittersweet.

"How long have you been here?" He asked, worrying that I had ended up in the exact same evil place. I sit on the edge of his bunk cautiously to not wake the other prisoners who could tell the guards for a reward that would never come.

"I'm not sure, a few months maybe, when did you get here? I never thought I'd see you again!" Lukasz looks over and puts a finger on his lips, indicating I keep my excitement levels down to not draw attention.

"I have been here over a year, I came from Auschwitz, they told me I'd be working but I never knew where until I arrived. These camps Jakub, they are just evil with death that always follows and little more." His eyes narrow, showing years of experience in such dreadful places that had taken away the boy he once was, leaving a man with very little life.

"Someones coming!" Whispers Lukasz in almost a shout. In a hurry we rush onto the bunks, squeezing amongst other prisoners and pretending to be asleep, just as the door of the hut swings open, an SS guard with his flashlight peering down the hut, looking for any sign of punishable movement. Pushing my head into my chest to calm my breathing we wait for him to disappear.

The unknown tension throughout the hut that night was so thick I'm surprised we didn't choke on it. I kept my eyes out of view as the guard walked up and down the hut, shining the light in sleeping prisoners' faces, looking for any slight indication that someone was awake. After minutes that felt like hours stretched to their rawest form, the guard left, banging the door behind him with intentional force. The cold and awful smells that rifled through the camp that night had become non-existent as I thought only of how my life had suddenly changed.

"We speak in the morning during *breakfast*." He says with bunny ears. The lack of food along with taste was at the back of my thoughts, I had countless questions I needed to ask that I needed answering, to piece together a life torn apart over the last five years. I nod in approval and hug him as tightly as I could without snapping his fragile frame.

*

The next morning I was up ready as the gong called to start the day. It would be a fair analogy to say that i had not really slept. Too many thoughts stabbed at my mind, possibilities of what could have happened over the last four years since he was taken. I was sure that he had probably done the same. Waking up before the rest of the prisoners meant that using the latrines and having somewhat of a wash was much easier than that of usual days, when waiting in line meant not always getting to the front before Appell. Much like Auschwitz with a possibility of being worse, the lack of nutrition and food meant that many prisoners suffered with diarrhea, resulting in terrible living conditions if not made to the latrines in time.

We had thirty minutes to eat what they called breakfast and during that time I looked for Kacper. He was sitting outside his hut with his tin bowl, barely touching its watery contents when I walked over and sat beside him. His stare to the ground did not move as I made my appearance, telling me that something was on his mind other than the daily conditions of camp.

"Do you know what happened to my Mama?" He asked, keeping his gaze down and swirling the watery contents around the tin.

"Unfortunately not," I say with a sigh, feeling guilty I could not give him the news he wanted. He remains silent. "Maybe that could be a good thing, no news is sometimes good news, right?" I try to sound enthusiastic and give him hope but it was evident he had lost that a long time ago.

"And yours?" He asks, turning to look me in the eye, waiting for a response.

"She died in Auschwitz, by the time we arrived there she was very weak, when I saw her I think that she had been beaten very badly." I hang my head in her memory with a prick of tears wanting to escape my eyes. I look over and Kacper is the same, yet I know his burdens had been burning a lot longer than mine. He was taken so early into the war that he had not seen his family for four years. Forced to become a man before his time was due. I pitied him, wanted to say words that would make him forget all the pain that he must have suffered all this time.

I had not put a pen to paper in so long I wondered whether words would ever be my forte again. "What happened to you all this time?" I ask, pulling my uniform tight around my chest as the rain began to hammer at our skin from nowhere.
"When they first took me for work, I worked on the railroads, fixing the lines and rebuilding roads that would lead to this place. I didn't know at the time, I just did what they told me. After a few months they sent me to Auschwitz, made me build the place up from nothing as if it would be a palace for them. We were building our own prison, nothing more." He sighs heavily and wipes his forehead, attempting to look stronger than he was, yet I could see inside he was close to giving up. "After six months I was transferred to the Motor Works factory to work on German war weapons, vehicles and plane engines. I knew nobody there, everyone was a stranger though I did befriend a man by the name of Leo, we were very close companions in Auschwitz." He looked into the distance as if capturing a memory inside his mind.
"What happened to him?" I ask, intrigued.
"They hung him in front of everyone. Leo and Hans believed they had produced the perfect plan to escape,

asked me over and over to join them yet I had seen what happened to attempted escapists, I tried to warn them, they wouldn't listen."

"Hans?" It was as though a lightbulb had been switched in my mind, *had this been the same Hans I had met in Auschwitz?*

"German Jew, sent to the camp in 42', he wasn't caught, he had tried to tell Leo that guards were coming but he wouldn't listen, kept on trying to dig through the fence anyway. Hans ran off knowing he couldn't get through to him. When they caught Leo they beat him until I could barely recognise him anymore. He was desperate, so desperate to feel the taste of freedom again it made him reckless." Kacper shifts his gaze from the distance and round to me as I sit next to him lost in thought, trying to put together the pieces of a broken puzzle of years lost to the war.

"I met Hans, we were good friends for a short time." I say, surprised how small the world had become in a war so big.

"He had a very strong spirit, held it together much better than me or Leo ever did. I am not surprised he was still there at your arrival."

"How long have you been here?" I looked again at his frail body and wondered how he had survived so long given his tiny matchstick frame.

"Eighteen months. I'm sent out into the city to repair the bombed roads and houses but sometimes they put me in the kitchen. For some reason they look at me as a trusted prisoner, they are very naive to think such a thing after all these years of beatings." He half smiles as he winks and looks down again.

"You can get food?" Shock floods over me, understanding how he had made it as far as he had. Before he could answer the Roll Call bell sounded that we had learned to not waste time responding to. As we walked away to take our positions in line I turned back.

"Kacper?" I shout, halted to the spot, "We will leave this place together, right?" At that moment he smiled, nodded and walked away, except now he had hope that rushed through his body once more, igniting his soul to believe that now, he had something to survive for and in Dachau, that was more important than anything.

November 1944 - March 1945 - Battle of the Bulge, Belgium

When we arrived back in France we were taken to Mourmelon-le-Grand camp on November 26th by trucks and despite the artillery craters and remnants of trenches left from the first world war, it was a welcoming sight. The hot showers and opportunity to wash our clothes that had built with mud, sweat and stench, was the most weightless feeling of all. We had been under heavy gun-fire so much in Holland that we had almost forgotten what it was like to not be constantly cautious of our surroundings. The most rewarding of all was the incoming mail four days into our arrival. We had repaired the barracks previously used by the German Infantry and light cavalry, taken down their posters and propaganda that had plastered the walls as well as repaired latrines and roads. As I sat on the edge of my bunk, the men of Easy that had not been evacuated back to England were playing poker and craps in the middle of the room, I opened the letter and smiled as I saw the writing of Jen.

"That was a 12!" Shouted Martin across the table, demanding his winnings be paid. He was an impressive soldier in combat, though when it came to getting along with the other men of Easy he found difficulty and that included when they were gambling their three months pay as soon as it touched their hands. Martin was one of the original Camp Toccoa men who jumped in Normandy though it left him shaken and while fighting alongside us in Holland his advice was often shunned.

The four men began to break out in a fight as I left the barrack and sat outside.

Peter,

I hope that this letter finds you well. I am missing you terribly and visiting my parents without your company is really quite painful. Mother insists that I move on while Father is constantly praising you. Some weeks I just don't bother going. It is nearly Christmas and I sincerely hope that they give you a pass to come home for the holidays. I understand there is a war but you also have a life here. I will cling on to the hope that your presence will meet me again soon and that this war is not being too unkind to you.

All my love,

Your Jenny

I couldn't help but laugh to myself at the thought of her enduring her pedantic mother on her own. I missed Jen just as much, though it gave me courage to keep fighting the fight until I could return to the States and hold her again. Returning for Christmas was not an option and I knew she would be incredibly downhearted about the fact. Inside the camp there were numerous opportunities for keeping entertained, including marching drills, movie theatres, a Red Cross Club and even games of basketball, baseball and football. Many men were trying out for the Christmas Day Champagne Bowl Game between the 506th and 502nd, including myself to keep my mind occupied from other affairs. We trained for three hours a day once we made the team and even privates such as Hiker, who had no time for such games began betting instantly on who would win. This encouraged us to prove them wrong, meaning our daily practise was taken seriously in order to cash in on winnings. Even some of the replacements to the company joined the team and even though they were only a mere year or two younger than us it was apparent that they were threatened by us. It was a running joke throughout the barracks yet some men would tease and torment them, it was army life, they needed to get their spines strong one way or another, we had to endure Sobel afterall.

We were under the impression that we would not see any further combat or fighting until March where we would then jump into Germany, followed by a move to the Pacific for combat in China or a jump into Japan. Winters had approached Hiker just a week into the return to France and offered him a promotion to Sergeant for his bravery in Holland and the fact he had been shot and wounded on numerous occasions and still carried on the good fight. Humbled, he had politely declined. As much as he wanted to do his part for this war, the responsibility of others lives on a higher scale than it already was was not something he could place himself under. He remained as a private, doing his part and returning to his girls at the end. On December 16, 1944, Hitler launched his last gamble in the snow-covered forests and narrow valley of the Ardennes in Belgium with the belief that he could split the Allies by driving all the way to Antwerp and forcing the Canadians and British out of the war. Although his generals were doubtful of success, younger officers and NCOs were desperate to believe that their homes and families had the possibility of being saved from the Red Army that was approaching from the east. Many were exultant at the prospect of fighting back.

We'd heard of Hitler's drive over the radio and just the next day on December 17th Eisenhower sent out 11,000 trucks and trailers carrying 60,000 men, ammunition, gasoline, medical supplies and other combat materials into the Ardennes. In just the first week of battle he was able to move 250,000 men and 50,000 vehicles into the fray. On the same day we were told we were moving out with the 82nd Airborne to approach north towards the city of Bastogne, seven and a half miles from the Luxembourg border. We were moved out on the 18th, under supplied with ammunition that we had brought back from Holland, which we were technically meant to have handed in though it was fortunate that we hadn't, we were still missing men that were recovering from wounds in the hospital and clothes and boots that were not sufficient for the snowy weather in Belgium. As we packed inside the trucks with little room to move from so many men inside, we wondered what Bastogne would have in store for us. All we knew was that the Germans had blown a hole in the line and it was our job to fill the gap. We were to head to Bastogne, the 82nd to the north near St Vith. The ride was uncomfortable, constantly banging into each other with every slight difficulty in the road.

We pulled up just over a mile outside the city, to which we complained heavily about the discomforting journey.
"That has got to be one of the worst journeys we've endured yet." Complained Hiker as he jumped out the truck and straightened his back.
"Think I'd rather of taken my chances cramming inside the Gooney Bird than taking that trip." I add, stretching my legs and heading off to relieve myself before we were lined up for formation.
"Not really sure what they want us to do out here with no ammo." Says Hiker with a tint of sarcasm as I return from a nearby tree.
"Good old fashioned fighting by the looks of it, did you bring your sword?" I laugh as I find my position in line. As we marched into the city and back out again we were approached by American troops running towards us away from the fight that we were heading into.

"You're not going to want to go in there I'm telling you!" Says one man with a look of horror on his face, running down the middle of the line.

"The Krauts have got everything! Tigers, air support, machine guns, they have it all!" Shouts another man.

"Anyone would think they are soldiers." I say to Hiker as we watch them make their exit in a hurry. "Hey! Do you have any ammo we can use? We've been sent up here dry." I ask one of the more relaxed and calm soldiers who had not completely freaked out.

"Sure, it stops us going back there if we don't have it." He says, emptying his grenades and M-1 ammunition into my hand, which was not a large quantity but was at least more than I had, that I shared with Hiker. The other men of the company were doing the same yet we still did not have enough ammunition and every one of us knew it, including 2nd Lieutenant George C. Rice from 10th Armored Division who drove to Foy and filled his truck with ammo as soon as he heard of the shortage. He met us as we were coming out of Bastogne and began giving out grenades and M-1 ammo to which he made two trips.

We headed towards Foy and the sound of the battle intensified as we drew closer. Of the 506th, 1st battalion were in Noville engaged in a serious fight that they were all but winning, while we were to protect Colonel Sink's right flank. Marching into the woods overlooking an open field just east of the Bastogne-Foy-

Neville road, Fox Company to our right, Dog Company in reserve, the sound of the fight began getting louder, indicating that it was approaching us and at a speed that worried us, we were low on ammo, food, appropriate clothing and had no artillery or air support. Between the 19th and 20th December we went into the line south of Foy as one part of the defense, engaged the 2nd Panzer Division at Noville northeast of Foy and had pulled back behind Foy after losing 13 officers and 199 NCO's out of 600.

As we dug foxholes in the woods, the 1st battalion and 10th Armored Division had taken out over 30 enemy tanks with over 500 German casualties. We were to form a mail line of resistance a handful of metres into the woods with several outposts on the edge and Battalion HQ behind us, just to the south on the edge of the woods. For the first night we spent a peaceful yet fully alert night. As the fight was in Noville two and a half miles away we slept in our holes with the occasional sniper fire. On the morning of the 20th a heavy mist fell over the woods that dampened not only the ground but our spirits too. The air held an icy bite that cut into our skin with clothes that offered no protection, we had barely enough K-rations to last a few days and medical supplies had started to run low. We waited in those foxholes for what felt like a lifetime of trying to keep warm and ignore the twisting pain of hunger that had started to cause havoc as we craved a hot meal. The 1st battalion had caused such a scale of destruction to the enemy that the Germans had focused their assaults on other areas of the defensive perimeter. The occasional artillery and mortar attacks came our way, however there was no infantry attack and sometimes we were not sure if we were glad of the rest or if we wanted them to come to just get it over with so we could get out of the cold.

Over the next few days it snowed in quantities that left us vulnerable to both freezing temperatures and in some men, trench foot from inappropriate footwear that left our socks and boots soggy and wet. We had attempted to wrap ourselves in burlap and blankets yet it did not stop the punishing bite of cold that our jumpsuits and trench coats could not protect us from. During the night of the 21st we watched from our foxholes as the German Luftwaffe bombed the town in an igniting display of orange and black smoke that tore down buildings and the people beneath it.

"I don't think I have ever been this cold." Shivered Hiker as he nestled down further into his trench coat trying to find warmth that was not available.

"Doesn't help with this damn wind." I was rubbing my hands together in an attempt to create heat but my body had been in the snow too long in temperatures below freezing that it did nothing but occupy my mind for a few short moments.

"When we got cold at home, Rosie would nestle into me and I think the body heat worked." He said looking at me as his body shook from the cold.

"We're not hugging!" I laughed, dropping down into the hole and wrapping my coat tight around my chest.

"Sharing body heat isn't it, not that I have any to offer." He managed a small smile but I knew he was desperate. Rolling my eyes I lay cramped next to him in a bid to share the limited heat we had between us.

"If you were at home right now, what would you be doing?" I ask, trying to keep the conversation going to avoid the thought of cold. Hiker sighs then laughs vigorously as a thought comes to him within seconds.

"We'd be sitting around a fire on the porch, Rosie and Laney wrapped up in a blanket as we talk into the night and eat the most amazing hot stew." He's lost in thought completely and part of me doesn't want to disturb him. "Y'know, I came here for them, to make a difference and show that I'm not always scared all the time. The money was obviously a big factor but I wanted my girls to be proud of me, not sympathising over the fact I'm hardly a man." He'd stopped shaking as his mind was occupied in saddening thoughts.

"How'd you work that out?" I almost shouted then remembered where we were. "You have been one of the bravest while being out here, you've been shot twice and been straight back in combat with no recovery."

"You know as well as I do, unless we have an arm or leg off we are required to come back fighting. That's how it works. '*Oh look, you have a leg off, you can go home while the rest stay out here fighting.*' He says with a high amount of attitude that I knew was full of longing for wanting to return home. "If I'm going into combat it's with Easy and no other battalion or company. That doesn't make me brave Mcclough"

"Well I think you see yourself in a much less light to what we do. Winters wouldn't have offered you a promotion if he didn't think so and I think his opinion was with good solid reason." I argue, trying to keep my encouragement to a low volume to not irritate the other men or alert the Germans of our presence.

"I turned it down! I couldn't even accept it." His most vulnerable side came out into the open that night, like a shadow that had been trapped inside his skin, finally seeping through the cracks. "I just want to be with my girls, that's all I care about, not promotions, not being brave or a hero, I don't care about anything else, just returning home to them." I knew how he felt almost down to the very word. I had thought about Jen every single day since I left and as much as I had tried to distance myself from the distraction, I just wanted what every other man of Easy wanted, to make it back home.

*

On the night of the 18th to the 19th December we were jammed into trucks and rushed into battle, destination Bastogne, Belgium. On the morning of the 19th we marched north and east from Bastogne towards the road from the town of Foy and Bizory in a place called Jack's Forrest. Between the Railroad line and Foy we had dug in during a gruesome cold winter with temperatures that fell to minus 28 degrees Celsius. Looking out of our foxholes we saw an open field between us and just below us a force majeure in the German occupied town of Foy. The 501st PIR was east of the railroad line and the 502nd was west of the tracks. The fighting in the coming weeks was harsh and brutal. The city of Foy changed hands at least six times as we gained control of the village, the Germans sent in tanks, battalions lost control, then other battalions gained it again. Easy company had lost a lot of good men during this period.

During one of the assaults on Foy, ordered by Easy Dick Winters, 1st platoon were sent in a flanking motion on the town. First platoon were ordered to halt and take cover by Norman Dike. They were sitting ducks at that moment without means of communication. The 1st platoon had to receive orders to move on to Foy before being slaughtered. 1st Lieutenant Ronald Speirs had ran to them, straight through the German lines, through Foy and taken the German soldiers by surprise. After delivering the orders he ran back towards the line, right through Foy once again and the still surprised Germans. The Germans were so surprised they had forgotten to fire on Speirs. Ronald Charles Speirs was named the Fearless Soldier. His nickname was Sparky, although nobody ever mentioned it to his face. Ronald Speirs and Bill Guarnere were the only two who were called 'natural Killers' by Dick Winters.

The first attacks on Easy came on 24th of December. Our position was bombed twice by friendly fire from American P-47s, or otherwise known as the Thunderbolt, with .50-caliber machine guns, and in the fighter-bomber ground-attack role it was capable of carrying five-inch rockets or a bomb load of up to 2,500 lb. On the 26th the Third Army, 37th Tank battalion had broken through German lines, meaning that we were no longer surrounded and supplies could be brought in of food, ammunition, medical supplies and blankets. The siege had been broken, though we were to stay on the line in our defensive positions. We were still outnumbered on the Western Front.

During January 9th and January 13th casualties were at its peak however on the 13th of January in 1945 Easy Company had captured Foy for the final time. We had left behind men like Muck, Penkala, Shindell, Hayes, Hoobler, Mellett, Neill, Hughes and Jackson. On 18 January we were moved 160 miles from Bastogne to the town of Alsace that was on the border of France and Germany, where we were to hold defensive lines until late February. The Germans launched what they hoped would be a distracting operation in Alsace in a bid to draw out American troops from the Ardennes. We headed in trucks that went at a pace we could have walked faster. Once arriving we stayed for almost two weeks, moving daily from one village to the next. The snow had started to melt, meaning spirits were beginning to rise at the blissful thought of saying goodbye to freezing temperatures. Not only was the passing snow a positive embrace we welcomed but also the supply truck that brought shoepacs, arctic socks and felt insoles, our clothes were sent to a laundry for cleaning and showers were provided and although not with hot water, it was not cold either, meaning complaints were at a minimum. We had endured six weeks of sweat, mud and dirty clothes that clung to our skin with no opportunity of getting clean, so the showers came as the most pleasing.

Come February 5th, we were moved into the line, relieving the 313th Infantry of the 79th Division in the city of Haguenau with a population bigger than any city we had engaged with so far. Our position was at the far right flank at the junction of the Moder river that ran aside the city as well as the canal that ran through town to cut off the loop in the Moder. Easy Company had occupancy of the buildings on the south bank of the river, while the Germans had the north bank. The river was high and was impossible to throw grenades over though machine-gun fire, rifle and mortar fire were in distance to fire at the Germans on the other side. Both sides had artillery support at disposal though the Germans had an advantage with a railway gun around the size of 205mm that was used in the first world war. We moved into buildings that had previously been occupied by the 79th Armored Division, the first time we had lived indoors on the firing line.

Moving by day was virtually impossible, as it would give visibility to the Germans and would encourage sniper fire, so we were to hold the line and set out patrols that would enable us to keep an eye on the Germans and serve as a forwarding artillery observer. Both sides encountered M-1 fire, mortar fire and sniper fire, we were chosen to go across the river in German rubber boats found by Nixon and Matheson, both old Easy Company men, to bring back prisoners and by the time February 20th came around Easy Company were moved into reserve as the 3rd battalion took over our position. Colonel Sink had sent down orders for us to follow a training exercise while we were in reserve.

On February 26th we had never been so happy to leave the front line and make our way back to Mourmelon, though this time we were not housed in our original barracks but in large green wall tents outside the village of Mourmelon. There we were able to shower and receive new Class A uniforms though our barrack bags that we had left behind when leaving for Bastogne, had been ransacked by the 17th Airborne, taking jumpsuits and parachutes, lugers and souvenirs we had gathered from Normandy and Holland. To say we were angry would be an understatement, though what could we do? Winter's, who had been promoted to Major before leaving Haguenau then called for a training programme to incorporate the new recruits.

The division was preparing for a daylight airborne mission, Operation Eclipse that involved a drop in and around Berlin. First, the Allied armies were to get across the Rhine. For quite some time we had expected a jump on the far side of the river though when the time came, Easy were not the ones to jump. Eisenhower handed this over to the 17th Airborne, the British 1st and the 6th Airborne Divisions. The 82nd and 101st were being saved for Berlin. We were disappointed and disheartened when we watched the C-47's pull away from the runaway and disappear into the sky, it was as though we were being left behind, yet most would have thought we would be happy to be out of combat after Normandy, Holland and the Ardennes.

Eisenhower needed men to strengthen the ring that was around Germany's industrial heartland in the Ruhr. As both the 101st and the 82nd were available our orders came towards the end of March that we were moving out by truck to the frontline on the Rhine River to eliminate the Ruhr pocket and advance across central Germany. It goes without saying that we had bared our thoughts on the German's for starting the war, though we never hated them, we didn't even hate the German soldiers we had fought against, some we even respected for the mighty soldiers they were but we were about to enter their territory and that is what unnerved us, yet exhilarated us. We would see for ourselves what the people of Germany were really like. This was the real and most dangerous fight so far and by god were we ready for it.

April 27th 1945 - Dachau concentration camp, Kaufering, Germany

I'd been in Kaufering for eight months when they arrived, troops of allied men making their way through the camp, horrified and distressed at the scenes playing out before their eyes. The SS had fled earlier that morning when they heard from the townsfolk that the allies were in town, taking most on death marches to Dachau, the sick and weak were left behind amongst the flames of the huts they had hoped would kill the rest of us off. I remember the first time I saw him, the man in the uniform that wasn't German but American. I remember the eagle on his arm, I didn't know what it meant other than that we were finally safe. He bent over my weak and frail body, too fragile to move but strong enough to not give in. I was laid in the mud as I saw the American soldier bend down and look into my eyes. He was horrified, distraught maybe but me, despite not being able to move, I felt the weight of too many years of war lift above me. I had been fourteen when the war started, I was now twenty years old and the war was still not over, yet for the first time since that first bomb fell on Warsaw, hope was now visible, not just a metaphor for getting through another day.

*

Earlier that morning...

"You need to wake up, they are rounding everybody up!" Shouts Gersw who had jumped down from the sleeping platform and was hobbling along the line trying to wake everybody up.

"What's going on?" I asked, squinting my eyes in the darkness of the morning trying to come to full wakefulness that was proving difficult. My body ached with every muscle working overtime, my chest pulled tight against my chest, making breathing almost impossible with my eyes refusing to stay open for more than a few seconds at a time. The lack of food and sanitation had begun to show within the camp long before now though it was my time to feel the harsh realities of it that morning. I lay within the walls of the hut with fifty other men, coughing, breathing hard against the cold that blustered through, some not waking at all, another night that had taken lives.

"Those who are able are to line up outside, come on, we need to go! They will kill us otherwise!" Shouts Gersw attempting to pick me up from the platform to which his own body strength fails him. I tried to lift myself out, pull against the deadweight my body was laying on me with no luck.

The sound of German orders rifles through the camp, demanding everybody to line up outside quickly, gunshots vibrated through the air in an array of panic and chaos with prisoners falling over in the mud in a bid to reach the roll call area before they were shot. The SS men were in more of a hurry than usual, taking any opportunity they could to fire their machine guns from the towers or from their backs as they lost patience with those that were deemed too slow. Men were dragged by the scruff of their necks and thrown into the line, being shot in the head if they fell over. Some of the prisoners had attempted to fight back, including Gersw who had pulled away an SS soldier who had pointed his gun at my head to which I barely flinched. The men that were able fought as hard as they could, it had turned into a battle between soldiers and prisoners, blood spilling onto the floor, through the mood, onto the piles of corpses fell bodies recently passed over. I'd been dragged onto the floor of the hut with many others, guns buried into our backs with strength we had forgotten existed. Frustrated by my old lack of teamwork from my mind and body I'd tried to stand up, to just stand up and make it to the roll call area and not lose my life to the bullet of the gun, not when I had come this far. As Gersw pulled on my arm to lift me up he was shot fiercely in the leg, causing him to drop to the ground in cries of pain. When the bullets had run out, so did the guards. Shuffling my body along the floor, I placed a hand on Gersw's leg, using what little strength I had to try to make the bleeding stop.

"No..no.." I cried, through spluttered coughs and tears, "Lukasz, Thomasz, please!" Lukasz hobbled over as quickly as his body would allow, taking off his shirt to wrap around the wound. Thomasz had been lined up with the other prisoners, beaten in the ribs and back for limping his way at a speed that did not satisfy the guards.

The SS had begun setting fire to the huts when they ran out of ammo, with prisoners still inside, too weak to outrun the flames that burned the huts to the ground. We could smell the flames and smoke before we saw them, overpowering the months of bad hygiene that had built up and bore tenancy within every inch of the camp. Men perished in the flames, coughing, screams and cries echoed through the air as the SS headed the able prisoners out of the gate in a march, locking us in as they did. The fire began spreading effortlessly, overflowing through the hut. I'd turned to Gersw who was sitting upright against the sleeping platforms, looking the most at peace I had ever seen him. His mouth did not hang open like those taken in the night, though his eyes were open, vacant, gone. Another friend I had met through the evilness of the war, that it had also taken away. As I reached to close his eyes I pictured him smiling, walking hand in hand with his family once more, just as Henryk had done. My hand remained on his leg as I sobbed all the heartache into the air, all the pain of all the years through the war pouring out of me in pitiful sobs with the flames growing higher, taking those who lay too ill to move. Lukasz pulled me outside by his boney fingers coughing into the smoke as I cried into his shoulder. We laid on the ground outside through the sun rising on the now half deserted camp, no guards patrolling the areas, no guards with machine guns pointing at us from the watchtowers, no noise other than that of the huts burning to the ground. It is uncertain how long I was laid on the ground with Lukasz beside me as we fell into a deep sleep, unaware of the surroundings around us.

I was woken by the sound of voices coming from the gate that had been locked on the departure of the German's and the prisoners. Lines of striped pajamas containing little more than skeletons were slowly making their way down the path of mud towards the voices, some aided by others. Emerging from the unburned huts were more, then more, all walking towards the gate. *Had it been opened? Was we now free?* Pulling up my aching head I peered over to see soldiers, distraught with the look of complete horror on their faces.
"Lukasz." I nudge him awake, pointing towards the herd of prisoners all heading in the same direction. He stares with his mouth open in shock, tears forming in his eyes that spill down his face. I didn't understand what was happening, my vision blurred with my body refusing to stand, I let the scene unravel around me as I watched in awe. The sound of trucks indicated more people were arriving. The gate swings open as I watch the line of soldiers walk in, holding their nose and mouths, some vomiting at the smell, prisoners looking to the ground in shame for their appearance to the soldiers.

They began talking, translating and looking around the camp, never the look of horror leaving their faces. I lay in the mud too weak to move yet paralysed by the overwhelming sense that maybe, just maybe, this was the end of the life we had grown to be so familiar with. Lukasz ruffled my shaven head with a smile.

"Told you we'd make it didn't I kiddo." He coughs into his jacket as the fumes and bad health refuse to be forgotten even under the blissful circumstances. I could feel my whole body take a deep breath, *we were finally being rescued*. I watched the men as they aided the prisoners, arms wrapped around the soldiers necks as they cried in overwhelment. We had pushed down emotion, grown to the idea of feeling nothing, leaving our lives behind when tattooed with the number that branded us and now, it was as though all that suffocated emotion and feeling was coming to the surface, not really knowing how to all get out at once.

I looked to Lukasz and smiled, "We made it, we really made it." He smiles back with tears falling from his face, onto his pajamas that had become a part of life. I turned to see the face of a soldier looking down at me, bending down to my level, no hand over his mouth, no vomiting, just the look of a man who had seen so much horror that it had embedded into his soul. What had been so real for us for so many years was an unbelievable shock to them. We wanted them to see it, all of it, to see the way we had been living. *Why?* I guess I don't really know the answer to that one, maybe I never will. His eyes looked down to see the bones of my body that were left.

"German?" He asks with a smile. I shake my head slowly as I remain curled up on the ground shivering.

"Poland." I say through a crackled broken voice. Papa had spent endless hours before the war teaching me English, reassuring me that one day it would be of use. I suppose he was right about that too. The man in the uniform with the eagle on his arm turns to one of his comrades and asks for a blanket, indicating that he was to find one from somewhere, he didn't care where. He reaches into his pocket and pulls out some chocolate that he breaks in half and hands to me and Lukasz. It was a miracle sitting right there in the soldier's hand, waiting for us to take it. I had not seen chocolate for many years, the taste was long forgotten, yet the knowing for its delicious flavor was not one to be removed from memory quite so easily. We take the chocolate cautiously, expecting it to be too good to be true.

"How long have you been here?" He asks, wrapping the blanket around me brought by another soldier who had turned on his heel to aid with other prisoners. I let the chocolate rest on my tongue for an agonising minute before biting down and feeling the solid texture of food that was not watery soup or grass we had started to eat in desperation for filling our stomachs.

"Eight months." I say, letting the chocolate slide down my throat and into the empty abyss of my stomach. He scratches his head and smiles as he hands me his water canteen, nodding his head in an indication to drink as much as we need. "You're going to be okay now." He says with a tear falling from his eyes and nodding his head, "You're going to be okay now." And for the first time in six years, I believed the man in the uniform.

April 1945 - Germany

The feeling of arriving in Germany was somewhat bizarre. We were housed in German homes rather than that of foxholes and trenches, with hot coffee at our disposal, hot and cold water and proper toilets unlike that we had seen in Holland or France. The German people took us by surprise the most, they were hardworking, clean and educated, quick to fill the streets to clear away rubble the morning after the battle and the German food and beer, it really was quite extraordinary. Unlike other countries we had faced in combat, German houses were more or less still in good shape considering. We moved by truck from Mourmelon to the Ruhr Pocket to which we set up positions on the west bank of the Rhine facing Düsseldorf. The 2nd battalion's quarters were from the north of Stürzelberg to Worringen in the south. The 82nd Airborne were on the 2nd battalions right flank facing Cologne, panning the Rhine River in western Germany. Out Posts were set every night in foxholes as well as standing guard at crossroads down the river bank where the men of the 101st stayed in homes in numerous villages. In terms of artillery shelling there was only minimal with no small arms fire at all.

On the evening of April 12th we were hit with news that took us completely by surprise.
"President Roosevelt is dead." Winters had told us as we sat around a table playing blackjack and drinking German beer one

of the men had looted from one of the nearby stores. The news came as a shock, the president had not only been a man in power but he had contributed to the war on a tremendous level, including the directing of troops at Utah Beach during the Normandy landings, for which he received the Medal of Honor. It came to light that he had suffered a Cerebral hemorrhage and it left us all downhearted and confused. Eisenhower ordered that all unit commanders were to hold a memorial on Sunday April 14th, to which Lieutenant Foley read out prayers.

By April 18th all German resistance in the Ruhr pocket had come to an end with over 300,000 German soldiers surrendering to the Allies. Easy Company were put to guarding a Displaced Persons Camp at Dormagen, with tens of thousands of people, including Czechs, Belgians and Russians. They were living in barracks divided by sex, overcrowded and in more than enough cases, severely hungry and starved. At our arrival they were overwhelmed and grateful, while being more than happy for us to pay them to cook, clean and wash our mess kits. They were fed and treated like humans, rather than starved and worked with no pay before we liberated them.

We were given passes to visit Cologne, the most heavily bombed city in Germany with a cathedral that stood tall and damaged yet managed to withhold the bombings that had ignited before it. The city was beautiful regardless, to which I wrote to Jen and told her all about the journey through Germany.

Jen,

It has been quite some time now and I have to admit I am craving your presence more than ever. On the other hand, Germany is quite extraordinary. The cities are beautiful, the people high class and intelligent. They are not afraid to get a broom out and sweep the streets straight after a bombing! The food out here is amazing yet it does not come close to your home baked bread I miss so much. The end of the war is so close we can almost touch it, just a little while longer. I hope your parents are not tormenting your nerves too much while I'm away however I do sometimes laugh at the thought, I know how good you are at hiding it. Until my return, I miss you terribly and I am thinking of you everyday.

All my love,

Your Pete

Hiker had written to Rosie at the same time, spilling his every emotion onto paper as though it would be the last letter he ever wrote. His letters were always the same, whether they were coming in or going out, they missed each other on a level I had not seen within any other man in the Company. Pride swelled inside me at the man he had become and the man he would be returning as that the 101st Airborne had made him. On April 19th we were paid for February and March in German Marks with the order to turn in all French, British and American money to trade for the German currency. Three days later the company was loaded onto German cars filled with straw, each of us receiving 5 K-rations each to head for Bavaria and the Alps. We had been assigned to the U.S Seventh Army with the objective of Munich, Innsbruck and the Brenner Pass with the purpose of getting American troops into the Alps before the Germans could produce a redoubt there that would perlong and continue the war we all wanted over so badly.

Within the town of Berchtesgaden Hitler's Eagle's Nest was located in the mountaintop and Eisenhower held the fear that Hitler would arrive there and be protected, with radio equipment that he could use to broadcast to the German people in a bid to keep the resistance going. The Germans however had no plans for building a Mountain redoubt though it was still a worry within the ranks. Towards the end of April on the 29th Easy Company stayed at Buchloe for the night in the foxhills of the Alps, close to Landsberg and it was here that we first witnessed a forced labor camp that was designed to produce war goods for the German war front.

As we marched towards the barbed wire fencing, hundreds of prisoners looking little more than walking corpses with the size of matchstick frames were looking out towards us, hanging their heads with their boney fingers through the barbed wire, trapped inside for a duration of time that was unclear. Before reaching the main gate the stench was overpowering, causing some of the men in the company to fall back and vomit on the ground before making their way back again.
"What in god's name is this place?" I said aloud, shocked and horrified at what we were seeing before us, unable to comprehend the sight of hundreds of people, half starved to death contained within the barbed wire fences.

Winters ordered that the fence be cut, the prisoners eyes watching our every move, longing in their eyes to be saved from the horrors they had been enduring inside. My chest felt tight and heavy, my stomach turning in knots. The place was nothing like I had ever seen before, nothing like what we had seen on the frontline in France, Belgium or Holland. The evil that had been at work here was on a completely different level and I found it difficult to wrap my head around it. Hiker stood perplexed with his mouth half open, confused and shocked as he took in the horrifying sights of men in striped uniforms littered around the camp from every direction, more stumbling and hobbling towards the fences at the sound of unfamiliar voices.

As the gate swung open we walked inside to see burnt and smoking huts half in the ground with men scattered amongst them, some lying on the floor motionless with their lives long gone. Winters had called for those who could translate to German to come forward as I walked down the huts with Hiker opposite. My feet carried me six huts down before they stopped. A young boy, looking no older than his early twenties was curled on the ground with another male prisoner sitting beside him. He was the youngest I had seen since stepping foot inside the camp, yet something told me he had experienced far too much for such a young boy. His body lay a pile of bones, fighting for the slightest grasp of life that could keep him going, his striped uniform bagging over his skin as though it had never seen a clean day.

"German?" I ask him, my eyes focused on him, distraught that the Nazi's could resort a human being to such evil and pain. He shakes his head as he lays shivering on the ground.

"Polish." He says with a voice that sounded so broken it almost shattered my heart at the very sound.

"Hiker! Ask Winters if there are any blankets, this boy is freezing. I don't care where they come from." Hiker runs off almost instantly, his rifle abandoned at his side. The two men before me look at me with eyes that hold years of pain, yet relief that they were being liberated. I questioned in my mind how long it had been since they had received a normal meal, their bodies indicated that it had been quite some time. Reaching into my K-rations I pull out the chocolate I had been saving and split it into two, handing it to the two boys whose eyes widen at the very sight.

"How long have you been here?" I asked, placing the blanket over the boy that Hiker had hurried over with, more in his hands for other prisoners that he wasted no time in wrapping around their shoulders, some of them hugging him tight, others shaking his hands as they cried tears of relief and heavy pain.

"Eight months." He says his English rather impressive. Taking out my water canteen I hand it to the two men, indicating that they drink as much as they need.

"You're going to be okay now." I reassure them. It was impossible for me at that moment to not feel every single emotion possible come to the surface. Suddenly, life on the front line, fighting back German armies and taking hits to the hand and legs by machine-gun and rifle fire were nothing in comparison to the suffering that we saw that day.

"My name is Jakub," He says, offering a shaking muddy hand, "What is your name?"

Wiping away tears I had not seen in a substantial amount of time, I take his hand gently and shake it, "Peter, Peter Mcclough." For the rest of the time at the camp I spent talking to the young boy and the man who sat beside him. Before long another prisoner hobbled over and sat beside him, stroking his head in an attempt of comfort as he looked at me with bold, tired eyes.

"This is my cousin, Kacper." Says Jakub as he smiles. Kacper holds out his boney and frail hand and shakes it with great effort. He looked skinnier than Jakub, I wondered whether they had arrived at the same time.

"Mcclough, Winters wants you up front." Came the voice of Hiker behind me. I leave the men the rations and water and smile as I walk to the rest of the company that had gathered around Winters at the main gate.

We were given the news that the prisoners were to remain inside the camp until suitable housing could be organised for them. We were also advised to stop feeding them, as their stomachs had strunk so small that they would overeat and most likely sentence themselves to a death by filling their stomachs with foods too heavy and rich for what they had become so accustomed to. The news would come as panic to them, they had tasted liberation with feelings of finally being free and now we were to lock them back inside so they could not disappear into the world without the right care and medical treatment.

I learned a lot about myself during that day of April 29th 1945. The war was still in motion and had not yet been ended and a part of me felt that we had already won. The liberation of Dachau Concentration Camp Kaufering made me realise that we had been living comfortably, even in foxhiles and freezing temperatures in comparison to the millions of victims who were detained within the camps. Over the next few weeks more and more camps were being liberated. In January, Auschwitz concentration camp had been liberated by the Red Army, which we had heard about through Major Winters and Colonel Sink, the largest of all labor and extermination camps across Europe. Hitlers plan for his perfect race and final solution had included the genoside and death of over one million people at Auschwitz alone. That day not only demonstrated to me that the world was much bigger than that of your back yard but that evil walks amongst us, disguised as people with their own beliefs that it is for the better good. The 101st Airborne changed me from a boy to a man, though that day at Dachau concentration camp opened my heart to those that had been unknowingly suffering at the hands of the Germans. For the victims who were liberated, the war felt over but for us we still had an objective. I never once stopped thinking of the boy who lay frail and broken on the ground, protected only by his striped uniform that had imprinted himself in my memory for years to come.

10 Years Later

I have spent many nights wondering of the strange possibility that many I had come to meet during the six years of the war across Europe had survived to tell the story afterwards. I have pondered at great length at what would become of the men in uniforms that fired not only machine-guns but evil in every direction that they saw possible. Nightmares are still a constant burden to my sleeping habits, yet I have become a man that knows I am not the only one. Many millions of people suffered at the hands of the war that raged on throughout Europe and the scars that it left are on such a substantial level that they will never be forgotten. Every man that fought hard on the front line in cold and bitter conditions, every civilian that was forced from their homes, every child ripped from their mothers, every single person suffered in some way and even though the war ended In September 1945, many hearts were left broken and missing fractions that could not be replaced.

Three days after the liberation of Dachau, Hitler and his wife Eva Braun took their lives by swallowing a cyanide capsule then shooting themselves in the head in his Führerbunker in Berlin. Since at least 1943, it was becoming increasingly clear that Germany would fold under the pressure of the Allied forces. In February of that year, the German 6th Army, approached deep into the Soviet Union and was annihilated at the Battle of Stalingrad, and German hopes for a sustained offensive on both fronts collapsed. Then, in June 1944, the Western Allied armies landed at Normandy, France, and began systematically pushing the Germans back toward Berlin. By July 1944, several German military commanders acknowledged their imminent defeat and had plotted to remove Hitler from power to negotiate a more favorable peace. Their attempts to assassinate Hitler failed however, and in his reprisals, Hitler executed over 4,000 fellow countrymen. In January 1945, facing a siege of Berlin by the Soviets, Hitler retired to his bunker to live out his final days. Located 55 feet under the chancellery, the shelter contained 18 rooms and was fully self-sufficient with its own water and electrical supply. This did not stop him growing increasingly frustrated, as he continued to give orders and meet with such close subordinates as Hermann Goering, Heinrich Himmler and Josef Goebbels. With the Allies fast approaching, Hitler and his wife had taken the decision of suicide as their only means of escape. Only eight days later, on May 8, 1945, the German forces issued an unconditional surrender, leaving Germany to be carved up by the four Allied powers.

On September 2 1945, formal surrender documents were signed aboard the USS Missouri, designating the day as the official Victory over Japan Day, otherwise known as V-J Day after their surrender in August 1945. The news of the war ending on 2nd September spread quickly and celebrations erupted across Europe on a scale that may never be seen again. Streets lined with civilians, parties like you had never seen before, finally, freedom had come to all those that had lived in the darkness and everybody emerged like shadows, stepping into a light that could never again be so easily dimmed.

Ten years later I made my way through America and headed for Coronado California. I had never seen such amazing sights before, the American's lived so differently to that of Warsaw, even after the 5 year reconstruction campaign by the civilians to raise Warsaw up once again from the ground. After many months of rehabilitation I was discharged and made my way back to my home in Warsaw. I suppose expectations were much to be desired, I knew that the city had taken heavy air raids, I lived through them but it was a closure that I needed to return. It had been almost four years since I had seen the city and over six since I had seen it in its original beauty. Walking through the streets felt eerie yet joyous. Memories of the bombs, the ghetto and the SS men that had once marched into the city with their Swastikas flooded back, along with the haunting memory of the family that would not be returning. Kacper had survived only two weeks after liberation, his body had endured years of abuse and trauma and had given in the fight. He had made it out of forced labor and camps, for his body to finally say it had had enough.

I was back in Warsaw for only a handful of days when I was reunited with Aunt Lena. She was under the impression that none of us had survived, just as I had, though telling her of Kascper truly broke her heart into pieces that would never again be the same. After several days she had told me of the painful experiments that herself and Mother were put through by Dr Josef Mengele who began working at Auschwitz in May 1943. Mother and Aunt Lena had been kept in a small wooden cage upon their arrival at Auschwitz and were given painful injections in their back. They hadn't known why but Aunt Lena believed it may have been an attempt to change the colour of their eyes. In another experiment they were given injections of bacteria that cause Noma disease that I realised had been the reasoning behind not only Mother's abnormal skin and chemical-looking skin but also her death. Mengele had fled West upon hearing of the Soviets approaching and was arrested by the US Army however he had no SS blood group tattooed on his arm, so he was released by a unit that was unaware that his name was on a list of major war criminals. He worked in Bavaria as a farmhand before being able to escape to Argentina in 1949.

Although the West German authorities issued a warrant for his arrest in 1959, Josef Mengele remained in South America before his death from drowning following a stroke in Brazil in 1979. He was buried in Sao Paulo under the name Wolfgang Gerhard. The experiments left Aunt Lena physically and mentally scarred, along with the loss of family that never really did restore her back to her pre-war self. We found housing and lived for many years surrounding ourselves with the memory of those that we had lost. It was not until now that I realised I had a hole that I needed to fill.

"Who are you?" Asks a woman with long brown hair standing in the doorway.
"I am looking for Peter, Peter Mcclough." I hand her the letter I had been carrying in my hand and as she skims the words she looks up at me and smiles.
"You are Jakub?" I nod and take off my hat in respect. "Please, come in."
As I walked through the home of the man that had saved my life, the man that had been fighting across Europe to put an end to a war we lived amongst in cages, I could feel my mind racing through past years. While Warsaw and the people within it were perishing at the hands of the Germans, this was the reality for America, so far away and living almost completely the opposite. The feelings were not ones of bitterness or hate but of bizarreness, how the world was living so differently.
"This way." Says the woman, smiling as I follow her into the next room.

Within just seconds of walking into that room my whole world began to spin in multiple directions. The closure I needed was finally in arms reach and it was impossible for me to find a middle ground in choosing just one way to feel.
"Jakub, you came." Peter was laid in bed, his eyes heaven and red as he watched me walk over to him. It was as though we

were living in parallel universes, he was now laid broken and fragile while I looked over him in the deepest of sympathy.

"I'll give you two some time," Says the woman heading out the door, "Can I get you something to drink? A lemonade? A beer?"

"A beer would be most wonderful, thank you." I turn my gaze to Peter as I sit in the chair beside his bed.

"It has been quite some time." He says ruggedly as he tries to control his breathing.

"Indeed it has sir, I got your letter." I say, sitting down and holding up the letter he was all too familiar with.

"Please, it is Peter." He says, holding up his hand with a smile. "You look a lot different to how you have been stored in my memories boy."

"Well the world has been much kinder since the war. I can now eat a full loaf of home cooked bread with no problems, though to be honest, I tend to steer away from bread if possible, there is only so much bread one can take." I laugh, as I take the beer from the woman who had reentered the room with a tray of biscuits and a cold beer. "I have to ask, as much as I have needed the closure myself, why did you ask me to come here?" He lets out a little laugh as though he had been expecting the question.

"Thank you Jenny," He says, shakily taking the water, "much the same as you I suppose. Until I saw you that day, the war was little more than front lines and artillery fire. I was so blissfully unaware of the evil that was seeping through Europe during those years, the real evil, not combat. I have carried the guilt every day since, while you were living in labor camps and suffering, I was complaining at the mere rations we had on the front line. Our lives were being led in completely different ways, running along in time with each other yet the circumstances so different. It has been one I had not been able to comprehend, or forget. I have blamed myself for not getting to you sooner." He sighs heavily and looks out of the window in distant thought. "The world, as much as we have experienced its bitter hand, is really an amazing place, I am lucky enough to have travelled it, despite the reasoning why." He sits up in bed and reaches into his bedside drawer, revealing an envelope that he passes to me. "Although it does not bring back the years the war took from you, nor does it bring back your family, I hope it at least offers some comfort to the years that are ahead of you." He passes me the envelope and I look at it perplexed.

The door opens just as I had found words to comfort him that it was not his fault. A young girl around ten years old comes running in the room and jumps onto the bed next to Peter.
"Uncle Pete!" She shouts, nestling her way in next to him and getting comfortable. "I won an award at school today!"
"Did you really? Now what did you win that for?" He smiles putting his hands around her shoulders and squeezing her tight as he kisses the top of her head.
"I answered all the questions right in class today." She beams, showing him the award that she throws into his lap. She looks at me wearily and retreats to being shy. "That man has a

uniform on just like yours and Daddy's." She says eyeing me up cautiously.

"Ah yes, I was meaning to ask you about that Jakub." Says Peter, indicating it was a question.

"When you found me," I began, trying to place my words right in the presence of a young girl who had probably not been exposed to such evils within the world, "hope and survival were not something I had felt for a very long time. I feared almost everything, orders, people, the men in uniforms. I never believed that a man in a uniform could bring good into the world after those six years, until you walked up to me that day, you restored faith where it had completely run dry. For that, I follow in your footsteps, I am a man of the Polish Army and that is thanks to you." I could feel every ounce of emotion working its way to the surface as I spoke the words, years of trauma that had had no place to go, saving itself for that very moment.

"My boy, you have made me the most proud man alive." He says, holding out his hand as I shake it with pride washing through me at the moment, not for myself but for the man who saved me.

"Daddy!" Shouted the young girl as she jumped off the bed and rushed to her fathers side.

"Jakub, I would like you to meet my very good friend, though you have already met once before. This is Bradley Hiker, my brother from combat who saved me on numerous occasions." Smiled Peter as he waved his hand over to the man making his way over to the bed.

"What have I told you about making me a hero Mcclough." He laughed as he shook my hand. "It means a lot to Peter that you could come here." Unsure of what to say I nod politely and smile.

"You were there wasn't you, at Dachau?" I ask, remembering his face as the soldier who had brought me the blanket.

"I was, that place has haunted us since we left, though I imagine it is a lot worse for you. It is good to see you looking so well." He eyes my uniform with a smile, "You are a man of the uniform?"

"Gentleman, sit with me." Says Peter as he sits back on his pillow, his breathing rapid and intense. "It means a great deal to me that you could both be here, I want to thank you both for your tremendous impact you have both had on my life." He says, eyeing the doorway then the young girl for her to go in the other room, which she does almost instantly with a kiss on his cheek and bounces out of the room. "Hiker, you showed me bravery, brotherhood and strength all those years that I have never forgotten, without you by my side through Normandy, Belgium, Holland and Germany I am not sure I would have made it as far as I did. Jakub, you showed me that even in the darkest of hours there is always strength that can be drawn from it. I live my final days in honor of the lessons you have both taught me." He shook both of our hands with a smile filled with nothing but pride.

1956 - Present day

As I sit at my desk writing these words, I am full of the most honorable memories of a soldier that saved my life and although we only met for the briefest of moments, they have carried me through some of the most testing experiences of my life. The war had lasted for six painful years, leaving burning scars that could never be healed. Peter, the soldier of the 101st Airborne, 2nd battalion of 506th PIR, Easy Company, inspired me to live out the rest of my days continuing in the footsteps that he could no longer. On our last visit he had drifted away into the night, peaceful so Jennifer had told me, though the cancer in his Kidneys had spread throughout his body like wildfire including his liver and lungs. For a man so young I felt he had many years of experience and life that he was denied, yet during his time he made an impact on so many lives. I have been unable to come to a reasoning behind why the world works as it does, why evil is so prone to drift into lives and cause havoc. I sit here now, at the end of my story, Peter's diary beside me as I tell his story, sharing his courage through times that offered only the darkest of moments. He was a great soldier, one that should be remembered for his contribution to the ending of a very dark war. I had opened the letter that Peter had given me upon my arrival back in Poland. He had left me $2,000 in hope that it would compensate for his unknowingness of the events of the Holocaust. I wished I had opened it before his departure from the world, I would have told him that it was never his burden to carry. Inside the envelope was another letter so fragile I worried it would evaporate at my very touch.

My darling Dorothy,

I am so incredibly overjoyed at the news that I am to be a father. If there is anything of purpose in this life it is to have a child and raise them with all the experiences and lessons that we have endured. If we are to raise a daughter, I will teach her of all the many lessons there are to ensure her heart is never broken. If we are to have a son, I will teach him how to be strong, to never give up on a fight that is worth winning. Maybe one day he will follow in my footsteps and be a mighty fine soldier too, though I know I am getting ahead of myself. This war is cruel and I intend to do everything in my power as both a man and a soldier to make it back to you so we can start our family. You have given me the greatest reason of all to fight harder and carry on living through these trenches so I can walk out of them at the end and reunite with you both at the end of it.

Keep holding on that little while longer, I will be home soon.

Your James

It is fair to say that this letter had played a tremendous part in seeing Peter through the long and dark days on the frontline of war. He wanted to make his father proud and I have no doubt whatsoever in my mind that he accomplished that. He respected the men he fought in combat with, saved lives on a scale that he never gave himself credit for and never once gave up when living amongst those foxholes and ditches with artillery fire that split the earth around him. He carried on because he knew that was his mission, he contributed to the end of Hitler's war and I do not believe there could be any greater achievement than that. I will keep the letters in my pocket during every jump and every time I feel like the world is too big I will take them out and remind myself of why I enlisted for the army. If I could say one thing to the man that saved me it would be this, *Peter, you undoubtedly made your father, Jennifer, me and your country proud, that goes without saying. I will walk through your footsteps and I will ensure that you are just as proud of me and that you saved me for a reason, to live out my days with only the greatest of purposes.*

The army serves me well, it is turning me into a man that I have always hoped to be, a soldier of the 1st Independent Parachute Brigade, a soldier just like Peter Mcclough, the man in the uniform that restored my faith and gave me hope when it had drained from me like a sink of dirty water. I sit here now, faithful to my Jewish heritage yet I stand tall for my country, so tall that I can now overlook all the horrors of previous years in the Warsaw ghetto, Auschwitz-Birkenau and Dachau, though I will never forget what happened. It is time for me to finally draw a close on this story, though there will never be a moment that it will not be held in my heart. We are jumping for Operation Musketeer tomorrow and I know as I jump, I will be jumping in his memory. The soldier of the 101st who made me who I am today, Peter Mcclough who made me a soldier. I am willing, I am determined, I *am* Soldier.